THE NUBIAN'S CURSE

Also by Barbara Hambly from Severn House

The James Asher vampire novels

BLOOD MAIDENS
THE MAGISTRATES OF HELL
THE KINDRED OF DARKNESS
DARKNESS ON HIS BONES
PALE GUARDIAN
PRISONER OF MIDNIGHT

The Benjamin January series

DEAD AND BURIED
THE SHIRT ON HIS BACK
RAN AWAY
GOOD MAN FRIDAY
CRIMSON ANGEL
DRINKING GOURD
MURDER IN JULY
COLD BAYOU
LADY OF PERDITION
HOUSE OF THE PATRIARCH
DEATH AND HARD CIDER

Silver Screen historical mysteries

SCANDAL IN BABYLON
ONE EXTRA CORPSE

THE NUBIAN'S CURSE

Barbara Hambly

SEVERN
HOUSE

First world edition published in Great Britain and the USA in 2024
by Severn House, an imprint of Canongate Books Ltd,
14 High Street, Edinburgh EH1 1TE.

severnhouse.com

Copyright © Barbara Hambly, 2024

All rights reserved including the right of
reproduction in whole or in part in any form.
The right of Barbara Hambly to be identified
as the author of this work has been asserted
in accordance with the Copyright,
Designs & Patents Act 1988.

British Library Cataloguing-in-Publication Data
A CIP catalogue record for this title is available from the British Library.

ISBN-13: 978-1-4483-1136-1 (cased)
ISBN-13: 978-1-4483-1137-8 (e-book)

This is a work of fiction. Names, characters, places and incidents
are either the product of the author's imagination or are used fictitiously.
Except where actual historical events and characters are being described
for the storyline of this novel, all situations in this publication are
fictitious and any resemblance to actual persons, living or dead,
business establishments, events or locales is purely coincidental.

All Severn House titles are printed on acid-free paper.

Typeset by Palimpsest Book Production Ltd.,
Falkirk, Stirlingshire, Scotland.
Printed and bound in Great Britain by
TJ Books, Padstow, Cornwall.

Praise for the Benjamin January series

"The historical backdrop is vivid, and the writing is exquisite. One of the best in a not-to-be-missed series"
Booklist Starred Review of *Death and Hard Cider*

"This masterly portrayal of smoldering racial tensions deserves a wide readership"
Publishers Weekly Starred Review of *Death and Hard Cider*

"One of Hambly's best mysteries combines historical detail, intense local color, and ugly truths about slavery and politics"
Kirkus Reviews on *Death and Hard Cider*

"Outstanding . . . Hambly's masterful historical detail, scrupulous character portrayal, and psychological analysis of human frailties contribute handsomely to her storytelling"
Publishers Weekly Starred Review of *House of the Patriarch*

"A fascinating, sadly timely tale of the hero's struggles with his rage over the treatment of Black people"
Kirkus Reviews on *House of the Patriarch*

"A stark and occasionally brutal story, and Hambly tells it superbly, in prose that is vivid and empathetic. For fans of this fine series, this is a must-read"
Booklist Starred Review of *Lady of Perdition*

"Deeply researched . . . Hambly's well-wrought denunciation of slavery and her skillful defense of women's rights resound from January's times to our own"
Publishers Weekly on *Lady of Perdition*

About the author

Barbara Hambly, though a native of Southern California, lived in New Orleans for many years while married to the late science fiction writer George Alec Effinger. Hambly holds a degree in medieval history from the University of California and has written novels in numerous genres.

www.barbarahambly.com

For Laurel

ONE

R*éveillon.*
　　Waking.
　　'But it's an ancient feast,' old Lucien Imbolt had said, back in Paris in the days of the restored kings. 'Older than the Evangelists who claimed it as the celebration of Our Savior's birth.' His dark eyes had sparkled in the candlelight of some nobleman's gilt-trimmed salon, the great chamber temporarily silent – like this dining room tonight, Benjamin January reflected, with the food spread waiting and the servants in pantry and kitchen catching a last bit of rest before their betters came in to feast.

In his mind he still heard the white-haired violinist's creaky voice, smelled the savor of goose and caramel and rich sauces above the honeyed scent of a thousand beeswax candles. The chilly whisper of draft that stirred the long velvet curtains tonight, sixteen years later (*Has it been only sixteen?*) and half a world away, reminded January of how deep snow had lain in the Paris streets that Christmas of 1824.

'It's the midnight of the year,' Imbolt had gone on, thin fingers adjusting the ivory pegs of his fiddle. 'The long dark, when the gates between the worlds stand open, and all the spirits walk freely back and forth. I don't think it was originally a celebration at all. I think it was a way of making sure that everybody was in the same room, with all the lamps burning, until day came again.'

Tonight – Christmas of 1840 – from his place on the musicians' dais, January surveyed the dining room of the Viellard townhouse on the Rue Royale in New Orleans, and smiled at the memory of his friend.
　　Réveillon.
　　Paris.
　　Was that really *me sitting at the harpsichord, waiting for all the cousins and uncles and in-laws of the Comte de Morens-Vrillière to come back from Mass?* It was hard to believe.

Jacques Bichet, the flute player who usually made up one of the little group of New Orleans musicians with whom January regularly performed, leaned across to him now, asking 'It true they got a genuine French princess coming here tonight?'

'I heard she was a marquise.' Cochon Gardinier slipped back into the dining room through the discreet pantry door, hopped up on to the dais with surprising lightness for a man of nearly three hundred pounds. He moved his violin, where he'd left it on his chair, with one hand, balancing in the other a plate full of vol-au-vents pilfered from the Viellard kitchen.

'A vicomtesse,' corrected the other fiddler, Hannibal Sefton, like an emaciated Celtic elf beside Cochon's comfortable enormity. 'Madame de St-Forgeux, kin to the d'Aumonts and Rochebarons and I don't know how many other aristocratic houses of France. She is escorting, I understand, one Daisy Emmett, of Virginia. A family less renowned in heraldry, perhaps, but with a dowry of half a million dollars and prospect to inherit six times that sum.'

He pressed his hand to his ribs to still a cough, while around him the other musicians – Jacques and his old uncle, Cochon and the handsome Philippe duCoudreau – exclaimed in awe. News of the heiress's arrival in New Orleans had been bandied among the whites of the town – both American and Creole French – for a week; among the free colored of the French town for twice as long.

'Quite a catch,' Hannibal concluded, when he got his breath, 'for the Viellards to celebrate Christmas with. *Gratias tibi maximus*,' he added, as January stepped down from the dais and brought him a champagne-glass full of water from the sideboard.

The master of Bellefleur – the plantation where January had been born – had in general celebrated Christmas by getting savagely drunk and finding a reason to horsewhip at least three of the house servants before passing out on the parlor floor. As a small child, January had spent two Christmases hiding in theciprière swamps when Michie Simon went on his customary Yuletide rampage down the 'street' of the quarters. He still recalled the piercing cold, the scorched-sugar smell of the fog mingling with the wet stink of the ash, where the men had burned over the harvested fields. The birdless silence of those winter woods.

The beauty of that stillness.

Stille Nacht, went the German Christmas carol. *Silent Night indeed.*

While the other musicians pressed Hannibal for further particulars about Miss Emmett ('Of course she's beautiful! What girl with a half-million-dollar dowry is ugly?'), January mentally placed the ancient houses of French nobility that the fiddler had mentioned. Even in New Orleans, even with the storming of the Bastille fifty years in the past, any Frenchman would have attested that such families as the d'Aumonts and Rochebarons were 'real' or 'legitimate' nobility, far superior to the ducs, comtes and barons granted their titles by Napoleon in exchange for 'services rendered' to the Empire. During the sixteen years that he had lived in Paris – working first as a surgeon, then as a musician and a teacher of music – January had listened to more details than he could ever possibly have wanted to know about why even the most impoverished 'legitimate' barons, half-starving in the countryside (to whom this evening's employers, the wealthy Viellards, were related), had infinitely superior 'blood' than those jumped-up Bonapartist *parvenus* . . . like their in-laws the Miragouins, for instance. The Miragouins were on the guest-list tonight.

('Two cents says Florentin Miragouin's gonna call out that cousin of M'am Viellard . . .')

'For sure somebody's gonna get called out,' prophesied Cochon, handing around vol-au-vents and keeping a wary eye on the pantry door. 'M'am Mabillet's gonna be here, and if she knows there's an heiress under this roof, she'll bring that nephew Gontran of hers – the one with the thing on his nose? And I *know* Ma'm Viellard's cousin Cèphalide gonna be here with her son Scaevola, that's been courtin' Mamzelle Ophèlie Viellard . . .'

'Who he's gonna drop like a hot potato,' opined Jacques, 'if this Miss Emmett so much as bats her eyelashes at him . . .'

'*Et genus et formam regina pecunia donat*,' remarked Hannibal, with an air of deep satisfaction as bets were laid on who would call out whom and why. 'What would the families of New Orleans do without Christmas?'

Back on Bellefleur, January recalled, Michie Simon's Spanish wife had usually taken her little son and gone to her family in town the minute the sugar harvest and the *roulaison* – the grinding season – were done. On the one occasion M'am Juana had spent the twenty-fifth of December on Bellefleur, Christmas Day had passed without comment, though that lady had held a little party, in the Spanish fashion, for the children of their nearest neighbors to celebrate the visit of *los Reyes Magos* on the sixth of January.

Benjamin himself had been eight years old, newly freed, and going to school in New Orleans before he'd even heard of the custom of *réveillon*. 'It's when you go to midnight mass and come home to a big feast and your mama gives you presents from Père Noël,' had explained one of the other boys at the St Louis Academy for Young Gentlemen of Color, adding for good measure, 'you dumb bozal.' At eight, January had been taller than most of the eleven-year-olds and stood out among those light-complected octoroon and musterfino boys like a lump of coal in a bucket of pale-brown eggs.

As he stood out still, among the other musicians, he reflected – except for Uncle Bichet and Hannibal. Hannibal Sefton, a stray Anglo-Irishman with his long, graying hair wound up over a woman's tortoiseshell comb, was one of the few white men in the companionable network of the free colored 'downtown' musicians. Uncle Bichet, with his tribal scars and thick-lensed spectacles, was another lump of coal beside his quadroon nephew Jacques, the octoroon Cochon and the ivory-fair Philippe duCoudreau.

By the time January was nine, he had made friends with most of the other boys at the Academy. He would go to midnight Mass with the family of Gilles Gignac, whose plaçée mother had been paid off by her 'protector' with a house on Rue Burgundy and enough of a settlement to set up in business as a dressmaker. M'am Gignac would let her cook go to early Mass in the afternoon, and January would come to help Gilles and M'am Gignac prepare the *réveillon* supper – oysters, turtle soup, grillades and a towering croquembouche glistening with threads of caramel sugar. His own mother rarely noticed whether he was at home or not, and after herself attending midnight Mass – sitting with the other plaçées at the back of the cathedral – would spend the rest of the night doing exquisite needlework beside the small but elegant feast that awaited her protector, whenever he could slip away from *his* white family's *réveillon* to join her for champagne and oysters in the small hours of Christmas morning.

January wasn't completely sure that his mother even knew that he'd gone to Mass with the Gignacs, much less when he returned to his room in the *garçonnière* behind the cottage. He'd certainly never gotten so much as a pair of shoelaces from Père Noël. His mother still attended Mass every Sunday and confession every Saturday and, so far as January knew, was a complete atheist.

When he was sixteen, January had started playing piano with the other musicians of the town, and after that date had been to twenty-nine *réveillons* celebrated by wealthy white people, either in New Orleans or in Paris. Not once in those twenty-nine years had he been able to attend a midnight Mass himself.

The pantry door behind the musicians' dais opened, disgorging three footmen and Visigoth, the grizzled, kingly Viellard butler. January glanced at the clock. It was one fifteen. Fingers were hastily cleansed of vol-au-vent sauce on handkerchiefs, music was opened, not that any of the six men needed reminders of how to play 'Adeste Fideles' or the 'March of the Kings'. Like January, they had all been playing for other people's *réveillons* for years.

The clock chimed the half-hour (*Everybody's standing on the cathedral steps talking . . .*). Then hooves clattered in the brick passageway that ran beside the Viellard townhouse and into the courtyard behind. The light of cressets jigged behind the curtains at that end of the room; voices exclaimed at the raw, foggy cold. Someone groaned audibly, 'I thought that old fly-trap would *never* shut up!'

At January's sign, Hannibal floated the first sweet notes of 'Laissez Paître vos Bestes'. Cochon's deeper viol, Uncle's cello, Jacques' flute widened and deepened the tune as more voices sounded in the passageway, and the courtyard French door opened to admit stately Madame Aurélie Viellard, like a dowager queen on the arm of Monseigneur Blanc, the Bishop of New Orleans. Her stout, myopic son Henri followed, blinking in the blaze of the dining room's three hundred candles, a slim, dark-haired lady on his arm who had to be the Vicomtesse de St-Forgeux. Henri's wife Chloë followed, dainty as a spider wrought of diamonds and glass, escorted by Madame Aurélie's brother Veryl St-Chinian in a coat and knee-smalls, which had seen their debut two decades before Napoleon had sold New Orleans to the Americans. Behind her, pink with self-consciousness on the arm of Madame Aurélie's Bonapartist son-in-law Florentin Miragouin, walked a mousy-haired, slightly pudgy girl of seventeen, her mourning black offset by the effulgence of her diamond necklace, diamond tiara, diamond bracelets, ruby-and-diamond earrings, and a ruby-and-diamond breast-pin the size of an artichoke.

Presumably, thought January, Daisy Emmett.

Other guests followed. A scrimmage of footmen in the carriageway to the street; flambeaux gleaming when the doors were opened. Men and women laughing as they came up the steps and into the long ground-floor room. Madame Aurélie welcomed them, Henri at her side, trying to pretend he recognized them without his spectacles; Visigoth showed them to the two long tables where they took their places with holiday informality. Jests and greetings rode above the sweetness of the music. After seven years back in New Orleans – seven years of playing for *réveillons*, Twelfth Night parties, balls and receptions at the houses of the French Creole upper crust and the wealthy upstart Americans uptown – January knew their faces and their names. After seven years of listening to his mother gossip about them, he also knew more than he really wanted to about their personal lives, families, finances, and how they treated their slaves.

So it didn't surprise him to see Gontran Mabillet, 'Scae' Viellard (who was engaged to Madame Aurélie's third daughter but clearly hoped he could do better), the dandified Evard Aubin and even M'sieu Brinvilliers – the Viellard family lawyer – practically shouldering one another aside to fetch Miss Emmett lemonade, in the hopes of gaining the seat at her elbow. Times were hard. It would be worth it, presumably, to listen to Miss Emmett's constant, squealing giggle, or to watch her fuss at the footmen over the best bits of duck in the ragout ('Maybe you could go check in the kitchen to see if there's any dark meat left there? The sausage is just so *nasty* . . .'), in order not to worry about one's rent again, ever. 'Of course I'm just heartbroken about poor Papa, and just when he'd promised we'd go to Paris in April . . .'

Footmen paraded in with pea soup, oysters, turtle soup, foie gras. The scents pinched January's hunger: he had foregone the vol-au-vents in preparation for Mass at dawn. Movement on the other side of old Uncle Veryl, as the vicomtesse leaned forward, trying to catch her charge's eye. (*As well she should*, reflected January. The girl seemed intent on engaging as much masculine attention as possible, and Cochon and Philippe were definitely going to collect bet-money on at least a couple of duels . . .)

Then he frowned, seeing the noblewoman's beautiful oval face by candlelight . . .

Is that . . . ?

He shook his head, returned to the old song, gentle as snow falling on Bethlehem:

> *Entre les deux bras de Marie,*
> *Dort, dort, dort le petit fils,*
> *Mille anges divins, mille séraphins*
> *Volent à l'entour de ce grand Dieu d'amour.*

He told himself, *It's only someone who looks like her. Someone else I saw in Paris.* As in New Orleans, he'd seen them all: faces of the old pre-Revolutionary aristocracy, of the financiers ennobled by Napoleon, of the *chevaliers d'industrie* who paid off the Duc d'Orleans – the cousin who'd scrambled on to the throne when the original line of kings had been unceremoniously booted out again.

It must be one of them who looks a little like her. That's all.

One of the first things January had been taught by old Herr Kovald – when his mother's protector had arranged for him to have music lessons ('Why on earth would you waste good money on that?' his mother had demanded) – had been a sense of occasion. At a ball, people wanted to dance. At the opera, the music would follow the singers' lead. Playing at a dinner, or a reception, people wanted to talk. They wanted the music to be there, but didn't really want to listen to it.

So he sank his heart into it, tasted again the layered sweetness of his memories of all those Christmas Eves, all those *réveillons*. The towers of Notre-Dame silhouetted against stars and snow-light; the haunted, exquisite stillness of the *ciprière* in fog. What that first Christmas Mass had felt like to a nine-year-old boy, accepted by the family of his friend.

> *Depuis plus de quatre mille ans,*
> *Nous le promettaient les prophètes*
> *Depuis plus de quatre mille ans,*
> *Nous attendions cet heureux temps.*

And what, he wondered, did Hannibal Sefton see, embroidering the old carols with fantasias of gold on his violin? The family he'd left behind in Ireland? His own memories of Paris in the twenties? What did Cochon Gardinier remember, of the rowdy jolliness of growing up in the French town with a sprawling family of libré dressmakers and plasterers and fiddle-players?

The doors between the worlds, he thought, stood open indeed, for the spirits of yuletides past to come and go as they wished.

Footmen brought in geese and grillades, lobsters in cream and spicy meat pies. Red wine, white wine . . .

'I don't see why Papa couldn't have arranged it for me to have stayed in Washington, when he died. There's always something wonderful going on there.' (Giggle) 'It was just selfish of him to make that awful man in Natchez my guardian . . .'

'Breeding? Pah! The only difference between those "Legitimite" d'Aumonts and Polignacs you worship and the imperial titles is that one bunch of them served a lazy king, and the others served their country and the emperor who brought it glory . . .'

(*Should I see if I can still get in on the betting of a duel between Miragouin and Aubin?*)

The clock struck three. Footmen returned yet again, to clear away dishes and bring in coffee and sweets. The guests moved their chairs about, or got up with polite excuses ('I will be back in one little minute, madame, but it has been weeks since I've seen my dear Madame Mabillet . . .') and mingled, taking each other's seats or leaning across chair-backs to laugh with old friends. At one end of the table, old Uncle Veryl retreated for a quiet chat with his only real friend at the gathering, an equally ancient English gentleman who was one of January's few medical patients – no white person in New Orleans (and very few of the free colored) being likely to choose a coal-black surgeon who stood six feet three and looked like a cotton-hand. These two aged gentlemen were joined by old Sidonie Janvier, the mother of the man who had been protector to January's own mother; she caught January's eye across the amber glow of the candlelit room, *Joyeux Noël* in her smile.

Rose, thought January – his beautiful wife – would be holding her own *réveillon*, with his sisters and their children, telling the littler ones of Père Noël, of shepherds and wise kings and angels singing among the stars . . . Not that she believed a word of it. She'd have ragout and pralines and callas waiting for him when he got home, on the threshold of winter dawn. And he smiled at the thought of her. Rose the logical deist, his sister Olympe the voodoo queen . . .

At the pantry door, the butler Visigoth appeared, caught January's eye, as 'Jesu, Joy of Man's Desiring' circled to its gentle close. There would be grillades and grits in the kitchen for the musicians – those who valued a free meal over the soul's union with God – before dessert and more music rekindled the feast. At *réveillon*, one did indeed stay 'waking' until daylight came again.

'Five cents says Brinvilliers challenges Gontran Mabillet,' whispered Hannibal, as the musicians rose from their chairs. And indeed the Viellard lawyer was bending over Miss Emmett's shoulder, recounting some courtroom enormity that made her giggle. Both Gontran and his mother, a few chairs away, were visibly planning murder. Jacques and Philippe both dug in their pockets as they stepped down from the dais.

'And five on Miragouin going after Marat Janvier over that remark about Miragouin's noble kinsman . . .'

A woman's voice said, 'Ben.'

January turned.

It is *her.*

The Vicomtesse de St-Forgeux hesitated, standing below the musician's dais. She was, he had seen when she entered the room, in mourning like the heiress in her charge, though unlike Miss Emmett her bombazine gown was in plain, exquisitely cut good taste, and she wore no jewelry (*First year of mourning*, he guessed). *No wonder I had trouble recognizing her.* In Paris she had worn yellow gauze, or apple-green, midnight hair piled like storm-cloud over a threaded glory of pearls.

'It *is* Benjamin, isn't it?' Her voice hadn't changed. Burnt caramel touched with salt. Nor had the whalebone loveliness of her slender form.

'Persephone.' He bowed.

Her smile hadn't changed either. It could still raise the dead.

'I should say *madame* . . .'

'For you it's still Persephone.' She moved her hand as if she would hold it out for him to kiss, then drew it back quickly, as if remembering that they were in America. In America, even a free black musician did not kiss a white lady's hand. Particularly not that of a bona fide French aristocrat. 'What are you—?' she began, and then shook her head at herself: 'I'm sorry. I just didn't expect . . . But you're *from* New Orleans, aren't you?'

'I am.' His smile added, *And we'll forget the dozen times I said that* nothing *on God's green earth would ever get me to return here.*

In the refulgent light of hundreds of candles, he could see her color a little, under rice-powder and rouge skillfully applied. 'I'm sorry,' she apologized again. 'But seeing you here is – not to be melodramatic about it – the answer to a prayer. The fact is—'

Miss Emmett's schoolgirl voice shrilled behind him: 'Oh, I *know* I can find some way of coming down here to New Orleans!' (Giggle) 'That *awful* guardian *can't* be so cruel that he won't let me come shopping!' (Giggle) 'And I have just *nothing* to wear once I get out of this *awful* mourning—'

Persephone Jondrette – *Her Ladyship Persephone de St-Forgeux*, he corrected himself – turned her head, red lips tightening, and in her eyes he saw the exasperation of weeks on ship-board from Virginia with the girl. He bowed again, letting her know he wouldn't take offense if she rustled off to corral her charge.

'Can I meet you somewhere tomorrow morning?' she asked. 'I know it's Christmas Day, and I'm sorry, but we leave for Natchez Saturday morning—'

'It will be my pleasure and my honor,' said January, 'to have you and Miss Emmett visit my family in the morning – I know you'll have invitations to Christmas dinner. We're on Rue Esplanade, the big gray house between Rue Burgundy and Rue Dauphine. You can't miss it. It's a girls' school. My wife runs it—'

'You married again!' Again, that radiant smile.

'I did. And she'll be delighted to make your acquaintance.'

'I'm so glad! I'd heard – I was in Switzerland by then . . .' Raised voices dragged her attention back to Miss Emmett, giggling behind her fan as Gontran Mabillet jostled Scae Viellard aside.

('How dare you, sir?' 'How dare *I*? And you with your engagement announced already to . . .')

'I must go,' she said. 'That girl . . . I can't tell you how glad I am to see you, Benjamin. I will come tomorrow—'

'And I hope you'll tell me what you were doing in Switzerland—'

She laughed a little, the sparkle of her eyes telling him that the memory was a good one. She sobered, and went on, 'The fact is that I've been at my wits' end, and you can be of enormous help to me. You knew Arithmus Wishart, didn't you? Well, I mean.'

'Arithmus—' Dark, strange eyes that wouldn't meet his or any man's, under a shaggy black mane worked with beads. Long, thin hands caressing the tiny bronze statue of a lion-faced goddess.

A man lying dead on the naked mattress of a carven bed, face twisted in staring-eyed agony and shock.

Imposuit dea manum – The hand of the goddess lay heavy on him . . .

'Did you find him?' he asked. 'After all these years?'

'I think so. It's why I—'

('A man who would so insult the family of his hosts deserves a horsewhip, not a choice of pistols or swords . . .' 'You know nothing of the business and nothing of my affairs, sir . . .' 'Gentlemen, gentlemen, there are ladies present . . .!')

'The thing is, I doubt I would recognize the man now, after sixteen years. I only saw him once or twice. And I don't know . . . Plague seize that girl!'

('I find your implications insulting, sir!' 'And I find you officious, sir, to say nothing of unprincipled and selfish—!' 'Gentlemen, please!')

'Go,' said January, half-laughing, though he knew that his old friend was in a very real sense responsible for her charge's reputation and, in a way, for the safety and perhaps the survival of the young men involved. 'I knew him, yes, and I would know him again. Did he come to America, then?'

'He's in Natchez,' she said.

('Oh, somebody help me!' cried Miss Emmett, fainting . . .)

'He's a slave.'

TWO

'Was that who it looked like?' Hannibal Sefton huddled deeper into a threadbare hand-me-down greatcoat as he and January walked downstream on Rue Royale in the thinning mists of Christmas morning. After *réveillon*, everyone in the old French Town was asleep – except the slaves, of course. Having stayed up from the previous morning preparing the white folks' feasts, they now washed dishes, dried silverware, and bundled table linen into wicker hampers for the laundry-women. By the time they were done with that, their owners would be waking up and sleepily demanding coffee.

Every carriageway and courtyard gate breathed scents of steam and wet bricks. Cathedral bells blessed the silent town.

It would be, January guessed, a very small morning Mass.

'Persephone Jondrette,' he affirmed. 'Did you know her?'

'I saw her dance.' Hannibal smiled in remembered bliss. 'And fell in love with her on the spot. Who in Paris didn't?' He and January had been in the French capital at roughly the same time, though in those days of the restored Bourbon kings they had moved in very different circles. He coughed again. 'But what's she doing here? And how did she get to be the Vicomtesse de St-Forgeux . . .?'

'You'll have the chance to ask her,' said January. 'After breakfast.'

'Oh, be still my heart! Did you meet her at the opera? Every man I ever spoke to would have lain down before her carriage-wheels to win her smile.'

'Actually,' January grinned at the recollection, 'she helped me hunt ghosts in a haunted chateau. She was the mistress of a friend of mine.'

The fiddler's eyebrows carried a whole line of parallel wrinkles towards his hairline. 'Fortunate man,' he said. 'And, from all I've heard, extremely wealthy man . . .'

'That's actually a very long story.' January's smile faded, as he recalled that story's terrible end.

And Arithmus Wishart's in Natchez . . .
A slave in Natchez.

They halted where Rue St-Pierre crossed Rue Royale, only a few hardy sparrows cheeping in the bare cathedral garden. A solitary cat materialized from the fog to trot before them down the damp pavement in the direction of the Place d'Armes. Vanished. 'Please tell Rose I'll be there within the hour. The early Mass is never very long.'

Though January had abstained from the kitchen feast of gumbo and grits in the Viellard townhouse – not to speak of pilfered vol-au-vents – he grudged nothing of the exhaustion, sleepiness, and mild headache of postponing the breakfast that awaited him, in order to kneel before the altar rail on the day of the Lord's birth and receive the Host. Monseigneur Blanc, who had preached the midnight sermon to a cathedral packed with fashionable worshipers, could be excused for accepting Madame Viellard's invitation to the *réveillon*. January guessed that the bespectacled Père Eugenius, officiating this morning, had spent the night in private meditation, on his knees. The young priest's voice echoed in the near-empty church as in a cavern, but January came away feeling that he had, in fact, in that stillness, touched the hand of God.

On his way from the building, he lit candles before the image of the Blessed Virgin, and whispered his prayers: for his young friend Artois St-Chinian, of the shadow-side of the Viellard clan; for his first wife, the beautiful Ayasha, dead of the cholera in Paris . . . *Has it really been over seven years?* For his sisters, his mother, his beautiful Rose . . .

For Arithmus Wishart.

So that's *what became of him* . . .

For a girl named Belle.

Remembering that long-ago winter – remembering Ayasha expostulating about ghosts in a dressing gown and boots – he found himself smiling again as he strode along the wet brick banquette, heading towards Rue Esplanade.

The cathedral clock was striking nine when January climbed the steps to the high gallery of the old Spanish house on Rue Esplanade. Ten thousand angel-wings of coffee-scent and ginger-bread wrapped him in blessings as he opened the French door into his study. If his mother had neglected to take him to Mass in his childhood, she had at least slapped into him the much more important fact that *no* self-respecting gentleman *ever* entered a house through the *parlor* French doors – the very idea! Only American animals did that!

He'd half-expected his niece Zizi-Marie to have gone to bed and to sleep by this time, leaving Rose and Hannibal to doze over a hand of picquet beside the breakfast dishes while they waited for him. But in fact, the whole household was awake. He heard their chatter as he crossed through his study and into the parlor. Even Gabriel was there, Zizi-Marie's seventeen-year-old brother, just packing up his white jacket and apron and the tall, starched 'toque' expected by his employer in the new restaurant on Rue St-Louis.

'*Joyeux Noël!*' The young man strode to catch January's hands. 'And now I've got to run, Uncle Ben . . . Every American in town's reserved tables – I'm not going to be back before midnight – I've left the menu Zizi and I worked out for Twenty-First Night—'

Zizi, sitting between Rose and Hannibal at one end of the table, threw a fragment of praline at her brother at this disrespectful reference to her upcoming wedding day, which was to take place on the fourteenth of January – eight nights after Twelfth Night; since, like every other musician in town, January would be playing for a white folks' Twelfth Night ball, and Zizi desperately wanted her uncle to be present. Gabriel caught the candy, threw it back, turned to hug Rose and then grabbed his things and dashed out through the study and thence out through the French door and down the gallery steps.

Half a foot taller, January reflected with a smile, than he'd been three years ago, when he and Zizi-Marie had come to live with him and Rose, following the bank crash that had ruined half the families in New Orleans. As Zizi sprang to her feet and came to embrace him, he caught Rose's eye: '*Joyeux Noël*,' she said. Her smile was like a kiss.

Happiness, he thought, as she too rose to be encircled by his other arm, didn't get better than this.

Three-year-old Professor John – as his elder son was called – staggered in Rose's wake; baby Xander, entangled in his long dress, crawled purposefully behind: *Joyeux Noël indeed.* The whole of his soul felt like a single prayer of thanks.

January strode to scoop up the Professor, swung him around as if he'd been a puppy and hurled him ceiling-ward. 'Throw me out the window!' screamed the toddler. 'Throw me out the window . . .'

'I'm gonna throw you out the window!' January roared in his best ogre voice, and ran for the windows, holding his son with gentle strength and spinning him in long swoops . . .

'Throw me out the window!'

'Uncle Ben—' Zizi caught up Xander on to her hip. ('T'row me window . . .' suggested the boy, his dark eyes wide.) 'Gabriel says he can roast a whole piglet for the wedding breakfast, like they did in olden times, with an apple in its mouth – Can we do that? Mama says—'

January – having opened and leaped through the French door on to the gallery, his son in his arms – now leaped back in again, settled down at the table, and turned his mind to these graver issues. In addition to the pig, there was the question of the rental of a carriage for Zizi's wedding, and how to seat Zizi's mother Olympe and grandmother at the same table without the wedding feast ending with Olympe – known among the voodoos as Olympia Snakebones – putting a curse on 'Gran'mère Levesque' . . .

'She wouldn't put a curse on her own mother, would she, Uncle Ben?' January could hear in her voice that the girl considered it a genuine possibility.

Hannibal paused in the act of removing a peppermint from behind the enthralled Xander's ear: 'I have three cents on it with Jacques Bichet that she does.'

Zizi threw a napkin at him.

'Do you know how difficult it was to find anyone to bet *against* it?'

Zizi threw another, harder.

'I'll talk to your mother.' January wiped the last dabs of the exquisite breakfast feast from his fingers. 'And to Gran'mère . . .' His mother would cut him to pieces with a clam-shell if she ever learned he referred to her as *Gran'mère* . . .

He glanced at the clock: noon. *Gran'mère* – and Olympe, Olympe's husband Paul, and the three younger children who had remained at home – were due for dinner at three: *Can I get some sleep between now and then?* Olympe and her ten-year-old daughter Chou-chou would undoubtedly arrive earlier, to help Rose with the cooking . . . Guilt gripped him, but he was playing for the Mabillet Christmas ball tonight at eight . . .

A form crossed the French windows that led out on to the gallery, and a moment later a light tap sounded on the French windows of the 'swamp-side' – or northern – front bedroom of the house: Rose's room.

He guessed at once who it was. *She must have inquired as to the local custom.* But of course, Persephone Jondrette had been an actress as well as a dancer. If she was currently playing the role of a widowed vicomtesse of the 'legitimate' French aristocracy, it went without saying that she would not put a foot wrong, even in the usages of a country and a society which she had never visited before.

He stood, and followed Zizi – with Rose at their heels – through the bedroom, to the French door on to the gallery.

'Madame la Vicomtesse.' This time he kissed the hand she extended. 'Welcome and more than welcome – *Joyeux Noël*. Permit me to introduce my wife, Madame Rose Janvier, and my niece, Mademoiselle Zenobie-Zuleimie-Marie Corbier. Madame la Vicomtesse de St-Forgeux.'

'Oh, but please don't curtsey!' Persephone had read the hesitation in Zizi's eyes. She held out her hand for a firm greeting, first to Rose, then to Zizi, very unlike the fashionable two-fingers touch popular among the upper social circles. 'I am *so* glad to meet you both, and I am *so* tired of people trying to guess what is the proper greeting for a "genuine French aristocrat" when all one really needs is a handshake. Thank you, Ben – *thank you*, madame! – for opening your home to me.'

January made a show of peering past her to the gallery. 'No Miss Emmett?'

'Are you the chaperone of this famous heiress, then?' Rose led the way back into the parlor, where a fire crackled in the small hearth. 'And can I offer you some coffee, and some of my nephew's pralines? I'm sorry to have to be the one to tell you, madame, that you – and your charge – are being discussed from one end of New Orleans to the other like characters in a serialized novel.'

Persephone rolled her eyes. 'I was afraid of that, the way the servants all peeped at us at the hotel. Coffee sounds wonderful, and please, *please* forgive me for coming here like this when I know you have to be getting ready for your own Christmas dinner.' She glanced around the spotless parlor, as if reading in the extra chairs and the glasses set on the sideboard the expectation of guests. 'I would never have done so, had we not been booked on to a steamboat for Natchez tomorrow, Miss Emmett and myself. I promise you, I won't keep Ben long. And good day to *you*, sir,' she added, as Xander stared up at her with sunny friendliness and said,

'He'o . . .'

'I feel like a monster,' she added more quietly, as January guided her to one of the chairs beside the hearth. 'Especially because I know you must be exhausted—'

'It's all right.' January seated himself across from her. His curiosity notwithstanding, Hannibal materialized as silently as a well-trained butler, bearing two cups of coffee and a plate of pralines, which he set on the small table at the lady's elbow. Then he retreated to the dining room without a word, to help Rose put away the newly dried dishes, intercepting Professor John en route . . . ('Throw me out the window . . .')

For a time they sat in silence on either side of the cheerful fire. In his mind, January saw again dark eyes flashing under the animal tangles of a beaded mane. The gleam of white teeth bared in a mad grin. The deep, hoarse voice growling over a tangle of unknown words.

At length he asked, '*Did* he kill Deverel Wishart? Do you know?'

She shook her head. The black of deep mourning suited few women, and she wasn't one of them. It showed her age, which he guessed at late thirties, though no gray as yet touched those thick sable curls. In the daylight the lines around her eyes were more visible – she had the good sense not to try to plaster them over with paint – and the soft, oval shape of her face still lay neatly tailored over beautiful bones. 'I don't,' she said. 'I don't see how he could have. It's one of the things I want – I *need* – to find out. And I won't know how to even proceed, probably, or what I need to do, if anything, until I get to Natchez, and – I hope – talk to Belle.'

'Belle?' January was startled. 'Belle . . . Miss Wishart . . .' He hesitated over the married name of the girl he'd known in Paris. 'Mrs Grice . . . is in Natchez?' The old sour sickness, the old anger of suspicions unproved and unproveable, drifted through his heart like the distant drag of chains in the dark of the Chateau Palongeux, sixteen years ago.

'When I was in Washington City in November,' said the former danseuse, 'a man named Travis Emmett died, and I assume went straight to Hell: he was one of the wealthiest slave dealers on the East Coast. He was also a moneylender, the landlord of I don't know how many properties in New York City and Washington, and the owner of five plantations in Virginia, three in South Carolina, and ten in Louisiana and Mississippi. Everyone was talking about it, even at the small gatherings suitable to my own widowed state: M'sieu le Vicomte had died in Washington on a journey to America in September, and I had come to put his American investments in order. M'sieu Emmett had been an only child, as his father had been before him. His American second cousins and cousins-once-removed were all outraged that he had left the guardianship of his only child – thank heaven somebody talked some sense into those two idiots last night to keep them from killing each other! – to the partner who manages his affairs in Natchez. I gather Natchez is a major center for the slave trade in this part of the country—'

'It is.' January's voice gritted on the words. 'The lowlands along the river there are the best cotton lands on the continent. The big dealers buy men and women – usually men – from the old cropped-out tobacco plantations in Virginia and Maryland, and walk them through the Cumberland Gap and down the valley of the Tennessee River to Nashville, then down the Natchez Trace to the Forks of the Road, just outside Natchez itself. If you're doing volume business, it's cheaper than taking them around by sea.'

He found himself – after the manner of the Kaintuck keelboat ruffians – wanting to spit, to purge the sour taint of even speaking of the trade, and settled for sipping coffee instead. It didn't help.

After a moment he went on, 'So Miss Emmett is no relation of yours? I wondered, when I saw you both in mourning.'

The vicomtesse shook her head. 'I am in mourning for my husband – whom I will miss, certainly, and whose family is being most kind. But my heart is not broken. But when my husband's uncle – also in Washington at that time – told me that M'sieu Emmett's partner, Creon Grice, had been made guardian—'

'*Creon Grice?*'

The man who had married Belle Wishart. He saw him again, as he first had done, in the twilight at the doors of the Chateau Palongeux: tallish, awkward and colorless, as if he had been wrought entirely of brownish dust. Dust-colored hair slicked back over a pate already beginning to go bald, dust-colored eyes, cold as the dead organs of a gutted sheep, considering him and Ayasha as if weighing up how much he could sell them for, back in the States . . .

A heavy chin and a mouth bracketed by lines of sour calculation, like the Third Rider of the Apocalypse on his black horse, with his balances in his hand and the prices of wheat and barley on his unforgiving lips.

A slave dealer. *Of course he would be . . .*

'I made it my business to seek out the lawyer for Mr Emmett's estate,' Her Ladyship went on. 'I've never felt easy in my mind about Belle's marriage to Grice—'

'How would you?' returned January bitterly. 'The minute he shipped her off to America, he sold off her father's property—'

'And I daresay' – Persephone seemed for a time to be absorbed in the reflection of the lamplight in the black surface of her coffee – 'that you had your own suspicions about how he forced her to marry him. But all I knew was that she'd gone to America. I know you and Ayasha looked for Arithmus . . .'

'We never found a trace of him. Nor,' he added grimly, 'did the police.'

Deverel Wishart. It had been years since he'd last thought of the man.

Now he saw in his mind, not the twisted horror frozen into the face of the man on the bed, but rather the first evening that tall, flamboyant Englishman strode into the upstairs room of the Café Beau Soleil. All January's fellow-members of the Brotherhood of Apollo turned in surprise as the newcomer tossed his crimson-lined cloak back from broad shoulders. 'Have a care, have a care,' he had cried, turning to gesture to the man who shambled in at his heels. 'He is a savage, but I can control him, through a combination of mesmerism and training. And because I hold *this*.'

He raised it up in his fingers. Very old bronze, January had thought at the time – or a very, very good imitation of ruinous age. About three inches high. The statue of a woman with a lion's face, and long braids of hair hanging over her back and her breasts – where jewels had once been embedded in those ropy locks gaped tiny pits. Her foot in its curled slipper rested on the neck of a crumpled man, who wore the crown of ancient Egypt on his head.

Wishart's companion had responded with a throaty ululation, and from his all-enveloping cloak a long, bare, black arm protruded, braceleted in beads and brass. Wishart held the image where his companion could touch it, caress it.

'It is his fetish,' said Wishart solemnly. 'His god. Holding it, *I* am his god.'

And Arithmus – 'the mysterious mathematical freak', the 'marvel of the dark continent', as he had been described in Wishart's letter of introduction to the Brotherhood – fell to his knees, and bowed his braided, shaggy head. '*Menhit*,' he had groaned. '*Sittina-Menhit.*'

'I know it's late in the day,' said Persephone Jondrette, and broke off a fragment of praline that she then set, uneaten, on the edge of her saucer. 'But I want – I have *always* wanted – to make sure that she's well. You never . . .?'

January shook his head, recalling the young woman herself, a brunette bespectacled fairy in a plain blue frock, a cameo of Athena's owl at her throat and a copy of Wolf's *Prolegomena ad Homerum* in her hands. 'I tried to write to her through the Wishart solicitor in London. But of course the property had been sold. I had no idea she was in Natchez.'

'I had no idea there was such a *place* as Natchez,' returned Her Ladyship, 'until I came to Washington. But my husband's uncle, the Marquis de Vallensonges—'

'*Vallensonges*?'

She smiled at his exclamation. 'The very one who was in the Brotherhood of Apollo with you. He was staying at the embassy in Washington, and had not the slightest idea of who I used to be in Paris . . . When I said that I had offered to chaperone Mademoiselle Emmett to Natchez, because, I said, I had met M'sieu Grice and his wife in Paris, he mentioned that she had brought "that frightful savage" of her uncle's to America with her.

And he shook his head and said that he'd always suspected the pair of them of the murder—'

'That's nonsense.'

'The Sûreté didn't think so. I think Belle must have insisted that Grice get Arithmus out of the country with her, when she came to America – even knowing that Grice's family must have claimed him as a slave, the minute he stepped ashore. M'sieu le Marquis said to me that Arithmus was a slave. It is why,' she went on, 'I need to ask you . . . Will you come to Natchez with me?'

'To rescue Arithmus?'

'If I can. To buy him from Grice – get him out of the country, if need be.'

January said softly, 'He may not go.'

'I know.' Half a smile touched her lips. 'I remember Belle telling me how stubborn he is. All the way here in that frightful ship, I've been wondering how to talk to him, how to talk to Belle, even. I only saw Arithmus two or three times – I don't think I ever spoke to him. He might not even remember me.'

'He'll remember.' January half-smiled in return. 'He remembers everything.'

'After sixteen years,' said the vicomtesse, 'I don't think I'd even recognize him. And I don't know if he's in the household with her, or in some other place. Then I saw you at the Viellards' . . .'

Behind them, Hannibal and Rose were spreading the table with the good yellow linen, the stacks of white queensware bowls, plates and bread plates on the sideboard a reminder of how few hours lay between the moment and three o'clock. Persephone glanced at the preparations, then at the clock.

'More than anything else,' she continued quietly, 'I want to make sure that Belle is all right. You saw that M'sieu Grice. I doubt *he* has changed much in the intervening years. But I don't know what the situation there is. Will you come?'

The bitter darkness of the Chateau Palongeux; the directionless crying that wasn't the wind; the clank of chains. Three fingermarks burned into Deverel Wishart's face, and Creon Grice's pale tan eyes. Grice's hand on Belle Wishart's elbow as he pushed her, weeping, into a cabriolet, the last time January had seen the girl who had been his friend.

'I'll come,' he said. And then, 'But only on the condition that you tell me how you went from being première danseuse at the Theatre Pelletier to being a respectable vicomtesse . . .'

She laughed, and as if suddenly released from a weight on her shoulders, picked up her fragment of praline and devoured it with a smile. 'Oh . . . *that*!'

'Daniel told me you left Paris—' He named the man who had supported her in luxury for seven years as a ploy to keep his parents from guessing that his preferences did not run towards women at all.

'That was – soon after the death of his wife.' Her brief silence stepped around that season of sorrow. 'I was approached by two financiers from Geneva, Laurent and Benedict Scudery; they were acquainted with Daniel. They said that their father's second wife had died, and he was grieving. He needed, they said, a young and lovely and *extremely discreet* bride to make him happy for what remained of his own life – he was at that time seventy-two.'

And January smiled, recalling with what *extremely discreet* perfection this woman had played the role of Daniel's mistress.

The laughter in her eyes matched his. 'Daniel said that I should do it. He even sent us a wedding present. In return, I received a new name, new parents – on paper – a new birthplace and education . . .'

'God forbid a respectable Zurich banker should marry a ballerina of the Paris opera, no matter how happy she made him.'

Her smile turned reminiscent, and a little sad. 'He was a sweet and kindly old man,' she said. 'And *he* made *me* very happy. Being a dancer isn't like singing with the opera, Benjamin. One can't keep it up past a certain age, and I did not wish to end like . . . Well, like other women I have known, in my position. I became another person – a young Italian widow, whose respectable family in Capua were more than happy to take a small stipend from the Scudery brothers to claim that yes, I was their daughter, should anyone ask . . . though no one ever did. From the stage, I knew how to behave among the *gratin* of Geneva and Paris—'

'When you came to Paris again,' asked January, 'did no one recognize you?'

'With the Scudery brothers swearing to my identity? Such chance resemblances are common.' She made an airy wave, and smiled again. 'Besides, do you think anyone who saw me on the stage was looking at my *face*? I'm surprised at you, Benjamin . . . And a little insulted . . .'

'I think your M'sieu Scudery was very fortunate,' said January, laughing. 'Both in his wife and in his sons.'

'Well,' she said, 'the boys were extremely good to me too – because I did *not* disgrace myself or run up outrageous debts or take lovers. I had had enough of that life in Paris. When my husband died, he left me extremely well off – which the boys invested for me. And more importantly, as the Widow Scudery, the relict of so respectable and *generous* a man, it was not long before I was able to take my pick among a dozen very flattering offers. Beaufils de St-Forgeux never had the slightest doubt that I was who I said I was – the well-bred Italian widow of a wealthy banker. I gave him the sons he wanted—'

Her smile returned, tender and joyful as he had never seen her, at the thought of her children. 'I was fond of him, and I'm sorry our time together wasn't longer. He cherished his family lands, and I hope my stewardship of them will not disappoint him. But you see that now, if Belle stands in need of a friend who does *not* owe money to her *Harpagon* of a husband – I can tell her that she has one.'

January said quietly, 'She has two.'

THREE

'Uncle Ben, you can't!' Another girl (*Daisy Emmett, perhaps*? reflected January) would have stamped her foot at the words. But Zizi-Marie only caught his elbow as he and Rose returned to the parlor after seeing the lovely vicomtesse down the steps and into her carriage. (He wondered who had paid for the vehicle, the St-Forgeux family or the late Travis Emmett's estate.) 'The wedding is on the fourteenth! You and Aunt Rose have both been so good to me, I want you there—'

'And I'll be there.' January placed his huge hand over his niece's long-fingered, slender one. 'It's only a day and a half up to Natchez, and less than that back. Three weeks—'

Her breath caught a little, with words unsaid, as if she'd unexpectedly pinched a finger in a closing door.

What's this? He had read in her restlessness at breakfast that something was amiss – though his niece was always a quick-moving girl. He had put it down to the approach of her wedding, and perhaps to the fact that Ti-Gall L'Esperance, his mother, and his sisters, were all going to be at dinner that afternoon.

But this is something else.

Before he could ask, footsteps clumped on the gallery again – no light-treading vicomtesse, this time. The way Zizi turned her head, the look in her eyes, told him it was Ti-Gall himself approaching the French door of the study (the 'men's side' of the house) . . .

For a moment, January read apprehension, guilt, uncertainty at the prospect of meeting her fiancé, not a bride's dizzy joy.

But the next instant she flashed into a smile – what his sister, Zizi's mother Olympe, would look like, should she ever shed the watchful aloofness that had armored her from tiniest childhood. And as Zizi fairly skipped toward the study door to let the young man in – January following, as custom dictated he should – Rose materialized to take his arm, the gray-hazel eyes behind the thick oval lenses of her spectacles showing neither surprise nor alarm.

'Will you go?'

'I have to.' January turned his attention from his niece and her sweetheart, to look down into the face of his own. 'Arithmus Wishart – only his true name was Asmerom Sudirja, and I have no idea what he's being called now – was unjustly accused of murdering—'

Rose laid three gentle fingers on his lips. 'It is almost one o'clock,' she pointed out. 'Your sisters will be here within the hour, and everybody else at four . . . And what time does the reception at Avidius Mabillet's house begin?' She drew him back through the parlor, to the door of their bedroom. 'Sleep. I can hear all about your elopement with Madame St-Forgeux at breakfast—'

'We are not going to elope! And we are leaving on the *Sarah Jane* at ten—'

'All the more reason you need to lie down *now*, sir. And don't stir until I call you. I guarantee you, being awake since two o'clock yesterday afternoon will do nothing for either your playing or your subsequent duties as a bodyguard.'

'And she does not want me as a bodyguard!' He was laughing as she pushed him through the bedroom door.

'I'll pack you a bag while you're out at the Mabillets'. Shall I include the girls' Christmas present to you—?'

January rolled his eyes. Rose's pupils had clubbed together to buy him one of the new oilskin 'raincoats': bright yellow, stiff as a suit of cardboard stage-armor, it could have housed two of him with room to spare.

'I'll hide it and tell them you did. I can even tell them you lost it on the way back. You—' Turning with gawky deftness, she caught Hannibal by the arm. 'By the time you walk back to The Swamp, the Keelboat' – this was the saloon in whose attic the perennially penniless Hannibal was camping that week – 'will be open for business and Miss Williams' – that establishment's formidable proprietress – 'will make you deal faro. Go upstairs and sleep in Gabriel's room. The poor boy isn't going to see his own bed until tomorrow morning, so somebody may as well get some use out of it.'

'"I go, I go,"' quoted the fiddler, kissing his hands to her and making a Shakespearean bow. '"Look how I go, Swifter than arrow from the Tartar's bow . . ."'

Laughing again, January kissed Rose, and looking up, saw Zizi-Marie standing a few feet away, that troubled pain back in her eyes. She began, 'Uncle Ben, I need to ask you—'

Rose took the girl's hand. 'Can it wait till later, dear?' And closed the door firmly behind her, leaving January alone.

He spent all of two seconds wondering if he should go out and deal with his niece's trouble – and it *was* trouble, he thought, and could be serious – as he walked to the bed, sat on it and took off his shoes . . .

And didn't wake until Rose called him at three.

He dreamed of Paris.

And of Arithmus Sudirja.

And of Deverel Wishart's body – face convulsed in open-eyed agony and horror, unmarked and still lingeringly warm – on the naked mattress of that haunted tower chamber at the Chateau Palongeux.

Paris – November 1825

'Behold him!' Deverel Wishart flourished with his cloak, great wings of night-black wool lined with orange-red satin, and gestured to the man who shuffled sidelong after him into the comfortable salon above the Café Beau Soleil. At the sight of that slumped, shapeless form, the members of the Brotherhood of Apollo 'scientific club' leaned forward on the chairs that formed a circle two-deep around the chamber. An eager whisper stirred them like wind in long grass.

Under a mop of hair like an unkempt black sheepskin, sharp dark eyes veered back and forth, then fled to stare at the floor. Standing behind the second row, January caught the white glint all around the brown iris. Half-hidden in the red African blanket, long, coal-dark hands fumbled and picked. Next to him, Floréal Michaux – January was surprised that in his dream he remembered the rotund little dandy so clearly – raised a lorgnette to his eyes and gasped, 'My God! Truly a savage beast!'

January reminded himself – in his dream, as he had on that evening in November of 1825 – that if all men were brothers, that included over-dressed idiots like Michaux, and curbed his impulse to shove the man over sideways.

'He speaks no known human language.' Wishart's deep, powerful voice was that of an actor, drawing in the little group in the salon. Not quite a scientific society, not quite a club, certainly not (they would all have sworn) *any* relationship to the Freemason's lodge to which most of them had belonged before the new king's expressed determination to close down all lodges in France. It was in fact illegal for even this group to be meeting, for the king's new laws forbade gatherings of more than five people, lest they speak sedition. But the presence of several members of the upper tier of nobility, like the Duc d'Aveline and the young Vicomte de Heyrieux, had granted a royal exception to the rule in the name of knowledge.

Not that His Majesty has ever opened a book himself in his life . . .

'I found him in an oasis west of Khartoum.' Wishart dropped his voice like an uncle relating a tale of mighty deeds. 'Living wild among the gazelles of the deep desert, upon a diet of dates and scorpions which he ate alive. Yet when I taught him a little French, I discovered in this strange, savage creature astounding gifts, gifts that are given to few men of the so-called civilized world. Arithmus!' he cried, and the bent form writhed around under its gaudy blanket of coarse red wood and animal tails. 'What is the size of this room?'

The shaggy head weaved to and fro. Three-quarters hidden in that rank mat of hair, the face was a strange one. Dark, African features contrasted with a long, undershot jaw and cheekbones too high and oddly shaped, making the eyes seem too close together. A young man, guessed January. And something in his eyes spoke to him not of savage bestiality, but of the porter in the house where he had lived as a medical student, who had collected keys, pins and buttons until his little room was filled with them; of the baker's assistant who lived upstairs from his friend Aristide Carnot, who would not speak to anyone but would hold long conversations with the stray dogs that he fed in the courtyard. Like this 'strange, savage creature', neither would meet any person's eyes.

'Three thousand cubits squared.' The words emerged flat and toneless; the dark gaze fixed on the salon's faded Aubusson. Long, dark fingers pawed and picked at his lips and chin as he spoke.

'What's that in feet, Arithmus?'

'Seven thousand two hundred.' He shifted from foot to foot as he spoke, as if seeking the quickest way to flee from the room.

To his left, January was aware of Louis Gounelle – one of the more obnoxious men of the Brotherhood – and his little coterie of hangers-on all scribbling in their notebooks, checking the 'savage's' assertion.

'And you, sir—' Wishart turned to scan the room, and nodded toward young Marius de Heyrieux, the scion of the House of de Vallensonges. 'What day were you born, if I may be so bold as to ask? It is in the name of science.'

'Thirtieth of May,' replied de Heyrieux. 'Eighteen hundred. Or as it was at the time . . .'

'Prairial.' The African's voice growled in with the name of the month in the calendar of the Revolution. 'The tenth day. *Strawberry Day*,' he added, because the makers of that calendar had replaced the names of the saints' days with the more 'natural' and 'uplifting' nomenclature of fruits, beasts and agricultural tools. He straightened a little – under that barbaric robe January realized he must be close to six feet tall – and looked as if he were about to say something else (*Point out that 30 May was formerly – and is now – the Feast of St Dympne?* January wondered).

But Wishart broke in quickly, 'How many days has this man been alive, Arithmus?'

And there was that momentary pause, not of uncertainty, but of confusion, like an actor forgetting his cue . . .

He's like Morel the porter, January thought. *Like Carnot's neighbor Bara. Not a mysterious savage, but a man of that strange type, playing the role of one . . .*

January found this infinitely more interesting. That this condition – whatever it was that some people manifested – was not limited to men in America or men in France. *Unless of course Arithmus – if that's really his name – actually is American or French, pretending to be a mysterious fetish-worshiping savage . . .*

'Nine thousand two hundred seventy-nine.' Arithmus retrieved his line.

More scribbling to January's left. Gounelle's square, strong-chinned face bore a look of smug annoyance, as if he were waiting for the chance to show up this mysterious mathematical savage . . . From other visits by men of science to the Brotherhood, January knew that the dandyish lawyer liked to show people up. He saw one of Gounelle's sycophants lean over and display his notebook to him.

'And how many seconds is that?'

'Eight hundred and one million seven hundred and five thousand six hundred.'

'And how many seconds,' asked Wishart, 'since the creation of the world?'

'Two hundred forty-seven billion ninety-five million eight hundred eighty-seven thousand two hundred . . .' His face suddenly very un-savage-like, Arithmus turned to look at the clock at the far end of the hall, as if to add in the number of seconds which had elapsed since six p.m. – that being the hour at which Bishop James Ussher of Ireland had calculated God had brought the world into being. Then he seemed to recall a lesson, and added, 'Two million eight hundred fifty-nine thousand eight hundred ninety-eight days.'

'He would calculate the number of camels in passing caravans with no more than a glance.' Wishart spread his hands in a gesture of awe. 'Or the number of bees in a nest. For what purpose has God fashioned such a man as this, in such a place?' From the deep pocket of his coat, he produced a schoolboy's writing slate, and used it as a tray to collect random objects from the men in the room: a seal, a pocket memorandum book, a ring, a candle end. January contributed his silver watch, and kept a sharp eye on it as the Englishman displayed the slate to his . . .

Slave? January wondered. *Servant? Confederate?* He recalled from the letter of introduction that Deverel Wishart was the younger brother of a Norfolk landowner, Stuart Wishart of Parchase. He recalled, in fact, reading the man's name a few years previously, on an article in the Proceedings of the Cambridge Geological Society . . . *Papyrus? Rare species of lotus?*

The mysterious mathematical savage was allowed to look at the display for one second, then Wishart turned his back on him and restored the objects to their owners. 'What was on the tray, Arithmus?' he asked.

Arithmus named them. Described them. A gold quizzing glass

with one sapphire on its rim. A gold card case whose lid bore a line of black enamel: he sketched the ornamental corner with a forefinger. A silver watch made in Paris . . .

He was halfway through this catalog when Louis Gounelle spoke up: 'You're wrong.'

Wishart raised his black brows, like a gentleman of King George's court confronted by an intransigent Jacobite in plaids.

Gounelle declared smugly, 'Since the beginning of creation – going by the good Bishop Ussher's calculation – I make it two million nine hundred . . .'

'I'm not wrong.' Arithmus straightened up. And yes, January saw, he was all of six feet tall, thin and weedy and stooped. 'Since the beginning of the world it's been two hundred forty-seven billion ninety-five . . .'

Gounelle lifted his chin. 'You forgot leap years.'

'I did not forget leap years.'

'Arithmus—' began Wishart, alarmed, but the young man wrenched free of his mentor's staying hand.

'I did not forget leap years!' shouted Arithmus, and Gounelle looked delighted at the expression of baffled fury on the 'mysterious savage's' face.

'You're wrong.' The lawyer's face beamed almost radiant with this petty victory. 'And you, sir' – he turned towards Wishart – 'are a fraud—'

'*I am not wrong!*' Arithmus's features contorted and he flung himself at Gounelle, seized him by the throat, weeping now with rage. 'I didn't forget leap years and I'm not—'

Wishart had already leaped to grab his protégé's arm. Arithmus, with the strength of a madman, flung him off, and January strode forward and caught the enraged youth's other arm. Wishart stepped in again as three other men yanked at the attacker's strangling fingers. January's friend Daniel ben-Gideon – nearly as tall as January and, despite his rouge, hair pomade, and excruciatingly fashionable rose-colored silk waistcoat, nearly as strong – caught Gounelle's wrist as the handsome lawyer attempted to wade back into the fray.

'Gounelle, you really are an ass.' And Daniel strode to the door of the little salon's pantry, flung it open for January and Wishart to drag the cursing, weeping Arithmus through, followed them in and closed it firmly behind them.

New Orleans – December 1840

January opened his eyes. Considered the gray light that now filled the bedroom, the cracks in the plaster ceiling and the hooks upon which, in summertime, the gauzy pink tent of mosquito-bar hung. From the parlor he heard his niece's voice, cheerful and laughing, and the deeper contralto of his sister Olympe: 'Oh, hell, no, they work as a team . . . She puts the cross on white folks' houses over in Third Municipality, gets the servants all in a panic, an' Vinegar John comes in an' takes the hex off. Thing is, it ain't really a cross, 'cause Vinegar John doesn't know a vévé from a valentine, but Americans see somethin' like that an' can't tell the difference. They call him in anyway . . .'

The light, comforting music of chinaware being set. The swish of petticoats and skirts.

Children's voices singing in the courtyard to the tap of their feet in a circle:

> *A la pêche des moules-moules-moules,*
> *Je n'veux plus y'aller Maman,*
> *Les garçons de ville-ville-ville*
> *Me pren' mon panier Maman . . .*

Christmas Day. In a few hours he'd be playing at the Mabillet townhouse on Rue Chartres, rather than sharing the circle of his family beside the living-room hearth. Listening to stout Hercule LaFrennière fulminate about the cost of shipping sugar to New York these days, and to Faisceu Mabillet – red-faced with cognac – wax loudly indignant over the iniquities of the current King of France and demand what right that whore from the House of Orleans had to sit on anything more distinguished than a *chez-percée* . . .

And he'd come home from that, to perhaps three more hours of sleep before he boarded the *Sarah Jane*, up-river to Natchez.

Natchez . . .

He closed his eyes.

Paris – November 1825

'Keep him quiet.' Deverel Wishart had patted Arithmus on the shoulder as a man would reassure a frightened horse. 'He'll calm down in a minute—'

'Will that – statue, that fetish – help?' January had asked, and Wishart had looked surprised.

'Good Heavens, no. It's actually . . . Please, wait.' And he'd darted out of the pantry door in a swirl of black cloak.

Standing between January and Daniel ben-Gideon, Arithmus had trembled all over, as if he'd been beaten. Tears still swam in his eyes and snot dripped from his nose. Daniel offered him one of the collection of spotless linen handkerchiefs he carried at all times, and the 'mysterious savage' took it – still without meeting the eyes of either man beside him – and blew his nose in a completely civilized fashion. He made as if to hand it back to Daniel, then stopped himself, like a child remembering someone telling him that one wasn't supposed to do that.

'Keep it,' said the banker's son in a friendly voice, and Arithmus had nodded.

After a long minute he remembered to mumble, 'Thank you.' And stood for a time, folding and re-folding the soiled linen in his hands. After another minute added, 'Thank you, sir.' Under the red blanket he wore a loincloth, sandals, and necklaces made of goat-hooves and huge black-and-white beads. January noticed that though the young man's dark skin was painted with all sorts of white lines and patterns, nowhere did he bear the tribal scars that so many of the men on Bellefleur wore: men who had been brought over from Africa.

Outside in the salon, Wishart's velvety baritone: 'Of course he miscalculated the number, sir. He would not have been familiar with the change-over from the Julian to the Gregorian calendar, and must not have made allowance for it. My fault entirely . . .'

'I didn't forget.' Arithmus kept his eyes on the floor of the little pantry. His voice – no longer the rough growl of the 'secret savant of the dark continent' – was a low, flat monotone, but not unpleasant, and his French was good. He wiped his nose again. 'That was eleven days, between 4 October and 15 October of the year 1582. It was the Christian Pope Gregory who did that. I don't know why. It was the year 960 back home, because you have to add six hundred and twenty-two years for the Blessed Prophet. But I shouldn't have got angry.'

'We all get angry,' said January.

'I don't want to get M'sieu Wishart in trouble. I don't want to be this way,' he added, moving his gaze to another portion of the floor beside Daniel's highly varnished boots. 'I don't know how not to be. I get angry sometimes, and I can't stop.'

New Orleans – December 1840

When he heard Hannibal's voice in the parlor, January got up. He and the fiddler crossed the yard to the kitchen (where Zizi-Marie, Olympe, Olympe's Junoesque mother-in-law Cassy Corbier, and Rose were poking the sweet potatoes boiling over the hearth, or chopping peppers and corn), borrowed a firkin of hot water from the boiler, and retreated to the tiny laundry room to wash and shave.

'Rose tells me you and I are accompanying the incomparable Persephone to Natchez,' remarked Hannibal.

January met his eyes. 'Thank you,' he said simply. 'That will make things a great deal easier. I could pass myself off as Madame de St-Forgeux's footman, but I don't know how trustworthy this young Miss Emmett of hers is about keeping her mouth shut. For all I know, she may resent the hell out of being given a chaperone and may tell everyone she meets that Madame didn't have a footman all the way from Washington City to New Orleans . . . And she may even recognize me from playing last night. You being my "master" will wallpaper over any number of holes in the story.'

'*Vivo solum servire.*' The fiddler inclined his head. 'And who am I to turn down four days in the gambling room of a steamboat filled with wealthy gentlemen on their way home from selling their cotton in town?'

January grinned, in spite of his annoyance (*No*, he corrected himself . . . *anger* . . .) at having to masquerade as a slave because it was safer for a black man to travel that way in America. Slave stealers, up and down the Mississippi, knew that the hunt for a missing free man of color would be considerably less assiduous than for a man who was worth twelve hundred dollars to somebody.

'Look upon it as your gift from Père Noël. Arithmus Wishart – the man we're going to search for – may or may not be in Natchez. He may be across the river on one of Creon Grice's plantations: Grice is owner or part-owner or manager of about seventeen of them. Arithmus knows me,' he went on quietly. 'He's . . . People call them *idiot-savants*, but he's no idiot. He just doesn't think the way other people do. He'll recognize Persephone, but he may not come forward, and she only saw him a few times, that winter of twenty-five. She says they never spoke. I don't know what he's been through, in the past sixteen years. I don't know who he'll trust, who he'll speak to, or who he'll believe.'

'To say nothing of what people will say,' remarked Hannibal, toweling his scrawny torso and slipping into one of Gabriel's clean shirts – the laundry room, despite its proximity to the kitchen, was sharply cold – 'if a white woman – and a French viscountess at that – tries to go up and have a conversation with a field-hand. Not a strategy to pursue if one wishes to be discreet.'

'That, too.' January pulled on his own shirt, buttoned up his good white satin waistcoat and tied his cravat.

From the kitchen he heard his niece denouncing her brother for abandoning them all to work today – 'Don't none of those hotel folks think that black folks may . . . oh . . . have *families* or somethin' that *they'd* like to spend Christmas with?'

(*Actually, no . . .*)

'And I swear it,' she added, as January and Hannibal emerged – scrubbed and shaved and point-device in black swallowtail coats and pale trousers – into the kitchen again, 'if Uncle Ben isn't back by the fourteenth for the wedding . . .'

'I swear I will rival Odysseus in my struggles to return to my home again!'

'Huh.' Zizi tossed her head, beautiful in a holiday tignon of pistachio-green and gold. Slim and tall, like her mother, the rounder contours of Paul Corbier's good-natured face softening Olympe's sharp bone-structure. 'Aunt Rose read me those books, and it took that man *ten years* to get his sorry butt home, and after he'd fooled around with goddesses and nymphs all from one end of the ocean to the other.'

'That's what you get for educating women,' sighed Hannibal, reaching around Rose to filch a cookie.

'Mama . . .' The dangerous glint in Zizi's eye reminded January all too sharply of Olympe – and of their mutual mother . . . 'If Uncle Ben doesn't come back here by the fourteenth, I want you to put a curse on him.'

'How bad of a curse, *cher*?' asked Olympe, hiding a malicious grin. 'Big curse or little curse?'

'Zizi!' exclaimed Gran'mère Corbier. 'Olympe! Shame on the both of you, talkin' of cursin' on Christmas Day!'

'Big curse,' declared Zizi. 'Biggest you got. Black salt double-cross goofer-dust with fish hooks in it.' Paul Corbier had made sure that all their children went to Mass and studied their catechism, but January reflected that a girl couldn't very well grow up in the same house with a voodooienne for a mother, and *not* learn at least something about black salt double-cross goofer-dust with fish hooks.

'That's not very fair to your Aunt Rose, honey,' replied Olympe mildly. 'But if *you*' – she turned suddenly, and pointed a long, thin finger at the startled Hannibal – 'don't bring Ben back safe, I'm gonna put a curse on *you*. A love-curse,' she added, as the fiddler opened his mouth to protest.

'You mean no lady's ever gonna fall in love with him again?' The girl looked distressed at the thought. January was aware his niece had had a tender spot for Hannibal since she was ten years old.

'Lord, no.' Olympe waved the thought aside. 'You'd have to change the motion of the stars an' planets to keep ladies from fallin' in love with that worthless *blankitte*. But if you don't bring Ben back safe . . .' She sank her voice, as she did when scaring the socks off her Corbier nieces and nephews with tales of the platt-eye devil, and made her eyes glitter, 'I will put the love-curse on you, that the ladies who fall in love with you will be possessive, an' troublesome, jealous an' wicked, an' will be crazy in love.'

Eyes wide with not-entirely-feigned terror, Hannibal whispered, 'I swear I will bring him home safe.'

Zizi grinned, and kissed him on the cheek. 'You see you do that.'

Rose slipped him another cookie, as the whole posse – less Olympe and her mother-in-law – trooped out of the kitchen and back across the overgrown little yard toward the house.

FOUR

'Uncle Ben . . .' Zizi-Marie caught his arm.

The others clattered up the back-gallery stairs, Rose with a platter of cookies, Hannibal indignantly pointing out that Odysseus and his crew had only themselves to blame for their misfortunes on the way back from Troy to Ithaca. (*'Vain toils! Their impious folly dared to prey/On herds devoted to the god of day . . .* If they'd obeyed orders, they'd have made it home in a week . . .')

The afternoon had grown cold. Already candles were being lit inside the house. From within, January heard his mother's smoky drawl, 'Pff! What's a vicomtesse? I understand that an actual *prince* will be at the Mabillet ball.' And Ti-Gall's booming threat, 'Fee, fi, fo, fum, I'm'a gon' get you an' *eat you all up!*' Thundering little feet: Professor John, little Ti-Paul Corbier, the youngest two of Ti-Gall's sisters, Charmian Viellard – daughter of January's youngest sister Dominique and Henri Viellard. Shrieks of terror as they fled the ogre . . .

Christmas light.

We all be together in one room, with all the lamps burning, as old Lucien said, *while the cold midnight of the year rolls over us and spirits walk the dark air.*

They stopped at the bottom of the steps, and January took his niece's hands. 'What is it, honey?'

'Can I talk to you – and—' She glanced back over her shoulder at the cheerful hell-mouth of the kitchen. 'And you not tell Mama? Or anyone?'

'You're a grown woman now, Zizi. What you choose to tell me – what you choose to do – isn't your Mama's business anymore.'

Her eyes ducked away from his. 'Thank you.' Then long silence, as she collected what she wanted to say, how she wanted to say it.

Don't tell me Ti-Gall's gotten her with child . . .

'Uncle Ben,' she said again slowly. 'How do you know if you're in love with somebody? I mean, when you meet them. When you haven't lived with each other, like you and Aunt Rose. How can you tell?'

How can you tell? He remembered his heart breaking, when he was fourteen and the beautiful girl he adored told him she was going to become plaçée to a rich white planter with seven children and barely twice that many teeth. (He and Rose had had her, and her beautiful daughter, and her faithful now-octogenarian lover to a holiday dinner last Sunday, his love for her mellowed to a friendship more precious than gold.)

Remembered laughter and summer evenings in Paris with the long-legged mistress of the opera ballet, love worn lightly as a chaplet of flowers as they'd walked out to St-Cloud for water-lily tea. Love mingled with laughter, pretty as candle-flame, whose nature he hadn't clearly perceived until he'd met Ayasha, like seeing the sun.

Ayasha.

And after that sun was quenched in abyssal darkness, he hadn't believed that day would ever dawn again. And when Rose Vitrac had turned to him in the murky shadows of the Charity Hospital, that rainy night in the fever season of 1834 – *I need a doctor . . . three of my girls are down sick . . .*

Had he known then?

He didn't remember. His own grief for Ayasha had still been raw flesh.

When did I realize I couldn't live without her?

He asked, 'Have you met someone?'

Someone other than Ti-Gall, tall and clumsy and so kind-hearted that he'd gently chase a bee out of the parlor rather than swat it.

Zizi-Marie's beautiful bronze lips tightened. 'I don't want to hurt Ti-Gall.'

How much more will he be hurt if you're unfaithful to him within the first year of your marriage? Or if you're not, but wish you were?

He put his arm around her, drew her to a rough-hewed bench set under the back gallery of the house, where the runaways he sometimes sheltered in the storerooms would now and then come out to take the air in late evening darkness, where nobody could see.

'There's this man – a white man – Marc-Antoine Picard—' She kept her eyes on her fingers, interlaced in her lap. 'He asked me to . . . to be plaçée. He's not some fly-by-night American,' she added quickly, looking up into January's face. 'He's related to just about everybody – to all the decent white folks – in town—'

'This would be one of Isaïe Picard's sons?' The Picards were indeed one of the oldest French Creole families in New Orleans, owning half a dozen sugar plantations among them, as well as ten cotton plantations up-river, town lots and rentals in New Orleans and Natchez, and shares in steamboats and cotton-presses. Years of listening to the gossip of his mother and sisters – not to speak of seeing every member of French Creole society at seven years' worth of balls and parties since his return from Paris – let him triangulate upon Marc-Antoine Picard with the exactness of a guide hearing a stranger's description of well-known territory. *There's a toy shop with two armies of lead soldiers in the windows, green coats on one, white coats on the other, across the street from a blacksmith shop . . . Oh, yes, that's Rue St-Philippe at Rue Bourbon . . .*

To his mind came the image of a good-looking youngish man in a modish Indian-red coat, joking with the other young gentlemen around the punchbowl at this reception or that, or leading one young lady or another out into a set of quadrilles. Someone who had never caught January's attention by being argumentative or drunk or loud or pushy. Someone who brought cups of lemonade to his mother and aunts.

Oh, yes, that's Marc-Antoine Picard . . . he would have said in the same tone.

'How do you know him?' When a girl was asked to become plaçée – placed – by a white man as a mistress, it was generally because her mother had been plaçée before her. Had brought her to one of the Blue Ribbon Balls at the Orleans Ballroom.

Olympe had run away from home at the age of sixteen, rather than let her mother take her there. She still had a way of lifting the left side of her lip, when such functions were mentioned.

'He and his parents used to come to Papa's shop.' Zizi turned her face aside again, as if the knuckles of her own hands were the most fascinating things in the chill slow-gathering shadows beneath the gallery. 'This was back before the bank crash. His Mama was having all their parlor furniture redone. He'd chat with me a little then. I liked him then,' she added, meeting his eyes once more, like one who fears her story will be doubted. 'Then a couple weeks – I guess a month – ago, I was at the market and he was buying flowers, at the next stall. He said, *Zizi!* And we . . . we talked. He walked with me a little ways back toward the house.'

Her glance dodged aside again, to the warm scarf of amber light that lay outside the kitchen doors. January didn't say, *That isn't usual, for a white man in his late twenties to walk with a librée girl up Rue Esplanade . . .*

But it wasn't unheard of. And he wanted her to go on, without breaking her train of thought.

'I told him I was engaged to be married. He asked, could he meet me, and walk maybe along the bayou? I didn't want to tell Mama.' The eyes fleeted back to his. 'Or you, I guess. Or Aunt Rose.'

No, thought January. *No. Rose, or I, would certainly have asked questions, and you may not have known the answers then.* Zizi-Marie and her brother had lived with them, since the bank crash of 1837 had made it impossible for Rose to hire the help she would need to keep a house clean without turning herself into a drudge. Impossible, also, for the upholsterer Paul Corbier to get enough work to support all five of his children. January's risky employment – finding missing persons, or unraveling puzzles that the City Police either wouldn't touch or couldn't be informed of (for one good reason or another) – had served to eke out the family finances during the two years that Rose's school had been untenanted and white folks' paying balls and musicales had been few and far between. It had been logical for Olympe's two oldest children to go share the big house on Rue Esplanade. Zizi helped with household chores so that Rose could get a little money by translating Greek poetry for local booksellers or publishers. Gabriel had quickly found work as a sous chef at the Hotel Iberville.

But there had been plenty of time when Zizi-Marie had not been at the house. When she could have been meeting, not her friends, but one particular friend. And that particular friend, not always Ti-Gall L'Esperance.

'Does he care for you?' One didn't – not in New Orleans or anywhere in the United States – speak the word *love* about a white man and a black woman. At dozens of balls, of course, January had overheard any number of white men casually boast of the intensity with which their librée mistresses adored *them*. But that – every one of those white men would have said – was 'different'.

'Yes.' The word came out like a fingernail flicked against the side of a tin pan.

'Do you love him?'

Zizi drew a deep breath. 'I . . . I guess I need to know if I love Ti-Gall.'

That isn't what I asked—

She went on, rather quickly, 'We've talked, we've been together – one night he came, quiet, to the gate, and we kissed in the passway . . . Uncle Ben, you know M'sieu Viellard loves Aunt Minou—' That was the family name for Dominique, and yes, January knew. Fat, timorous Henri Viellard did love Dominique and was passionately loved in return – a love he didn't get from his precise, cold-blooded little wife.

'And you saw Sunday, how old M'sieu Motet loves M'am Clisson—'

January couldn't help smiling again, at the recollection of the girl who'd broken his fourteen-year-old heart, all those years ago.

But you still didn't answer my question.

'And Ti-Gall . . . Uncle Ben, this sounds terrible, *terrible* to say, but the more I look at it, the more I think about it . . . Our children, Ti-Gall's and mine, would be . . . would be like I am. Like Gabriel's going to be, struggling all his life, because Mama and Papa have so little. You go out and risk your life, only to keep a roof over your family's head. If anything happened to you . . . You know what would happen to the Little Professor, and to Xander, in spite of everything Aunt Rose could do.'

Her words stumbled over each other, and he could see how she quivered with the effort of bringing them out at all. 'I know I shouldn't be thinking like this about getting married and falling in love, but it's true! I can't . . . You know Ti-Gall! You know he's not like you, he's not like Madame Metoyer—' She named their neighbor, the sharp and successful owner of a chocolate shop . . . who had been plaçée and had gotten the capital for the shop from her white lover. 'Ti-Gall will be good, he'll be faithful . . . but he'll never be more than what he is.'

'He will, in fact,' pointed out January. 'He's apprenticed to his Uncle Ghis, making harnesses. There's no reason he won't make his living at it.'

'He'll never own his own shop.' Zizi turned to face him yet again. 'You know that. He just doesn't have the money for that. None of his family do.'

January knew that his niece spoke the truth. Knew, too, that he and Rose had only wed when the issue of money had been resolved – by a chance windfall of cash, which had let them buy the house that could be used as a school. Otherwise, what could he have offered her, beyond a room rented in the house of yet another ex-plaçée?

'*Do* you love Marc-Antoine Picard?'

'Yes.' He saw something – some heat, some memory of passion – flicker in her eyes.

She went on very quickly, 'He's offered me a contract, in the old way. He'll buy me a house – in the Faubourg Marigny – and settle six hundred dollars a year on me.' She took a deep breath, steadying the flood of her words. 'Our children can go to proper schools. Can learn surgery, the way you did. Or learn things like Greek and Latin, like Aunt Rose, so he can teach, or work in a bank. Ti-Gall—'

She couldn't go on. From overhead, Ti-Gall's voice called out, 'Mama?' across the yard, where the three French doors of the kitchen had begun to glow more strongly as shadows collected. January heard on the gallery the voices of their neighbors, the Metoyer sisters, laughing at Hannibal's outrageous declarations of devotion. ('*Doubt that the stars are fire/ Doubt that the sun doth move . . .*') Paul Corbier, his deep voice protesting, 'What's the big deal about a prince anyway, m'am? Bet he doesn't have half the money this Miss Emmett's supposed to, that Ben's going up-river to protect . . .'

Light still filled the sky overhead, but in the yard, within its high walls, it was twilight, and would soon be night.

The glow of the kitchen doors outlined Olympe's slim figure, gleamed on the lid of a covered dish. Behind her, Cassy Corbier called, 'Ben? You out there? We got us a goose in here needs be carried—'

In less than three hours, January knew he and Hannibal would be leaving for the Mabillet townhouse.

'Does Ti-Gall know any of this?'

Zizi-Marie wiped her eyes, and shook her head.

'Don't do anything until I get back from Natchez. Are you still sewing for Madame Trulove?' For weeks now, Zizi had earned extra money for her wedding by doing embroidery for the English planter Fitzhugh Trulove's wife. 'Keep working for her if you can,' he went on, when Zizi nodded. 'Don't give up that bit of money for right now – or burn any bridges. All right?'

She managed to smile. 'All right.'

And maybe when I get back, reflected January, as he crossed the yard to the kitchen's warmth and his own duties as host and goose-bearer, *you can tell me what it is you're lying about.*

He turned to look back towards the house, in time to see Zizi-Marie reach the top of the steps, and let Ti-Gall take her in his arms.

At the Mabillet ball that evening, he watched for Marc-Antoine Picard. The Picards hadn't taken sides in the ongoing affray between Royalists and Bonapartists that periodically exercised the Creole French community, and so were welcome at the festivities on both sides. The man was as he recalled: good-looking, dark-eyed, his hair a mingled bronze and gold. He squired all the bright-gowned, marriageable girls – Aubins and Mabillets, Pitots and Crozats, Trepagniers and Maginots – on to the dance floor with not the smallest hint that it was not a pleasure to partner each and every one, regardless of their family fortunes, and gave the impression of a man who wouldn't *dream* of taking a mistress.

Music like gold and light, except for the thought that returned to January again and again, of the choice that his niece faced.

And the sense, deep in his heart, that Zizi-Marie wasn't telling him the whole of the truth.

The custom of plaçage was waning, but there were still men in New Orleans who made these shadow-marriages with free women of color. Who bought them houses, paid their bills, settled pensions on them, educated their children and gave them money to get a start in life. He recalled with affection his mother's protector, St-Denis Janvier, who had had the kindness to buy both her children when he had purchased her from Simon Fourchet. He had paid for their education, though they were another man's get and that other man, an African cane-hand with 'country-marks' cut into his face.

And he knew that Zizi was right. What, indeed, could Ti-Gall L'Esperance offer a bride, save hardship shared, and children raised in borderline poverty if no worse . . . and a heart like the ocean and the sky?

Would I want to see Rose lying in another man's arms, if I knew that that man would give her children all that I have not the wealth to provide?

Across the Mabillet ballroom, grass-green and gilt and sparkling in the light of two huge chandeliers, old Sidonie Janvier caught his eye again and smiled. He knew the matriarch still had coffee with his mother on Sundays, and regarded him as 'one of the family' – 'from the shady side of the street'. Close beside her, Henri Viellard – his sister Dominique's 'protector' – stood dutifully by, ignored until his mother and the dowager Madame Mabillet exchanged kisses, then bowed himself – had January been closer he could have heard the young planter's corsets creak – and kissed his hostess's hand. 'My *dear*,' effused Marie-Honorine Mabillet, 'you simply *must* introduce me – and my dear nephew Gontran' – she almost pushed her stout young protégé into the group – 'to your lovely Miss Emmett . . .'

Over dinner that afternoon, January recalled, his mother had remarked that the Mabillets still didn't have a pot to piss in.

And Madame Mabillet – and the eligible but impecunious (and wart-nosed) Gontran – were going to be out of luck this evening, as most of the Bonapartiste Mabillets had little use for such Legitimiste nobility as the St-Forgeux and Vallensonges and hadn't invited the vicomtesse and her charge. Presumably in trade for promises of future introductions to the heiress, however, the dowager Madame Mabillet was leading her friend Madame Viellard – still trailing Henri and his two unmarried sisters – to meet the 'genuine prince' previously advertised.

January had noticed the young man earlier, resplendent in a clearly non-American crimson dress uniform plastered across the chest with rows of bullion. Gold tassels winked from his boots.

'Hungarian Imperial Hussars,' whispered Hannibal. 'Wonder if it's his or if he rented it for the occasion?'

'His Highness, Prince Serafin Corvinus.' Madame Mabillet made sure everyone nearby heard the title, and plumed herself like a pigeon as all the Viellard ladies, including the senior madame, sank into the deep curtseys that Zizi-Marie would have executed that morning for the vicomtesse.

The young man himself – tall and wide-shouldered, dark-haired, dark-eyed, and splendid of thigh – made a gracious reply, and the older man who followed him in a rather Germanic swallowtail coat and the blue ribbon of some European order, glowered behind his monocle. 'My tutor, Doktor Boehler,' the prince introduced.

Sent by Papa and Mama back home to keep His Highness out of trouble? Such pedagogues had not been uncommon, January recalled, trailing the sons of minor Germanic royalty in Paris.

Madame Mabillet glowed with triumph, at the coup of having procured such a guest for her Christmas ball.

Olympe, January knew, held him and his fellow musicians in scorn for their fondness for gossip about the wealthy whites of the town – 'Like you don't have families an' wives of your own!' But completely aside from the entertainment that January and his friends derived from the never-ending intrigues among the French Creole aristocracy, as they maneuvered for social superiority and the acquisition of money, credit, and land, January was also aware that these were the people who held power. These were people whose crotchets and whims could quickly translate into work – or trouble – for him and for everyone he knew. He kept an eye on them, the way he'd check the edges of a cornfield for tracks, if he farmed next to a forest where wolves and lions roamed.

This came as second nature to him, and it had not been different in France under the last of the Bourbon kings.

And to this day, he recalled, there were tracks and signs he'd seen at that haunted chateau near Paris, that he hadn't been able to interpret – but that had told him even then that Arithmus Wishart was innocent of the crime that all had said he'd done.

FIVE

'So tell me, *amicus meus*,' Hannibal closed the minuscule stateroom's door as January set the fiddler's shabby carpet bag on the bunk, 'how did this all start, in the winter of 1825?'

The woodwork of the *Sarah Jane* shuddered as the big side-wheeler backed away from the wharves. Dimly, January heard the deck-hands shouting down below, as luggage was stowed in the hold, and the boxes and bales of goods bound for Bayou Sara, Natchez, and Vicksburg were dragged into better position around the deck. Morning sun glared around the edges of the small window's faded curtain, and through his boot soles, January felt it when the port wheel stopped, the starboard wheel changed direction, to the dim clanging of bells.

The pilot's voice yelled, 'Snatch her! Snatch her, God damn it – pull her down! Where the *hell* you think you're goin' . . .'

The heavy hand of the current pressed the vessel's side as the *Sarah Jane* pivoted slowly in the water. The *Sarah Jane* was a fast boat: they'd be in Donaldsonville by dinnertime, Bayou Sara at midnight, depending on how many riverside plantations had flags out on their landings. November and December saw the harvest of both cotton and sugar; every planter on the river had spent the past weeks in New Orleans buying everything from hair ribbons to sugar boilers. Those who weren't actually on the boat with their purchases would be waiting on a thousand plantation wharves from Carrollton to St Louis, squinting down-river and muttering, *Where the hell's that goddamn boat . . . ?*

The yellow-brown waters around them churned with torn-off branches and the stumps of trees. Wind from the north blew cold.

'It didn't really start in 1825,' January said after a time. 'You could say it started in 1798, when Napoleon invaded Egypt . . . or maybe in 1789, with the Revolution. If one wanted to be obnoxious about it—'

'Oh, please do!' Hannibal urged, perched tailor-fashion on the end of the bunk.

'—you could say it started in 1484, when the Sieur de Palongeux swore fealty to the Marquis de Chalon-Neuf.'

The fiddler's dark eyes sparkled. 'Do I detect a lawsuit over King Charles X's reparations for lands confiscated by the Revolutionary government from some – but not all – of the French nobility?' He, too, had been in Paris in 1825.

Drowned in a lake of laudanum at the time, reflected January. But surfacing once in a while, presumably, to read a newspaper.

'You do. Or you might say,' he went on after a moment, 'that it started sometime in the second century AD. Or even seven centuries before the birth of Christ, when the armies of Nubia might – or might not – have marched into the realm of the pharaohs from the south.'

Paris – November 1825

Deverel Wishart came fairly regularly to the meetings of the Brotherhood of Apollo after that, that winter of 1825.

The men of the Brotherhood liked him – with the exception of the (Bonapartist) Duc d'Aveline, whose contentions about certain inscriptions on the upper reaches of the Nile he disputed. His graceful apology to Louis Gounelle, and an admission of error before all the Brotherhood, had won him that young lawyer's condescending camaraderie, though every man in the room had later laboriously calculated years and days and seconds and it was fairly obvious to them all that it was Gounelle (or rather Gounelle's cousin Olivier, whose family had been living off the gifts of Gounelle's father's coal mines and railway shares for years) who had been in error. Like most of the Brotherhood, Wishart was a Freemason, and he attended the much-reduced meetings at the Lodge. In this, his elder brother Stuart Wishart joined him, when that stout, unobtrusive scholar came to Paris to meet his daughter, who had traveled to Egypt in her flamboyant uncle's company. Like most of the Brotherhood, Deverel Wishart's learning was wide-ranging and his interests wider still: education and political theory some evenings, chemistry and the strange botany of the Asian islands and the farthest coasts of Africa on others. And sometimes just the ankles of the newest danseuse at the Theatre Pelletier.

Wishart was good company. For all his exuberant showmanship – he exhibited Arithmus's skills at street fairs and society drawing rooms all over Paris – he was a good listener, whether to Abelard Bourgeois – whom January had met during his time as a surgeon at the Hôtel-Dieu – speculating about the medical knowledge of the ancient Romans, or to foppish Floréal Michaux holding forth about the smaller size and 'degenerate' nature of American animals as compared to those of Europe (not that the man had ever set foot in America in his life).

Stuart Wishart was well-liked also during his short visit. Equally erudite in his self-effacing way, he was more apt to discuss the laborers' housing on his own property in Norfolk than of the unfortunate citizens of Pompeii or Atlantis. He came to Paris to escort his daughter home – seventeen-year-old Belle ran the house her uncle had rented on the Rue St-André des Artes and presided over a sort of salon for the Brotherhood on Sunday afternoons. But Belle (named for a Mesopotamian goddess rather than for the warrior-queen of old Spain) coaxed her father into allowing her a few more weeks in Paris, to argue theories of art with Marius de Heyrieux and the gods of Greece with Daniel ben-Gideon. Stuart Wishart – a moderately wealthy property owner with aspirations to one day acquire a baronetcy – compromised by hiring a beefy Breton Amazon named Citoyenne-de-la-République Thibaut as the girl's maid, and every man of the Brotherhood guessed that the elder Wishart was deeply proud of the scholarly, bespectacled little sylph who shared his – and his brother's – love of knowledge for its own sake.

'Stuart's the head in our partnership,' explained Wishart, at one of those Sunday afternoons over some very good Merlot that de Heyrieux had brought up from his uncle's estates in Burgundy. 'The head and the pocket book. The journey up the Nile was his idea – he's wanted to explore the temples of Egypt since the pair of us read the *Egyptian Memoir* of Napoleon's band of scholars. But he left it to me to plan it, and in the end, with our father's death last year, the poor old fellow had to stay home after all.'

'So he is the head and the pocket book,' smiled stout Sardou the apothecary, 'and you're the soul?'

Wishart thought about that, while the winter rain clattered on the closed shutters of the salon's long windows, and Bloque

– one of the servants who'd been hired with the house – brought in coffee that smoked a little in the gold of the candlelight. 'Rather you could say,' he raised a forefinger as though pointing out some detail to himself, 'that Stuart outlines a sketch in pencil, and I'm the one who fills in the colors. And Belle' – he glanced across the comfortable, white-paneled room towards his niece – 'is the one who points out to me where I've missed a spot.'

Dressed in her schoolgirl frock and hair ribbons, her spectacles flashing in the light of the hearth, Belle laughed at some tale January's wife Ayasha was telling – either about her appalling family back in Algiers, or the extravagant excesses of her wealthy customers here in Paris, it was impossible to guess. With Ayasha, it could have been anything.

'Our Great-Aunt Caroline – Father's old aunt – was speechless with horror at the thought of Belle going to Egypt with me.' The explorer smiled like a mischievous elf at the recollection. '"She'll miss the queen's drawing room!"' he squeaked in imitation, and flung up his hands. '"It will mean she won't come *out* for another year! How *ever* will Stuart get her married off?"'

And Belle's head turned for a moment, half-protesting, as she caught the mimicry of the family dowager's tones.

'And his business manager nearly had an apoplexy at the idea – not over Belle's reputation, but over the cost of the journey . . .'

On other evenings, when the Brotherhood gathered at the Beau Soleil, Wishart was sometimes accompanied by Arithmus, whom he described as his 'servant'. In addition to his uncanny skill with numbers, the young African would reproduce drawings made on the spot by the artist Aristide Carnot after being given a one-second view of them, or repeat back – in French considerably better than his own usual speech – conversations improvised between January and Daniel on the subject of waistcoats and hats. For an experiment, on one occasion January and Daniel carried on a conversation in German, a language January had learned on the wharves of his native New Orleans, pretending to be two market women arguing over whose son was going to marry the daughter of a wealthy acquaintance. This, too, Arithmus reproduced exactly, down to Daniel's affected gestures and January's exaggerated eye-rolling.

'Did you actually know what we were saying?' January asked

Arithmus later, when he emerged – earlier than the others that evening, because he had to give piano lessons the next morning to the daughter of a financier in Louveciennes – by the gates of the Palais-Royal gardens. It was the busy part of the evening, fiacres and carriages dodging one another like ponies in a circus exhibition on the wet pavement of the *place*: Wishart, on the edge of the steps, was performing a sort of human version of a military semaphore tower in an effort to catch the attention of the jehus. Around him, patrons emerged from the restaurants, gaming parlors and shops in the galleries that surrounded the ancient royal garden and dashed in pursuit of one vehicle or another. Carriage lamps and gaslights threw flickers of color on the blue or black coats of the men, the too-bright gowns of the ladies. Wrapped in a baggy black greatcoat, Arithmus kept back, his barbaric scarlet robe in a discreet bundle beneath one arm, a wide-brimmed hat jammed down to hide the bones and feathers braided in his hair. He had washed the white paint from his face, after – January observed – leaving the Brotherhood's meeting, presumably in the interests of making it easier for Wishart to signal a vehicle.

The young man glanced once, furtively, at January's face, then looked away, as he had that first evening in the café's upstairs pantry. All evening, as he usually did, he had kept silent unless spoken to; now, in his heavily accented French he mumbled, 'No. That wasn't French, was it?'

His own French, January had already observed, was good – far better than he used during his turn as a 'mysterious mathematical freak'. The flat monotone of his voice gave the impression of something learned by rote, but January knew by this time that it was just how he spoke.

'German,' said January. And, seeing Arithmus trying to fit that together with things he'd heard before, he added, 'It's the language they speak in Bavaria, and Prussia, and Saxony.'

'It's different than French.' Arithmus thought about it some more. After their first conversation in the pantry, January was always careful to speak to the 'mystery of the dark continent' when none of the rest of the Brotherhood could hear. Arithmus, he had gathered, was not a servant at all, but a sort of partner to Wishart, playing a savage barbarian because it got them a better audience and more paid exhibitions of the young man's truly astonishing skills. 'There's some of the same words. *Factory* and *hairdresser* . . .'

January recalled the portion of his scene with Daniel that had dealt with the fictitious wealthy heiress's fictitious father's fictitious factory . . . And the need to consult a hairdresser . . .

'*Alley* and *lover* . . .'

Another long silence. Though nearly January's great height, when not imitating a mysterious savage, Arithmus seemed to shrink in on himself, and though he'd been in Paris for some weeks at this point, he still seemed to be looking for a place to hide from the noisy crowds in the *place*. Wishart glanced back at them, half-hidden in the shadows of the arcade, then nodded a little to himself and went on with his arm-waving. The Englishman had been wary that first time he'd returned to the upstairs room at the Beau Soleil, listening and watching for any sign that any of the men there – besides January and Daniel – knew of the imposture. When Daniel had asked him to recount the details of his discovery of the 'barbarian savage' and everyone had nodded and listened, it had seemed to reassure him that neither January nor Daniel would peach.

'Back home everybody has different languages,' said Arithmus at length. 'Ethiopians speak one thing and Arab merchants it's all different. They all use a lot of the same words from each other's languages – *tea* and *sugar* and *blood*, and *four* and *seven* and *ten* . . .' He ticked these loan-words off on his fingers and looked on the point of going on to enumerate an entire catalog of similarities, then stopped himself, again recalling some lesson about keeping his mouth shut. Then, after long thought, 'Mama and Papa speak Nubian at home and Somali to the clerks. I speak Arabic too.'

And January smiled. 'I'll bring you to my home for dinner one Sunday, to meet my wife,' he said in that language. 'She's from Algiers.'

Arithmus had glanced up, shyly, as if confused, then away again. 'I'd like that.'

Mississippi River – December 1840

'Dev Wishart had a blood-and-thunder tale of finding Arithmus living alone in a jackal's den in an oasis in the Libyan desert.'

Persephone, Vicomtesse de St-Forgeux, chuckled as she leaned her back against the railing of the *Sarah Jane*'s upper deck, turned her head to view the dark-green monotony of the cypresses on the riverbank, the bright squares of the plantation houses visible through the trees. Chilly sun splattered on the steamboat's paddles, and the pilot – who, as far as January could tell, hadn't shut up since leaving New Orleans – was cursing at the leadsmen measuring the depth of a sunken bar.

'Quarter-twain . . . quarter-twain . . . quarter less twain . . .'

Looking ahead, January could see yet another white flag fluttering on a plantation landing, and sighed. It was four in the afternoon and they stood to reach Donaldsonville just before sunset.

'In fact, his name was Sudirja, and he was the oldest son of a merchant named Berhane al-Tajir, whom Wishart came to know when he was exploring up the Nile. The young man had a perfectly good education – Berhane shipped ivory and hardwoods out of Asouan across to the Red Sea, and to ports all over the Indian Ocean. But Arithmus was . . . odd. Rather like Uncle Veryl St-Chinian's friend Mr Singletary. Brilliant with mathematics – he was doing the books and banking for the family firm before he was twelve – but unable to be around people. He would panic in gatherings, and weep if pressed to speak to strangers. His temper was ferocious and uncontrollable. He used to speak to ants by clicking his fingernails, and would tear at his own skin with scissors. His father beat him to teach him better manners, and that only made him hide for days, until he grew strong enough to fight back.'

'There was a lad like that near where I grew up, in County Mayo,' remembered Hannibal. 'He learned Latin at some astoundingly early age, and for days at a time refused to speak anything else. He was forever cataloging things, I recall. Buttons and horseshoe nails and the whiskers of the neighborhood cats. He'd go wild with rage if anyone disarranged his collections.'

He frowned a little at the memory. So crowded was the *Sarah Jane*'s hold and decks with goods en route to St Louis that two-score of these crates and bales had been craned up to the deck usually reserved for passengers, half-filling the space at the boat's stern. Tucked behind this rampart was a narrow clearing, protected from the wind; still more protected from the view of those passengers who would have made it their business to comment had the lovely Vicomtesse de St-Forgeux been seen coming and going from Mr Sefton's tiny stateroom . . .

Or in conversation with Mr Sefton's black valet. Her own servants – the Swiss footman Herr Sigerist, and the stout, pink-faced Westphalian maid Fräulein Hauser – would have been the first to raise an outcry. Such things were 'not done'.

So January leaned idly on one corner of the little fortress, and kept an eye on the narrow deck that lay along the starboard rail, in case anyone strolled in their direction.

'He wasn't stupid,' Hannibal went on after a moment. 'Or insane, as people would label insanity. Just . . . very, very odd. His parents, God bless them, had the wits to realize he wouldn't last a week at a public school, so for about twenty months they'd send him over to our place, so my tutor could educate us both, before I was packed off to Eton. God knows he profited more from the instruction than I ever did.'

'Good for his parents.' The vicomtesse sighed, and gathered the velvet of her cloak closer about her throat. Even within the protective wall of crates, the afternoon was bitterly cold. 'Poor Arithmus's family had not the slightest idea what to do with him. Dev was fascinated by him – not by his talents, with numbers or with memory, but with the person who was trapped in this . . . this strange mental maze of perceptions that weren't like those of anyone around him. As if he were going through life with faceted lenses over his eyes, and a spell on him, that he would hear words spoken to him one day as Tahitian, and the next day as Chinese, and the next as Turkish, never the same twice. Dev offered to take Arithmus with him when he went back to Europe, to teach him how to get along in the world of men.'

'Wishart told me once,' said January, 'that he looked on it as if he were trying to teach a deaf man to get along in business, and make his living. He and Stuart had had a deaf brother, who died very young – I think the boy's sight was impaired also. Wishart spoke of tutoring the lad, of the challenge of figuring out what the child was capable of seeing, was capable of learning, and how to get through to him. For him, finding a way to the center of the maze – to the young man who was the real Arithmus – was the same as exploring the ruins along the Nile, or searching for ancient legends in the old libraries at Asouan and Khartoum. He was as hungry for knowledge as any dilettante in Paris was hungry for sensation and surprise.'

Movement caught the corner of his eye, and he shifted his position, to cover the opening in the crates and any view of Hannibal and the vicomtesse perched on a trunk inside. With the casual air of a man taking a rest from his duties, he gazed idly out over the green-brown water as Prince Serafin Corvinus emerged from the stairway that led to the lower deck, a young lady on each arm. His dark, curly head was bent to the right, listening to what Daisy Emmett had to say. Miss Emmett's mourning costume was more stylish than any woman's day-frock on the boat, with the possible exception of her chaperone's. In Miss Emmett's case, however, the ruching on the bosom, and the tight, low-cut sleeves were not flattering, plastered though they were with immense appliqués of jet beads and sequined lace.

The girl on the prince's other arm, of much the same height and plumpness, was plainly dressed in a turkey-red frock many seasons out of date. Persephone had discreetly pointed her out that morning as Creon Grice's niece Josephine, summarily ordered to cut short her visit with school-friends in New Orleans ('Her father's trying to marry her off . . .') to accompany the heiress to Natchez. Judging by her sycophantic eagerness to nod and exclaim at her companion's remarks, she didn't seem to be broken-hearted over the situation.

Or maybe, reflected January, she simply rejoiced in the chance to stand next to His Highness.

'. . . *nothing* ever happens in Natchez,' complained Miss Emmett. 'That's what they all said at Madame Viellard's. Marie-Thérèse Almonaster said, all anybody *ever* talks about up there is cotton and niggers and the weather, and *everybody* comes to New Orleans to buy their clothes because there's nobody decent up there making them.'

'But you're in mourning, honey—'

'Even in the depths of her grief,' put in the prince – who seemed already to have gauged those depths as far as the heiress was concerned – 'a lady remains true to her quality. I'm sure your poor father would not have wanted his beautiful daughter to be one atom less than the cynosure of every eye.' He raised Miss Emmett's hand reverently to his lips.

'Your uncle can't be so stingy – so heartless,' proclaimed Miss Emmett to her companion, 'as to condemn me to imprisonment in some horrible little village—'

'But Natchez isn't!' protested Miss Grice. 'And my Uncle Creon is one of the richest men in town—'

'A slave dealer!' sniffed the heiress, and stamped her foot. 'How am I going to *endure* the shame of it? But everyone in New Orleans was so different, so *kind*, as if they knew how much my soul loathes such a nasty profession!'

'No true man would hold against you . . .' Their voices faded as the prince escorted the two young ladies away along the deck.

Et genus et formam regina pecunia donat, Hannibal had earlier remarked. *Money makes anyone both brilliant and beautiful*.

And January reflected that the low social position of slave dealers probably had more to do with the heiress's 'shame'. He guessed, too, that the money her father had made from that 'nasty profession' was the reason for the kindness she had universally met in New Orleans.

His mind went back to Creon Grice, who had been Stuart Wishart's man of business before he had become Travis Emmett's Natchez business partner. An undistinguished clerk, who sixteen years before had brought the news of his employer's death to his employer's daughter.

And had married her, upon her guardian's death.

SIX

Paris – early December 1825

'Have I the pleasure,' inquired the red-nosed gentleman, when one of the Beau Soleil waiters opened the door that led downstairs, 'of addressing the Brotherhood of Apollo?'

January, sitting at one of the salon's several small tables studying the strange old second-century manuscript Wishart had acquired in Asouan, half-turned in his chair to regard the newcomer. Most of the men in the room were looking also, but from the corner of his eye he saw Wishart himself give a violent start. 'What the—?' the Englishman exclaimed.

'I trust that it will be your pleasure.' The physician Abelard Bourgeois, who was chairing the meeting that evening (insofar as meetings of the informal Brotherhood were ever 'chaired'), rose from the group nearest the salon's door and bowed. 'It is our honor, sir.'

Louis Gounelle looked down his long nose, at the idea that a stoop-shouldered little stranger who was by his shabby dress so obviously somebody's clerk could possibly 'honor' the gathering, and the Duc d'Aveline muttered, 'Well, *really* . . .' Bad enough – his stiff back and flushed face proclaimed – that Jews like Daniel ben-Gideon, and even *Negro musicians*, were admitted to the Brotherhood. And as for mountebanks like Deverel Wishart, who *dared* to contradict *his* researches into the mystical greatness of ancient Egypt . . .!

'My name is Sylvestre Mouche.' The visitor held out his card to Bourgeois with a little bow, then performed a second bow to the room in general. 'I represent Monsieur Charles-Xavier Grezolles, a broker on the Bourse—'

'Mouche!' Wishart sprang up and strode to the door, hand stretched out in welcome. 'What the devil are you doing here, man? Is everything all right?' His face clouded with sudden concern. 'You haven't had word—?' The most recent letter from Norfolk had contained reassurances from Stuart Wishart that he was on the mend, after a fall from a horse that had broken his collarbone and left him dazed and disoriented for several days.

'No, no, quite all right.' The clerk raised both his hands, in an attitude rather similar to prayer. 'But Monsieur Grezolles has been reflecting upon what you told us all at dinner the other evening, regarding these friends of yours here and their wide learning of the world.' He looked around the room.

With the end of the formal meeting, the Brotherhood had broken into threes and fours to chat over coffee and wine. It always amused January to see that, Brotherhood of Man notwithstanding, the men had divided exactly as they did back in New Orleans. The Napoleonistes tended to cluster around the Duc d'Aveline – who was still fizzling about Wishart's so-called proofs that the Nubian kings had conquered Egypt some eight centuries before Christ – while those connected to the old Versailles nobility – the 'Legitimate' 'nobility of the sword' – sneered even at those whose titles dated from the purchase of judicial office under the kings. Men who looked back to the early ideals of the Revolution unobtrusively avoided both.

In its way, this proved to January that indeed all men were brothers. But as Abel had found out in Chapter Four of Genesis, not all brothers got along.

The current controversy had its root in Deverel Wishart's interpretation of certain inscriptions that he had studied in and around Asouan, just north of the First Cataract of the Nile. Some of these involved a very ancient, polytheistic sect of Jews, but the Duc d'Aveline had taken violent exception to others. He particularly objected to the second-century Roman manuscript Wishart claimed to have acquired in Asouan, which – entwined with a dire tale of an ancient curse – contradicted his own theories about the enduring greatness of the Pharaohs of Egypt. ('*Negroes*? Subdue the greatness of Egypt? Preposterous!'). Charles-Auguste Choquet, Duc d'Aveline, as he never failed to remind everyone in the Brotherhood, had been part of the band of scientists which had accompanied Napoleon's expedition to Egypt in 1798. He had in fact written a book on the subject of Egypt's downfall having been brought about by a conspiracy of Jews during the reign of Manasseh of Judah (and published it at his own expense).

But since d'Aveline's grandfather had manufactured boots for Napoleon's army, the 'Legitimite' nobles all supported Wishart's contentions: How could anyone believe anything a *nouveau-riche* profiteer's offspring had said? In keeping with the tenets of Freemasonry, they were scrupulously polite to the duc – but their relatives in the prestigious (and royally sponsored) Société Académique de St-Cloud refused to admit him to their ranks. Not a meeting of the Brotherhood had gone by in the past month, that had not involved at least one debate about Wishart's Roman manuscript, which proved – in conjunction with the strange little bronze of the goddess Sittina-Menhit trampling a pharaoh underfoot – that Nubia had conquered Egypt.

And when Wishart got to his feet and went to welcome Monsieur Mouche at the door of the upstairs meeting room, January noticed that he swept the little packet of carefully re-enforced papyrus into his pocket before he left the table. Noticed, too, how the duc edged his way toward the table while everyone's attention was distracted by the little group at the door.

'And what may we do for you, Monsieur Mouche?' Bourgeois asked. Monsieur Sylvestre Mouche relaxed a little at the friendliness in the physician's voice. The looks he was getting from Gounelle, and from the clique of 'enlightened' aristocrats around the Vicomte de Heyrieux, January reflected, would make anyone nervous.

The clerk executed another graceless bow. 'Monsieur Wishart has spoken often to my employer about your Brotherhood being a scientific society. Is this true?'

Bourgeois – who had a thriving practice on the fashionable Rue St-Germain – smiled a trifle ruefully. 'We hope we are, sir. We try to be.' He glanced around at the gathering, about a score of men that evening: the presence of de Heyrieux, and of the old Comte du Plessis-Méjarnesse, whose family crests boasted a dozen quarterings and who had known the king when His Majesty was a dashing young prince chasing beauties at Versailles, guaranteed that the royal ban on gatherings of more than five people would not be enforced here. 'We learn, and we keep an open mind.'

His blue glance didn't even twitch toward d'Aveline, who was gazing innocently around him like a man who would never in his life have snatched from the table a piece of evidence that disagreed with his theories, had it by some chance been left unwatched.

'How can we help Monsieur Grezolles?'

'It is a question of ghosts, monsieur.' Mouche's sparse brows puckered. He looked up at the tall physician, then over at Wishart, who was now rather pink with embarrassment about the ears. 'Do they in fact exist, and how does one drive them forth from their haunts?'

Mississippi River – December 1840

'The problem was this,' said Persephone, while January maintained his pose of idle contemplation of the riverbank and kept an eye on the flirtation, now at the far end of the deck, between the young heiress and the prince. 'The Marquis de Chalon-Neuf and his family fled the Revolution in 1790. Their estates were confiscated, and sold – you remember what a mess the finances of the country was in then—'

'I remember being told about it,' said Hannibal, 'by the sons of the émigrés I encountered at school. At great length – *Ploratur lacrymis amissa pecunia veris*. By the time I was twelve I had heard more than I ever imagined I would want to know about *assignats* and *mandats* and the tax on doors and windows.'

'Then when the kings returned in 1817 – and every émigré with them – the first thing all those ducs and comtes and de Noilleses and d'Aumonts did was sue to get their lands back. And everyone who had bought those lands, in good faith, from whichever government was in charge of the Revolution at the time . . . How many constitutions did they have, between the fall of the Bastille and Napoleon taking over as emperor?'

'Five, I think. I was drunk at the time,' added Hannibal apologetically. 'But I gather that was why Charles, when he finally became king in 1824, pulled almost a billion francs out of the treasury to pay the nobles for the lands they'd lost. So they'd renounce their ownership of those lands, and clarify the legal situation for the purchasers.'

'The fact that those nobles were all his friends,' said

the vicomtesse, 'no doubt had something to do with it. And maybe he was afraid they'd lose the lawsuits.' On the deck below, men leaned on poles and cast ropes to the wharf of a plantation, while others manhandled crates into position to offload. Miss Emmett pointed out something to the prince, who laughed again with his white teeth and released Miss Grice's arm, to press his other hand over Miss Emmett's, and smile down into her eyes.

'Be that as it may, there was a legal distinction between lands that were the *actual* property of a noble house, and those that were the property of their *vassals*. One of these vassals was the Sieur de Palongeux, who had sworn fealty to the Marquis de Chalon-Neuf – the Good God-only-knows how many centuries ago . . .'

'Fourteen eighty-four,' provided January.

'Show-off. Furthermore, some of those nobles – and some of those vassals – renounced their titles with the August Decrees. Whatever the case, the Chateau Palongeux – it's out near Argenteuil, a few miles from town – was confiscated, and sold to a speculator in wheat and firewood named Villefranche, who stripped the lead off the roofs and the boiseries off the walls and sold off all the furniture, and eventually sold the chateau itself, and its lands, to a contractor, who in turn sold it to this lawyer, Monsieur Grezolles.'

Farther along the deck, the glum, dark shape of Doktor Boehler appeared at the head of the steps that led down. He didn't approach the prince and the two girls, but only stood, arms folded, frowning. The prince guiltily disengaged from Miss Emmett, made some hasty excuse. The heiress flung up her plump, black-gloved hands, her playful retort a coy symphony of cocked head and coquettish pokes with her fingers; the prince tried to explain, anguish in his face. January wondered if the pedagogue's brief extended to nightly reports to the young man's noble – royal? – parents in Hungary, with financial consequences in the next bank-draft.

Miss Grice, left standing alone a little ways off, watched the exchange with her hands clasped sympathetically before her breast. The pilot's cursing dyed the air blue as the boat closed with the wharf down below.

'The problem was,' Persephone continued, 'that the Chateau Palongeux – actually, there were two problems. One was that just as Monsieur Grezolles had arranged to sell it to a manufacturer in Bordeaux named Souscayrac, the heirs of the Sieur de Palongeux turned up and sued for the return of the property. They said it had been held by their grandfather outright, and not in vassalage to the Chalon-Neufs, and thus it had been illegally sold in the first place.'

'*Fortuna humana fingit artatque ut lubet*,' remarked Hannibal. 'I suppose all the Chalon-Neuf records had been burned in '89? – I thought so. And the second problem?'

'Was that the chateau was haunted. Badly haunted.'

Paris – December 1825

'There were always family tales, evidently,' explained Monsieur Mouche, that rainy autumn evening at the Beau Soleil's upper room. 'The peasants in the village remembered some of them – it was the reason you wanted to have a look at the place last week, wasn't it, Monsieur Wishart?'

He glanced across at the explorer, who, like everyone else in the room, had gathered around Mouche's chair near the Franklin stove. Bourgeois had poured out coffee and cognac, and set cup and glass on a small table at the guest's elbow. Blue whiffs of tobacco smoke suffused the air.

Wishart looked around him in some embarrassment. The Brotherhood of Apollo, to a man, decried peasant superstitions and belief in elves, fairies, witches, and *croque-mitaines* that haunted pools and streams and ate children's noses and fingers. D'Aveline inquired nastily, 'Looking for a boyfriend to go with your little bronze harpy, Wishart?'

'I should hardly term the Lady Menhit a harpy.' Wishart reached into the breast of his coat to produce the image. 'To judge by the Egyptian pharaoh lying broken beneath her feet, I should say she was a goddess of no small power.'

As d'Aveline's face flushed and his mouth popped open for an angry retort, Wishart held the statue up to the glow of the oil lamps overhead, gleaming between his long fingers. 'According to the Curse Manuscript, she would avenge without pity wrongs done to those who only love. No – I'd heard some strange tales in the neighborhood, about a white horse that appears on the grounds and lures men to ride him, or a woman – a *voirloup* –

who moves about the chateau at night, sometimes in the form of a fox, or a cat, or a goat . . . And honestly, I was curious.'

His dark brows pulled together and he folded his hands around the image of Sittina-Menhit, gathering – January thought – what he could and couldn't say.

'We had a *voirloup* at our chateau at Lac d'Argent,' put in old Comte Plessis-Méjarnesse. 'And I think a white horse as well, now that I come to think about it, on the road that ran nearby – to say nothing of the old woman one would sometimes see in the corridors, feeling her way along in the darkness. Looking for a child, my *granmère* always said . . .'

Wishart produced a light-hearted grin. 'Well, they did say there was a headless woman in white who walked the corridors of Palongeux . . .' He shook his head. 'I never saw her. Or any of them,' he added. 'There was a room in one of the towers that was . . . cold.'

'Every room in my *granpère*'s chateau at Montbassange was cold!' laughed de Chapponnay – Heyrieux's cousin and a member of the prestigious Société Académique de St-Cloud. 'Especially the ones over the moat!'

Wishart's gesture conceded the point with grace.

'But the blood you spoke of,' said Mouche diffidently. 'And the . . . and what you saw in the corridor. The footsteps, and the hand, writing on the wall . . . and what happened to your French manservant—'

'That has to have been an accident,' said Wishart quickly. 'The man could have been drunk – or an eater of hashish, for all I knew, though he'd seemed sober enough when I hired him . . .' He fell silent.

'Did your Negro Arithmus see anything?' asked Bateux, who was a recorder in the law courts, his voice genuinely curious. 'I have heard that naturals, and the mad, can see and hear . . . well, *differently* . . .'

'And did your *granmère* tell you that?' scoffed Gounelle.

January replied mildly, 'Do you say it isn't true?' He turned back to Wishart.

'Arithmus wouldn't step across the threshold,' said the Englishman quietly. 'He stopped dead, like a horse will when there's a bridge washed out. He said there was a smell – I didn't notice it – and begged me to leave him outside. The caretaker of the place won't go in, either, after dark,' he added, glancing at the men around him. 'Nobody in the village will. At one time, I understand, the rumor went around that there was treasure buried in the castle crypts . . . but now most of the villagers won't even put a foot on the grounds. Some of them say the digging woke something up.'

He looked down at his folded hands, his mouth closed tight at the corners. Gounelle sniffed. D'Aveline, usually a sceptic, didn't appear to have heard. He had been edging closer to Wishart – and the brown corner of the Roman manuscript that protruded from his pocket – but when he observed January watching him, he backed quickly away.

'Alas,' said Monsieur Mouche, 'word of all this has reached Monsieur Souscayrac, and now he has said he will not buy the chateau. Unfortunately, money has already changed hands. Between that, and the prospect of dealing with the lawsuit himself, my employer is . . . My employer would like to know, if you gentlemen of understanding have – or know of – some method of . . . what they used to call "laying" a ghost.'

De Chapponnay flung up his hands with a crack of laughter. 'But this is priceless!'

Dr Bourgeois made a shushing gesture. Scientific enlightenment and logic were all very well, but bad manners to a guest were not something he tolerated, even in the eldest son of the Marquis de Vigonet.

Very softly, Wishart said, 'I think there are more than one.'

January was interested to note that, despite the new king's devout new laws concerning respect (and submission) to the Church, nobody suggested sending for a priest.

SEVEN

Paris – December 1825

Fourteen of them went, in all.

Among his Freemason lodge-brothers, many of whom were in the Brotherhood of Apollo, January was recognized as a man of sharp observation, with the practicality of one who had both a country childhood and medical training. 'Let's see what we're talking about,' he said, 'before we start sowing the ground with salt.'

Everyone agreed that this was probably the best course. Daniel ben-Gideon volunteered to assist: his parents were bent on arranging a meeting between him and the daughter of a Bonapartiste baron the following Saturday, and he was in quest of a previous engagement. His valet, Freytag, accompanied him: the thought of even a few nights without a freshly pressed nightshirt, perfectly made breakfast chocolate, or a barber sufficiently skilled with razor, curling irons and pomade was not even to be considered. Besides, Daniel said, someone had to look after Musette, the little Italian greyhound who was, he claimed, the true love of his life. For good measure, because he was fairly certain his father was having him watched, he also brought his mistress, the beautiful opera dancer, Persephone Jondrette.

Also unthinkable was the notion that the *première danseuse* at the Theatre Pelletier should spend four or five nights in a haunted chateau without her maid, a thin, red-haired girl named Clémence, who came from Moirans-en-Montagne in the Jura mountains, and appeared to be terrified of everyone in the party except Freytag and Belle Wishart.

Mademoiselle Wishart accompanied her Uncle Dev, with Citoyenne-de-la-République in tow to discourage masculine advances; not that Belle couldn't easily have trounced so mild an assailant as Monsieur Mouche unassisted, should he have offered the slightest liberty. The likelihood of seduction by ben-Gideon was recognized by all to be non-existent. Mouche's valet, Brachet, was, like Freytag, a votary of some penitential Protestant sect and glared his disapproval of all the women of the party alike: Belle (a heretic), Persephone (a dancer), both their maids (Catholics!) and January's wife, the beautiful dressmaker Ayasha, who had invited herself along. ('You go spend the night in a haunted chateau with thirteen people, Malik, and see what happens.')

Both Mouche and Brachet brightened perceptibly when they saw that the party also included Daniel's chef, Señor Antonio-Ismael Castillero (accompanied by *his* assistant, Conejo), and eleven crates of jellies, wines, cognacs, Westphalian hams, cigars, chafing dishes, cherries bottled in brandy, truffles, and pâté de Strasbourg. Wishart, by contrast, had brought only two valises and a brass-cornered trunk full of equipment for botanical experiments, and volumes of Aristotle and Goethe. It was Citoyenne who had remembered to bring a change of clothing for Belle.

Monsieur Mouche was the only one who suggested – viewing the pale-ivory walls of the chateau at the end of the pot-holed and muddy drive – that someone should fetch a priest.

'It's been done, I gather.' Wishart stepped from his rented fiacre, which had stopped beside the dilapidated lodge gate, to follow the clerk's nervous gaze. 'Repeatedly. One story goes that the son – or nephew – of the original builder abducted a young woman and held her captive in that turret room there on the southeast corner of the main block. The poor girl died, either trying to get down from the window on the ivy – you can still see it growing there up the wall – or by suicide, to keep herself out of his hands and, I should imagine, the hands of his friends. Other stories I've heard are worse. About ten years later a priest was summoned – they say – to make the screaming stop, which was heard in the tower at dead of night. The man's body was found the next morning, below the tower window.' He shrugged. 'Or so they say.'

Mouche looked alarmed, and took a hasty swig from his silver pocket-flask, presumably to ward off specters. Brachet did his best to appear above heeding such tales, and Arithmus, sharing the fiacre's box with Wishart, seemed puzzled at implications which he did not understand. Clémence stared down the drive at the dilapidated walls in undisguised terror.

The Englishman shook his head. 'Other attempts to exorcize

the ghosts – and some rather unpleasant happenings over the years have only added to the reputation of the place – have been undertaken, one in 1692 and another in the 1720s, without much effect. The last one was in 1775.'

'From all my mother told me of the priests in the days of the kings,' remarked Persephone, elegant in a very military-looking pelisse in Daniel's black and primrose landau, 'the men sent to cleanse the place probably could have done with a little moral scrubbing themselves. The face of truth can drive a man to leap from a window, as surely as the face of lies.'

Mouche opened his mouth to protest this view of the pre-Revolutionary clergy, but the dancer had already signed the *fourgon* – bearing Daniel's five trunks, her own three, Señor Castillero's kitchen paraphernalia, Freytag, Clémence, the chef himself and his assistant, plus three footmen and two grooms who would lodge, with the coachman, in the village – to proceed to the rear courtyard and begin unloading.

'Drive on,' she added. 'Let poor Benjamin have a look at the place before dark.'

January leaned around in the landau's rear-facing seat – he and Daniel having very properly taken the less attractive places, to leave Persephone and Ayasha to face forward – and studied the walls of the haunted villa, the shuttered windows and the bare and shabby battens of its denuded roofs.

Persephone sized the place up at a glance. 'One can only hope that sufficient rooms remain more or less under shelter.'

'The turret roofs look intact,' pointed out January. 'And according to Monsieur Mouche, part of the east wing was thatched a few years back, when the slates and leading were sold, to protect the floors.'

'Protect the value of the wood, I daresay.' Daniel, too, turned in his seat, like a great, soft, over-fed cat. Musette, cradled in the breast of his greatcoat, reached up to lick his chin. 'Would you mind very much sharing a chamber with me, if necessary, Dark Goddess?' he added, with a glance back at Persephone. 'I'm virtually certain one of the footmen is sending reports of all this to my father, and it would make the poor old man so happy.'

Daniel had been the dancer's protector for eighteen months now, paying the rent on her seventeenth-century *hôtel particulier* in the

Rue des Francs-Bourgeois and buying wines, provisions, and a wardrobe that was the talk of the Paris demi-monde. The Hôtel des Camellias was large enough for Persephone to retire comfortably to her apartments whenever Daniel would discreetly meet male friends there who shared his preferences, and her own discretion was absolute. What she was being paid for, she understood, was to take part in a masquerade. The banker and financier Moses ben-Gideon – and Daniel's coterie of well-off uncles – saw nothing amiss in a man of twenty-nine being out all night, or nearly all night, with a dancer from the Theatre Pelletier.

('It keeps everyone happy,' Daniel would say, spreading his hands like a wise monarch offering peace to the world. 'Where is the harm?')

The remainder of the afternoon – while Daniel's servants swept and tidied bedrooms (looking nervously over their shoulders all the while), Señor Castillero began work on dinner (after thrashing Conejo for refusing to be left alone in the scullery), and Daniel's coachman took the horses, carriage and *fourgon* down to stabling in the village – January spent looking over the chateau. Monsieur Mouche had come in a cab (January wondered if his employer had paid for that), with Brachet sitting up beside the driver, his modest satchel of clean clothing and shaving soap wedged between his feet. When the driver departed, and Wishart paid off the post-boys of the fiacre he'd come in and they, too, took their leave, January sensed among his companions an odd feeling of being stranded, though it was only a mile and a half to the village, and less than an hour's drive to Paris.

But the shrubbery and young trees that had been suffered to grow up close to the chateau's walls in the decades of its desertion, the stained walls of its great rooms, and the shutters that guarded windows long since denuded of glass, gave the place an atmosphere not only of desolation, but of shadowy threat. In what seemed to have been a library – to judge by the marks where bookshelves had once been bolted to the walls – the fireplace had been bricked up, and a curious collection of cracked dishes, some still containing the stains of what could have been either food or blood, had been left on the hearth-tiles. On the bricks themselves, a number of different hands had written '*Reste tranquille*' and '*Silence, au nom de Dieu*'. Nearly eradicated beneath them could be made out the scrawl, '*Quia caritas Dei in pace relinquit nos.*' It may have been his imagination, and it may have been the holed and dilapidated state of the damp walls, but it seemed to January that the space before that sealed hearth was colder than the rest of the chamber – which was cold enough, he reflected, to put bears into hibernation.

Painted gods gazed sadly from the flamboyant ceiling, leprous with water stains and mold.

He found another such collection of offerings in a corner of one of the attics. Smaller, the Lord's Prayer chalked on the wall beside a place where a floorboard had been taken up and nailed back, and several crosses drawn on the wall and the floor, in chalk, or ink, or blood. 'Reminds me of what the voodoos draw, back home,' he said, and remembered his sister Olympe, who had run off with the voodoos when she was sixteen. Salt had been scattered over the floorboard, and when he took it up, he saw beneath it, between the joists, the scattered bones of what looked like a dog and a bird, and the finger bones of a human hand. A rosary was tangled among these last, also scattered with salt.

'Looks like whoever is here didn't pay any mind to those priests,' Ayasha commented, hugging her shawl about her and shivering with cold. She looked around at the walls of the small attic cell – one of those whose roof-slates had been partly pillaged for sale. 'Myself, I'd have left the bones on the doorstep downstairs, rather than come up here with all these doors behind me.'

January nodded thoughtfully. The tiny chamber had at least seven doors, the entire space beneath the chateau's rafters being broken up into more than a score of servants' rooms, few larger than eight feet by ten. Using the chalk that he carried in his pockets, he marked the doorways behind him as he explored ('Wait, look! There goes a Minotaur, Malek!' 'That isn't funny, Ayasha . . .'). After all these years, no glass remained in the dormer windows, and the holes in the roof had left the floors warped, rotting, sagging under mats of dead leaves an inch thick, or gaping with holes a sofa could have dropped through. Other cubicles simply smelled of rats.

Downstairs, Daniel had chivalrously insisted upon Persephone getting one of the few rooms that showed no signs of leakage, water damage, or offerings to malevolent spirits – the northwest turret chamber, physically as far from the southeast 'murder' chamber ('And it may all be a legend . . .' had temporized Wishart uneasily) as was possible within the main block. The room beside it was also in fairly good shape, and Daniel claimed it for his own – the next room to the south being uninhabitable. After that stretched a sort of suite which included the southwest turret, of which only a small part of the roof had been pillaged. 'If Mademoiselle Jondrette has no objection,' suggested Wishart, when the explorers foregathered for coffee and wine in the least dilapidated of the chateau's three salons, 'perhaps Belle might wish to share quarters with her . . .' He was aware by this time of the nature of Daniel's chaste relationship with Persephone, 'In the interests of . . .'

He hesitated, clearly not wanting to say, *not being left alone after dark.* But Citoyenne – who with Freytag had been distributing cups, glasses and little plates of macaroons – set down her tray on the table (which had been fetched, like the chairs, that afternoon by Freytag from the village) with a ferocious clatter. 'Not while I have breath in my body, m'sieu!' She rounded on her employer like a Saracen preparing to make mincemeat of Godfrey de Bouillon. 'Mademoiselle Belle, share a room with a woman who dances on the public stage? What are you thinking? What would your brother say?'

'Stu knows as well as I do that Mademoiselle Jondrette would be as safe a chaperone as yourself—'

'I do not speak of safety,' retorted the maid. 'I speak of the girl's reputation. You' – she jabbed a finger at her startled charge – 'you will say no more of this. There is a room down in the west wing where the roof is well thatched, where you and I will be perfectly safe, no more than ten strides down the corridor from these rooms here—'

She swung around to glare again at Wishart, who backed away in alarm. 'And you, monsieur, you know as well as I do that there is no such thing as a ghost.'

'I wouldn't—' her employer began uncertainly.

'Then shame on you!'

In the end, it was agreed that Belle would sleep with Ayasha in the small parlor of the southwestern suite, while January slept in the southwest turret itself. The west wing chamber referred to boasted not only a thatched roof, but the words, *Dieu me sauve!* scrawled, in the faded stains of old blood, on the wall beside the fireplace. Even the least superstitious of the party found good, rational reasons not to slumber within its walls.

Citoyenne and Clémence shared the little dressing room on the far side of the southwestern turret – Clémence carefully chalked crosses on the room's doors and hung a rosary around the door handle – and Monsieur Mouche took a leaky, but otherwise sound, chamber twenty feet down the western corridor, and retired to it with his flask of cognac immediately following dinner. Brachet tried to volunteer to sleep in the kitchen with the chef and Conejo, but was instead installed in the dressing room next to his master's chamber ('Nonsense, man, it isn't raining now and that floor is perfectly sound!'), and Wishart took the room beyond that – despite six rat-holes in the walls – and proceeded to unpack his brass-cornered trunk and spread its experimental paraphernalia everywhere in sight.

Arithmus categorically refused to sleep in the chateau at all, and made a bed for himself under the table in the kitchen, Castillero having claimed the table's surface (he'd brought the table itself from the ben-Gideon townhouse on Rue de Vaugirard). Conejo claimed the stone hearth and refused to share.

Freytag and the two maidservants then brought in an excellent dinner of *poulets à la ficelle*, *potage de Condé*, fricassee of partridge sausages, cauliflower with cheese and olives, patisseries, wafers, cognac and coffee, while darkness gathered in the corners of the haunted rooms, and wind began to cry among the overgrown trees outside. Among other comforts, Daniel had brought three Carcel lamps, but even their brighter flame didn't go far, and the fire in the salon's soot-blackened hearth smoked and shuddered in the drafts. 'I should have brought some screens,' lamented Daniel, in the middle of Wishart's account of the astonishing effects of ingesting the blue lotus of the Nile, or the roots of certain white African flowers that bloomed only at night. 'And a larger table, while I was at it. And extra coal.' He glanced regretfully over his shoulder in the direction of the small salon's struggling fireplace. 'And a chimney sweep.'

'You'd have to feed him and his boys,' January reminded him, and Daniel sighed.

'So I would.'

'Instead of the chimney sweep,' offered Persephone, 'you could have brought a billiard table.'

In the last of the twilight, they took the lamps and made a final patrol of the hallways, filled now with the coming night. Nobody offered to investigate the bloodstained parlor, the old library, or the southeast turret, before seeking their beds.

Mississippi River – December 1840

'And did you,' inquired Hannibal, when he and January met in his 'stateroom' (*Read, 'closet'*, January reflected) late that evening, for further details of the Haunting of Chateau Palongeux, 'actually see a ghost?' The *Sarah Jane* would reach the thriving little river-port of Bayou Sara at midnight – through the thin wooden partitions on both sides of the tiny room, January heard the shufflings and murmurs of passengers either preparing to go ashore, or to go to bed. He had spent a few hours after dinner playing the piano in the boat's main salon (and had received nearly eight dollars in tips), while at the gambling tables, Hannibal politely tripled what Persephone had given him and listened to gossip from all along the river.

'In a manner of speaking.' January thought back upon that first night in the southwest turret, wrapped in four quilts and with a hot brick providing a very poor substitute for Ayasha against the bitter cold. The room's ceiling had long ago crumbled away beneath the place where the roof slates had been pillaged, and for a part of that night diluted moonlight had trickled through. When the wind had come up, that feeble gleam faded. He'd been waked, the first time, by the gale's roar in the trees all around the house, a sound like a rainstorm beating on the leaves.

Chateau Palongeux – December 1825

The second time he'd been waked by crying.

Or wailing. Or . . . He wasn't certain what to call it. A hollow sound, soft but seeming to fill the blackness of the room, the blackness of the corridors, with eerie, indescribable menace.

Silence, au nom de Dieu, pleaded the chalked scribble on the library wall.

He'd heard whispering in the room next door – the door between it and the turret was open. A moment later, the firefly speck of a candle. He'd gotten up, collected Ayasha and Belle, and for a time the three of them had stood, a draft like Job's whirlwind plucking at their nightclothes, in the absolute darkness of the corridor, listening to that sound in the dark. Once he thought he saw something moving in the blackness, but with their hands curved close around the flame of their candles against the torrent of moving air, it was impossible to tell.

Mississippi River – December 1840

'And considering the number of holes there were, in the roofs, in the walls, where doors had been taken off chambers, it could have been leaves blowing along the passageway. Or a rat.'

'One can,' said Hannibal thoughtfully, wrapping a blanket around his own thin shoulders (the 'stateroom' was nearly as cold as January's recollection of that dark and wind-haunted corridor), 'use sounding boards in conjunction with an aeolian harp – especially if one's got a metal sound-box. Or supposedly with what's called a wind-organ: I've never heard one myself. But it sounds like there were plenty of drafts in the attics of the chateau, and enough holes through the ceilings to the rooms below for the sound to carry.'

'I know,' agreed January. 'I knew it at the time – standing barefoot in that corridor with only a couple of candles, listening to *that* . . . I spent the next two days looking for it.'

'Did you indeed?'

'Those chalked prayers on the walls, in the old library, and in the attic room,' January said. 'The handwriting was different, the color of the chalk was different . . . But they all looked fresh. Even the blood in the west wing chamber. You could get the same effect by diluting the original application. And even where the grammar was a little dodgy, the words were all spelled correctly, both the Latin and the French.'

'Oh, shame! I concocted better forgeries than that at Eton!'

'The writing in the attic . . . You know how rats will leave a dirty trail, where they habitually run along a wall? One of the chalked crosses impinged on such a trail. The chalk wasn't even smudged by further rats. And the bones underneath that floorboard were old, but not as much as fifty years old. The salt was fresh, too.'

'*Fronti nulla fides*. Do I detect the elegant hand of the litigious Sieur de Palongeux?'

'Somebody's elegant hand,' said January. 'Somebody who could get into the chateau, and who knew its reputation.'

Voices murmured, passing the stateroom door. January leaned away from the single candle Hannibal had lit when he'd come in from the *Sarah Jane*'s gambling parlor, touched the window-curtain's edge. Moonlight showed him the gold lacing that decorated Prince Serafin Corvinus's fur-collared greatcoat. Lamplight from a stateroom further along the deck brushed the girl's skirts with an edge of red. A few steps further the couple halted, the prince turning toward the girl, kissing first her hands, then her mouth, her throat, her breast through the fabric of her frock. His fingers tangled in her chignon and released dark curls.

'And was there treasure,' inquired Hannibal, 'buried in the chateau's crypts?'

January let the curtain move back into its place. 'During the Revolution, the Committee of Public Safety went over the place pretty thoroughly. It was searched again during the Directorate – the Directors would have searched a naked beggar if they thought he had any money on him – and Villefranche, the speculator who originally bought the place, went over it from sub-crypt to rafters without finding so much as a dropped sou. The first day we were there, Ayasha, Belle and I went down to the cellars. The flagstones had been taken up and were heaped around the walls, and it looked like every mole and miner in France had been turned loose in the place. Wine-vaults, storerooms, the chapel crypt: holes gouged five and six feet deep, half of them half-full of dirty water. If anyone had ever found anything down there, they hadn't said so.'

Hannibal said, 'Hmmn.'

Did Miss Emmett, January wondered, nudging the curtain aside again, know that Miss Grice was betraying her? Or was the girl he saw Miss Emmett, in her companion's borrowed dress, so that nobody would tell tales to Persephone? Dark-haired like the heiress,

Josie Grice was square and stocky rather than softly plump, and barely an inch taller. Both had danced with His Highness, turn and turn about, during the informal festivities in the boat's 'saloon' earlier in the evening. It crossed his mind to wonder whether Miss Emmett's maid Linney would be sleeping on the floor of the stateroom that the heiress – and Miss Grice, and Persephone – shared on the other side of the boat. Many slave holders required this service as a matter of course.

Fräulein Hauser, he knew, had been purchased a bunk in the 'Ladies' Cabin' among those half-a-dozen white women who could afford such an amenity. The Swiss footman Sigerist had one in the men's common cabin downstairs. Miss Emmett's middle-aged manservant, Joe – who would have been called a footman in Europe but who in America was simply referred to as a 'boy' – would be sleeping on the planks of the stern deck with the other people of color, slave and free.

And where, he wondered with an inner grin, did the good Herr Doktor Boehler have to lay his head tonight? Did his duties include sleeping on the floor of His Highness's stateroom, to make sure he wasn't sneaking out for assignations with heiresses (or their dewy-eyed companions) in the dark? Or did he delegate that task to the prince's ferociously mustachioed valet, Gaspar?

For that matter, had Miss Emmett instructed her companion to keep Doktor Boehler, and/or Persephone, busy while she stole out of her cabin wearing her friend's red frock, to keep this rendezvous?

As Belle Wishart had, he recalled, when she thought Ayasha was asleep.

EIGHT

Chateau Palongeux – December 1825

They caught Belle the third night.

That second night at Palongeux there had been no eerie, half-heard wailing in the darkness. A second search of the chateau on the day in between – undertaken by the Wisharts and Mouche while January, Ayasha, and Daniel returned to Paris to respectively teach piano, fit a ball dress for Madame d'Espinasse-Bellegarde, and deal with correspondence at Gideon-Duvallet-et-Frères regarding the financing of joint-stock canal companies in Gascony. Persephone had slept late, and gone in around noon, to rehearse *Didone Abbandonata*, and would not return until very late.

The search had yielded no evidence of aleatoric instrumentation. But January had been waked in the darkness of that second night by Ayasha slipping into his blankets beside him, wrapped rather discouragingly in her heaviest greatcoat and three pairs of knitted stockings (and in spite of that, more desirable than Venus in a silk hankie).

'*Malek*—'

He gathered her to him, devoured her with kisses. But the coat was buttoned up to her chin and she was wearing stoutly laced shoes as well as the stockings, which told him that she'd been up and about in the freezing dark, so he regretfully decided against demanding marital rights then and there. 'What is it, *zahar*?'

'Belle. She's gone.'

'What—?'

'I felt her slip out of bed. But instead of just using the pot and getting back in, I heard her put clothes on and leave. I dressed – well, as dressed as you can get in the dark – and followed. She'd lit a candle when she got into the west corridor, but she was far ahead of me. I followed the light – lost her on the grand stairway, then saw the light again going up one of the backstairs, and followed her to the attics. *Uslub ta'ajjub*, what a maze up there! I would hear her footsteps, then they'd be gone. See a light, then it would be gone. Down here, did you hear the chains rattling?'

She sounded perfectly cheerful and matter-of-fact – she would have done so, January knew, had she encountered the Four Horsemen of the Apocalypse in the hall.

'Did you see anything?'

'A white shape, like moonlight in the mirror. That was when I was on my way back down here. I heard footsteps down here that weren't hers, unless she put on Citoyenne's boots. When she slipped from the bedroom I don't know what she had on her feet, but it made very little sound. And only saints and angels would know where she would have got the chain, because she and her uncle and Monsieur Mouche all went through every room here today . . . and I don't think it was her anyway.'

'Persephone?'

Ayasha shook her head. 'I looked in her room. She's back already, and asleep. I need to get back to bed,' she added, sliding from out of his arms and out of the blankets. 'When Belle returns, I don't want her to know that we know she went out.'

She pressed her chilled fingers to his lips. 'You'll wait outside in the hall tomorrow night and follow her.'

His hand closed around her wrist. 'What if I meet the ghost?'

It was too dark to see her face by the little moonlight that leaked through the broken ceiling, but he heard the impish twinkle in her voice. 'Tell him to come back the night after. Tell him you have more important things to think of.'

She ducked away and was gone, leaving him smiling, too. Some time later, he surfaced from the shallower shoals of sleep to hear the soft closing of a door in the room beyond, and the faint creak of bed ropes as Belle Wishart slid under the covers beside Ayasha. Cloud had veiled the moon. He didn't know how long it had been.

Mississippi River – December 1840

'A handsome footman?' Hannibal folded his skinny knees, tailor-fashion, beneath the blankets of his stateroom cot. The wind that sighed down the Mississippi Valley that night breathed unbroken from the North Pole. 'Don't tell me she developed a passion for the Spanish cook. Was he handsome?'

'He was fifty-five years old, mostly toothless, and had a nose on him like a mangel-wurzel. He had been extremely handsome in his day.'

'Don't speak ill of a man in the prime of his life!' Hannibal drew himself up with dignity and stroked his graying mustache. 'Did the beautiful Belle have an insane passion for confits and cream?'

January shook his head, smiling again at the recollection of those icy hours, the following night, of waiting in the doorway of his room. Of seeing Persephone and her maid come in after the opera, of listening to the sound – infinitely far-off, picked up by the echoes of the corridors and of the holed ceiling from the attics overhead – of what could have been dragging chain. Even the strong suspicion that no ghost was involved hadn't kept his heart from beating quicker.

'It wasn't that kind of love.'

Chateau Palongeux – December 1825

Belle twisted around with a gasp when January opened the door of the tiny chamber: 'Who's there?' But Arithmus, with two quilts wrapped on over his gaudy African blanket, didn't seem in the least surprised or upset to see January in the doorway of the little cubicle near the kitchen where in former times the lamps and silverware had been cleaned. Two tapers, set between them in saucers on the floor, augmented the light of Belle's bedroom candle. The bare chamber was like an ice-house.

'I was afraid he'd be lonely,' said the girl, a little later, regarding January with a trace of wary defiance in her eyes. She, too, was wrapped in blankets over Citoyenne's stout (and enormous) winter pelisse. 'We weren't doing anything wrong.'

'Citoyenne would think we were,' put in Arithmus. 'I don't know why.' He frowned for a moment, pulling and twisting at his own fingers, then added, 'My mother, too, I think. But it is scary, there in the kitchen, when the rats come out. I hear them. Castillero doesn't. But he's up on the table. I'm on the floor underneath.'

January nodded. He knew all about rats, when one is obliged

to sleep on the floor. 'Are you afraid of the ghosts?' he asked, hearing in his mind Wishart's account of their earlier visit.

Arithmus shook his head. As always, he avoided January's eyes, looking instead at the spoonful of light that wavered on the floor around the candles. His long fingers stroked at his own hands and wrists, as if there were something scrabbling beneath the skin. But January had learned by this time that what he would interpret in another man as signs of unease and untruth were, for Arithmus, simply how he made his way through the world. 'There aren't any ghosts,' he said. 'And if there were, M'sieu Wishart lets me keep this.' From around his neck he drew out a thong, from which hung the image of Sittina-Menhit, knotted firmly into the leather as if it had been a randomly shaped bit of wood.

He turned her around and held her right-side-up. 'My Uncle Tafiq says, the living and the dead both run from her in fear. Even if she is only a piece of metal.'

'Did your Uncle Tafiq give her to you, then?' January settled on the floor between Belle and the African, the cold of the flagstones seeping through his greatcoat to freeze his bones.

'He gave her to M'sieu Wishart,' Arithmus affirmed. 'Along with the scroll – the Curse Manuscript. I think M'sieu paid money for them.' He thought about that for a time, arranging the events in his mind. 'I didn't see that happen. M'sieu Wishart told me later. Back sixteen hundred and ninety-four years ago, one of my ancestors – Dejen – had this statue with him when he was made a slave to the Romans.'

He held the image out, the leather thongs dangling. The lion-faced goddess stared out straight ahead of her, one foot on the neck of the crumpled figure which lay before her in the dust.

'I read that,' agreed January. '*Diebus Tiberii Caesaris in provincia Aegypti Nubianus servus factus est . . .*'

'*In the days of Tiberius Caesar, in the province of Egypt, a Nubian was made slave,*' repeated Belle softly. 'And he was descended from the Kings of Nubia, and worshipped Sittina-Menhit, the Queen of Night.'

'He was,' said Arithmus prosaically. 'His whole family did. The king's name was Pankhy and he invaded Egypt and conquered it. The image was made then, of Sittina-Menhit treading the pharaoh under her feet, though she really doesn't exist. But her hand lay heavy on them: *imposuit dea manum* – that hat the pharaoh's wearing is the one all the pharaohs wore.' He pointed to the tiny details of the bronze. 'Uncle Tafiq studied in Mecca and Fez and Timbuktu, and he knows all those old stories. One day I want to be like Uncle Tafiq.'

'The manuscript said the king carried the goddess's image with him into battle,' continued January. 'And his descendant carried it, when he was made a slave of the Romans.'

'He did. And when his Roman master, Publius Antius, took Dejen's wife away from him, Dejen told him, the Night Queen protects those who have only love, whose only wish is to love, and he'd better give her back. But Uncle Tafiq said, the Roman's wife fell in love with Dejen—'

Arithmus frowned then, stumbling over an idea he barely understood. 'Her name was Calpurnia Tertia,' he went on quickly. 'And she was so angry Dejen still loved his wife, that she poisoned her husband, and told everyone that Dejen and his wife had done it. Then Dejen's wife killed herself because she didn't want the Roman soldiers to get her, and Dejen buried the statue under his master's house and the Romans killed *him*, and the evil wife and all the family and everybody in the house came to a really bad end.'

'*Imposuit dea manum*,' repeated Belle. 'The wicked wife was found with her face so twisted with agony and fear that they almost couldn't recognize her: *Vultus eius a dolore et timore transfiguratur*. The sons of the household, and the daughters and I think one of their husbands, came to terrible grief, some of them years later.'

She poked her spectacles straight on the bridge of her nose, and the lenses caught the gold of the flame. The faint, fishy smell of the rush baskets in which that evening's dinner had been brought from the village drifted from the kitchen. Somewhere in the darkness, thin voices seemed to cry with a distant, silvery moaning.

'So how did Uncle Tafiq come to have the statue again,' January asked curiously, 'if it was buried under the house?'

The African shook his head. 'He said the house burned down, after misfortune destroyed the whole family. *Magnum malum omnibus habitantibus in domo illa*.'

'Supposedly,' provided Belle, 'one of old Publius's soldiers found the image in the ruins, and carried it all the way back to Nubia, to take the curse off the last child of his old commander's family. There the priests of Elephantine propitiated the Night Queen.'

'But Uncle Tafiq says,' Arithmus concluded, 'that the Night Queen looks after those who love with pure hearts. She revenges herself on those who . . .' His dark eyes lost their focus for a moment as he saw again – January was certain – the old scholar beside the slow green waters of the Nile. When he spoke again it was with a different inflection in his voice, a different timbre, imitating exactly what had been said . . . *Where? When?* '"Lies in wait for those who make mockery of loving, and spill the blood of loving hearts."'

'*Vindicatur in eos qui amantis ludibrium faciunt*,' agreed Belle, and January recalled those words from the last page of the brittle, faded packet of vellum that Wishart had unfolded for him at the Beau Soleil, half a dozen nights before. '. . . *et sanguinem cordis amantium effundunt*.'

'Which is what happened here, I suppose.' January considered the darkness around them. 'If the story of that poor girl in the tower is true. But if you have no fear of the ghosts, why do you refuse to sleep in the chateau?'

Arithmus wriggled all over at that, fingers pawing at the lower part of his face. 'I won't go in the chateau,' he announced. 'I-I don't want to.'

'And you don't have to.' Belle held his bulbous, bony wrist, rubbed the back of his hand comfortingly. 'Nobody's going to ask you to. And tomorrow I'll talk to Uncle about getting a bed and some coal so you can sleep in here and not in the kitchen—'

'I want to sleep in the kitchen,' said Arithmus quickly. 'It's scary in here, and those men might come back.'

'Men?' January frowned.

'I don't mind the rats. Really I don't. And not even the smell of the fish baskets. And maybe I don't have a heart pure enough that the Lady Menhit will protect me.'

'You have the purest heart,' Belle touched again the back of his hand, 'of anyone I know.'

She turned back to January, spectacles again catching the candle-gleam. 'Arithmus told us that men broke into the house on Rue St-André three weeks ago, just before Father went back to England. Father took me to the opera – *La Clemenza di Tito*. We even saw

Mademoiselle Jondrette dance on the stage,' she added, with a chuckle. 'And she is *very* good. Citoyenne was up in the gallery with Gatewood – that's Father's valet, Father got them both tickets – and said later she hoped I'd had the decency to close my eyes.'

And January, who had also seen Persephone Jondrette onstage, laughed.

'But when we got home,' she went on, 'Arithmus swore that men had broken into the house and held him at gunpoint in the scullery, though the cook and the footman both swore that nothing of the kind had happened. That Arithmus had been asleep and dreamed it all. There was nothing missing, not even the money from Father's desk. But the thing is, I know Arithmus doesn't lie. He can't,' she added, with another smiling glance at the 'secret savant of the dark continent'. 'The thought of anything in the least bit different from what he remembers drives him crazy.' Her hand closed affectionately, again, around the skinny African's fingers.

'I didn't lie.'

'It's all right,' she told him. 'If those men come back, they'll go back to the house in Paris, not to here. And we're not there.'

He nodded, as if he didn't quite follow this train of logic, and Belle deliberately changed the subject, getting her friend to tell her instead of the events of Uncle Deverel's latest 'exhibition' of 'the mysterious marvel of the desert', at a dinner given by M'sieu Grezolles the previous week for no less a person than the great financier Jacques Lafitte himself. With his usual abruptness, Arithmus then announced that he was sleepy. Belle and January silently followed him back into the kitchen and tucked him up under the table in his quilts and blanket – the fish smell was worse there and yes, there were indeed rats skittering with cold little feet over the dishes on the shelves.

'Why would your father's servants have lied about robbers breaking into the house?' asked January softly, as he and the girl followed the long passageway from the kitchen back to the main house.

'They were probably paid.' Belle tugged her borrowed blanket more tightly around her shoulders, the bedroom candle she carried bobbing erratically in her hand. 'You see, M'sieu J . . . the Duc d'Aveline has tried two or three times to buy the Curse Manuscript – and the statue that shows the pharaoh defeated by a Nubian goddess – from Uncle Dev.'

'Ah.' He recalled the intent gleam in the duc's eyes, and how d'Aveline had angled to place himself behind Wishart, watching that brown corner of manuscript protruding from his pocket, when he thought the Englishman's attention distracted. 'To lose them, you mean.'

The duc's voice returned to his mind, screaming at Wishart on a previous occasion, *The greatness of Egypt would never have bowed to a pack of Negroes out of the desert, and that manuscript is a forgery!*

Belle Wishart nodded. 'I think that may be what happened to that manservant Uncle Dev told everyone "disappeared" in the chateau. That he really fired him because he was working for d'Aveline.' With stray dark wisps working loose from her braid in the frozen drafts of the corridor, and her thick spectacles, she had something of the look of a pale small spook herself. 'His Grace has been trying for years to get into that Société Académique de St-Cloud,' she explained.

'Yes, I knew that,' he returned. 'They've endowed a chair at the Académie des Sciences, in the king's name. I know His Grace considers himself not only qualified, but entitled to the position because of his participation in Napoleon's expedition to Egypt.' It was a qualification that he had heard about at least once a week for seven years.

'I think that's one reason why they won't even look at the book he wrote about the pharaohs.' She sighed. 'Other than the fact that it's all tosh, as far as I can tell. He's sent copies of it to every member of the Société, along with reams of additional notes and things.'

'Believe me,' January shook his head, 'I – and every man in the Brotherhood – has heard all about that book.'

She chuckled. 'Oh, dear . . . my condolences, sir.'

'I think he believes that the president of the Société thinks that Napoleon and his scientists made everything up, that they found in Egypt . . .'

Belle rolled her eyes. 'Well, Uncle Dev has also been trying for years to be invited as a guest to one of the Société's meetings.

I gather it's like trying to insinuate oneself into the king's *petite entrée*. That's part of the reason he chose Egypt as our destination.'

'To get into the Société de St-Cloud?'

'To . . .' She stopped, held up her hand. January halted, too. They stood for a moment in the doorway that led from the kitchen passageway to the pantry, listening in the icy darkness. Far off, the inhuman wailing echoed and re-echoed, impossible to track, in the ruined strutwork of the attic.

Then, barely on the edge of hearing, the dragging clank of chains.

The girl's small hand closed around January's arm. She drew close against his side, the light of her candle wavering in the drafts. 'That isn't – that isn't real, is it?' she whispered. 'I mean, that isn't someone who's . . . who's really dead . . .?'

He looked down at her consideringly for a moment, then asked, 'You didn't encounter anything of the sort when you went up to the attics last night? Or along the corridors of the western wing?'

Her eyes widened in shock. 'I . . . What?'

'That wasn't you?'

She shook her head. 'I came down here – just to keep Arithmus company. And you know he'd never – that is . . .' Her words stammered to confused silence. Then, 'I thought Uncle Dev was making it all up. About finding blood on the walls, and hearing sounds . . .'

They stood in the darkness for a time, listening as the sounds died away.

At length he said, 'We won't know what it is, Mademoiselle Wishart, until we confront it.' Only the ground-in threats of half his lifetime kept January from putting a comforting arm around the slender shoulders. And though the sounds made his own flesh creep, he kept his voice wryly cheerful. 'Like most things in this life. And I think you and I have both had enough excitement for one evening, without chasing ghosts. I'll tell you tomorrow what I think might be going on.'

He took the candle from her hand. 'You're freezing,' he said. 'And Ayasha will be worried about what we might have met in the hallways.' And, seeing her eyes dart nervously at the skitter of something – a rat? – in the passageway's colonnaded shadows, he asked her, with deliberately matter-of-fact curiosity as they walked on, 'And does this business with the book go back to your uncle's theory that the Nubians were a great people back in ancient days? Great enough to defeat the Egyptians?'

Belle's hand relaxed around his elbow, and she half-laughed again. 'Oh. *That.* Not only defeat them, but rule Egypt for a time. It's why we went to Asouan, and then down to Khartoum – there are ruins on the Blue Nile south of there that he wanted to see.'

January held open for her the stout oak door which led into the chateau itself, held the candle high to look all around him at the pantry on the other side of it, as Belle closed it behind them, and locked it with a very modern Bramah lock.

'In Asouan, al-Tajir – Arithmus's father – introduced us to old Uncle Tafiq and the other scholars at the madrassa there. And they said, yes, Nubians had conquered Egypt and ruled it for a couple of hundred years. That's why Uncle Dev bought the Curse Manuscript and the statue of the Night Queen defeating the Pharaoh of Egypt—'

'All of which,' sighed January with mock ruefulness, 'directly contradicts d'Aveline's contention that the pharaohs ruled Egypt in unbroken glory until they were betrayed into the hands of the Assyrians by a coalition of Jewish merchants in 652 BC. I think he even claims that the version of events given in Exodus was a lie cooked up by Moses—'

'What Jewish merchants?' protested Belle, appalled. 'I've never heard Father or Uncle Dev or any of their friends at Oxford mention Jewish merchants in Egypt! I don't know nearly as much about Egypt as Father or Uncle Dev do, but even I know that they were crumbling for a long time before the Assyrians took them over.'

'I suspect,' said January, 'the Jewish merchants who hold positions on the boards of Paris banks now.'

At the other side of the dark pantry, he pushed open the double doors of the dining room, a ruinous cavern smelling of mold and the decaying plaster of the stripped walls. 'He worked on that book for twenty years. No wonder he's trying to buy the evidence from your uncle.'

'For *fifty thousand francs*?'

'Is that what he offered?' Rent on the rooms January shared with Ayasha on the Rue de l'Aube was less than five hundred francs per year.

'More, I think.' Belle's lips tightened. 'And the thing is, I don't trust Bloque, or Mr Daucourt – that's our cook at the house – or . . . or any of them, really. I know they'll try again. If Arithmus loses his temper – which he does . . .'

The distress in her eyes made him stop, and ask gently, 'You care for him, don't you?'

She looked quickly aside. Had they been in daylight, he thought, he would have seen her blush. And it flickered through his mind that on Stuart Wishart's last day in Paris, nearly three weeks ago, there had been, beneath the affection of father and daughter, a note of constraint.

He had put it down to her pleas to have more time in Paris, and had not wanted to pry. Since that time, he had sensed a sort of hesitancy between uncle and niece, as if there were things the girl didn't quite have the nerve to bring up.

Now she said, 'Arithmus and I . . .' And hesitated. 'Before he left, I asked Father—'

Somewhere in the vast blackness beyond the dining-room doors a man's voice cried, '*No!*'

And the tumbling clatter of something falling down a long flight of stairs.

NINE

Chateau Palongeux – December 1825

Deverel Wishart lay crumpled at the foot of the grand stairway. Daniel, Persephone, Ayasha, Citoyenne, and Freytag were clattering down the stair as January and Belle charged through the dining-room doors and into the hall; bedroom candles fluttered in the draft like anemic fireflies and did nothing to illuminate the great hall's all-swallowing dark.

'Don't move him.' With strong fingers Freytag pulled a couple of threads free from his own linen sleeve, and held them before the half-parted lips. '*Peste.*' A first-class valet, be he never so German, would have gone to the stake before he'd have sworn in anything but French. 'The wretched gale in here—'

Ayasha dropped to her knees beside the unconscious man as January and Belle reached the place, turned over the lapel of her greatcoat – everybody had clearly paused long enough to grab outer garments and footgear after lighting their candles, not wanting to succumb to frostbite on their way to the rescue. As usual, she had four needles (threaded in different colors) and a row of pins stuck through the underside of the cloth. One of these she drove into Wishart's hand. The scholar twitched and gasped, half-turned his head and immediately lost consciousness again.

'Here.' Freytag dug in the pocket of his own robe for a crystal phial of smelling salts (presumably Daniel's), held them under Wishart's nose.

Persephone and Citoyenne reached the bottom of the stairs last of all, bearing two massive candelabra.

Wishart gasped, '*She*—' and flung up his hand before his face.

'Uncle Dev—!' Belle reached instinctively for the swatch of bleeding flesh on the left curve of his skull's frontal bone, where his head must have struck the marble baluster as he fell. But she drew back with a gasp, as maid and dancer brought their brighter lights closer. Very faintly – almost invisible in the darkness – three small burns marked her uncle's left cheek, as if demon fingertips had been laid on the flesh.

His eyelids fluttered, and he whispered, 'Did you see her?'

'Can you move your feet?' asked January.

The explorer opened his eyes then, and managed a shaky smile. 'I will if that harpy of yours sticks a pin into my hand again.' He flexed his ankles, then his knees. Then slowly, wincing, half-rolled on to his side. 'My God, it feels like every bone in my body is broken—'

The Italian greyhound Musette, who had been sniffing interestedly all around the lower hall, now came pattering up to Wishart, and licked his face. January regarded the little dog for a moment, then turned back to help Wishart to sit up. 'How many fingers am I holding up?'

'Two.'

January took back the candle that he'd handed Belle, held it close enough to the injured man's face to see that the pupils of his eyes immediately contracted with the approach of the light. No concussion. 'What did you see?'

'She . . .' Wishart's brow twisted, partly with pain, partly – January suspected – with an effort to remember. 'She came at me. Tall, taller than Belle.' (This meant little. Everybody was taller than Belle.) 'She wore white, something . . . Her hair unbound. Dark. There was blood on her face, and her clothing, and her hands.' He shut his eyes, turned his face away. 'Her eyes . . . She was mad. Insane. There was . . . nothing human in them. She came at me . . .'

His hand moved toward the burns on the side of his face, but flinched away.

January helped Wishart to his feet, supported him as he climbed the stair. Like the rest of them, Wishart wore a quilted robe over his nightshirt and a greatcoat over that, thick bed socks under curly-toed Morocco-leather slippers. 'I heard sounds in the corridor,' Wishart explained as they climbed. 'Someone crying, and what sounded like the dragging of a chain. When I came out of my room I saw a light, far down at that end of the gallery—'

He pointed towards the southeast, where the locked door of the southeast turret was invisible in the darkness. 'Then she came . . .'

January passed what remained of the night on a chair brought to Wishart's room from Daniel's. Monsieur Mouche – who peered shakily from behind his chamber door as the little party passed and asked what all the noise had been – ordered his valet Brachet to sit up for the remainder of the night at the foot of *his* bed to guard him.

In the morning – rising at first light and forgoing breakfast, since he had to be at the Pillet house on Rue de la Pépinière at noon, and at the opera for rehearsal at three – January and Ayasha inspected the upper gallery near Wishart's door, the long curve of the grand staircase, and the room in the southeast turret where, legend said, the haunting was the worst. On the wall of that chamber, words had been scrawled in fresh blood that had not been there before.

The air in the room still smelled of it.

Sauve-moi, au nom de Dieu.

Musette, pattering at their heels, sniffed interestedly at the blood and tried to lick some. She seemed no more conscious of unseen presences than she had at the foot of the haunted stair the previous night.

Mississippi River – December 1840

'Was it d'Aveline?' asked Hannibal.

January glanced across at him in the feeble candlelight. Bayou Sara lay behind them. The 'staterooms' on either side were like tombs. Vast darkness lay on the river, silent now save for the half-heard throb of the engine, the churn of the paddles and the pilot's distant, untiring cursing. The night was moonless, the banks – and the obsidian waters – barely outlined in the thin gleam of wind-dried stars. January had heard pilots extol this wan illumination for night travel: *Damn moon throws shadows, you don't know what the hell you're lookin' at . . .*

Now and then, through the little window, he glimpsed disembodied dots of light on the black wall of the banks, the Christmas season still holding sway in these empty lands.

They would reach Natchez just after noon.

He raised his brows inquiringly.

'After the attempt at robbing his house,' the fiddler surmised, 'I'm guessing Deverel Wishart would keep his manuscript on his person. Or maybe under his pillow. Even if the chateau's doors were kept locked, I'm sure the servants back in Paris could have been bribed to copy the key. It could have been the Sieur de Palongeux behind the assault, of course . . . Behind the whole haunting, for that matter. Or even this what's-his-name, the chap who wanted to buy the place cheap and sell the home woods for lumber, looking to drive the price down or spook Grezolles into selling quickly. A man who could offer fifty thousand francs would have no trouble suborning a footman.'

'I heard later that d'Aveline eventually ran the price up to two hundred and fifty thousand,' recalled January quietly. 'Wishart wasn't the only man who had challenged his view of Egyptian history, evidently—'

'Oh, gods, no. I knew one of d'Aveline's nephews slightly – this was years after the stirring events you describe. Poor fish sat me down in the corner of the Café Procope one night and told me all about d'Aveline's *Secret Empire of the Golden Desert*, which his mother had made him read in an effort to get on the good side of "Uncle Guste", as he called the duc. They rather needed a contribution from His Grace at that moment . . . He was drunk as a drowned sailor's ghost, and weeping with pity for his own plight – I gather he'd been tasked with bearding the Comte de Chapponnay about looking with favor on Uncle's tenth application to the Société de St-Cloud, who were still having none of him. If I hadn't been so thoroughly embalmed myself, I couldn't have sat through it. But he was buying. *Did* Wishart habitually carry the document in his pocket?'

'I don't know,' said January. 'Believe me, I tried to find out. And of course d'Aveline was at a ball at the Sieur Petiet's that Friday night, where four hundred people could see him. But as you say, if a man can offer two hundred and fifty thousand francs for a document – and a three-inch statue, presumably – he can afford to hire his dirty work done for him. The same goes for the Sieur de Palongeux,' he added. 'Although with less money involved. And for the unknown M'sieu Souscayrac.'

'*Auri sacra fames*,' murmured Hannibal, and leaned down to pick up his now tepid cup of tea from the floor beside his bunk. 'Money may not be the root of all evil, but possession of staggeringly large amounts of it can have strange effects on people's definition of the word "good". Look at Miss Emmett, something I'm not entirely unwilling to do. She's a well-enough-favored girl, but every man on the boat has been going on about her beauty, charm and wit, as if she were Cleopatra and Ninon de L'Enclos rolled into one. Even one or two of the married ones have made what looked to me, at least, like serious approaches to her.'

'So I saw.' The prince and his beloved – whoever she was – had long since left the deck outside. 'I felt a little sorry for them,' he added, recalling the scrimmage around the plump heiress in the earlier portion of the evening, 'getting themselves into a lather, only to have Prince Serafin step into the room – in uniform – and clean them out like a handful of aces.'

'*A substitute shines brightly as a king/Until a king be by* . . . I've known men who would divorce a wife if they saw the chance to marry an heiress. I've even been offered money to be the Other Man. Did your friend Daniel's little greyhound sense anything amiss in that haunted turret chamber? Or anywhere in the chateau?'

'No,' said January. 'Not a thing.'

Chateau Palongeux – December 1825

'Blood.' January touched the baluster halfway down the grand stairway. Though morning's gray light had begun to suffuse the great well of the hall, Ayasha brought her candles close. Around them, hushed footfalls and the chink of toilet articles could be heard: servants executing the preliminary rites of day. One of Daniel's footmen emerged from the backstairs with a brass can of hot water, then glanced nervously in both directions before he would tiptoe into the hall. Arms full of linen, Clémence followed him, clinging close, as if the young man were a match for women in white whose touch left burns on the flesh.

Word, January reflected, had obviously reached the service areas of the house. At a guess, it had been communicated to the footmen and groom when they'd come up from the village at first light. He wondered where Arithmus had been during the commotion last night. *I'll have to ask* . . .

'His head was cut.' Ayasha touched the place on her own brow. 'Not scraped.' January had put two stitches in the place last night before everyone sought their couches, and had closely examined those three small burns on Wishart's cheek. Oval, like a woman's fingertips . . .

Now he took his wife's hand where it closed around the gilt porcelain stem of the girandole she bore, angled the lights closer yet to the smear of browning red on the marble. A smear, he thought, and a curiously shaped one, as if a finger had daubed blood on the stone – which was itself rounded, without any edge on it that could have cut the flesh, as Wishart's had been cut.

The wound itself had more resembled the quick hack of a razor.

'Keep the light close above me.' He moved on down the stairs on his knees, a single step at a time, studying the marble with the attention he had once directed towards cleaning infinitesimal fragments of gravel and wood from the wounds of market women who would come into the night clinic with their husbands swearing, *Oh, she fell . . . fell in the courtyard, she did . . .*

What he sought, he did not find.

Nor had he really expected to.

And any vessel that had contained the larger amount of blood used to write in the turret chamber could have been easily dropped down the disused well in the yard.

Close by the foot of the stair, a small door opened into a chamber barely larger than a cupboard. This contained nothing but an empty and much-battered wooden crate, and Wishart's brass-cornered trunk, also empty. Musette pattered in at his heels, sniffed these items all over. Presumably the niche had once housed a footman charged with taking the cloaks and hats of the Chateau Palongeux guests, before they either passed into the ballroom, or climbed the stair. The trunk, he observed, was new – he'd helped Wishart unpack it on the evening of their arrival. He frowned, something about its appearance tugging at his memory.

'What is it?' Ayasha followed him back up the stair, and down the gallery towards the haunted chamber at the chateau's southeast corner. Morning light now filled the well of the stairway. Freytag passed them on the opposite gallery across the open well of the hall, point-device and armed with a towel, razors, some discreet pots of rouge, and scented Spanish soap. Musette bounded to greet him. Belle emerged from her uncle's room, hastened toward the head of the stair with a worried expression.

January said, 'Mademoiselle Wishart—' and she stopped and turned as he and Ayasha came back to her.

'I have to see Arithmus.' Her dark hair had been stuffed haphazardly up under a cap, and her clothing bore every sign of having been hastily donned. 'All he'll have heard of this is what the servants heard from each other . . .'

Her distress was evident. January stepped closer to her, a hundred small details coming back to him from the previous night.

'You've known him for some months now, haven't you?'

This time he could see the color rise in her face. 'Almost a year.' She glanced back into her uncle's room. Wishart was asleep, but on the corner of the bed – distant from his hand – a letter lay, presumably (January hoped) bearing news that his brother was recovering from his fall hunting. It had arrived on Thursday, two days before. She looked up at him, short-sighted brown eyes pleading for him to understand. 'He's . . . Please don't judge him by how he sometimes acts, M'sieu January. He can't help that. People seem to think it's like madness, but it's not. He'll learn . . .'

He thought of those fingers constantly twisting, the averted gaze and toneless, flat voice. The moments of uncontrollable wrath. The way her hand had touched his wrist, calming him. 'It's no more to me than if he had a lame foot.' January shrugged. 'You just . . . work around it. Why does he refuse to come into the chateau?'

'I don't *know*.' Her black brows pulled together; genuine concern mingled with bafflement in her eyes. 'The other thing people assume is that all Africans are superstitious barbarians . . . Oh!' she added quickly, with a glance at his face, as if she'd suddenly remembered that he, too, would fall into this category. 'I mean—'

'That's no surprise to me, mamzelle.' He smiled.

'But you're not. Arithmus isn't. Completely aside from the education he had from his Uncle Tafiq, I don't think he has the imagination to believe in ghosts. And the first time Uncle Dev came out here with M'sieu Grezolles, Arithmus *did* go inside with him. When they came back to the house that afternoon, nobody said anything about Arithmus not wanting to set foot inside.'

'Did they know it was haunted then?' asked Ayasha.

The girl nodded. 'That's why they came out here. M'sieu Grezolles does business with Father – he owns the house we're renting in Rue St-André, you know. He told him about the tales of the ghosts, and the buried treasure, and asked him to take a look at the place. People from the village are always trying to break in and poke around in the crypts, he said. But neither Uncle Dev nor Arithmus ever said anything about seeing or hearing anything . . . untoward.'

Sounds in the courtyard made January turn his head. It was the smallest of the baggage-transport vehicles Daniel had brought along, a shabby chaise that Conojo the assistant cook took into the village to do the marketing. It was time, January knew (with a pang of regret about breakfast) to go bespeak a seat on it for a ride into Paris. *Dammit* . . .

'Thank you, mamzelle.' As he bowed, his eyes were drawn again to the blood-smudge on the banister. 'What you've told me has been very interesting.' And he went down the stairs at a run, to catch the groom and the assistant cook before they could leave.

Mississippi River – December 1840

'Why the burns on his face?' inquired Hannibal.

The night was now very deep. Somewhere beyond the black of the window a lone prick of light broke the darkness.

Someone sick, thought January. *Dying, maybe.* On a moonless night, it was long past the hour at which even the most lively holiday gathering broke up.

He recalled going out with Dr Gomez, his old teacher in New Orleans, to an isolated plantation near Bayou Sara. The master of the place, a repellent and abusive Spaniard, had inexplicably fallen down a flight of stairs, sustaining internal injuries that the Feliciana Parish sheriff had ruled were the cause of his death. He remembered the man's young wife, with the marks of a beating discoloring her jaw, weeping in terror, because she knew she'd be accused of pushing him. *I was nowhere near him, m'sieu*, she had whispered, over and over again to Gomez, that endless night of sitting up beside the man's bed, the darkness outside as if the plantation house had been sunk to the bottom of the sea. *I was nowhere near!*

And indeed, Gomez had said – to her, and to the fifteen-year-old January, and later to the sheriff – that the man showed every sign of having had a stroke, from running up the stair in pursuit of the frightened woman. Choleric, red-faced, and given to rages, Señor Verruta had indeed suffered severe injuries in his fall. But Gomez gave his opinion at the wife's trial that what had killed him was a second stroke eight days later, as he lay in bed.

The woman had been hanged.

'I don't know.' January turned from the window, as the speck of gold disappeared behind some obstruction on the inky wall of the river's bank. 'And when – and *how* – they could have been produced by an attacker . . . It isn't like running up to someone in a sheet and shoving them downstairs.'

'Not to speak ill of the dead . . .' Hannibal clasped his thin fingers together, settled back against the wad of shabby pillows by the wall of his bunk. 'I do have to ask – was your friend M'sieu Wishart sober at the time? I can't say that I have never been assaulted by women in white whose touch burned the skin, but I *think* that attack actually happened. It's a long story. You don't happen to know if the man was in the habit of imbibing specialized North African candies or Smyrna cocktails after he retired for the night?'

'I don't think so.' January cast his mind back, to the candlelit chamber on the western corridor as they'd helped Wishart to bed. The full panoply of Wishart's botanical experiments had been stacked along one wall: alembics and presses, bottles and vials, two braziers obviously stolen from the kitchen – one of which had clearly been in recent use for heating the room – along with an assortment of more mundane objects. A shaving mirror balanced on a stack of Wishart's books. A couple of candles and a salt spoon (for measuring chemicals?) occupied the room's single, broken-down stool. The letter from his brother had then been folded and tucked between the shaving mirror and the bedside candle, the red wax of its cracked seals gleaming like blood.

Belle must have come in and read it while he was still asleep . . .

Mold and the faint smell of rats, and of charcoal smoke from the brazier, but nothing of the queer flowery fumes of opium. And among the flower presses and tins, the notebooks and packets of dried leaves, he saw nothing that resembled – or smelled like – the little packets of brownish-black paste that the doctors at the Hôtel Dieu had kept so carefully under lock and key.

'When I looked at the pupils of his eyes after his fall, they reacted normally. They weren't pinpoints, the way they'd be if he'd had that much of a drug. And in the weeks he lived in Paris, I never saw him act . . . intemperate.' He glanced apologetically at his friend, who had in the past given an entirely new dimension to the word. 'And I think either Mademoiselle Wishart, or Arithmus, would have spoken of it.'

'Loyalty and love on the one hand . . .' The fiddler shook his head. 'And innocence on the other. From what you tell me, your Nubian savant could have described the minutest symptom of recreational ossification from any occasion for the previous nine months, without having the slightest idea what it meant. Did you ask M'sieu Wishart himself?'

'No.' January sighed, some part of him aching anew at the recollection of that exhausting defeat. 'I did not have the chance.'

He and Ayasha had returned to the Chateau Palongeux in the long chilly hour between sunset and full dark. Neither Daniel nor M'sieu Mouche had had business in the city that day, so once January's rehearsal was done – Persephone having a performance that night – it was a walk of nearly two hours to Palongeux, even including getting a lift on an obliging farmer's cart. They left the shabby ruin of construction materials and the remains of Napoleon's wooden triumphal arch behind them, and entered the bare, cold shadows of the Bois de Boulogne, where the road to Argenteuil led to the Pont de Neuilly and the woods around Palongeux itself. Wind muttered secrets through the remains of the old forest of Rouvray which hid the village; dark trees and overgrown ponds infinitely more creepy, in the gathering dusk, than the pale walls of the chateau itself. The bell of the village church, tolling for evening service, reminded him that he had not had time to go to confession that day, as he'd hoped to do.

'Auntie Jeanne back home,' January said, 'told me about a h'ant that would walk the River Road carrying a lantern, a woman with a great long neck but no head – like a decapitated giraffe, I suppose. If you saw her she'd chase you into the swamp, and leave you there to die . . . If you made it into your house and locked the door, she'd come down the chimney – first a disembodied foot, then a leg, then a hand, maybe, or an arm . . .'

'*Bisharafak!*' Ayasha sniffed. 'My aunt Farida would sweep those things out of the house with a broom. But if you're walking home past a ruined building at night, or a cemetery, the *ubir* might be waiting there. The blood-drinkers, with burning eyes, and long fangs . . .'

January said, 'Pff! If one of your *ubir* even once saw the red eyes of the platt-eye devil coming at him in the dark, he'd run like a bunny rabbit till morning! And if the hag-witches caught him, they'd put a bridle in his mouth – long fangs and all! – and ride him three times around the . . .'

He stopped. In the thickening twilight he could make out, against the ghostly walls of the chateau, a small cabriolet of the kind Stuart Wishart had rented when he was in Paris in November. Men clustered around the groom's seat – he could just make out their forms in the gloom. Too many for a casual exchange of gossip.

He caught Ayasha's hand, quickened his step. *What now?*

As they came near, January heard one of the footmen say, 'M'sieu Bloque said – the butler, you know – said he was supposed to be getting better.'

And the groom, still seated on the box, shook his head. 'And so he was, I hear. Me, I think there was somethin' else in it. I mean, M'sieu Wishart always said how M'sieu Stuart was a crack rider. Me, I think he was took ill, sudden-like, in the hunting field, and that's why he took faint and had that fall in the first place. From what I hear, he never really rallied – I mean, what's a broken collarbone, to a hunting man . . .?'

The great hall, with its up-curving stairway, was empty and dark. But the dim glow of candles outlined the open door of the small salon, and within, Deverel Wishart sat on one of the chairs that Daniel had brought to the chateau when the whole business had been simply a ghost-hunt, holding his niece rather awkwardly on his knee. His arms were wrapped around her, and his face, bent over hers, was pale and very still, as men's will get when they have had news that they're still trying to tell themselves is untrue. When they lose an arm, or a brother, and can't quite realize yet that the loss will be for ever.

Belle was weeping. Arithmus, standing behind the chair, looked down at her, hands hanging at his sides and his face expressionless, save for the inarticulate grief in his eyes.

Mouche, Daniel, and Citoyenne grouped nearby, Mouche clearly trying to think of a way to leave the room and the other two wrung with helpless pity. Before them stood a tall, stiff, clerkish man, with sandy pomaded hair and unmistakably American tailoring. That ill-fitting, utilitarian black coat practically screamed *Made in Cincinnati*, the trousers bound at the crotch and fell in an awkward line to the thick, many-times-mended black shoes. The pale tan eyes that flicked briefly to January, then to Ayasha, held a cold interest that January hadn't seen since he'd left New Orleans, then returned to the couple on the chair.

That was the first time January encountered Creon Grice.

Ayasha gently coaxed Belle to stand, held her wrapped close in her arms. Grice said, 'I think it would be best if Miss Wishart returns home tonight.' The flat glance rested for a contemptuous moment on Ayasha's dusky brown face, then moved on to Deverel Wishart. January remembered someone – Belle, or Wishart himself, on one of those Sunday afternoons on the Rue St-André des Artes – telling him that, as business partner, Grice not only managed Stuart's property, but Deverel's modest investments as well.

To Deverel, Grice went on, 'There's a great deal of paperwork to be settled at the house, sir. Creditors and agents were waiting for me when I arrived this morning. They'll want to talk to you.'

Wishart's mouth flinched, as if driving back nausea. 'Yes, I . . . I suppose so.' Against the brownish linen of the bandage on his forehead, his skin had the pallor of shock.

'I can have your expenses and the notes from your trip put into order for you, to go over with the representatives of Lafitte.' Grice spoke in English, as he had from the beginning, though January guessed, from what he said, that his French had to be fluent to deal with those creditors and agents. He simply didn't bother with the other people in the group. 'If you like, I can brief you on what you need to say to them—'

'Yes, yes!' Wishart slashed with his hand in front of his eyes, like a man chasing a cloud of pestering flies. 'Tomorrow, or . . . Tell them I'll be there . . . I'll be there Monday—'

'It would be better if you could address the problems right away, sir. The man from Baring Brothers is particularly—'

'I'll be there Monday, dammit! I have things to finish up here, you know.' By the way he waved around him at the bare darkness of the chateau, January guessed he simply wanted time to catch his breath, away from the partner's intrusiveness. 'Belle . . .' He turned to his niece, held out his hands to her. 'Belle, I'll be there in a . . . I'll be there soon. Monday. I promise.'

Belle nodded, in a way that told January that Uncle Dev had broken promises before.

Many times.

'I think it probably best . . .' Again Grice looked Ayasha up and down, grimacing either at her complexion or at the working-woman's gown and demure cap, which did nothing to hide the desert-witch beauty and intelligence of her face. 'It would be best if Miss Wishart comes back with me now. Her maid can bring along whatever she needs for tonight. I'll send a man for the rest of her things in the morning.'

Belle threw a look of agony at her uncle, who seemed so dazed by his own grief – so sickened by the thought of dealing with his brother's affairs – that he could not help showing the relief he felt. Relief that he wouldn't have to deal with anyone's pain but his own.

'I shall start making arrangements for your return to Norfolk at once,' Grice continued. 'As soon as your brother's affairs are concluded here. When shall I tell the men from Lafitte's, and from Baring's, that you will—?'

'You'll deal with that when I get there, damn it!' Wishart shouted. 'I said Monday. Or maybe Wednesday. I don't know. I'll be there.'

'Sir,' pestered Grice, 'I need to know—'

'You need to know bloody all! I'll write you tomorrow. Belle, I promise—' He took his niece in his arms, kissed her quickly, and as quickly almost shoved her into Citoyenne's arms. Then he snatched the bottle of cognac that stood, in the evenings, on an up-ended crate near the fireplace, and strode from the room.

Mississippi River – December 1840

'He was drunk the whole of the next day,' said January. 'And on the Monday morning his body was found, in the bed in the south-east turret room, unmarked, his face twisted with an expression of the most ghastly horror and shock.'

Hannibal sighed, and leaned back into the pillows again. 'A stroke could do that,' he said. 'Or a seizure brought on by alcohol poisoning. Or fright, at something he saw, or thought he saw. *Etiam fortes viros subitis terreri*. Given the amount of money involved with the sale of the chateau, I expect someone thought it worthwhile to accuse Arithmus of the deed, rather than a ghost. Or did they say Belle did it?'

'Both.'

TEN

Natchez proper stood on the crest of the high golden-red river bluffs, nearly three hundred feet above the devastation of half-rebuilt cotton presses, wrecked houses and coffee shops, and incompletely reconstructed warehouses that last spring's tornado had left of Natchez Under. Amid the shambles of building sites and ruins, wagonloads of cotton crunched the muddy gravel; steamboats clogged the repaired wharves and the chill wind that streamed down the Mississippi Valley did little to dissipate the smell of privies, cook-fires, streets long uncleansed of decaying garbage and dung.

On the stern deck a few yards away, Miss Emmett and Josie Grice gazed cow-eyed at the handsome figure of Prince Serafin, while the vicomtesse chatted with Hannibal. January stood a few feet further off, with the luggage; a trifle compared to the ten trunks being guarded by Miss Emmett's 'boy' Joe. Miss Emmett's maidservant Linney, and Persephone's stout, pink-faced Fräulein Hauser, stood nearby, almost elbow-to-elbow, the German woman ignoring Linney as resolutely as the buxom little octoroon ignored the very-much-darker Joe. It was difficult to tell whether they were in their turn being ignored by the fierce Gaspar, or whether he was simply concentrating all his attention on defending Prince Serafin's three trunks and two carpetbags from all-comers: the man appeared to have spent the entire thirty-hour voyage closeted in his master's cabin polishing his master's boots. Doktor Boehler, at his side, and like Fräulein Hauser clearly of the opinion that servants were – or should be – invisible, watched the prince like a bearded mother hen. When Miss Emmett would make artless attempts to stroll over and speak to His Highness, the pedagogue would step in front of her: 'His Highness wishes to be left in peace, Fräulein.'

Had he stabbed the heiress with Cupid's golden arrow, January reflected, Boehler could not have more thoroughly inflamed Miss Emmett's infatuation for her royal charge. Sleepy though he was after only a few hours' repose on the floor of Hannibal's cabin, January couldn't keep from shaking his head at the little three-way melodrama being played out by the rail: the prince's pleading glances at the black-veiled girl, dark eyes begging beneath long lashes: *Please understand! I can't explain now, but know that I adore you . . .*

What would you call it if it was played at the American Theater on Camp Street? January wondered. *A Forbidden Crown? American Princess?*

'My parents would never accept an American . . . My heart is at your feet . . .'

'Our love will find a way . . .'

And of course Miss Emmett was nearly swooning with the heady emotions of thwarted passion.

His eyes returned to the Natchez bluffs. A line of leafless pride-of-India trees fringed the top, the black lace of mourning against the pale afternoon sky.

Arithmus.

Belle.

I could have done more . . .

But he had no idea what that might have been.

'His body was unmarked,' he had told Hannibal, early that morning over the coffee he'd brought up to the stateroom. 'His eyes were bloodshot, and all the subcutaneous capillaries of his face had ruptured. There was mucus in his throat, where he'd tried to breathe, but his hands showed no sign that he'd tried to defend himself.'

'Sounds like a stroke to me.'

'That's what the man from the local prefecture of police thought. Stroke brought on by excessive drinking – there was an empty cognac bottle in the room, and the whole bed smelled of liquor. He'd just had news of his brother's death,' January added, shaking his head. 'I've wondered since if his brother might have died from the same cause – stroke, I mean. That he'd had one out hunting, which was what caused his fall and injury, and then a second one a week later. And of course the village priest was of the opinion that Wishart died of the "vexations of demons." Only what was to be expected of a heretic.'

'*Shadows tonight/Have struck more terror to the soul of Richard,*' Hannibal quoted in his plummiest imitation of the great Edmund Kean, '*Than can the substance of ten thousand soldiers* . . . I'll wager that was what put Grezolles or the Sieur de Palongeux or whoever else looking for an actual person to blame it on, rather than something he saw in the dark. Even a stroke wouldn't do. And since they had a "mysterious savage from the dark continent" conveniently on the premises, who'd flown into a rage and tried to strangle what's-his-name – your friend from the Brotherhood . . .'

'Louis Gounelle,' said January. 'And yes, the man from the Sûreté talked to Gounelle – and to half a dozen other men of the Brotherhood who'd been there that night. It might not have mattered, had they not found the letter Wishart had received the morning before his fall down the stairs.'

'About Miss Wishart,' asked the fiddler softly, 'and Arithmus?'

January nodded. 'When her father came to Paris to take her back to Norfolk,' he said, 'both she, and Arithmus, spoke to him: Arithmus asked for her hand.'

'Considering the Titanomachy which ensued when my cousin Godwin married a Catholic – a perfectly sweet and respectable young lady, I might add – I can't imagine the prospect met with Papa's approval. I doubt that even a charming and personable Nubian with ten thousand pounds a year would be welcome in London society: we all saw how much good it did Othello.'

'According to the letter, at the time Stuart Wishart asked his daughter to do nothing rash, and promised to consider the matter. Having considered, he wrote, he forbade the match and commanded his brother in no uncertain terms to prevent further familiarity between his daughter and Arithmus by sending Miss Wishart back to England at once.'

Hannibal sighed, a whisper of breath, his thin hands curled around the coffee cup that January had brought him. 'And did Miss Wishart know the contents of the letter?'

'She claimed she didn't. But the man from the Sûreté who came out later in the day – before the undertaker's men arrived to take the body back to town – he found the letter in Wishart's room.'

As he'd spoken the words, January had recalled seeing the letter himself in Wishart's room, during the few hours he'd watched by the explorer's bed after the ghostly attack. Remembered how the cracked red wax of the seal had caught the edge of the candlelight, propped on the rickety bedside chair between the shaving mirror and the salt-spoon. Ayasha, he reflected, would have read it – and after Wishart's body had been found, would have slipped back into his room and burned it.

Ayasha would have guessed what lengths men would go to, to keep M'sieu Souscayrac from backing out of the sale before the lawsuit with the Sieur de Palongeux came on.

Could I have saved them, by that simple act?
Or wouldn't it have mattered?
He had never known.

Belle, he recalled, had remained in Paris, numb with the shock of losing her father and her uncle within the space of days. Creon Grice had arrived at Palongeux only minutes behind the undertakers' men, bringing Charles-Xavier Grezolles' notary and a clerk from Gideon-Duvallet et Frères with instructions about placing the chateau under seal. In his will, made in 1821, Stuart Wishart had named his deceased wife's cousin – who had died in Provence of pneumonia shortly after Deverel and Belle set forth for Egypt – as the girl's guardian, should Deverel die before Belle came of age. His business partner, Creon Grice, had been named fourth on the list.

'I suppose it was a convenience,' surmised Hannibal, 'to have a man legally qualified to make decisions there in France at the time—'

'If the man hadn't been a crook,' January snapped. The light outside the shabby muslin window-curtain had been broadening by then; he'd guessed they'd be sighting Natchez soon. 'I have my suspicions about how he forced her into marrying him – which he did, a week later. He packed her off immediately to the United States – he had family in Baltimore, presumably Miss Grice's father – and spent the next month selling off her father's property.'

'Which must have been considerable, if he was able to go into partnership with Travis Emmett dealing slaves—'

January shook his head. 'According to Deverel, it consisted of a modest estate in Norfolk, worth probably around five thousand pounds. Enough to give Grice a stake to make a start in something, though.'

'And was there any explanation' – Hannibal rubbed the side of his nose – 'of why he'd gone to the southeast tower room? Was there writing in blood still on the wall? Though God knows how many times *I'd* lie down in one bed with a bottle of cognac and wake up in another, sometimes with someone I had never seen before in my life . . . What did Miss Wishart say about the matter?'

Quietly, he said, 'I didn't see her again.'

A voice outside, on the deck below, shouted that they were coming up on Red River Landing, Red River Landing ahead . . .

'Arithmus went back to the house on Rue St-André des Artes with Grice when the undertaker's men took the body away,' he went on. 'The next day he vanished. I suspected that Miss Wishart had heard something – possibly Grice told her – that she, as well as Arithmus, were under suspicion for murdering her uncle—'

'*What?*' exclaimed Hannibal in mock horror. 'Men in the Sûreté accept *bribes*, to alter a charge that might complicate the sale of property? Benjamin, you shock me!'

January made a rude gesture, and divided the last of the coffee between them, before setting one cup on the tray he'd brought from the kitchen, and another half out of sight on the windowsill, lest anyone suspect that a black man had shared a meal with a white one. Both men knew that, sixteen years ago, most members of the Paris Sûreté had been former criminals themselves.

'Daniel, Ayasha and I spent the next year looking for him,' he said. 'For any word of him, or for any word of who might have had the means to get into the chateau on the Friday night, when Deverel was pushed down the stairs, or the Sunday night when he was killed.'

'Keys can be copied,' repeated Hannibal with a sigh. 'Or there's always a ladder and a low place on the garden wall, if you don't fancy being blackmailed. I suppose several hundred other people saw the Duc d'Aveline dancing at a ball Sunday night as well?'

'At the Comte de Lentilly's.'

'μὰ τὸν κύνα . . .'

'One difficulty was, all the people that we spoke to later – Daniel, Persephone, Ayasha, the little street urchins that Ayasha paid to chat up d'Aveline's stable help – all came back with the same story. Everyone – his grooms, his mistress, his priest nephew, his secretary – they all agreed that the Duc d'Aveline was the pettiest, stubbornest, vainest, most arrogant and obsessive man in the Western world . . . and that he would not have paid, or commanded, anyone to harm another person.'

'Well . . .' Hannibal had leaned back against the wall behind his bunk. 'Hell and seventeen devils. I suppose they *all* couldn't have owed him money. For the sake of his soul, I ought to say I'm delighted to hear that, but if such was his reputation – deserved or not – I expect it made things extremely awkward for poor Miss Wishart and Arithmus.'

'Over the course of that next year we did learn that the Sûreté had men out looking for Arithmus the night before he disappeared – it was "common knowledge" among half the people who'd seen him exhibited in Paris that he was Wishart's slave, and savage, and dangerous – and that they wanted Belle as well. We traced Souscayrac, de Palongeux, even Grezolles, but it was the same story: all of them could be accounted for on the Sunday night, and each of them had the means to hire the crime done by someone else. We never uncovered a trace of who that might have been.'

At that point the chilly morning shadows had darkened the curtain on the door, and Miss Emmett's voice outside had exclaimed, 'If he's still asleep, can't you waken him, then, Your Ladyship? I *must* get a note to His Highness somehow! We're landing at two! And that horrid guardian of his won't let me get near him – won't leave his side when I so much as speak to him!'

'That's almost certainly Doktor Boehler's job,' Persephone had pointed out.

'That's no answer! And what should his parents care, if he marries a good American girl? In five years all Papa's money will be mine – and *please* don't tell me any stuff about old families and blood! I guess an American girl's blood is as good as any ugly German princess's . . . and I saw him playing cards with Mr Sefton last night! He's got to . . .'

January had raised his brows, and gathered up the tray. Gently, he slipped from the cabin, bowed to the two women on the promenade outside: 'Michie Hannibal will be out by and by, Miss . . .'

'But you have to give this to him *now*.' She wedged the note between his fingers and the edge of the tray. 'It won't take you but a minute. It's desperately important—'

January gave her a conspiratorial grin. 'I will, miss – but if I hand it to him 'fore he's out of bed, he'll just blaspheme, and chuck it away without reading.'

Persephone chuckled at Miss Emmett's exasperated frown, and cut off her upcoming command with, 'Now, *ma cherie*, the first thing a lady needs to learn about conducting a clandestine *affaire* is to trust the word of a man's valet about what he's like in the morning.'

'It's *noon!*'

It wasn't – January guessed it was no later than ten thirty – but the dancer laughed again and gestured for him to go. As he walked off, he heard Miss Emmett behind him: 'Any decent person *should* be awake at this hour! And I for one didn't like the way that scoundrel talked about his master. My daddy would have whipped a man who said . . .'

Thankfully, January rattled down the stair to the galley on the lower deck. *Et genus et formam regina pecunia donat* . . . Royal parents or no, he reflected, even a quarter-million-dollar dowry couldn't be worth living with that young lady for so much as a week.

Now, clustered on the bow deck as the *Sarah Jane* put in to the wharves, January watched Miss Emmett elbow her way to Hannibal's side. She asked him something: he raised his old-fashioned chimney-pot hat with gentle respect as he replied. Miss Emmett stamped her foot at him, then threw an agonized glance at the prince (*to see if he witnessed the show of ill-temper?*).

His Highness appeared to be being scolded by Doktor Boehler.

Miss Emmett flounced back to Miss Grice, snapped something at her, and then started ordering Linney and the harassed-looking Joe to move the luggage to a spot more convenient to the gangway. Then she turned to view the shambles of the half-repaired riverfront with balled fists and tears of disappointment in her eyes.

The paddles ceased their turning; the deckhands leaned on their poles. The *Sarah Jane* inserted herself neatly between the *York and Lancaster* on one side and the *Old Glory* on the other, so close that an active man could have leaped from the rail of one or the other on to the *Sarah Jane*'s decks. January saw Josie Grice rise up on her tiptoes, wave her handkerchief at a group on shore. Her one attempt to speak to her companion was met by foot-stamping rebuff.

For all the ruin the recent tornado had wrought, however, Natchez remained a brisk, lively, wealthy little town perched on its bluffs. Set amid all those miles of swamp, cotton fields, woodlands, mosquitoes, and dense summer heat, in midsummer it would be an oasis of breezes, fifty miles from the bucolic Vicksburg and seventy from St Francisville.

Belle has lived here for sixteen years. January saw again in his mind that scholarly young lady who had traveled with her uncle to Egypt and the Red Sea, who had studied in Paris and gone up to London, as a child, to see the king. No older than Miss Emmett was now.

And, he thought, as much in love. Probably more, for the man she cared for wasn't a Hungarian prince whose attentions to her had put every other girl in the Mississippi Valley firmly in the shade.

'And where was Creon Grice,' asked Hannibal softly, 'on the night of Mr Wishart's death?'

'At a concert at the Tuileries Palace, sponsored by the queen to raise money for a monument to her parents. He apparently claimed that Belle was with him – I can't imagine she would have been, the day after she heard of her father's death.'

'And did the police believe that tale?'

January shrugged. 'I have no idea. I heard that within a week of her father's death – her uncle's death – she married Creon Grice, in a private ceremony at the home of the American minister, and the following day set sail on the *Sophie Hallam* for Baltimore. It was only this Friday – Christmas – that I learned from Persephone that Arithmus went with her, probably posing as her slave—'

'An impersonation that became reality,' the fiddler's voice was grim, 'the minute he stepped ashore, I daresay.'

Better than running the risk of being guillotined? January could just imagine the impression Arithmus would have made on a *juge d'instruction*.

Like the taste of wormwood on his lips, those bitter winter weeks returned to him. Days when he should have been sleeping, knowing he'd be up all night playing for the Christmas entertainments of the Duc de Polignac, of the financier Delessert, of the banker Jacques Lafitte and the Comte de Beaupoil. Freezing rain the night he and Ayasha had broken into the locked-up Chateau Palongeux and found that yes, there was an arrangement of windpipes, Aeolic wires, and curved metal sounding-boards hidden in a sort of belvedere above the attics, where none of the searchers, nor the police, had found it. Even by candlelight he had formed the impression that the machinery, while many decades old, had been put into working order recently . . .

Meetings with Daniel between opera rehearsals, for worried exchanges of information about what the young banker had learned from his disgruntled father (and from assorted gossipy boyfriends) about the progress of the Sûreté's investigation. The efforts to trace Citoyenne, who had either abruptly resigned her post after bringing Belle's effects to the house on the Rue St-André on that Saturday evening, or been dismissed for theft . . . stories differed.

And the whispered suspicion in the back of his mind that he was missing something. That the pieces didn't fit together.

I could have done more . . .

Could I have done more?

'In any case,' said January, 'I don't see how it could have been Grice, who didn't arrive in Paris until the Saturday – the day after Wishart's first encounter with the "ghost".'

The gangplank was run out. The man who greeted Josie Grice had the same nondescript, sandy coloring January recalled in Creon Grice, but save for that, and for his height, he couldn't recall Grice himself well enough – after sixteen years and only two brief encounters – to trace a resemblance. The man wasn't sufficiently well dressed to be Grice himself, and though they embraced, there was clearly awkwardness there. January recalled Persephone saying that Miss Grice had been ordered to accompany Miss Emmett, family duty cutting short a holiday visit to friends in New Orleans. The man, if it was her father, had the air of a clerk.

Persephone, Vicomtesse de St-Forgeux, passed over the gangplank next, and nobody crowded her. Evidently the glamor of French nobility held its charm here up-river, and be damned to American democratic principles. Daisy Emmett, following behind, had drawn her mourning veil over her face and walked with bowed head, in a fair imitation of Mary, Queen of Scots, at Fotheringhay. She didn't even glance at Miss Grice.

A smart green-and-yellow landau, and a sturdy wagon, waited for them amid the jostle of carriages and cabs at the back of the crowds on the wharves; Sigerist was helping the vicomtesse into the former, where Miss Emmett already sat enthroned. The coachman, a little black beetle of a man with shoulders like a cotton bale, extended a hand to assist Fräulein Hauser up to share the box with him – the customary perch of servants – and her eyes widened with shock, as if at the prospect of getting into a dung cart. January forced his face straight at the way her horrified glance cut to the alternatives – either standing on the footman's perch with Sigerist (not something you wanted to do, January reflected, if you were not used to hanging on that way and were about to go up that very steep hill to Natchez proper), or (*a fate worse than death!*) riding in the wagon with the luggage and four other people of African descent.

For a moment Miss Emmett's display of martyrdom was rivaled by the stoic heroism of the German maid. Then Persephone asked gently, 'You won't mind if Fräulein Hauser rides inside with us, will you, *cherie*?'

Miss Emmett turned her face aside with an almost audible sob – *How can you ask such a sacrifice of me when you can see me in agony over my exile to this place?* – and shook her head, a tiny gesture. *Yes, I'll bear the blow with bravery . . .*

January didn't dare meet Hannibal's eyes as the fiddler handed the maid into the carriage. Gales of laughter over the ongoing histrionics would have severely complicated any effort to speak to Belle – and there was no way of knowing what waited for them at Grice's household. Miss Emmett's maid Linney clearly shared Fräulein Hauser's opinions of riding on the same box with a man as ebony-complected as the coachman – like many house servants, the young woman was fair-complected and obviously considered the man beneath her – but had no choice. It was ride on the box or in the wagon with Joe, January, twelve trunks, and the driver.

Yet when they reached the top of the hill of Silver Street, and turned along Main through the business district of the town, January could not find it in his heart to have contempt for the Virginia maid's squeamishness about riding with a coachman so much darker than she. At the corner of Main they passed a tall brick building – newly repaired after the tornado – with a high wall behind it on whose top glittered a line of broken glass:

GRICE & EMMETT
Cotton Hands – House Niggers
Fancies

On the benches beside its doors, a line of men and women watched the passing traffic, the women clothed in bright calico dresses and neat head-rags, the men buttoned stiffly into cheap blue suits. The women's skirts mostly covered the chain that joined them at the ankles, but the metal links gleamed between the men. There probably wasn't a day, thought January, that Linney – for all her stuck-up airs – wasn't aware that nothing, literally *nothing*, stood between her and a bench outside some establishment like that one. Travis Emmett had been a slave dealer.

No wonder the girl tried to tell herself that with her fairer skin she at least wouldn't come to *that* . . .

And Belle, he thought, as he watched the women in the line whose children clung to them. *Had Belle borne children to Creon Grice?* Even if he'd forced her into marriage, by fear of arrest or, it now seemed to him, fear for Arithmus's safety, over the past sixteen years it was impossible to think that she hadn't.

One thing every owner knew: a woman with a child is less likely to flee.

Who's going to take in a woman with a child? Or more than one?

The bells of Sunday worship floated over the town, like angels singing the praise of God.

Since the chaperonage of the Vicomtesse de St-Forgeux would end once Miss Emmett was deposited on the doorstep of her guardian and his wife, Persephone had written ahead to reserve rooms for herself – and for Hannibal – at the Magnolia Tree Hotel on Pearl Street. Their little cortege stopped there long enough to unload Persephone's trunks, January's and Hannibal's modest wicker grips, and Sigerist and Fräulein Hauser, then made their way out past Pine Street and along St Catherine's Road. The town buildings gave way to winter-bare woods dotted – at long intervals

– with town villas and country estates within easy reach of the town itself. Ostentatious gateposts bore names like 'Traveler's Haven' and 'Hollywood'.

To their right, just outside the limits of the town, brick or clapboard buildings clustered on a small knoll, and January's hair prickled on his nape as he read the names on the signs there. *Franklin and Armfield. John D. James & Co. William Pullum, Trader.* Names known – and spoken with bitter fear – by men and women of color from Baltimore to Texas.

Another for *Grice & Emmett*.

Forks of the Road. The biggest slave market north of New Orleans. Bigger, in some ways, with the cotton lands of Mississippi and Missouri opening up, and credit reviving after the bank crash. Livestock was sold there as well as men and women; even in the cold, the place smelled of horses and mules . . . and privies left uncleaned too long.

And, it seemed to January, the spiritual stink of slavery. Of rage fettered, and grief disregarded, and hate that went straight down like a well to the lowest depths of hell.

The knoll was hidden by the winter trees, but the smell followed them for a mile. The darkness of his soul, further yet.

The driver of the landau turned down a gravel drive, and drew up before an impressively porticoed mansion named 'Laburnum'. Two magnificent specimens of that poisonous tree flanked the pillared porch, naked now of their golden chains of blossom. If Belle had borne her husband children, January wondered, had any of them died of eating the berries that dropped in autumn from those boughs?

He remained beside the wagon while Hannibal escorted the vicomtesse and her charge up the three shallow steps to the gallery. A beribboned wreath of holly and ivy decorated the front door. Even as the fiddler raised his hand to the knocker, the door was opened and January had a glimpse of a spry, slender, silver-haired man in butler's livery. A moment later – as January himself offered a hand to Linney to step down from the high seat of the wagon – Creon Grice emerged from the front door.

'My Lady St-Forgeux.' He bowed like a man impaled on a stick. January recalled the man's barely concealed sneers at Persephone, on the Monday afternoon that he'd arrived at Palongeux in the wake of the Sûreté; it was clear that he did not recognize her now. 'And Miss Emmett! Welcome to your new home, my dear. I hope that it will be a home to you. I cannot say how grieved I was to hear about your poor father . . .'

The door closed. Grice himself hadn't changed much, January reflected as he picked up Linney's small suitcase. The slave dealer still carried his head thrust forward, peering with those sharp, colorless eyes. His snuff-brown hair had thinned and retreated yet further up his forehead, and he wore it shorter. His mouth retained the look of a man who charged for every word he spoke.

January followed Linney around via a neatly bricked pathway to the rear of the house. The butler met them by the kitchen steps: 'The wagon will be along in about fifteen minutes with the rest of Miss Emmett's things,' January told the man. 'Lady St-Forgeux is staying at the Magnolia House . . .'

'There may be a change of plan about that.' The butler held out his hand to January – 'Quincy,' he introduced himself, 'Quincy Taylor,' – and then bowed to Linney, and signed to the youth who'd come out of the kitchen behind him to take her bag. 'Miss . . . Linney? Very pleased to make your acquaintance, miss. Corena's had a room made up for you in the attic, if that'll be all right with your young miss. Geordie here'll carry your things up.'

He turned back to January as Linney and the boy Geordie disappeared into the house. 'Fact is, sir, Mr Grice is pretty near for certain going to ask Her Ladyship to stay on here for a time, if she'd be so kind. He's sent for one of his cousins from Lexington, to come stay with Miss Emmett, now that she'll be his ward. But he needs someone here now – tonight, in fact – a lady with a good name.'

'Mrs Grice—'

Quincy's mouth flexed into a thin line. 'Mr Grice turned Mrs Grice out of the house, day before yesterday. He . . . found her with another man. Soon as everybody gets back from Christmas, he'll be calling on his lawyer to start divorce proceedings.'

ELEVEN

'So you may as well come inside,' concluded Quincy Taylor. 'It's warm in the kitchen, if you don't mind Corena tellin' you to stay the hell out from under her feet.'

Like many American houses, Laburnum had kitchen quarters within the main house, rather than in a separate building in the French and Spanish Creole fashion. It was, as the butler promised, warm, and large enough that it doubled as a dayroom for the servants. A battery of kitchen knives lay neatly spread on a clean towel on the long table at one end of the room, beside a knife-block, a pair of white cleaning gloves, and a jar of pink emery powder. At the other end, a stack of the household day books, a kitchen slate and chalk, and an inkpot and pens showed who had gotten the task of settling up the year-end accounts with the departure of the lady of the house: January could see the ink on Quincy's right cuff. Beside the new American cast-iron stove, a thin woman with a face wrinkled like a dried date patiently stirred a custard. She gave January a friendly smile as Quincy said, 'This here Ben, Ruby. He's Mr Sefton's man, that escorted her ladyship and Miss Emmett here. Ben, Ruby – best cook in Natchez.'

'He only says that 'cause he thinks I'll bake an extra apple for him,' responded the cook mildly. 'Do you know, Ben, if Her Ladyship will be staying here to bear Miss Emmett company, until Mr Grice can get her a regular governess? It's turned everything upside-down, Mrs Grice leaving as she did, with everyone in town coming tomorrow night to meet Miss Emmett—'

'Do you know where she's gone?' asked January. 'Mr Sefton knew her father in France,' he explained, seeing the startled reaction of both servants. 'And is Arithmus still here?'

'You know Rithmus?' Quincy's eyes – that curious silvery hazel, like many of mixed ancestry – narrowed a little, his amiable features suddenly watchful. And, when January nodded: 'He always been like that?'

'I don't know what he's like now,' said January. 'Sixteen years ago, he took some getting used to.'

The butler considered that reply, then nodded, and led him back to the rear door. 'Right over there.' He pointed catty-corner across the yard to the rear wing of the house that contained, by the look of it, the laundry, a potting room, and what could have been a storeroom or a pantry, closest to the main house. 'He been doin' the books for Mr Grice's business – both the town office and the main jail out at Forks of the Road – for fifteen years.' His voice was carefully neutral as he named the slave market, but January saw something flicker behind those gray-turquoise eyes.

'After all this time he still can't look a man in the eye or carry on a conversation,' Quincy went on. 'But he can tell you to the penny how much Mr Emmett's cotton press made back in December of '32, or what the profit's gonna be on any one of Mr Grice's – or poor Mr Emmett's – plantations across the river, off the top of his head. I think Mr Ulee Grice – Mr Grice's brother – would have gone bankrupt about three times, if Mr Grice hadn't put Rithmus in to look after his affairs. Don't be surprised if he don't even look up when you go in. He's got his year-end books to do an' Hell itself won't stop him before he's tracked down where every penny went.'

January made himself grin for the benefit of Quincy and Ruby. 'Sounds like the man I knew.'

But he thought about the young man he'd known, as he crossed that corner of the yard. Those winter months of 1825 beat around him like wings: Belle Wishart's tiny smile tucking down the corners of her lips as she said, *Please don't judge him* . . . The way they'd both looked up, each wrapped up in a blanket, sitting across from each other on the floor of that icy little room behind the chateau's kitchen. Startled and innocent, like brother and sister, the bedroom candles between them. *I was afraid he'd be lonely* . . .

The wailing of the ghost of Palongeux, and Deverel Wishart lying at the bottom of the grand staircase, with demonic finger-marks on his face and a cut on his forehead whose severity didn't quite match any of the blood found on the stair above him. Arithmus screaming, *I am not wrong!* as he lunged at that imbecile Gounelle in the salon above the Café Beau Soleil, weeping with rage and frustration.

I knew that the haunting was being faked. There must have been something, some sign . . .

Quincy was right. Arithmus didn't look up when January – after knocking twice at the door of the office – opened it and stepped inside. For a moment January was reminded of those German legends, in which a sorcerer creates a homunculus to perform a task: a creature which then performs that task and nothing but that task, come high water or the gates of Hell.

He said, 'Arithmus,' and the man at the desk stopped his scribbling. Sat for a long moment, his position unchanging as an automaton of brass, one big hand stilled around the black stalk of his pen. 'Arithmus,' said January again, and the man turned around in his chair.

A grown man. Still skinny, but with a man's filled-out frame.

The eyes touched his face, then ducked away again at once. The long face with its too-heavy chin, its too-high cheekbones, hadn't changed, save for more lines around the eyes. His hair had been cropped to a fuzz, replacing the unruly mass of kinks and beads that had proclaimed him a 'savage mystery of the dark continent'. The flat, expressionless voice was the same. 'Hello, Ben.' Though he'd been living in Natchez for sixteen years, he spoke to January in French, as if under the impression that this was the only language January knew.

In English, January asked, 'What happened?'

Arithmus frowned. 'The police came the day after the men from Benoît and Sons took Mr Wishart away to fix him up for the funeral.' He still ticked events off on his fingers, as if reciting the progress of a play he'd seen. 'Mr Grice told me to go down in the cellar and told the police—'

January gestured him quiet – which of course didn't work, Arithmus being still nearly impervious to gestures – and said, 'Not back in Paris. Now. Where is Miss Wishart?'

'Venezuela.'

January stopped himself from saying, *What?* with the recollection of some of the more exotic names that Americans tended to give plantations: Carthage, Fontainebleau, Rienzi, and Tally-Ho sprang to mind. 'That's a plantation?'

'Yes. It's across the river in Concordia Parish. You take the river road above the Vidalia landing three-quarters of a mile, and when you come to the big bayou . . .'

'Did she leave with a lover?'

Arithmus thought about it for a long time, his usually inexpressive face working with distress. At last he said in a strangled voice, the first time January had ever heard that flat monotone break, 'Mr Grice hit her. Quincy, and Barnabas – that's Mr Grice's valet – and Corena all grabbed me and dragged me into the kitchen and across the yard and locked me in here.' The words tumbled out, like matter spurting from a lanced wound, frantic at the memory which, like all his memories, was crystalline and exact.

Then he seemed to catch himself in hand, and looked aside. In his customary tone he continued, 'Later Belle – Mrs Grice – came and told me not to do anything, not to raise my hand against Mr Grice, not even to look him in the face or anything. She said she was leaving, but I was to be good and stay here and be good, and she wouldn't forget me, and she'd be at Venezuela for now, and she didn't know where else later but she wouldn't forget. Then that night Mr Grice came in and told me to write up a letter to his lawyer, so he could divorce her.'

His fingers clenched up as he spoke, and his eyes remained on some point just to the left of January's elbow, but on the whole January saw that the man's mannerisms had toned down over the years. He wondered if Arithmus had been beaten for them, or if that had been from contact with his fellow slaves. Or with Belle.

A dealer, of course, would have ways to make a bondsman more 'likely'.

'Quincy and Corena were all upset, and Mr Ulee Grice – Mr Grice's brother – and Mrs Meadows whose husband owns India Tree Plantation and Still Waters and Beersheba and thirteen percent of the stock in the Planters' Bank, all said, the reception Mr Grice was going to hold to welcome Miss Emmett here to Natchez on Monday night couldn't be held, and Miss Emmett couldn't stay with him unless he had a respectable woman to stay with her. He said that was fine because she was coming with a French lady, so they could hold the reception. But later he was so mad he went out and beat Barnabas with the buggy-whip, just for not ironing his shoelaces right. He beats his horses,' he added, hands suddenly stilled and a dangerous glint in his eyes.

'Belle – Mrs Grice . . .' again his voice caught on the name, 'told me not to hit him or anybody else about the horses, not ever. Their names are Aethon, Eous, Phlygon, and Pyrois. He used to have a dog named Ares, and he killed him when he was angry. He beat me, too, when I didn't lock up the inventories of Mr Emmett's sales office out at Forks of the Road, after he got the letter Mr Emmett had died.'

Arithmus frowned at that, as if some recollection of the incident were stirred.

'Who does Venezuela Plantation belong to?' January asked, when the strange savant had been long quiet, pursuing that memory.

The crease of concentration vanished from between those sparse brows. He even looked surprised at the question. 'Mr Grice,' he said.

Quincy knocked at the door then, with the news that Mr Sefton wanted to speak to his 'man'. As January suspected, Persephone was indeed accepting Grice's earnest entreaty to remain as Daisy Emmett's chaperone for as long as it took for him to find a suitable governess/companion for the girl – 'And to locate Mrs Grice and her absconding lover, I daresay . . .'

'According to Arithmus,' reported January, glancing around the pillared front gallery – well aware that out of sheer self-defense, many bondsmen became habitual eavesdroppers – 'she's staying at one of Grice's plantations in Concordia Parish.'

'The hell you say.' Hannibal's eyebrows laddered up in pursuit of his hairline. 'I couldn't get a single detail this afternoon – it's not a thing one asks one's host, you understand. But I expect I – or the lovely Persephone – will be able to find out all the facts at the reception tomorrow night. I gather every lady in town with a marriageable son was paralytic with dread that the event would be canceled. I've volunteered you to play, by the way—'

January mimed an elaborate bow of delighted assent.

'—and Grice appeared to be tickled pink at the thought of having his ward introduced to Natchez society by a genuine French viscountess – it being obvious he doesn't recognize the quondam toast of the Paris opera stage. I have been asked to dine here tonight, so I've also volunteered you to go back to the Magnolia Tree Hotel and arrange to bring up Persephone's trunks, my evening dress, Sigerist, and the charming Fräulein Hauser.'

From his pocket he dug a small handful of silver. 'And any information you can pick up on the way as to why a man who's divorcing his wife for adultery would then offer her the shelter of one of his – apparently several – roofs . . . Presumably because her money paid for it – or at least compound interest on her money paid for it, though I'm not certain what Mississippi law has to say on the subject.'

'Under the new Married Women's Property Act in Mississippi,' said January, 'she might have some claim on it – provided she could prove that the money he used to purchase the properties came from the sale of her father's estate in England . . . and that's *after* he came up with the funds to go into partnership in the slave business with Travis Emmett. And Married Women's Property Act or no, I suspect a judge would look at the words "divorce" and "adultery" on the brief and rule that whatever happened in 1826 – which is when Grice went into business with Emmett – in Virginia, is no business of his. I take it,' he added quietly, 'since there's no nanny or governess in the household, there were no children of the marriage?'

'Mrs Grice had five miscarriages.'

January recalled Deverel Wishart's workroom on the Rue St-André des Artes, the scrubbed pine table with its gleaming array of alembics, pestles, bottles. The leather trunk with the brass corners, in which even to a haunted house he'd brought the little presses and jars, scales and distillation equipment necessary to his study of plants . . . very like, he reflected, equipment similar to that which Olympe used to prepare everything from love potions to abortifacients. In the months that Grice had remained in France – with Belle gone and Arithmus vanished – had he packed up Wishart's laboratory and shipped it to Baltimore with everything else?

Had he – or Belle – brought it to Natchez, when Emmett had sent his new partner there to manage the western end of the business?

His voice was dry. 'Did she indeed?'

The front door of the house was yanked open; January glimpsed a flash of black in the hall beyond. Persephone's voice said, 'Now, my sweet, is that any way to behave? And if you ran away, where would you go?'

'*Anywhere!*' cried Miss Grice. 'Back to New Orleans! Anywhere but this . . . this one-horse village! There's nobody nice here, nobody I want to meet—'

'Now, how do you know if you haven't met them?'

'Just a bunch of country boys! Like when I had to go stay in Richmond when Papa went off buying niggers! There's no theater here in town, and you saw those dull little shops along Main Street – like that's the best they could do! And the way the ladies we saw were dressed! I'll bet the balls here – if they have them! – everybody falls asleep and goes home at ten o'clock! And anyway I have to wear this ugly black like something out of a haunted house . . .'

'Now,' said Persephone soothingly, 'tomorrow evening you'll be the best-dressed girl at the reception, and you'll get to meet everyone in town, and you'll see how the young gentlemen will flock at your feet—'

'Because they want Papa's money!' The black skirts visible around the edge of the door jerked as she stamped her foot. 'They all do, except . . . except . . .' She took a step forward then, so intent upon her own personal tragedy that she didn't see the two men standing at the side of that long pillared space, threw back her head and pressed the back of her lace-mitted hand to her forehead, à la Juliet in Act V. 'Oh, what it is to be loved for oneself!'

But she allowed herself to be drawn back into the house. The door closed. Hannibal leaned one shoulder against a pillar, considered the portal as if he could see the two black-clothed ladies as they crossed the hall to the stair.

'Is it just my suspicious mind,' he remarked, 'or does Mrs Grice's adultery – if in fact she committed any – seem singularly well-timed? A man gets word that he's about to become the guardian of an extremely wealthy young girl—'

'Who will be completely dependent on him,' finished January grimly, 'for at least the next four years . . . Yes.'

'And anyone who's read *Pamela* – not that I would ever sully my chaste eyes with such trash – can probably tell you how much of a fight the servants will put up to defend the honor of a damsel against their employer.'

'Who literally owns them. Yes.' January's own suspicions returned, of how Grice could have forced Belle Wishart's consent to his suit. 'On the other hand, he doesn't own Persephone. And he can't very well eject *her* from the household, as I'm pretty sure he fired Miss Wishart's maid in Paris.'

'Not if he wants to keep his reputation in this town. Take the word of a slave dealer – be he never so wealthy – against that of a bona-fide widowed French noblewoman? My *dear!*' Hannibal mimed the raised hands of a society matron shocked by the horror of the thought.

'The girl's a spoiled pest,' said January. 'But she deserves at least the choice. As to whether she has the brains to *make* a choice . . .' He shook his head. 'I will say I'll be extremely curious as to whether Grice manages to get Miss Emmett to marry him by this time next year, though. Care to bet on that?'

Hannibal drew himself up with dignity. 'πολλαὶ μορφαὶ τῶν δαιμονίων, πολλὰ δ᾽ ἀέλπτως κραίνουσι θεοί· καὶ τὰ δοκηθέντ᾽ οὐκ ἐτελέσθη . . .' he quoted Euripides. 'Not on your life.'

Long before Hannibal returned to the Magnolia Tree that evening – via a cab the Viscountess Persephone surreptitiously paid for – January had collected all the information anyone could want concerning the circumstances of Belle Grice's sin. The youthful wagon driver Geordie, the yardman at the hotel, Nestor – Grice's sturdy, bandy-legged coachman – and four of the hotel servants, when January himself returned from unloading the trunks at Laburnum, fountained out the tale of the scandal, with corroborative detail about Grice's wealth, his ventures into moneylending ('Even his own brother!'), and his partnership with Travis Emmett back East. ('He gotta been stealin' from that Mr Emmett 'fore he ever came to Natchez,' opined the desk clerk of the Magnolia Tree over supper in the hotel servants' room. 'God knows he's stole from pretty much everybody else in town when he had that bank.') None of the hotel servants – or the servants of the guests who shared the meal – seemed to know where Mrs Grice had gone after her husband had turned her out of the house with nothing but the clothes she had on, and January didn't enlighten them. But he did, at least, learn the name of the man in whose embrace she had been surprised.

'*Clay Bryce?*' Hannibal stared at him – behind the locked door of the fiddler's chamber that night – in disbelief. 'The gambler?'

'That's what everyone says. And everyone,' added January, 'seems to be as shocked about it as you are. Needless to say, every woman in town has cut her – women whose friend she has been for the past sixteen years, women she's worked with on church committees, and in the relief efforts after the tornado. I don't wonder at it, that Grice is desperate to recruit the most socially prominent woman for ten counties around to introduce his ward to Natchez society. My guess is that all those second-cousins-once-removed back in Maryland are already clamoring to the nearest judge to name *them* the guardian of Miss Emmett's person and fortune.'

'From what I heard at dinner this evening,' returned the fiddler, 'that was precisely the reason Emmett named his partner in his will to be his daughter's guardian – though I suspect the man didn't think he'd die while she was still unmarried. Of course Grice was married at the time, and word of Mrs Grice's possible involvement in her uncle's death doesn't seem to have reached America at all. It's astonishing,' he added, 'how difficult it is to get information even from places like England and France, let alone the remote corners of Italy – no wonder nobody was ever able to find out that Her Ladyship's supposed parents in Calabria never had a daughter at all.'

Or that the 'mysterious marvel of the dark continent' was in fact a well-off, well-educated merchant's son from an African trading town that nobody in Europe would ever dream of visiting? Around them, the hotel was quiet – footsteps occasionally creaked in the corridor, now and then a door opened and closed. Once a man said something that made a woman laugh. At this time of night, most guests were back from dinner and preparing for bed, and those who weren't, would not return until late.

His mind turned again to that young white girl with her spectacles and her books, traipsing cheerfully after her father and her uncle to Italy and Africa and distant Red Sea ports, searching for the sources of the Nile or the truth about Nubian legends of conquest – or ghosts in haunted chateaux. A girl who looked beyond the strange mannerisms and odd behaviors of the young man whose family didn't know what to do with him; the young man her uncle had taken under his wing, to teach about the wonders of the world.

At last he sighed. 'What time do I need to be back tomorrow for this *fais-do-do* at Grice's?'

With the river high, it took the little steam ferry *Vidalia* nearly half an hour to thrash its way through the yellow-brown water to the opposite bank. Crossing Waverly Point to the plantation Venezuela, deep in the flat, low cotton lands of northern Louisiana, took nearly twice that long, in a rented gig. Venezuela Plantation itself was typical of that country. Like Bellefleur Plantation on which he'd been born, it was strictly a money-making operation, the 'big house' barely more than an office, for occasional use by the owner while the family lived in town. High on its bluff, Natchez was cooler than these sweaty bottom-lands. Though here and there they passed larger, half-built, pillared houses reminiscent of Laburnum – and of the other urban estates that lay behind Natchez's bustling downtown – most buildings glimpsed through the trees were plain, businesslike structures, raised to avoid the periodic floods that inundated the land, but no place a man would bring up his family.

As in New Orleans, 'home' was the townhouse. The overseer looked after the plantation, and kept the 'hands' at their work.

The cotton harvest was done. It was the season for repairs, for clearing weeds from the fields, for winter plowing and cutting wood. A surly overseer came down the steps of his own small house and demanded their business as Hannibal drew rein in the yard; the fiddler handed him a sealed envelope, said, 'Mr Grice told me to bring this out here.' It was addressed – in a fair imitation of Grice's hand (a sample of which Hannibal had evidently abstracted from the man's desk the previous day, when Grice's back was turned) ('You never know when something might come in handy,' the fiddler had explained apologetically to January) – to B.G. – *Venezuela Plantation*. 'He told me to wait for an answer.'

The overseer studied him for a moment – a youngish sandy man with a jaw like a rat-trap – then yelled into the cottage behind him, 'Nettie!'

A girl appeared, eyes defensive.

'Take this up to the house.'

It was twenty feet, up the steps to the front door. The overseer watched Hannibal and the door alternately, until Nettie reappeared.

'M'am say, yes, they's from Michie Grice.'

Belle waited until Nettie's footfalls had retreated across the porch and down the steps before she sprang to her feet, crossed the parlor and almost – but not quite – took January's hands. She'd lived in America for sixteen years. But her voice shook as she said, 'Ben!' and tears swam in those dark eyes.

'Mrs Grice.' January bowed. 'Please allow me to introduce my friend Mr Sefton; he can be trusted like a brother. How can we help you?'

She hesitated a long time before replying. 'If you're here,' she said slowly, 'you know my husband is divorcing me. I'll be leaving Natchez soon – going to New Orleans . . .'

'If I may be permitted to ask . . .' Hannibal bowed deeply. 'And I realize it's none of my business. But Clay Bryce has left town already, hasn't he?'

Color stained her cheekbones in the dimness of the parlor, but her voice remained even. 'I'm afraid that he has.'

'Then permit me the honor of escorting you.'

'Thank you – I appreciate your offer, sir. But your reputation—'

'My reputation has been going downhill steadily since 1819 and is currently somewhere between Tartarus and Erebus. The very pigs would spit on me as they stepped over me in the gutters of Bourbon Street – *Oderunt peccare boni virtutis amore*. Fortunately not recently, but mud sticks. You behold a man pargeted to the eyebrows with it.'

Belle clamped her lips together to keep from giggling, but tears continued to flow from her eyes.

'Persephone Jondrette sent us here,' January said. 'She's a full-fledged bona-fide French viscountess these days, with a different name and a cast-iron reputation. She can help you find a place to stay in New Orleans, where at least you will be unknown.'

She whispered, 'Thank you. Oh, Ben, I had no idea you were back in America! You said you'd never return . . .'

'And Julius Caesar said that the Ides of March had come and that nothing awful had happened to him. Life . . . leads us to some unexpected destinations.'

'*As here we see.*' She quoted the ending line of one of the most horrifying plays Ancient Greece had produced. 'Are you happy?'

'I am.'

Her smile reflected her gladness at that news.

'I'll tell you about it another time. I don't know your circumstances – and as Mr Sefton says, it's none of my business – but I'm fairly certain that money can be raised to pay your passage back to England, should you so choose.'

'Thank you,' she said again. 'The fact is that I have nothing in England to go back to. My . . . Mr Grice has been generous enough to promise me an allowance . . .' Her voice stumbled on the words.

'In exchange for not causing him trouble over the divorce?' asked January just as softly. 'Since it's obvious to me, at least, that he has every intention of marrying Miss Emmett as quickly as it can be . . . arranged.'

For a moment her lips set, at some terrible recollection, and it again crossed January's mind that once Persephone returned to France, Daisy Emmett would be spending nights under the same roof with Creon Grice. Who knew how much protection that 'cousin from Lexington' the butler had spoken of would be – would dare to be? Had Grice chosen to rape his ward – knowing her to be an heiress, knowing that a rumor of unchastity would effectively preclude any other marriage for her, even if, in Belle's case, she weren't facing possible accusations of murder – what recourse would she have?

As if she'd wiped her face with a damp cloth, the expression was gone. Belle drew a careful breath, let it out, drew another, propped her spectacles on her nose and said in a well-rehearsed tone, 'There is of course nothing I can say in mitigation of my sin. My affair with Mr Bryce is of long standing, as he has already deposed to Mr Grice's lawyers. I can only be thankful for Mr Grice's extreme generosity.'

The dark eyes went to Hannibal, and in a more normal voice she went on, 'I won't compromise you by going openly on the boat with you, sir. But if you would be so good as to . . . to watch over me from a distance as we go down-river, it would ease my mind a great deal. And if it's true,' she turned to January, tears glimmering in her eyes again, 'as you say that Miss Jondrette – that Her Ladyship stands ready to help me, I will . . . I will be more grateful than I can possibly say. If I may trespass on your patience long enough for me to write a note to her . . .'

'Of course. Mr Sefton and I will be playing for Miss Emmett's reception at Laburnum this evening—'

'They're still *having* it?' Her expression was almost comical. 'I'm sorry,' she added quickly. 'It's just that . . .' She paused, then blew her breath out in a gust of exasperation. 'Of course he is. Of course he is. God forbid he should get on the wrong side of Natchez society.'

'We'll be leaving tomorrow morning,' January went on – it not being his business to comment on a white man's enormities of conduct, particularly to that white man's soon-to-be-discarded wife. 'On the *Vermillion*, if that will give you time to get ready—'

'More than enough.' Her features, her straight slim shoulders, relaxed, and she shook her head once again – *Of course he is . . .* For a moment she was almost the girl he'd known in Paris. 'It isn't as if I have a great deal to pack. Thank you.' She glanced around her at the plain whitewashed parlor walls, the simple brick fireplace and the red-brown ravaged rug of the cotton fields visible through the windows. Again, an expression of pain flickered across her face – a pain years deep – instantly replaced by matter-of-fact calm.

'I daresay you're thinking what a . . . a mess I've made of my life,' she said. 'And I have. That makes me all the more grateful – you'll never know how grateful – for the help you've offered. Thank you.' A long hesitation. Then, 'Have you seen Arithmus?'

'It was he who told me you were here.' Something in her eyes, and in the tone of her voice, caused January to add, 'I would be more than happy to give him a message from you this evening as well. He looked well,' he added. 'He was at work on Mr Grice's accounts when I spoke to him, and he mentioned several times that you had told him to be good, and hold tight, and that you wouldn't forget. He didn't seem to be in any doubt of that.'

She closed her eyes briefly, let out her breath like a woman relieved of overhanging fear. 'Thank you.' Glancing up at him again, she half-smiled. 'He still has a temper, though he's . . . he's learned to control it, over the years. It isn't his fault, you know. My husband—' She paused, in a way that made January think of Arithmus saying, *He beats his horses . . .* That glint of deadly anger in his eyes.

Of course Grice would try to 'beat the temper out of him', as the slave owners said.

'The other servants didn't mention that he'd made any trouble after you left,' January said.

He studied her face, that thoughtful look, as if she speculated about some future action. Not worried, *What will happen to him when I'm not there to protect him?* A serious question, in the case of Arithmus. But, *How am I going to do this?*

It crossed his mind that Arithmus's freedom – or at least a change of ownership – might well be part of Grice's 'generosity' towards his departing wife, should she sign the divorce papers quickly.

If the man could be trusted.

His mind went back to the lines from Euripides' *Bacchae* that Hannibal had spoken the day before under the bare branches of the poisonous laburnum trees: πολλαὶ μορφαὶ τῶν δαιμονίων, πολλὰ δ᾽ ἀέλπτως κραίνουσι θεοί· καὶ τὰ δοκηθέντ᾽ οὐκ ἐτελέσθη. *The gods bring frightful gifts, and the ends men sought never came.*

It was not something he himself would want to bet on, with the life of someone he loved.

TWELVE

Heavily veiled, and bearing only a small carpetbag, Belle Wishart Grice boarded the steamboat *Vermillion* at Natchez-Under-the-Hill on the morning of Tuesday 29 December, a small figure in her dark dress, alone in the world.

January and Hannibal watched her from beside the stairway that led to the upper deck, but did not sign to her as she glanced in their direction. She gave them the briefest of nods, and looked away just as quickly. 'You think Grice'll actually send her any of the money?' asked the fiddler.

'When Hell freezes.'

'*Per ch'lo mi volsi*,' quoted Hannibal from Dante's Inferno, '*e vidimi davante e sotto i piedi un lago che per gelo avea di vetro . . .*' a reminder that portions of Hell were indeed solidly frozen over and had been so, presumably, for millennia.

'How would you like to swim back to New Orleans?' January glanced at the nearby deck railing.

'*Omne supervacuum pleno de pectore manat*,' apologized the fiddler. 'Forget I spoke.'

Throughout the previous evening, January had had plenty of opportunity to study Creon Grice. The slave dealer had moved about the lavishly decorated ballroom at the rear of Laburnum, introducing his ward to the wealthy and socially influential of the town. In deference, perhaps, to her wails of protest at dressing like 'something out of a haunted house', her guardian had permitted her to wear 'half-mourning', mauve silk so silvery it appeared almost the color of twilight, veiled and trimmed with black lace and ribbons of black velvet. Probably, January guessed, purchased in New Orleans, against such time as it would be appropriate for a girl of seventeen to put off complete mourning for a parent – a full year after that parent's death.

Persephone, in full black crape unrelieved by so much as a grisaille brooch, stood close to her charge's shoulder, her whole attitude an ebony statue of Duty Overriding Grief: not for nothing had she been an actress as well as a dancer. Fiscal Necessity Overriding Disapproval seemed to be the theme of the ladies of Natchez society: they had sons to marry off, after all. The two score or so young gentlemen ('country boys', Miss Emmett had sniffed) clustered around the heiress and did their best to claim her attention, but though she returned their admiration, she did so with the wan air of a princess in exile.

After each encounter with a would-be swain – sons of the Natchez planters, sons of bankers and judges and even a Congressman – Creon Grice would draw her close and whisper something in her ear: '"That one was raised by wild hogs in the forest,"' surmised Hannibal in an under-voice, in a deadly imitation of Grice's nasal, slightly drawling voice. '"Don't look at that one, honey, he don't change his drawers more'n once every four months – I know his laundress."' The other musicians on the dais – two slaves belonging to the owner of the local livery stable, on fiddle and flute, and a solemn young freedman whose master had had to petition the state legislature (with the signatures of all his neighbors and two thousand dollars bond) to manumit him (no one else in Natchez, enslaved or free, could play the bull fiddle half so well) – nearly stifled, trying not to laugh.

Grice, for his part, held close to his ward's side, her hand tucked firmly between his elbow and his ribs. His offers of lemon ices, cakes, and negus being rejected, he had clearly set himself out to please her. 'What, courting already?' whispered Hannibal, between sets of mazurkas, and January nodded significantly toward the ballroom's door, and the splendidly uniformed figure that stood there, like a gold-and-crimson macaw against Herr Doktor Boehler's dark bulk.

Rather grimly, Grice drew Miss Emmett aside and spoke to her, with a determined attempt to look like a man hiding the bleeding wound of his broken heart. She pulled away from him, stamped her foot – the raised dais of the musicians gave even January, seated at the piano, a fairly good view of the proceedings between the kaleidoscopic passes of the quadrille. Grice shook his head, Miss Emmett showed signs of bursting into tears, and the vicomtesse moved disapprovingly closer.

The dancers hid them.

'What do you want to bet she gets him to take her back to New Orleans for Mardi Gras?' said Hannibal, as the dancers swirled into a grand right-and-left.

'Only if His Highness goes back before then.'

As the sets re-formed, January glimpsed them like a little tableau: Grice stepping back from the chaperone's quelling glare, the shimmering silvery figure of the girl between them; the way she turned her head to gaze across the ballroom, into the eyes of the prince. Herr Doktor Boehler moved to draw His Highness away, with a scowling head-shake which clearly served only to fan passion's flame behind twenty dollars' worth of black point-lace ruffles.

And by the line of gilt-trimmed chairs along the wall, Josie Grice – semi-resplendent in a gown clearly passed along to her by Miss Emmett – followed the by-play with hopeless eyes.

The prince, too, strode across the *Vermillion*'s gangplank this Tuesday morning, trailed by Gaspar and Doktor Boehler and a line of trunks that put the vicomtesse to shame. He'd obviously been shopping in Natchez. He paused with well-executed casualness and turned back, letting the others of his party go on ahead. January glimpsed a flash of dark-gray skirts, a black shawl clutched tight around plump shoulders, and saw a girl emerge from the press, an envelope held out in one hand. Before he could decide – given the thickness of the scrimmage around the gangplank – whether this was Josie or Miss Emmett herself, his view was obscured by a stern Natchez Polonius delivering a hogshead of advice to a young man in a bottle-green greatcoat. The prince took the note, kissed it, then caught the withdrawing hand of the girl and kissed that, too, with a lover's tenderness.

Herr Doktor Boehler thrust his way towards them through the confusion on the deck, but by that time Miss Emmett – if it had been Miss Emmett – was back over the gangplank and gone in the crowd.

January shook his head, recalling the remarks he'd overheard back in Paris, from the 'legitimate' 'nobles of the sword' concerning the hopeful daughters of wealthy financiers. *Does she think Prince Charming's family is going to permit him to wed a commoner?* he wondered. *Even if they elope, it will be annulled the minute his parents – or all those hopeful second cousins back in Virginia – get word of it . . .*

But as the *Vermillion* – hold and decks roof-high with cotton bales – was poled from the makeshift wharf, and the great twin paddles began to turn, January thought he glimpsed another face in the crowd: long, jutting jaw, cheekbones that seemed too high, on a neck too long, a thin awkward frame. Dark eyes that watched expressionless as the woman he loved – the woman with whom he'd come to America to be enslaved in an alien land – melted into the chaos of passengers and luggage and cotton bales, leaving him alone.

Then Arithmus – if that *was* Arithmus – was gone.

The next time January saw him was when he was called to locate Creon Grice's body.

In retrospect, it seemed to January that the week before Creon Grice's murder (if it *was* a murder) he spent in observing what later turned out to be pieces of the puzzle, like the alphabet blocks that Rose hid all over the house to teach Professor John 'word-making and word-taking'. By the time he returned on the evening of the thirtieth, the house had been turned inside out: Christmas holly boughs refreshed, paper garlands repaired after the depredations of Ti-Paul, Zephine, his own boys, Charmian, Ti-Gall's four little sisters, and all the Corbier cousins. Crèche figures sacred and silly wrapped and put away; table linen and chinaware washed and ironed and readied for Zizi-Marie's wedding (if there was going to *be* a wedding).

The boarding students – Cosette, Germaine, Marie-Evaline, Alice, and Aglaëa back now from their own families – were in a constant flutter of excitement, planning what they'd wear for the wedding and comparing notes about ribbons and gowns. (Rose put them to writing essays in Latin about what their own weddings would be like.)

Ti-Gall was there daily – when he had finished his work with his Uncle Ghis – helping Chou-chou wash the floors, scrubbing the gallery steps with brick-dust, sorting out preserves and nuts to be used when the cooking started, and good-naturedly running errands for the girls so that Rose could have more time to prepare the lessons which the girls were almost too distracted to do. January caught him sometimes watching Zizi-Marie with troubled eyes, or breaking into smiles of relieved joy when she teased him or touched his hand, or behaved towards him as she once had done. Once or twice he thought the young man on the verge of asking him something, or asking Rose something. Saw him step back from that precipice, afraid of what he might hear.

Zizi-Marie wasn't often there, that week. With the money that Persephone de St-Forgeux had slipped Hannibal during Daisy Emmett's reception in Natchez, Belle Grice rented a tiny cottage far out between Bayou St-John and the lake – two rooms, and a kitchen in a sort of shack out behind. At January's suggestion, his niece went out there daily, to sew for the young woman, her Christmas work for Mrs Trulove being accomplished. Belle had not exaggerated when she'd said her husband had turned her out of the house with nothing. January had seen the small wicker grip that was the woman's only luggage when she'd come aboard the *Vermillion*, and none of the promised funds had come yet from Natchez.

Suspecting that in fact they never would, January solicited from everyone he knew to purchase cotton for petticoats and chemises, wool for two new dresses, thread, and several pairs of stockings. Zizi offered her labor gratis, but Belle insisted on paying her: 'There's a little left over from what Her Ladyship gave me. *My husband*' – in relating the conversation to January, his niece put in something of her new employer's dry good manners when speaking of Creon Grice – '*should be sending me something any day now* . . . An' if he does, Uncle Ben,' Zizi broke character to say, 'somebody better have smellin' salts on hand, 'cause I'm gonna faint with surprise . . .'

'"A woman always needs to have a little money tucked away someplace where nobody else can get it," she said to me,' Zizi went on. '"Not her husband, not a priest, not some scoundrel who says he can double it for her, not her own child. Don't ever let anybody even know you got it. You can't know – an' that money may be your one chance, between living an' dying; between freedom an' bein' trapped as a slave".'

'I'm sorry she had to learn that,' said January quietly. He had come out to the cottage, deep in the marshy siprière where the tiny Bayou P'tit-St-Jean formed a desultory chain of stagnant ponds, bringing firewood and some of Gabriel's new-baked bread. 'Because it's true.'

'But if you truly love someone,' began the girl hesitantly. 'You wouldn't keep something like that from Aunt Rose, would you?'

He grinned. 'I hope your Aunt Rose has a little cache hidden away from *me*.'

'You are *bad*, Uncle Ben!' She pushed at his shoulder, then looked past him, and her dark eyes widened as her breath caught with joy.

With love.

January turned, and saw a young man – not Ti-Gall, nor yet Marc-Antoine Picard – walking up the path that straggled back toward the bayou road. A tall young man, with the broad shoulders and strong build of Wolof ancestry – like his own – but features that were nearly European. His well-cut, but slightly old-fashioned clothing marked him as somebody's valet, but he walked as if he owned the ground that he trod. Zizi caught up her skirts and hastened down the path to greet him, but when he took both her hands and drew her to him to kiss, she put a staying hand on his chest, glanced over her shoulder at January.

He let go of her hands, followed her to the cottage. With forced, friendly calm, Zizi said, 'Uncle Ben, this is Starke Hagan, Michie Picard's valet. Starke, this's my Uncle Ben.' Her voice was breathless, and her dark eyes searched his face for sign of approval or distaste.

Hands were cordially shaken, Starke Hagan radiating friendly confidence and a beaming smile. When January carried his basket of wood into the cottage he traded words with Belle – engaged in trying to lay out the cut-newspaper pattern pieces that Dominique had lent her to get a bodice out of the smallest quantity of fabric she could manage (he'd seen Ayasha do the same, times without number). When he glanced through the single small window beside the door, he saw Zizi in Starke Hagan's arms.

On the second day of 1841, January visited his sister Olympe at her dark-red cottage on Rue Douane. He had called the previous day – everybody in the French town called on everybody else on New Year's Day, and the place had been filled with Corbiers, neighbors, friends, fellow-musicians, and members of the Faubourg Tremé Free Colored Militia and Burial Society. But mainly he had spent his time there helping his brother-in-law Paul make punch before going forth to play at a ball given by cotton factor and stockbroker Samuel Hermann, over on Rue St-Louis. Zizi-Marie had been at her mother's house earlier that morning, with Chouchou, helping Olympe clean up – the two girls had passed him on Rue Burgundy, on their way back to his own house to help Rose clean up . . . pretty much everyone who'd visited Olympe had visited Rose and January either earlier or later the previous day, including Olympe and Paul themselves and their children. Every small cottage on Rue Burgundy had its windows open, despite the hard cold of the afternoon, the steam of clean-up wafting forth. Every shallow doorstep gleamed with soapy wet.

'Tell me about Marc-Antoine Picard,' he said.

Those velvet-dark eyes slid sidelong to him – sometimes she looked very like their mother, the redoubtable Widow Levesque. 'You've seen him.'

At the Hermanns' ball the previous evening, and at that given by the Destrehans on New Year's Eve, the French Creole matrons had been in stiff competition to make sure young Marc-Antoine danced with their daughters – few of whom had had eyes for anyone but the Hungarian prince.

Yet unlike many of his contemporaries, Marc-Antoine had displayed no pique at the universal adoration of foreign royalty. He had chatted with his male friends; helped break up two arguments that could easily have resulted in duels; talked business with his uncles and hunting with the prince himself. ('Shoot a *cougar*? There hasn't been a cougar in the ciprière in twenty years!' His Highness had looked as crushed by this news as if he'd been told that prostitutes had become extinct in Louisiana. Doktor Boehler had inquired, could not one perhaps be imported?)

'His Uncle Luc brings him to the balls at the Salle d'Orleans,' January said now, 'and introduces him to the young ladies there, so I assume he hasn't a mistress yet.'

Olympe showed no sign that she knew of the young man's offer to her daughter. 'He's twenty.' She gestured indulgently with one hand, and went on sorting the dried leaves and roots that had hung, wrapped in paper, all autumn from the rafters of the little kitchen.

Deft, bony fingers stripped the crinkled foliage from desiccated stems, and dropped the leaves carefully into small crocks that had once held butter or salt. Feverfew to ease headaches. Cohosh and pennyroyal, to prevent pregnancies or to end them before term. Willow bark for fever, asafetida – 'the devil's incense' – to drive enemies away. Black mustard seed to sow quarrels, and 'Cruel Man of the Woods'.

'He's visited the Countess Mancini's . . .' She named one of the higher-class parlor-houses in the Second (American) Municipality, 'and Madame Piaget's in St-Mary. Neither of them has ill to say of him. He never hits the girls, they say, nor curses them, and tips them money they don't have to show their madames. Drinks enough champagne to sing songs but not enough to get into fights. Only gambles with the money he brings with him. A nice boy.'

Watching that dark, thin face with its prominent front teeth, its self-sufficient stillness, January wondered if she knew. *She can't not . . . Does she not take young Picard seriously?* But Olympe, who knew all the secrets in New Orleans, never asked.

Maybe Madame Araignée, the spirit she claimed lived in the black-painted gourd bottle on the little altar in her parlor, told her.

'What about his valet?' he asked. 'Starke Hagan?'

This time she was silent for a long while, velvety African eyes considering him. He thought for a time she would say, *What do you seek to know, brother?*

'The ladies like him.' That phrase could have carried any number of inflections – she gave it none. Careful fingers, protected with small squares of tissue-fine notepaper, rolled the delicate white blossom of snakeroot. 'I hear tell, a year ago, a market girl was caught pregnant by young Picard – he'd gave her presents for months, and talked to her sweet. The boy sent Starke to make the arrangements with Mambo Yejie, for he knew the girl's father would take it out hard on the girl. I hear tell it, Mambo Yejie asked three dollars to rid her of the baby, and Starke told his master it was four. Four is what Picard paid, and three is what Mambo Yejie got.

'Beyond that . . .' She paused, and turned her hand over: *Nothing on this side, nothing on that . . .* 'He's a man who knows how things work. Knows how to get things done and who'll do them and keep quiet about it. He gambles some, and word is he's taken money off his master, on bets and cards. Young Picard looks up to him a little, if he needs advice, about bets on a horse-race or where to buy good hounds. Starke's a man who knows things.'

Again, that dry little twist in her voice.

It was January's turn to say nothing. Sourness coiled in his chest, as he recalled his niece's slim tallness clinched tight in Starke Hagan's arms, when they thought themselves unobserved. How much would Starke glean of the money Marc-Antoine Picard would spend on buying a cottage somewhere in Marigny for Zizi-Marie? Of the money he'd give her for dresses, for food, for pins and rings and ear-bobs? And what would he do with that money when he got it?

How do you know if you're in love? she had asked him. And she hadn't meant Marc-Antoine.

And how was that different, he wondered, from Starke being his niece's pimp, for his unsuspecting master?

Would Zizi believe him if he told her?

And if she believed him, would she mind?

He realized he'd been quiet for a long time. Olympe, tapping the paper over the little crock to shake the powder from it, watched him under her eyelashes, waiting for his next question.

'And what do you know about Creon Grice?'

'Ah.' She fetched out a small, sharp knife from the half-unwrapped bundle of knives on the table beside her, and unfolded the knobby gold-brown fingers of poke-root from their paper, as careful as Deverel Wishart had been in the handling of his exotic African berries and barks. Like Rose, when she weighed and mixed chemicals for her opera pyrotechnics.

'A Baltimore man.' Her voice was neutral still. 'You met him, too, I hear. Went to England to seek his fortune in '17, as soon as the shooting was over; hooked up with Travis Emmett as soon as he came back in '26, with the fortune he'd made selling up everything his wife's family owned—'

'Fortune?' He knew that unlike most of the poor *sang-mêlés* at the back of town, Olympe didn't automatically see a few thousand dollars as a *fortune*. *Fortune* was what the Destrehans had, the Marignys, the Almonasters. The Heywards of South Carolina, the Lloyds and the Blairs of Maryland, the Schuylers and Van

Rensselaers of New York. 'I understood Stuart Wishart's lands didn't realize that much.'

She picked a fragment of earth from the root. 'I heard tell it was near to seventy thousand dollars, brother.' Her eyes met his again, reading the shocked astonishment there. 'So that poor woman's daddy must have owned *something*. Plus whatever he's made since, selling slaves with Emmett, and lending money at twelve percent. He holds mortgages on one in ten of the plantations north of Baton Rouge – one in twenty of the slaves. And I hear tell it,' she went on, 'that he's divorcing your English girl, now that he's guardian of Emmett's child. She that has all the young bucks and their mothers kissing her shoes.'

'He is,' said January. 'He promised he'd send her money – and I think, said he'd give her the manservant Arithmus, who's been her friend since girlhood . . .' He had the sensation, from the way she glanced at him on hearing the name, that she knew all about Arithmus, too, '. . . and marry the girl himself. But I don't see him sending her a silver dime, much less a man he can sell for fifteen hundred dollars.'

'No.' Her glance returned to the poison root, the silver blade. 'He bought a girl named Clytie, right after they settled in Natchez for him to handle the trade there, and set her up as his wife's maidservant. Then sold her on when he was done with her, and bought another. It was his third or fourth girl who came to me, one year when Grice came down here to sell cotton and pick up a cargo from Armfield and Franklin to take back to Natchez. Fancy, her name was. She wanted to buy poison and I wouldn't sell. She went and got some from Doctor Yellowjack that used to do root-doctorin' out on Bayou St-John. I thought it was for Grice. I'd heard about him from others. But she took it herself.' With the edge of the knife, she scooted the poke-root into a little pile on the cutting board, slid it into another jar. 'That Grice, he's not a good man, brother. You watch your dealings with him.'

Rising from his chair, January kissed her cheek, stepped over baby Zephine – who all this time had been braiding ropes of jasmine vines where she was leashed by one ankle to a leg of the kitchen table, at a safe distance from the hearth and from any possible debris of her mother's work.

As he passed through the parlor on his way out to Rue Douane, he paused before the little shelf there, like an altar high on one wall and half-hid in the dim room's shadows. A cheap plaster statue of the Virgin stood near a strange-shaped root that had been dressed in scraps of purple silk and white lace. Another statue of St Peter with his keys January recognized as representing Papa Legba, guardian of crossroads and doors, rough X's marked with charcoal on his bright orange robes. Candles surrounded them, and bunches of tobacco – all the gods love tobacco – and three elaborately wrought balls of knotted string that smelled faintly of stale rum. Small plates of sugar, the skull of a mouse, and signs chalked in red and black and blue: the serpents of Damballah-wedo, the ornamental heart of Erzulie, the emblems of the Twins, and of the drums.

Signs that had come from Africa, all those years ago. Dreams that even the ships, and the whips, and the murderous grind of years in chains could not take away.

And at the back of the niche, a black-painted gourd bottle covered with gleaming black beads and sealed with wax.

Madame Araignée, Olympe called the thing that she said lived inside; the thing that spoke to her in her dreams.

And what, January wondered, had Madame Araignée – who both his confessor and his teachers in Paris had assured him did not exist – told Olympe about Starke Hagan? About Creon Grice?

Above the smells of stale rum and tobacco, he caught the whiff of fresh blood.

Outside in Rue Douane, a market-woman sang a long, wailing song about the oranges she carried in a basket on her head. The voices of children sang clear and sharp and distant in the cold. Chilly afternoon sunlight laved him as he walked towards his home, to shave and wash and change his clothes, to play for white folks to dance tonight, drawing to his heart the golden music of Mozart like healing sunlight. Healing light, like the healing music that it was his gift to make – secure in the delusion that none of any of this really had anything to do with him.

THIRTEEN

Twelfth Night approached. Planters and their families were coming back into town.

The girls in Rose's school (and the three day-students) chipped together the slender allowances their fathers sent them, to purchase a Sheffield-plated coffee pot as a wedding gift, which they sneaked into January's custody amid blood-curdling oaths of secrecy. He concealed it in one of the empty oil jars that nearly every New Orleans household had somewhere in their ground-level storerooms – concealed, too, his uneasiness as he observed his niece in the approach to the day.

Dominique took up a collection among her friends to purchase fifteen yards of French silk (*At two dollars a yard!* she cried in horror), and lace for collar and cuffs, a gift Zizi-Marie received with exclamations of delight which to January's ear seemed just slightly forced. It was not lost on him that his niece ran quickly from the parlor, and when she came back, beaming, he saw the wet edges of her tignon, the spots of damp on her collar, that told him she'd splashed cold water on her face to hide evidence of tears. His old friend Catherine Clisson came one evening, while January was out playing for a subscription ball at the Theatre d'Orléans, to cut out the dress – an accomplishment beyond either Rose or Olympe – and a dozen of Zizi's friends descended on the house for the next two evenings, twittering like a tree-full of birds, to help sew under the direction of Madame Clisson. January's mother, the elegant Widow Levesque, put in an appearance on those occasions as well, to tell them they were all doing it well enough, but not what *she* was accustomed to.

She herself used the scraps of silk and lace to fashion a diadem of silk blossoms that reduced the girls – and her son – to speechlessness at its frail beauty.

Zizi-Marie wore bridal joy like a pair of too-tight shoes, and January could almost see invisible blood seeping out with every smiling step.

Twice Starke Hagan came to the house – snitching the time while on errands for his master, or bringing Zizi notes from young Michie Picard. He came early in the day, when Rose was instructing the girls, and January preparing for the lessons he himself taught, either to the girls at the school, or in the homes of his piano pupils on Rue Royale or Nyades Street or out in Faubourg St-Mary. The girls – Germaine and Cosette, Aglaëa and Alice and even the elegant Marie-Evaline – all thought Starke Hagan was the handsomest man they'd ever seen and teased Zizi ('What, are you *flirting* with Starke?' 'We're gonna tell Ti-Gall!'), as girls do, not knowing that he was more to her than a friend. They had not seen Zizi locked in the young man's arms beside the kitchen shed of that tiny cottage of Bayou P'tit-Jean. Not seen the desperation of her grip, as if she would not – could never – let him go.

Chou-chou – at ten impervious to masculine charm (with the notable exception of Hannibal's) – said simply, 'I don't like him.'

It was not lost on January that his niece was spending a good deal of her time at the tiny house in theciprière, and avoiding the one in which she might encounter Ti-Gall. And more often now he saw the pain and puzzled grief in Ti-Gall's ox-brown eyes.

Creon Grice arrived in New Orleans on Monday – two days before Epiphany would usher in the Mardi Gras season of parties and balls – and took an elegant, countrified house called Les Cyprès, on Bayou Gentilly near the raceground. Since the prince had returned to the city for New Year's, nobody was really surprised. The heiress was effervescent at being back in a city whose society ladies thought it perfectly acceptable behavior to attend the opera – and even balls – in mourning, and it was obvious that Grice, under the Vicomtesse Persephone's watchful eye, was trying to demonstrate to his ward how obliging he could be.

He made no effort to get in touch with his former wife.

'I know she wrote him.' Zizi-Marie licked a fingertip, touched the surface of the iron she held, then swung it deftly a few times, to get the coals in the little firebox stirred to newer life. Outside the tiny kitchen shed, the cypress swamps along Bayou P'tit-Jean lay hushed in the birdless stillness of winter. January had brought Miss Wishart – as she asked to be called – a packet of coffee and a half-dozen rolls that Gabriel had baked that morning: in every kitchen in town, housewives – or cooks – would be baking king cakes, soft brioches sprinkled with colored sugar and cinnamon, into which a bean – or a thimble, or a coin – would be mixed. Whoever got the bean, said the tradition, became King of the Feast.

And whoever got the bean – or the thimble or the coin or sometimes a tiny image of the Christ Child – had to host the next party. Back at the school, January had left the girls giggling about whether this would mean somebody other than poor M'sieu Corbier got to pay for Zizi's wedding breakfast.

'And she said he promised her,' the girl went on now. 'Said he'd send her money every month, if she signed the papers saying she really did commit adultery with that Mr Bryce. She wrote that lawyer of his near a week ago, and hasn't heard back.' Dark eyes went from January – across the chemise that lay spread on a clean towel on the kitchen table before her – then past him, through the open door, to the little cottage that faced on to the bayou proper, and the shell path from the greater Bayou St-John. Despite the day's cold, every door and window of the kitchen shed stood open, filling the rickety hut with the dry scent of fresh linen, and of last night's rain.

'And I suppose,' said January quietly, 'that he didn't put his promise in writing, because it could be used as evidence of collusion when he marries Miss Emmett.'

His niece said nothing for a time, driving the hot steel square of the iron across the garment. Then: 'It's not like he can't afford it. The man's rich already.' In her bitter voice, January saw again the men in their cheap blue jackets sitting on the benches outside *Grice & Emmett: Cotton Hands – House Niggers – Fancies*. The women with their skirts not quite hiding the chains. Heard Olympe's voice again: *That poor woman's daddy musta owned something* . . . 'After he marries Daisy he's going to have all the money he can spend and a whole river of it left over.'

She shook her head, kept her eyes on her work. Around her neck, bright against the faded green calico of her blouse, January saw she wore a thin gold chain, with a pendant cross of gold, just thick enough to be more than a plain girl's parents could afford. He half-opened his mouth to comment on it, to ask her if Marc-Antoine Picard had given her this. To warn her that if she said yes to the young man's proposal, she had better make sure that the contract he offered was in fact in writing, and in proper form.

But who would look over this contract, to make sure her rights – and those of their children – were secured? Who would negotiate with her would-be 'protector'?

Olympe – who had run away from her own mother rather than be pushed into such a contract with one of St-Denis Janvier's business partners – would tear up any document her daughter suggested and spit on young Michie Picard. *Probably bury a ball of black wax, goofer-dust and pins under the front steps of his house into the bargain.*

And the thought of himself having any hand in drawing up such an agreement made January queasy with disgust.

Dominique, I suppose . . .

He thought again of Zizi-Marie, clinging to Starke Hagan's muscular arms. Seeing nothing, knowing nothing, except that she loved him.

'I want to respect her choices, as a woman grown,' he said that evening, when he encountered Persephone de St-Forgeux in the torchlit courtyard of the de Macarty townhouse as everyone at the evening's gala was going in to supper. The musicians who had played at the reception – and who would play for the dancing afterwards – had a table set up beneath the abat-vent outside the kitchen doors. Like those of Belle Wishart's tiny kitchen earlier in the day, these doors all stood open, and the heat from the huge fireplace and the range of stew-holes streamed out, bearing on it the savor of onions and garlic, of caramel and coffee. (Bearing the cook's voice as well: 'You pay attention to what you're doin', Leah! You burn that sauce an' I'll take a cane-stalk to you . . .')

'But I see her acting like a girl in love, and I want to warn her to watch her step. And until I know what she's made up her own mind to do, I can't go tattle on her to her parents. I'm pretty sure I know what they'll do, and I'm pretty sure that's only going to make matters worse.'

Since Christmas he had had a front-row view of how the grim Doktor Boehler's opposition had whipped Miss Emmett's original desire to outshine every other girl in Louisiana into (as the Duke of Aragon had put it in *Much Ado*) 'a mountain of affection' that would not be shifted or denied. The spectacle of Grice's efforts to keep them apart – while pretending to be a man in love himself – made him shake his head and wonder to what lengths the slave dealer was prepared to go to secure the girl's hand.

Persephone sighed. The ball was fancy-dress, and with deliberately insipid care the vicomtesse had arrayed herself as a fully rigged seventeenth-century Spanish duenna, like something out of a Molière farce: black bombazine stomacher, stiff plain bodice, towering comb and trailing curtains of mantilla, maintaining her own mourning as a deliberate foil to her charge's exiguous silken chiton and beribboned artificial doves. 'Don't look at me for advice, Benjamin. My mother died when I was twelve and if she'd lived, she'd have peddled me to the highest bidder – which is exactly what my aunts tried to do.'

She looked around the courtyard, where the lights of the dining room, and the double parlor above it, shed secretive pools of glow and shadow among the bare tangles of the jasmine, the straw-wrapped towers of the pruned-back roses. 'At least your girl is nineteen, and has a brain in her head. You should try looking after a spoilt chit barely out of the schoolroom who subsists on a steady diet of romantic novels. She seems to believe that *Love in Excess* and *The Mysteries of Udolpho* are based on actual events, and that the handsome Lord Orvilles and Count d'Elmonts of the world don't have families and responsibilities of their own—'

She turned her head sharply, as the unmistakable form of Doktor Boehler blotted the light of one of the dining-room doors in a Pierrot costume that made him look like a monstrous loaf of unbaked bread. He took two strides into the courtyard in the direction of the tall water-cistern that stood nearly hidden in the shadows, and another figure hastened out behind him, to catch his puffed white sleeve.

For a moment January thought it was Miss Emmett, until he recalled that the heiress was dressed as (presumably) Aphrodite – in addition to her doves she'd carried a large seashell . . .

Josie Grice, resplendent as a fairy princess (her wings snagged on the winter-bare stems of the bougainvillea that grew over the balcony above), looked up into the pedagogue's face and asked him something. Clung tight to his sleeve and refused to be put aside. Persisted. Pestered. From the corner of his eye, January glimpsed a blur of white, the wink of reflected gold, in those shadows, and a moment later, on the far side of the kitchen building, he saw Prince Serafin move off through the gloom, heading back toward the dining room.

From playing at other de Macarty entertainments, January knew that one could get from the vine-draped cistern around behind the kitchen unseen. He was just pointing this out to Persephone, Miss Grice having drawn the prince's governor back into the dining room, when Aphrodite herself, her hair in disarray and trying to reposition the rather drunken-looking doves upright on to her shoulder again, emerged from the darkness and foliage behind the cistern.

Miss Emmett was still engaged with the recalcitrant doves when Grice – who at least had had the sense to wear evening dress instead of cavalier frills – emerged from the dining room and strode to her across the yard. She looked up as he neared her, hastily pulled a dead leaf out of her disordered curls, and he took her hands. Looked down into her face, oblivious to the musicians who sat a few yards away around the kitchen work-table, he said something to her, earnest.

She shook her head, replied, head up and chin out.

His gesture was that of a kindly guardian with one hand, but with the other, he drew her closer. Shook his own head, reached to touch her hair with a kind of clumsiness, like a man making a movement he has learned by watching lovers on a stage.

Beside him, January heard Persephone whisper, 'Damn the man—'

Mantilla billowing, she descended on the pair like a very well-dressed crow, called out, 'So there you are, dear! You shouldn't . . . Oh, Monsieur Grice! I did not see you.'

Grice dropped Miss Emmett's hand. The girl stood uncertainly, looking from her duenna back to the dining room's light. Her pale mauve chiton, nominally trimmed with bits of black embroidery, would not have been considered mourning in any city in the United States except New Orleans – and then only among the French ladies.

'Come in to the supper, Daisy, darling,' Persephone cooed. 'You must be freezing out here, and' – she leaned playfully closer – 'we mustn't give all those jealous mamas here reason to whisper about you, even if you're only out here with your guardian. Here . . .' She unwrapped her own black shawl from about her shoulders. 'Your poor little birds look like they've had a night out on the tiles.'

Miss Emmett giggled nervously, as Persephone herded her back toward the house, repositioning the doves and draping the girl's lightly covered arms with the more substantial silk. 'Oh, don't, m'am,' protested the heiress. 'It doesn't go with my dress! I'll bet Aphrodite never *ever* wore a bundly old black shawl.' (Giggle.)

'Well, Aphrodite was a goddess and never caught cold, either . . .'

She didn't look back at Grice. The planter stood gazing after them for a moment, the hand he'd had raised to his ward's hair closed into a fist.

Then he followed them into the house.

'If you're not interested in your beer, *amicus meus*,' called out Hannibal's scratchy voice from the table, 'please say so before Cochon slays me for defending your rights.'

It's not my business. January returned to the makeshift supper in a somber mood. *If he rapes the girl the minute Persephone gets replaced by someone who can't afford to stand up for her charge . . . there's nothing I can do about it.*

He was well aware that he would probably be beaten up – or lynched – for even mentioning such a thing.

Heiress or not, Daisy Emmett was alone.

The de Macarty cook had even baked a small king cake for the musicians. Uncle Bichet the cellist was the lucky finder of the traditional bean . . . which in the white folks' larger and more elaborate version had been replaced by a silver coin.

'Ah, Uncle gets to give the next party!' triumphed Philippe duCoudreau.

'I always get the bean,' complained the old man with a grin, setting it beside his plate. Dark eyes twinkled behind the lenses of his spectacles. 'Next time I'm gonna just swallow it, and let you all give your own parties!'

* * *

Twelfth Night came. Thin, bone-chilling rain.

January suspected – having played at the entertainments of Hubert Granville for seven years now – that whatever was in the king cake he served to his guests, it probably wouldn't be just a bean. Possibly not even a coin: a silver thimble, or some other valuable trinket. Costly, like everything else in the banker's ostentatious town palace on Rue Chartres, although his musical colleagues were taking bets (unenforceable) on which of the guests would swallow the 'lucky' item rather than pay for the next party. Jacques Bichet took up a collection among his colleagues to suborn the dining-room servants for a report.

Because of his business dealings with the Bank of Louisiana, Hubert Granville was one of the few Americans accepted socially by both Americans and French. The musicians jestingly referred to his pink stucco mansion, with its balconies of the new-style curlicues of cast-iron trim, as the 'Fourth Municipality' – New Orleans having been divided into three separate cities over the inability of the Americans and the French to collaborate in government (or in anything else). In practice, this meant that bets were running high among the musicians as to who would challenge whom to duels, and over what. Politics was always a fruitful incitement to bloodshed – particularly in the wake of the recent election – but there was also much jostling and glaring among the men around the Widow Redfern.

That stout relict, like Madame de St-Forgeux last night, was clothed as a Spanish duenna, but even veiled in yards of gauze-fine black point-lace, there was no chance of mistaking the one for the other. Emily Redfern – determined to outshine even a bona-fide French viscountess – had enlivened her somber gown with a good four thousand dollars' worth of diamonds: necklace, bracelets, earrings, pins, and rings on every chubby, lace-mitted finger. Purchased, Hannibal surmised, to console herself for the passing of the extremely wealthy Mr Redfern six years previously.

And as the fiddler had earlier observed, there was no such thing as an ugly heiress. January was hard-pressed to hide his smile at the expression on the widow's face as every scrawny Hercules, paunchy Mohican and fustian Musketeer turned from her, as one, with the entrance of the even-more-wealthy Miss Emmett . . .

. . . on the arm of Prince Serafin Corvinus.

At the sight of her, his amusement faded. *So it's true*, he thought. He felt shock, but no real surprise.

'Five cents says Ophélie Viellard calls Miss Emmett out by ten o'clock,' jested duCoudreau.

'Ten?' Cochon Gardinier mimed astonishment without dropping a note of the elaborate double fantasia of his and Hannibal's fiddles. 'I'll bet you a fip Henriette Crozat pulls her hair out by nine thirty. That is Miss Emmett, isn't it, under that mask?'

January said, very quietly, 'It is.' Anger burned him, like a hot needle driven into his chest. He had suspected as much since his conversation six days previously with Olympe, about where Creon Grice had gotten the 'fortune' he'd brought back from France with him in 1826. Now he was sure.

Miss Emmett was clothed and masked as the goddess Sittina-Menhit.

He looked away from her, back to 'The Lancer's Quadrille', the dancers skipping and bowing in the great gilt box of the Granville ballroom. But he was aware of Miss Emmett, moving from group to group around the room's edge, gazing adoringly up into His Highness's handsome face. There was nowhere else she could have seen – and ordered copied – that close-fitting dress of bronze silk, the wide, beaded collar and the bronze-gilt head of the papier-mâché lioness that masked her own face.

The bastard.

Whoever it was who had killed Deverel Wishart – and for whatever reason – it was Grice who had stepped in and married Wishart's niece. And as her husband, he had acquired the right to her uncle's property as well as her father's. The right to sell the proof of that ancient invasion of Egypt to the man who would offer almost anything to destroy it. A quarter-million francs ... somewhere in the neighborhood of ten thousand pounds. No wonder even a plutocrat like Travis Emmett had welcomed the man as a partner.

Miss Emmett even had the shoes right. Curl-toed red slippers, and a scepter that looked suspiciously like a Nubian war club. It was a weapon she looked like she would cheerfully have used to brain Mrs Redfern, as the men crowded around the older woman again, like puppies wagging their tails, hoping for a treat.

* * *

'It's Sittina-Menhit,' he said to Hannibal, when the musicians descended, at ten, to the servants' 'hall' for supper. 'That means he has the statue that went with the Curse Manuscript. It's the only way Miss Emmett would have seen it.'

'I wondered where the girl saw ancient Egyptian garb. They mostly masque as Romans or Greeks.' Turning in his chair, he took the hand of the servant girl who set a bowl of gumbo before him, and gazed up into her face like a Covent Garden Romeo: *'With eyes that were a language and a spell/A form like Aphrodite's in her shell* . . . Although no Egyptian, goddess or otherwise, would be wearing her hair in curls down her back like that.' He released the giggling servant, picked up his spoon. 'Do you think that was his price, for hiding Arithmus and getting him out of the country?'

'It could have been.' Bitterness made his voice hard. 'Or he could have simply searched the house once he'd put her on the boat. He had a day, between the Saturday that he arrived in Paris and drove out to Palongeux to tell Wishart of his brother's death, and hearing of Wishart's own death Monday morning. During that day, d'Aveline could have called on him, and offered him money to steal the manuscript. Then, when he heard of Wishart's death, he realized what a chance fate had put in his way.'

Outside in the courtyard, beyond the protective shutters, rain had begun to fall, rattling on the leaves of banana plants and palmetto with a noise that reminded January of that board-stiff, ridiculous raincoat the girls had given him.

'And he had to act fast,' murmured the fiddler, 'before somebody else got to the manuscript first: the servants, or someone working for d'Aveline. Maybe even whoever was faking the haunting and killed Wishart. Miss Wishart must have guessed what he'd done, when he showed up in Baltimore in the New Year with the statue in his pocket. I wonder why he didn't sell that to d'Aveline as well?'

January shook his head. 'He could have gotten it from Arithmus easily enough, if he was hiding him at the house in Paris.'

He made himself smile his thanks as the servant girl returned and set a bowl of gumbo – and an extra plate of croquembouche pilfered from the kitchen – on the table. But he felt no appetite; nothing but the sour rage in his heart.

How easy it would have been, he thought, for Grice to go to the distraught girl's room in the middle of the night. A quarter of a million francs would certainly make the effort worthwhile. How easy to say, as you climbed out of her bed and did up your flies, *You're a fallen woman now. No virgin – who's going to marry you now?* Maybe he'd even thrown in the obligatory, *You know I've always loved you, my dear.*

Or maybe he'd just arranged to drip a little laudanum into her wine at dinner. Dinner *à deux*, with no one else there to chaperone or protect or protest . . . Even had she not been facing the possibility of being charged with murder herself, by whoever it was who wanted to scotch the rumors of the Palongeux ghosts. Or the knowledge that the man she loved – strange and inarticulate and by this time known the length and breadth of Paris as a 'mysterious barbarian' – was being sought by the Sûreté for the crime.

Had Arithmus been locked in some cubicle in the cellar at the time of the rape? Not even aware of what was going on?

In sixteen years, had Belle ever told him?

If it happened at all, January told himself. *It might not have. She might only have yielded to verbal coercion – Marry me or I'll tell the police you and your little black friend cooked it up between you . . .*

But he felt as if he had seen it. Had heard her crying in the darkness, like the eerie wail of the wind-harp in the attics of Palongeux . . .

He shook his head again, and dragged himself back to the present.

'Blackmail?' Hannibal poked with his spoon at the ball of rice that floated in the gumbo. '*Five thousand francs a month will keep me from sending this to the Société Académique de St-Cloud*?'

'I wouldn't put it past him. But with that much money in his pocket already, and returning to the United States . . . Why would he need to?'

'So who really faked the haunting?' asked the fiddler softly. 'And why? Why pitch poor Wishart down the stairs? What had he seen? What did he know?'

January was silent. Beside him, Cochon Gardinier started to ask, 'You gonna eat that, Ben?' but took a look at his face and stopped with the words half-said.

Hannibal moved the soup plate a little closer to January's elbow, put the spoon in his hand. 'It'll be a long night.'

It was.

January had played at balls in Paris with riots going on in the street outside; at receptions three hours after hearing that the first cases of Asiatic cholera were sweeping the city. For the first eighteen months after his return to New Orleans, he had played, and played well, even as grief at his wife Ayasha's death swamped him in unexpected waves as certain songs, certain phrases of music, brought back to him with agonizing clarity the memory of her leaning on the side of the piano in the rehearsal room at the Theatre Pelletier when he'd practice there. The line of sunlight on the edge of her hair, the folds of her dress. The music – Mozart, Gluck, Auber – was more to him than light that cleansed away grief, more than the golden wall of a magic fortress that no shadow could pierce.

It was life itself. Like the harp of Orpheus, it could indeed resuscitate the dead.

In the early part of the evening, he could always tell where Daisy Emmett was in the ballroom, by the tall pennants of Miss Grice's green fairy wings poking up above the heads of the crowd. Neither the vicomtesse nor Creon Grice appeared to have accompanied the girls to Granville's. (*Did Persephone murder Grice in defense of Miss Emmett's virtue? Did Grice murder Persephone in quest of it?*) Twice he saw the commanding young matron Euphèmie Miragouin – clothed as a Herculean Red Riding Hood, with a small stuffed wolf beneath her arm – break off her conversations with bankers and sugar growers to squint near-sightedly around the ballroom, and stride in pursuit of those selfsame green wings:

'I think La Miragouin is playing chaperone to the girls this evening,' confirmed Hannibal, as the circle of waltzers broke up with the conclusion of a Chopin piece. 'It would make sense, I suppose, if Persephone *did* murder Grice and is now burying him in theciprière . . .'

About halfway through the evening, the tall green wings disappeared as well.

'I wouldn't put it past Miss Emmett to take scissors to them,' surmised the fiddler, adjusting the ivory pegs of his instrument.

'It's the only way their guardian dragon can keep track of where they are . . . Maybe she murdered old Boehler herself and told Miss Grice to bury him in the garden.'

The shadowy forms of prince and goddess, nearly hidden by the curtain of a window embrasure, merged closer to one another. Madame Miragouin, deep in what looked like negotiation about the purchase of something – land, slaves, shares in a cotton press – with old Jacques-Francois de Livaudais, didn't even glance in their direction.

Ordinarily, January, like the other musicians, found a good deal of entertainment in the behavior of their 'betters'. This evening, as the rain rattled against windows misted with the cold outside, he couldn't put from his heart the anger he felt towards Creon Grice, towards the Duc d'Aveline. As he walked along Rue Chartres with the other musicians – four o'clock on a bitterly cold morning, the rain just ceased and getting ready to fall again, by the smell of it – his thoughts returned, again and again, to that unprotected girl lying in the darkness of the house on the Rue St-André des Artes, ill with grief at the deaths, first of her father, then of the uncle who would have protected her. In his mind, he heard a man's stealthy step on the waxed floorboards outside her door, then the soft creak of a hinge.

He was barely aware of the joshing of the other musicians, about what uses the stiff, enormous oilskin raincoat that he carried over his arm *could* be put to. ('You could put a couple poles under it, use it for a house . . .' 'The ancient Persians could have sealed up all its openings and inflated it for a boat . . .')

The carriageways they passed, beside the big townhouses, glowed with cressets and lamps. Voices drifted forth – *Blessings of this day . . . May the Wise Kings bring you blessings . . .*

It's not my business, he told himself. *There was nothing I could have done then. And there's nothing I can do now.*

But the sense nagged him still, that there was something he could have done. Something he should have seen and didn't.

He tried to remember whether the vicomtesse had ever seen the little image of Sittina-Menhit, knew of its connection to the Curse Manuscript. Whether she recognized the costume Miss Emmett wore. She had had, as she'd said, little acquaintance with

Arithmus himself in France, for he had refused to enter the chateau and she'd spent her evenings in town . . .

The brown vellum of that shabby little codex returned to mind, the ink faded to near-invisibility and the warm light of beeswax candles playing over it. Rain falling then as now, outside the windows of the Beau Soleil. The old Latin, laboriously copied from some earlier document and barely readable, relating the interwoven tales of Great-Grandpa Pankhy's invasion of Egypt and poor Dejen's unmerited death at the hands of his Roman master. *Imposuit dea manum . . . Vultus eius a dolore et timore transfigurator: the goddess laid her hand on him, and his face was transfigured by agony and fear.*

The goddess whose power had been as strong in the days of the Emperor Tiberius, as it had been when she had fought at the side of King Pankhy, to grind the pharaoh's forces into the dust.

That was what Grice had wanted from her. That, and the Curse statue that corroborated the tale. The image of the goddess whom that silly girl had dressed up as tonight, down to her curly red slippers.

And how can I prove a thing?

And what would it matter if I did?

Persephone will be going back to France soon. To her children, and the family lands she will administer for them. After that, it isn't my affair. I can no more help anyone than I could have helped the slave Dejen when the Roman stole his wife.

Just an ancient tale. *Diebus Tiberii Caesaris in provincia Aegypti . . .*

Freezing wind drove the rain before it down Rue Chartres. The musicians sprang on to the brick banquette as carriages passed them, men and women laughing, or humming snatches of Chopin, of the 'Amazon Galop' and 'The Light of Other Days'.

Diebus Tiberii Caesaris in provincia Aegypti Nubianus servus factus est . . .

And in the dank cold of the following winter forenoon, when January crossed through the boys' nursery behind the bedroom, and thence to the rear gallery – he could hear Rose taking the girls through their math exercises in the dining room – and descended to the yard and the warmth of the kitchen, he found that someone had left a note for him on his small plate, on the worktable beside the open hearth. There was coffee in the pot just within the glowing range of the coals, and leftover king cake in one Dutch oven on the hearth, half-covered with embers. Another contained grits and two sausages.

Two notes, actually, he observed as he returned to the table with his breakfast.

One was from Rose, carefully embellished with curlicues drawn by Aglaëa – who at eight had an artistic technique beyond her years – surrounding the motto, JOYEUX MARDI GRAS and signed by them all.

The other was from Persephone.

Les Cyprès
Bayou Gentilly
7 Jan.

Dearest Benjamin,
Something very strange has happened. Monsieur Grice has disappeared, and Mademoiselle Emmett insists that he was murdered, and has sent for the City Guards. Some advice from you – and ostensibly from your friend Monsieur Sefton, as my experiences in this country make me doubt the Guards will listen to a man of your complexion – would be deeply appreciated.
Yours in the Brotherhood of Apollo,
Persephone de St-Forgeux

FOURTEEN

'Maestro.' Abishag Shaw, Lieutenant of the New Orleans City Guard (First Municipality), ambled down the steps of the house called Les Cyprès as January and Hannibal came up the shell path from the road along the levee. 'Her Ladyship told me as she'd sent for you, or I'd have done it myself. Sefton . . .' He held out his knobby-knuckled hand first to Hannibal (who was after all white) and then to January. 'Says she knowed you in France.'

'Madame did indeed.'

With Shaw and Hannibal, January entered the house by its front door, something he'd never have been permitted to do (and would never have risked doing for a number of reasons) had he been by himself or with another man of color. In the imposing front hall, Quincy the butler took his hat and coat as well as Hannibal's without comment or change of expression, placed them on the hall rack, and said, 'This way, sirs,' as if he had never seen January before in his life. But when they passed Nestor, and the buxom housekeeper Corena, emerging from the parlor, the coachman shot Quincy a startled look.

Persephone was alone in the parlor, immaculate in her somber bombazine and crape. Her smile was one of gratitude mingled with exasperation: 'Thank you, beyond what I can say – and poor Mr Sefton, bless you for coming also. Though Mr Shaw tells me' – she turned her rueful expression on the Guard – 'that he has worked with you before, Benjamin, and respects your opinions and observations highly.'

'Just as well.' Shaw scratched under the breast of his sorry wool waistcoat. 'Bayou Gentilly bein' the Third Municipality, m'am, Cap'n Barthelmy's in charge, an' I may get turned out of this duty any time.' As usual in the Mardi Gras season, the Kentuckian bore the appearance of a man who'd been to the wars, with a half-healed cut on one cheekbone and a bandage across the knuckles of his right hand. He added, 'If so be there's a case at all, that is.'

January glanced from Shaw's face to Persephone's. Noted the woman's unhealthy pallor.

'I suspect there was something amiss with the oysters last night at supper,' Her Ladyship sighed. 'We had been invited to the Granvilles' Epiphany ball, but when the time came to leave neither I nor Monsieur Grice felt in any case to attend. At least, I know I didn't, and Monsieur Grice claimed, with every appearance of distress, that he didn't either. But Mademoiselle Emmett had so set her heart on going that I sent a note to Madame Miragouin – the sugar broker's wife, you know, who has been most kind to us this week we've been in town – asking, would she chaperone the girls and bring them home? A most disinterestedly helpful lady,' she added with a smile. 'Her son being too young to be thinking of marriage to anyone, and her daughter still in the schoolroom, there is a refreshing lack of awkwardness in her friendship.'

January recalled the horse-fly persistence of those mothers – French Creole and American alike – who *did* have marriageable sons, as they maneuvered to position their young men close to Daisy Emmett. No surprise, that the girl had fallen head over ears in love with a European prince who clearly *wasn't* after her for her money – and whose parents, Herr Doktor Boehler made clear, would *not* welcome even a seven-figure dowry and seventeen cotton plantations.

'I had hoped,' Persephone went on, 'to wait up for the girls, but the medicine I took for my indisposition was stronger than I'd anticipated. I slept like a baby through the night. Josie tells me she also felt the effects of the Monsters of the Deep rather suddenly a little later in the evening, and left the Granvilles' early.'

(*So* that *accounted for the disappearance of the wings*, January reflected.)

'Prince Serafin told his valet, who was acting as his coachman last night, to bring her home, and she came in quietly through the back. She had torn her gown and didn't want to be seen,' she added, in a voice that told January that in fact she had probably vomited on it. Any lady, young or old, would hang herself rather than admit such a contretemps . . .

And he recalled a number of meetings witnessed between the prince and a girl who could well have been Miss Grice, and wondered if it was Miss Emmett who'd gotten His Highness to pack her – *rival?* – off so promptly.

Poor girl.

'At breakfast I felt better,' Persephone continued after a moment. 'I inquired of Quincy if Monsieur Grice was convalescent as well. He said he thought so, because Monsieur had risen early – before even the servants were up, evidently – and gone out walking, without so much as a cup of coffee to invigorate him. He should be back, Quincy guessed, at any time. But he didn't come back. The girls came down at about eight, and Mademoiselle Emmett seemed most startled to hear that her guardian had recovered and gone out, since he had seemed so very ill the night before. At ten she sent Nestor and Joe out to look for him – we'd already ascertained that he hadn't taken any of the horses – and when he couldn't be found, she took it into her head that he was dead. It was she who sent for the City Guards,' she finished, with an apologetic glance at Shaw. 'I didn't know anything about it until I saw Geordie riding away with the message.'

Without a word, the Kentuckian drew a crumpled piece of notepaper from his pocket, slapped it clear of lint and tobacco fragments on his thigh, and handed it to January.

> *Les Cyprès*
> *Bayou Gentilly*
> *Jan 7*
>
> *Captain, I beg you to send an officer AT ONCE to Les Cyprès on Bayou Gentilly. Mr Grice has DISAPPEARED WITHOUT A TRACE, and I believe there has been FOUL PLAY.*
> *Miss Daisy Emmett*

'She sent it to the Cabildo,' explained Shaw to January, 'on account of her thinkin' that's the headquarters for all the police in town. I sent a note to Cap'n Barthelmy, what's head of the Third Municipality force, if you can call 'em that, an' came on here.'

'At which point . . .' The vicomtesse took the note from Hannibal, to whom January had passed it, and re-read it with a glance, 'I sent for you, Monsieur Janvier. That would have been . . .' She frowned, held up a finger, calculating, 'ten thirty or eleven, I think. It's now nearly one. Some of the men have been out looking through the cypress marshes behind this house for nearly four hours, and I am indeed becoming concerned.'

'He didn't take no horse nor no carriage,' said Shaw thoughtfully. 'Not from his own stables anyways. I understand' – he turned those mild, pitiless gray eyes on January – 'that the wife he's divorcin' lives over to Bayou P'tit-Jean, not four miles from where we're standin'. Her Ladyship tells me you're a friend to her, too.'

'I am.'

'Might you be so good as to come with me to her place? Just wantin' to make sure,' he added, as if he read the sudden wariness in January's eyes, 'where everythin' stands, 'fore we go ridin' off in all directions. Sefton, maybe you'd escort Her Ladyship over there by carriage, if'fn she feels able for it? The maestro an' I'll walk along the bayou, where a man afoot mighta gone. That sit with you, m'am?'

'Thank you.' Persephone held out her hand to him. 'I will be very happy to go along, so poor Mademoiselle Wishart – as she has asked to be called now – will not feel . . . *descended upon* . . . by the police.'

Shaw bowed like a broken puppet. 'That bein' the case,' he said, 'an' if'fn you don't mind, m'am, I'd like it if Mr J here could have a look at Mr Grice's room 'fore we go, 'case there's anythin' I mighta missed.'

Persephone rang for Quincy, who sent word to the stables that the light chaise would be needed; January followed Shaw up the backstairs. Les Cyprès was the antithesis of Venezuela Plantation in Concordia Parish, an American-style house, with a kitchen on the ground floor of an attached servants' wing, close to town and designed for the plantation's owners to live in most of the year. The plantation itself, Belle had told January on one of his visits to her, had been divided between the two sons of its late owner, Auguste Villeré. The elder had elected to continue living in the old, Creole-style house – which was crowded with not only six children but two sets of uncles, aunts and cousins – about two hundred yards down-river on Bayou Gentilly. The younger son, having built this handsome American-style dwelling for himself, had discovered that his share of the land was in fact marshy, low-lying and swarming with mosquitos. He had settled for renting his soggy acres back to his brother, hiring out the house to such wealthy Europeans and Yankees as wished to winter in New Orleans, and living modestly on the proceeds in town.

Creon Grice's room overlooked the porch, one of the two most handsome chambers in the main block of the house. Its furnishings were expensive and meant to be recognized as such, the bed without a mosquito-bar, as it was sharply cold winter, the candles on the bedside table burnt down nearly to their sockets. 'Tallow.' January sniffed the greasy odor of them even as he stepped into the room.

'Ever'body I talked to says the man named his pennies.' Shaw reached a long finger to turn over one of the several brownish 'winding sheets' that had accumulated on the side of the candle. Someone had broken them off and laid them on the rim of the holder, rather than get a fresh light and send the candle back down to the kitchen half-burned.

The hearth was cold, and clean, a new fire laid but unkindled. The bed had been made. January turned back counterpane and blankets. Slight creases showed in the middle, where someone had lain, but the sheet had been freshly washed and ironed, its sides still crisp with starch. Whoever had lain there, he thought, had not lain long. When Shaw – hearing Quincy's approaching step – turned to look out into the hall, January set his hand in the middle of the bed and pushed gently down.

The moss stuffing was new, springy.

He crouched quickly, felt the underside of the bed where the stretched ropes held up the mattress, and those, too, felt new.

He was on his feet again before Shaw and Quincy came back into the room.

'The bed had been slept in, as I was telling Mr Shaw,' said the butler. 'Naturally the housemaids made it up when they cleaned the room. Mr Grice's walking boots are gone; his hat, his outer clothing, his shirt – the things he'd wear to go walking—'

'But he didn't *go* walking!' Scurrying clatter in the hall, and Daisy Emmett flounced through the door – taking advantage, January assumed, of Persephone's preoccupation with the carriage. In its frame of mouse-brown side-curls, her round face was pale, her eyes almost frantic, like a slightly chubby Cassandra prophesying the doom of Troy. 'I keep telling Persephone that, and these *idiots* . . .' Her lace-mitted finger stabbed at the butler. 'You *know* it's true, Quincy! Mr Grice *hated* to go walking! Something's happened to him. I know it! I feel it in my heart!'

She pressed her hands to the organ in question, for emphasis. 'Are you all that *stupid*?'

After last night's masquerade, she had resumed her proper degree of mourning, and black did not become her. She looked haggard, too: nervy. As what girl wouldn't be, January thought, living under the roof of a guardian who had cornered her, as he had seen her cornered in the Macartys' courtyard? A girl desperately enamored of someone else?

'An' no one saw him leave the house?' asked Shaw.

Quincy shook his head. 'When Susie – she's the housemaid, sir – came in quietly, to light his fire early this morning, he was gone. As I said, Mr Shaw, it didn't look like he'd left in a hurry. He'd drawn up the blankets to cover the bed, his clothes were in order, not like he'd grabbed or fumbled with anything. One of his cravats is gone, too, so he took the time to tie it.'

'Someone could have lured him away!' proclaimed Miss Emmett. 'Ambushed him . . .'

Quincy looked as if he would have pointed out that there were no signs of ambush, either, but wisely held his peace.

'Where was his nightshirt?' January studied the monumental black-walnut dressing table, the handsome swivel-mounted mirror. He ran his finger lightly along the inside of the shaving mug, then opened a drawer to look at the brush and razor, though he guessed they'd be dry as well.

'Hung over the end of the bed like he usually leaves it.' The butler threw a quick glance at Shaw – *probably checking to make sure it's all right if he answers the question to someone who isn't white*, thought January. 'Susie took it an' brought it down to the laundry, Mr Grice liking a clean nightshirt a couple times a week.'

'He's dead!' Miss Emmett stamped her foot. 'I *know* he's dead! Why won't any of you *believe* me?'

She followed Shaw and January as Quincy escorted them around the other rooms on that floor. 'That should have been my room.' She pointed proudly into the other handsome chamber beside Grice's. 'He had my things moved in there, only Persephone – that's my *companion*' – she twisted the word with contempt – 'got all starchy and made me take a poky little *cell* clear at the other end of the house . . .'

Glancing around him, January had an impression of two heavily carved armoires stuffed with petticoats and chemises, a dressing table large enough to erect a medium-sized house on, one of the new full-length German mirrors in a corner. The score or so of books on the shelf bore witness to the heiress's literary preferences (*If 'literary,'* January reflected, *is the correct word . . .*): *Pamela, The Mysteries of Udolpho, Love in Excess* (Persephone seemed to have guessed her charge's tastes with great exactness), *Glenarvon, The Vampyre, Clermont*. He'd seen most of these titles either in his sister Dominique's house, or cached about his own in what the boarding students fondly believed to be deepest secrecy. (He and Rose had spent several hilarious evenings reading the choicer portions of these to each other in bed.)

One of the other two bedrooms on the upper floor of the main block was devoted to storage. In the fourth – and he felt a curious catch of anger in his throat – Deverel Wishart's chemicals and laboratory equipment crowded the dressing table. Some of them he recalled from the Englishman's room at Palongeux: presses and pestles and jars of dried leaves, very like Olympe's pharmacopeia – jumbled together, as if they'd simply been taken out of the trunk and left there.

By whom? One of the servants, searching for herbs to quiet protesting stomachs last night?

Had Grice brought these here to keep the servants left behind at Laburnum from tampering with them? Or because he was searching for something of his former wife's, not quite knowing what it was?

The brass-cornered trunk was there, too, the corners tarnished and dented: beside it, even the candles and the pilfered salt spoon. Other things he recognized from Wishart's workroom at the rented house on Rue St-André des Artes – retorts, lamps, alembics, a barometer. Pots of greenish paste and a jar of bodkins that had at one time been sealed with red wax.

He followed Shaw down the hall, to the smaller door that led, he guessed, to the wing where Miss Emmett's 'poky little cell' was situated, probably next to an equally poky chamber relegated to Persephone.

And when Grice returned with his ward to Natchez – and some impoverished cousin from Lexington or Baltimore arrived to take over the duties of companion – would she, whoever she was, be given a 'poky little cell' in some corner of Laburnum, far from the handsome chamber that Miss Emmett would then be offered? The implications of which she obviously had given no thought . . .

Again, he felt the prickle of anger at the roots of his hair.

This isn't your business . . .

But as competition for his ward's hand crowded on Grice's heels, January felt in his bones that it might indeed become his business, very soon.

'If you'll excuse me a moment,' he said to Shaw, as they descended the backstairs again. Miss Emmett had taken the main staircase down to the hall in a frou-frou of black silk taffeta petticoats, and he heard her voice – and the softer tones of Miss Grice – from that direction:

'They won't *listen* to me . . .'

'Uncle will turn up, honey! I can't believe anything terrible has happened—'

'It has! It *has!*' January could almost hear her stamp her foot.

'Quincy . . .' He fell back to join the butler, lowered his voice. 'Did Arithmus come down with the family from Natchez?'

He almost had the feeling – in the pause that ensued – that the man was going to respond with, *Why do you ask?*

'He did, sir. You'll find him in that little room there at the back.' He pointed to the rear wing of the house. In a lower voice, with a slightly forced grin, he added, 'You didn't think Mr Grice would actually quit keeping up his accounts for a little thing like Twelfth Night, did you?'

He led the way out to a sort of loggia at the back of the house, between the kitchen wing and that which, upstairs, contained the two smallest guest rooms. Through the long French windows, January saw that one of the downstairs chambers was also a guest room – plainly furnished and plainly intended for the lowest-status person on the white side of the household, governess or maiden aunt or whoever might be contagiously sick. It wasn't made up. The ticking mattress was rolled up at one end of the bed, the lattice of bed ropes stretched naked in the frame of the bed itself.

The other contained only a small desk and an assortment of what looked like document boxes. Arithmus sat hunched exactly as he had been a week and a half earlier in Natchez, this time copying a letter. There was no fireplace in the room. The Nubian's breath puffed almost invisibly in the cold. Fingerless mittens sheathed his hands.

He didn't look up when January tapped at the window. Only when January opened the door and spoke did he sit up and turn, and the instant before he did, January saw the younger man's shoulders tighten, as if readying himself for an accusation or a blow.

When he saw who it was his eyes widened, first with delight, then with apprehension as he glanced past January's shoulder to see Quincy standing behind.

'Have the Guards gone away?' he asked.

'Lieutenant Shaw is just now leaving,' said the butler. 'He says others may come from town later today, but that's nothing you have to deal with, Rithmus. You just stay here and get on with Mr Grice's work. He hasn't come back yet.'

Arithmus thought about that for a moment. 'Oh. All right.'

If it hadn't been Arithmus, January would have wondered why the man didn't ask, *Is Miss Emmett still in a state?* or make a suggestion about a locale that might have been missed. But it was clear that, though the man was now much improved in his dealings with others, such polite conversational tropes still had no place in his thought processes.

'Mr J wants to ask you a few questions, I think,' said the butler. 'He's working with Lieutenant Shaw and the City Guards.'

Arithmus's eyes darted from one to the other.

'Nothing to worry about,' January assured him. 'I just want to know if anyone might be able to give me some idea of when Michie Grice left the house.'

'I was asleep,' said Arithmus promptly.

'When?'

'When Mr Grice left the house.'

'What time was that?'

'Five minutes after four o'clock in the morning.'

'Couldn't have been much after four,' pointed out the butler smoothly, "cause Susie went into his room at a quarter of five to light the fire, and he was already gone.'

Arithmus nodded vigorous assent. 'And Mrs Miragouin's carriage drove up at ten minutes after four,' he said, starting to tick off times on his fingers. 'She has two bay horses with one white stocking each; their names are Figaro and Susanna. Prince Serafin was escorting them because it's so far from town. He was riding a black horse – I don't know the horse's name. Mr Backhall in Natchez says that a bay horse with only one white foot is supposed to be bad luck, because the white foot will make him trip, but I've never—' He caught another glare from Quincy, and added, 'But I was asleep.'

'Most all of us were,' said Quincy. 'Poor Linney was asleep by the fireplace in the drawing room, where her ladyship had sat before dinner. It had been banked down, but the coals were still plenty warm. Mr Grice doesn't hold with servants keeping fires in their rooms,' he added, with a wry glance toward the empty hearth to his right. 'Nor with keeping the fires up in the kitchen after dinner's cooked.'

And with Persephone ill, January reflected, Fräulein Hauser would have gone to bed as well, leaving poor Linney to watch alone.

'When she came in, Miss Emmett said not to wake her. She said she didn't want her chattering, as she helped her undress, for fear of waking Miss Grice. Miss Grice shares the Yellow Bedroom with Miss Emmett. She said she could do for herself, which she could,' he added with half a grin. 'That gown that goddess of hers was wearing was no more than one of those dresses ladies wore back when I was a little boy in Virginia, that was more like a nightgown than a dress.'

'Maestro?' Shaw's tall form appeared in the window behind Quincy. 'If'fn we plans to get a look at the ground 'twixt here an' Bayou P'tit-Jean, best we get a move-on 'fore whoever Captain Barthelmy sends out clumbers all over it.'

As January was turning away, Arithmus spoke up again. 'The dress wasn't really like the goddess,' he objected pedantically. 'She found Sittina-Menhit in the room with Mr Wishart's things, just after she got to Natchez, and Mr Grice told her it was from ancient Egypt and there was supposed to be a curse on it. Miss Emmett said it was romantic, and got Miss Grice to help her make the mask, out of papier-mâché. Miss Grice did most of the work. But Sittina-Menhit was from Nubia, not Egypt, and it was she who brought the curse. The Duc d'Aveline sent it to Mr Grice,' he added. 'He said it brought him bad luck.'

January said quietly, 'I hope it did.'

He and Shaw crossed the yard behind the house, and then the kitchen garden, the route a man would take who, rising in pre-dawn blackness, set forth afoot to the tiny cottage, four miles off, where his former wife slept. The rain that had fallen in the first hours of last night had resumed shortly after five; January had waked, sleepily, to hear it for all of five seconds before falling asleep again. Whatever tracks had marked the muddy earth between the beds of tomatoes and lettuces had been obliterated.

The same would hold true, he guessed, for any tracks around that arrogantly grand house on the bayou. He looked back at it, with its pillared portico – the very newest fashion, on display in the wealthier villas behind Natchez as well – and its long windows, wanly silver in the cloudy afternoon light. On the way from the shell road along Bayou Gentilly he had, out of sheer habit, studied the ground, and had seen little. But the bayou itself was deep enough, wide enough, to carry a pirogue or a raft. At this season of the year, with the river high and the lands behind it half-inundated, a man who knew the territory could probably pole his way in a few hours, from Bayou Gentilly to the Fisherman's Canal a few miles to the south, and thence to the river itself just below the race-course downstream.

He held his peace, however, as Shaw led the way into the filtered gloom of the cypress swamps. Once they heard the crash of a gun, distant in the somber cathedral of the trees. *His Highness in quest of a cougar?* His companion muttered, 'Consarn it. Somebody been along here last night, but if they was comin' or goin's, more'n I can tell right now.'

To January, the ground-marks were barely scrapes in the mud. In one place, where the ground was high near what had been a Chickasaw camp, a squishy indentation showed where leaves of jewelweed had been trodden into the clay.

'You think Grice was really sick?' Shaw bent to examine the broken stems. A clump of swamp-laurel overhung the place, growing near the decrepit wall of what had been some swamp-rat's family cemetery, most of the brick tombs now crumbling back to the soil. 'Or fakin', so's he could have a night when nobody knew for sure where he was? Be easy enough to put a dose of somethin' in dinner, to lay Her Ladyship out so's she wouldn't haul them girls home early . . . An' she didn't look any too peart this mornin'. I can't see a man truly sick takin' a stroll in the swamp in the rain, wife or no wife.'

No. January suspected that it was Arithmus who had left the tracks. Arithmus taking the opportunity, while Grice was ill, to visit Belle – whatever his relationship to her was, whatever it had been for the past sixteen years. Whatever promises concerning him that Grice had made or broken.

He was fairly certain what had happened last night.

What had caused the household servants to change, not only the bedding but the mattress and even the bed ropes.

The only question was, how it had happened, who had done it, and where the body was to be found.

FIFTEEN

Zizi-Marie's yellow dress showed up bright against the gray-weathered lumber of the back of Belle Wishart's cottage, as January and Shaw drew near the edge of the trees. The tangle of yellow on the ground near her feet, January knew, was her tignon, pushed free by the hands of the man who held her so tightly near the corner of the little kitchen. Who kissed her so devouringly, his hands buried in the springy cloud of her hair.

Starke Hagan.

Beside him, Abishag Shaw halted, then deliberately broke a branch from the nearest clump of swamp-laurel, snapped it loudly between his hands, and stamped on the pieces. 'It much further, Maestro?' he asked in a carrying voice, and the couple sprang apart. Zizi snatched up her tignon and vanished into the kitchen. Her lover – (*The soul of gallantry*, reflected January sourly) – dodged around the far side of the cottage. An instant later, January glimpsed a flurry in the marshy tangle of winter-brown fern that spoke of ignominious retreat.

And yes, he reminded himself, there were men who'd beat a valet who was glimpsed kissing the girl to whom he'd simply been told to take a letter of more-or-less love. Some who'd sell a valet who romanced that girl as a means of bettering his own position – others who'd simply cancel the transaction and seek for a less compromised mistress.

The cottage faced south, towards the little bayou and the neglected shell path along its rim. Belle sat close enough to the window beside its door to see the two men come around the corner of the house; she opened the door even as they drew near. Her eyes went past January to Shaw, and the pleased welcome in them turned to apprehension.

'Miss Wishart.' January bowed. 'Please allow me to introduce Mr Abishag Shaw, of the New Orleans City Guards, First Municipality.'

'M'am.' Shaw raised his spavined old hat and bowed also, as she stepped aside from the doorway.

'Won't you come in?'

'You'll excuse us comin' in on you like this, m'am. But I needs to ask you about your husband, Mr Creon Grice. Seems he's gone missin', an' Miss Emmett – his ward – is swearin' blue-blind there's been foul play.'

She started at that, the apprehension changing to surprise in her face. 'Missing? I ̇ . . . Good heavens,' she concluded weakly. She had been, January saw, sewing in the chair by the window. A half-finished bodice and half a score of muslin petticoat-flounces lay across the small table. A row of pins glinted where she'd stuck them through her cuff as she worked.

'You know he was down here in New Orleans?'

'I knew that, yes. I-I had hoped to arrange a meeting with him, on matters pertaining to the divorce.'

'Nuthin' set up?'

She shook her head.

'Nor nobody come to you from his house?'

Arithmus. January could almost hear the man's name in the stiffening of shoulders and back.

Behind her, the door to the lean-to opened and Zizi-Marie slipped through, her tignon restored to its tidy and complicated folds.

'You have any idea' – Shaw's gray eyes held hers – 'of any who'd wish Mr Grice harm, m'am? He have enemies?'

'Creon Grice' – for all its hardness, Belle's voice was half a sigh – 'was hated by men from St Louis down to New Orleans, and I think in Alabama as well. In England and in Paris, too. He and his partner, the late Mr Travis Emmett of Virginia, in addition to dealing in slaves, lent out money for mortgages, both on property and slaves. You would have to look at his account books for the details. Or Arithmus would know. My . . . husband . . . was perfectly willing to foreclose, or to evict tenants from the properties he owned, with little notice and no observable compunction.'

She turned her face aside for a moment, her lips compressed again. Then, in a lighter tone, 'And that was *before* he became guardian to Miss Emmett, and let every hopeful suitor in the state know that he intended to marry her and her money himself. Miss

Emmett's father and grandfather were both, as I understand, only children, but there are second cousins and step-nephews in the East who would be more than willing to . . . to step into his place.'

'It's somethin' we'll surely look up, m'am.' Shaw scratched his long, greasy hair. 'If so be it turns out that he really has been snatched up by somebody, or kilt. Though at this distance, writin' letters back an' forth to Virginia, God knows what kind of information you're gonna get. He left his house 'tween four an' five this mornin', afoot . . .'

January did not miss her expression of surprise at that.

'. . . an' men been out lookin' for him since eight. You wouldn't mind savin' us a little time, tellin' us about this divorce, m'am? You don't have to,' he added, when she hesitated. 'But somebody's gonna look it up in the state records in Jackson, if'fn, as I say, he don't turn up today. You don't happen to know if he had a lady friend, do you? Here or in Natchez?'

She began, 'I don't know of any woman who would willingly . . .' and stopped herself, as if hearing the anger in her own voice. Carefully selecting her words, she explained, 'He tended to acquire female servants for their looks – at least I assume it was for their looks, it certainly can't have been for their housekeeping abilities. He would sell them on, when they . . . they began to show with child. He dealt in slaves,' she added, her eyes turned away. 'There was no shortage of opportunity. And I have heard – though I do not know it of my own knowledge – that he . . . sometimes took advantage of the situation if a woman – or a man with an attractive wife or daughter – was so unfortunate as to fall behind on his loan payments.'

Had he been chewing tobacco – the policeman had very properly expelled his wad before approaching a lady's door – January suspected Shaw would have spit.

'As for the divorce . . .' Belle Wishart drew a deep breath and straightened her back. 'Six weeks ago I very foolishly let myself be compromised by a . . . by a plausible scoundrel. I will not hide the fact that I was deeply unhappy with Mr Grice, but there is no excuse for my conduct.' Her face, rather than pink in the gloomy afternoon light that came through the windows, had gone very pale. 'I did not contest the divorce, and I believe that with my signature on the final papers, he and I are no longer man and wife.'

Zizi-Marie, silently sewing petticoat-ruffles in the chair by the other window, raised her eyes, and January saw the flicker of outrage in her glance that reminded him strongly of her mother. But her father's – and grandmother's – training in manners held good, and she returned her attention to her work.

But if she'd had black wax, graveyard dust, and fish-hooks to hand at that moment, January guessed she'd have used them.

Harness-chains jingled outside, and a confusion of hooves, far more than could be accounted for by a single-horse chaise. Through the window, January saw not only the chaise from Les Cyprès – Persephone's Swiss footman Sigerist springing down to help Persephone descend – but two mounted men just stepping from their saddles.

One wore the unmistakable militia-style uniform of the New Orleans City Guards. The other, in a well-cut frock-coat and tall hat, January recognized as Captain Nicholas Barthelmy, in charge of the Guards of the Third Municipality – a strong-built, fair-haired man who tipped his hat to the vicomtesse and ran a contemptuous eye over Hannibal, having not many years previously stepped over him in every gutter in town.

Barthelmy entered the cottage without knocking. 'Ah, M'sieu Shaw.' He had, January knew, been one of Shaw's co-lieutenants when the City Guards had been a single organization, before New Orleans had calved itself into three 'municipalities'. Barthelmy had been promoted to become part of the Third Municipality's force, owing to his French and German Creole birth and his education, as much as to his connections with the American business community.

His pale eyes went to Belle: 'Mrs Grice?'

And barely waiting for her assent, he turned to Shaw. 'Captain Tremouille tells me you were so good as to respond to Miss Emmett's note.' His English was perfect; far better than Shaw's alley-cat French. (Or the Kentuckian's English, for that matter.) 'If you would remain and enlighten me as to your findings thus far. Did you in fact discover evidence that Mr Grice came here this morning?'

'The lady says not.'

'Hrmn. Well.' He ran his glance over her again – thoughtfully – and then turned to study Persephone with quick, suspicious interest. 'And this is Madame the Vicomtesse de St-Forgeux, I believe? I understand you knew Mrs Grice in France, madame? Listolier . . .' This in French to the uniformed guard. 'Please be so good as to wait with Her Ladyship in the other room while I speak to Madame Grice.' He gestured to the bedroom door; literally *the other room*, as the cottage had only two. And in English again, with a dismissive gesture, 'The rest of you may leave.'

January thought, *Shit*, as he, Hannibal, and Zizi-Marie retreated out the front door. *Damn it*.

He knew perfectly well what conclusion Barthelmy was bound to come to.

To his niece, he said softly, 'Were you here last night?' He had not seen her when he'd returned to his own house at three o'clock that morning, but that yellow dress was the one she'd had on yesterday afternoon.

She glanced at Hannibal, looked aside in some confusion, then murmured, 'No.' Hannibal, with prompt good manners, strolled off in the direction of the chaise, gazing around him as if he'd never seen cypress trees before.

Looking down at her, January said quietly, 'You don't have to tell me where you were.'

'There was a dance,' she breathed. 'At the brickyard on the Rue Dumaine . . .'

He raised two fingers, as if about to touch her lips. 'Be careful.'

She looked aside, and he saw again the sheen of tears in her eyes. Then she shook her head, turned her face back to him as if closing one ledger book and opening another to a fresh page. 'That stripe-eyed *pichou* never sent her the money he promised,' she whispered. 'She can't go on living off Her Ladyship – Madame's got to go back to her children in France soon, and nobody's going to hire a woman that's been divorced. You know they're not, Uncle Ben!' Anger and distress twisted her brows. 'Is old Grice really croaked?'

'No,' January said quickly. 'But he is missing. I don't think Barthelmy would be here if they'd found any sign of him. And Lieutenant Shaw found traces – and they're only traces, because of the rain – that someone either walked from Les Cyprès to here, or from here to Les Cyprès, sometime between three and four thirty this morning. Has Arithmus been here, at any time, to see Madame Wishart?'

Zizi hesitated. 'That old snake promised he'd give her Rithmus,' she said at last. 'And send her money, the nasty old toad. You didn't really think she'd played kiss-and-hug with some riverboat gambler just for fun, did you?'

January shook his head. 'No, I think the minute Grice knew he'd have Miss Emmett as his ward, he started scheming how to get rid of his wife so he could force the girl into marrying him. I think Madame Wishart made a deal with him: she'd give him cause for a divorce, in return for her own freedom, and that of Arithmus – who was enslaved illegally in the first place – and enough money to go back to Europe. Maybe even back to Arithmus's family in Africa. She does love him, doesn't she?'

Tears flooded the girl's eyes again, 'Like life. All these years . . .'

Enough to murder her husband, for backing out of their deal? Or to get Arithmus to do it?

And how long will it be, before Barthelmy contacts the Paris Sûreté and learns this isn't the first time they've been suspected of collusion? Six weeks? Eight weeks?

How long do they have?

'Don't tell anybody that.' Zizi's glance flicked towards Hannibal, sitting in the chaise reading his grimy copy of the *Iliad*. 'If anybody knew about that – *anybody* – you know who they'll say killed that old bastard. He really is dead, isn't he?'

'I don't know,' lied January doggedly. 'And nothing can be done, legally, until they know if he is alive or dead – including getting Miss Emmett another guardian, or permitting her to marry. At this point I don't know who'll be in charge of the day-to-day running of the household, or his business interests—'

'I bet somebody'll figure out it's all right to sell his slaves.' She almost spat out the words. '*Including* Rithmus . . .'

'Let's see what the next few days turn up.' January glanced at the sky, visible through the gloomy screen of the cypresses in the direction of the bayou. *After three* . . . He was due at Caldwell's American Theater on Camp Street at five, for the first rehearsal of *Semiramide*.

Dammit . . .

The cottage door opened. Barthelmy strode forth like Alexander the Great at the head of his army – and, like an army in his wake, his single Guard. The captain turned back and said something to Shaw, a disreputable straggler bringing up the rear. Only when Belle and Persephone emerged, the vicomtesse's arm protectively around the younger woman's shoulders, did January relax. But Belle looked scared. Bowing stiffly, Barthelmy said, 'My apologies if I was forced to be unpleasant, mesdames. But I trust you understand my request that neither of you leave New Orleans for the time being, until Monsieur Grice's return.'

'Of course.' Belle dipped a curtsey. Persephone merely looked down her nose at the man.

'Species of pig,' she said, as the two men rode away.

'Can I take you back to Les Cyprès, Benjamin?' the vicomtesse asked, as the three men crossed the muddy yard to the cottage door. 'You can cling on to the back of the chaise, and save yourself wading through long grass and muck—'

'Thank you, madame. But we – Mr Sefton and myself – need to get back to town . . .' He glanced at Shaw, who nodded, hands shoved in the pockets of his scarecrow coat.

'As do I. Thank you kindly, m'am, for the thought.'

'I'll stay here for a time.' Hesitantly, Zizi came to Belle's other side. 'If you're not too tired, Belle – m'am,' she corrected herself. 'We can still get some of your sewing done, if those carrot-pulling tooth-drawers haven't pulled you through the blue sky . . .'

'If I may . . .' With a small gesture, January beckoned the two white women to the shelter of the kitchen. Within its warm, smoke-smelling confines, he warned softly, 'If they don't find Grice in a day or two, they're going to start going through his papers. Here first, but they'll send someone up to Natchez within days. Madame . . .' He turned to Belle. 'Is there anything they might find there that would . . . harm you?'

Behind the thick spectacle-lenses, her dark eyes were sad now and infinitely weary.

'That would cause someone who wanted to prove that M'sieu Grice was in fact dead, to think that you had something in your past?'

'Like the Paris Sûreté thinking I might have murdered my uncle?'

'Something like that.'

'Or that I'd got Arithmus to do it for me? Or that *he'd* got *me* to do it?'

And when January made no reply to that, she said in a small and hopeless voice, 'We didn't kill him.' As if she knew that any accusation of the former 'mysterious barbarian marvel' of Africa would involve her, too, as the brains of the operation.

'I never thought you did, mamzelle. Did Grice get the Nubian Curse Manuscript from you?'

'No. I don't know where he laid hands on it. I didn't know absolutely that he'd done so, until a few years ago, when d'Aveline sent him Sittina-Menhit's statue. After the house was burgled, Uncle Dev said he was sure the servants had been in league with the thieves, and that he was going to hide the manuscript. But of course everyone in the Sûreté must have heard that the duc was offering a hundred thousand francs or more for it . . . When Mr Grice came to America, and with enough money to buy all that land, and the house, and lend out money at interest and go into partnership with Mr Emmett, I thought the only place he *could* have gotten the money was from d'Aveline. He wouldn't tell me, but I'm certain it's the reason he . . . *asked*' – she picked the word carefully – 'me to marry him, when Uncle Dev died. I thought at the time it was about Papa's land . . .'

Her voice shook as she said the words, and in his mind January saw again the dark of her bedroom, the sable tangle of the girl's hair on the pillow. The man standing up over her, adjusting his clothing. *You're a fallen woman now* . . .

And who would have permitted her to marry an African 'savage freak of the dark continent' anyway?

'Then when the duc sent back the statue, I knew. His son had just died – had hanged himself—'

'I heard about that.' He remembered, too, that when his friend Carnot the painter had told him this piece of gossip, his first thought had been, *Serves him right* . . . 'Didn't his daughter die as well? Fell down some stairs . . .'

'That's what they put about,' said Persephone. 'She died in

childbed, at the convent where he'd sent her when she was discovered to be pregnant.'

Pity softened Belle's voice. 'That was only a few months before the son's suicide. The duc sent the image back to Grice, saying it had brought him bad luck. I think he must have just destroyed the manuscript. But that's when I realized that – that Mr Grice . . .' Her voice faltered again on the name, '. . . *had* to marry me – to get me to marry him – so that he could legally sell the statue and the manuscript to the duc. I think that's why he stayed in France, when he sent me – and Rithmus – to America. To give him time to find it, wherever it was hidden.

'I don't know how much of a record was kept of all that.' She sighed again. 'But you're right. Combined with my letters last week asking him to honor his bargain after the divorce – which I know they'll find in his desk – and the letter my father sent to Uncle Dev about . . . about Arithmus asking for my hand, all those years ago . . . It looked pretty damning then, and now . . .'

'Why would Grice have brought all the things from your Uncle Dev's workroom down here?' he asked quietly. 'As I understand it, he was only going to be here until Mardi Gras.'

'Oh.' Color flooded to her face. 'I think that has to have been Quincy.'

And, when he regarded her with lifted brows, she went on, a little self-consciously, 'He and Corena . . .' For a moment she could not meet his eyes. Then she took a deep breath, raised her head. 'Corena guessed I was using some of those herbs to . . . to prevent conceiving by Mr Grice, or to bring on miscarriage. The ones Uncle Dev had collected and dried in Egypt weren't the same as those that grew around Natchez. I-I couldn't take the risk with plants I didn't know as well. Corena started stealing them, for the other women on Laburnum, and when she'd go out to Venezuela and Camelot Plantations across the river. I'll bet you ducats to cribbage-pegs that Quincy pretended he'd gotten his instructions wrong – he's very quick with a story – and packed up all the workroom things by mistake, so Mr Grice wouldn't guess what was so important in that workroom, and why the women on his plantations weren't bearing "pickaninnies" for him to sell. Arithmus told me . . .'

She bit the words off, and the flush returned.

'I'm not going to ask you when.'

In a hurried voice, not meeting his eyes, she said, 'Arithmus told me Mr Grice got angry with Quincy on their first day here, and beat him with a riding whip. He didn't know for what.'

'Can we beg you,' Persephone stepped closer, with a glance through the open door; Lieutenant Shaw had disappeared, Sigerist was sitting like a statue of Duty at the reins of the chaise, and Hannibal, beside him, had gone back to the *Iliad*, 'and of course the good Hannibal . . .'

The tell-tale, tiny smile in the corner of her mouth made January inwardly roll his eyes.

'. . . to make the journey to Natchez again, if M'sieu Grice hasn't returned by tomorrow morning, and hunt through M'sieu Grice's papers? I have the keys to the house, and can write a note to his brother Ulee – Miss Grice's father – who's looking after the place.' Her dark glance went from January to Belle, and January had the uncomfortable suspicion that she, too, guessed – or knew perfectly well – that Creon Grice was dead.

But how 'perfectly well' does she know?

'I'm sure we can convince Daisy to let Arithmus go with you, too. The girl can't add two and two and has no idea why anyone would want to keep track of money anyway. And *I'll* bet you ducats to cribbage-pegs that if there are threatening letters – or incriminating ledger books – Arithmus remembers not only what box they're in, but how many pages in from the front *and* from the back of the box . . . *And* the date and time he put them in that box, and what the weather was like outside and what they had for dinner that night in the servants' hall . . .'

'No bets. I don't care how many cribbage-pegs you offer me.'

They all laughed at that, but January was already calculating in his mind: Rehearsals for *Semiramide*. And upcoming rehearsals for *Der Freischütz*, and *Abduction from a Seraglio*. But they'd have to go soon. There was the first Blue Ribbon ball at the Salle d'Orleans, and the musicale at Madame Redfern's on the tenth, and rehearsals for the ballets of *Semiramide* et al., not to speak of the lessons for the boarders and the lessons for Flora Cullen and the Savonière children and little Carrie Paden . . .

A pang went through his heart. *And Zizi-Marie's wedding on the fourteenth?*

He saw the girl again in Starke Hagan's arms, her yellow tignon tumbled around her feet like a forgotten promise, a discarded flower.

'All right.'

'I'll make the arrangements,' said Persephone briskly. 'With our luck, that lying rascal will show up after they've – *jailed*' – she visibly stopped herself from saying, *hanged* – 'poor Belle for his murder . . .'

Very quietly, January said, 'He won't.'

Their eyes met again, but neither spoke.

But the fact that Grice was dead – unless it could be proved *how* he died – wouldn't keep Belle Wishart from the gallows.

Nor the others, he reflected, who would, as a result of finding the body, die as well.

SIXTEEN

Semiramide was a recent opera, its lush score requiring January to play the cornet rather than the harpsichord, which was his usual contribution to the works of such composers as Mr Mozart; he enjoyed the change. Moreover, at the rehearsal that evening, he was delighted also to renew his acquaintance with the soprano Consuela Montero, singing the role of Azema. Madame Montero, after making eyes at Hannibal throughout the evening, asked them both up to her dressing room for coffee afterwards: 'You understand that I am faithful eternally to my beloved Don Julio de Montmejor,' she purred to Hannibal, who replied that his heart swooned with gladness only to behold her beauty once again. The wealthy gentleman for whom she had left Hannibal in 1836 had been someone else entirely.

'Two sons!' she cried, when January answered her question as to Rose's health and spirits. '*Mis mejores deseos – Dios los bendiga!*' She seized his hands, kissed him on both cheeks. 'Give her all my best love!'

'If you would care to make that gift yourself,' replied January, 'you will be more than welcome to dine with us tomorrow evening – *this* evening,' he added, with a glance at the dressing-room clock, 'at five. You can meet the boys yourself – and my niece and nephew, who now live with us . . .'

'*Dios mio!* From a new bridegroom to a patriarch in four short years . . .!'

'And Rose's students will be awestruck to meet you.'

She laughed. 'So long as nobody tells their parents she had an actress to dine with them – do they know about Hannibal?'

'I'll have you know, *mi corazón*, that I am a perfectly respectable teacher of Greek these days . . .'

'Hannibal and I have an errand late in the evening,' said January, as they walked Madame at last up Julia Street towards her hotel. They had sat for hours in La Montero's tiny cubicle drinking coffee, eating beignets, and telling stories of their respective adventures since they'd parted four years ago on the quai at Vera Cruz, and the streets were finally beginning to quiet down. Julia Street – like many in this part of New Orleans – was still a mix of American-style houses and vacant lots where ancestral trees still grew, and most of the houses, Carnival notwithstanding, were now dark. His glance crossed the fiddler's and Hannibal nodded, a little grimly.

'Dark deeds afoot?' inquired the soprano, whose previous acquaintance with them had involved a certain number of such deeds. January turned the question aside.

'Only something that needs looking into, for a friend.'

She sniffed. 'A likely tale.' The men bowed her into the lobby of her hotel on Nyades Street, and she offered Hannibal her hand to kiss, like the Empress of Babylon in Act One.

As they emerged on to the steps again, the fiddler asked softly, 'Midnight?'

January nodded. The evening's warm pleasure faded at the prospect of what had to be done.

'You really think we'll find him?'

'I think so, yes.' A carriage full of young men passed them as they turned their steps back toward the French town, its occupants banging tin pans and singing.

'*Plaisir d'amour ne dure qu'un moment* . . .'

From the big houses on the far side of Lafayette Square, music could be heard, pianoforte and the drift of merriment as parties broke up. The ladies homeward bound, the men – undoubtedly – en route to rowdier entertainments, or to visit their mistresses ('Oh, George and I are just going to have a drink or two, aren't we, George? I'll be home directly, dearest . . .').

Fog blurred the gaslights along that wide central corridor of the Second (American) Municipality, hid whatever moonlight there was. 'Arithmus could have told me the exact number of times an owl hooted in the trees outside his window last night,' said January. 'And the time to the minute when the rain started and stopped. He didn't. He has no imagination whatever, I think it's very hard for him to lie. He met Madame Wishart last night . . . and I think he saw something when he came back to Les Cyprès at four o'clock this morning. Yesterday morning,' he corrected himself. (*No wonder I feel like I've been pulled through a mangle.*) 'The question is, *What?*'

They walked on in silence for a time. 'You think one of the servants did it.' There was no query in the fiddler's voice.

'Or Persephone.' January tucked his cornet case more firmly under his arm, huddled deeper into his rather shabby greatcoat. 'Or Arithmus and Belle together. Or when Arithmus came out of his room at four in the morning, the first thing he saw was Belle murdering her ex-husband, after she'd left a trail to Les Cyprès through the ciprière. I won't know until I see the body.'

'Why would the lovely Persephone . . .?'

'I don't know. Think about the people you've met, Hannibal. Think about the situations they get themselves into, things we know nothing about.' He gestured down the retreating darkness of Lafayette Street as they crossed it. 'It isn't just a question of the servants being sold when the master dies, if he's mortgaged them. Whoever killed him, if a man is murdered by one of his slaves, the law will hang the whole household. If Arithmus discovered Belle in Grice's room with Grice's corpse; if Arithmus discovered Quincy or Barnabas or Corena holding a pillow over Grice's face; if Quincy or Barnabas discovered Arithmus strangling Grice for striking Belle . . . Whatever the configuration, Persephone sleeps at the other end of the house and by her own admission took paregoric. Miss Grice was laid up ill – probably she took paregoric when she got home, too. Miss Emmett was still at the Granvilles'.'

Making sheep's-eyes at Prince Serafin under the nose of her near-sighted chaperone.

'A body will void itself at death,' he went on quietly. 'In most cases, in any household that can afford it, some or most or all of the bedding of a deathbed has to be destroyed, or at the very least boiled repeatedly. The bedding on Grice's bed had been changed: sheets, mattress, even the bed ropes, in case something soaked through.'

Hannibal made a face. '*Give me an ounce of civet, good apothecary, to sweeten my imagination . . .*'

'Once Grice was dead, all of them – Quincy, Barnabas, the maids, the cook, Nestor and Corena and all the others . . . they had to hide his body. I don't think they'd risk dumping it in the river. Even at high water, these things get washed up. Whether they did it – together or any one of them by him- or herself – or just found the body, they *had* to hide it, and all evidence that anything had happened, and make preparations to flee before it could be found.'

'*Culpam poena premit comes*,' murmured the fiddler thoughtfully. 'And I suppose if Grice dealt in slaves, any one of them—'

From the dark of Perdidio Street, away to their left, a man's voice proclaimed loudly, 'Take your hand off me, you scum.'

January paused, looked – it was the tone of voice white men generally used in addressing black ones, but the man's accent caught his attention: European.

Slavic . . .

A group of men had surrounded a light chaise, its lamps dimly outlining their forms. Two men had pulled the chaise's occupant out, while another held the frightened horse. A gold gleam flickered on the head of a cane as the driver lashed at those who surrounded him.

Idiot . . .

The next second, as the men closed in, the European shouted 'Help me! Help! Murder!' and in the chaise, a woman screamed.

Damn it . . .

As one, January and Hannibal stowed their instruments in the dark doorway of a lawyer's office on the corner, and strode towards the melee.

There were only four of them, one of whom had released the rein of the horse to drag the woman from the vehicle. January fell upon this attacker from behind, ducked a savage punch as the man writhed free, and the woman twisted like a snake in her assailant's arms and grabbed a double-handful of the man's hair. She jerked, hard, sideways, giving January a perfect shot at the bearded jaw; the attacker fell back into the horse which reared, screamed, and took off at a gallop up Perdidio Street, taking the chaise – and its lamps – with it.

January plunged into the struggling mass beside him, caught a pair of shoulders and hauled their owner into another punch. A blackjack clipped him across the bicep, and he heaved his opponent in the general direction of the fracas, then ducked as the driver's cane whistled past his head. Someone yelled, 'This ain't the last you'll be hearing, Prince!' and there was a bumbling scramble as the attackers fled.

January could barely make out the movement in the darkness, as the 'prince' collapsed to his knees in the mud beside the roadway. He wiped the blood from his own lip and looked around for the pale blur of the woman's dress, but she, too, had taken to her heels *whoever she is – I hope she makes it home all right . . .*

Far down the street he heard the horse scream again, and the clattering din of the chaise coming off its wheels and connecting with something-or-other – *the corner of a building?* – in the dark.

He fumbled a candle from his pocket, and the little brass tube of matches he habitually carried – 'Hannibal?'

'Oh, God, help me,' moaned the 'prince', and when January managed to strike a match, his hands trembling, he saw that this was, indeed, Prince Serafin Corvinus, blood trickling from a gash on his chin and more streaming from his nose.

Hannibal lay like a broken doll in the ditch.

The ambush had taken place next to one of the many empty, wooded lots that still lined the streets behind Nyades. The nearest building was nearly a hundred feet away, where one of the several cotton exchanges marked the business premises of Carondolet Street. All empty and dark, of course, at this hour of a foggy morning. January called out, 'Over here, man!' and the prince staggered up, hand pressed to his ribs.

'Is he all right?' He knelt again at January's side, and obediently took the candle January pressed into his hand. 'Thank you.' He looked around. 'Liesel – Mademoiselle Gautier—' he corrected himself.

'She ran for it.'

'Good for her.' Prince Serafin flinched again with pain. 'I'll have to look for her tomorrow, make sure she's all right.' He added, a little self-consciously, 'She impresses me as a girl – er – well able to take care of herself.' He looked down anxiously into Hannibal's face, as January gathered the papery skin on the back of the fiddler's hand and pinched it sharply. Hannibal twitched but didn't open his eyes; January gingerly slid his hand under the back of his friend's head, ascertaining that his skull hadn't been cracked nor his neck broken. The candlelight showed him a bloodied cheekbone, rapidly swelling, and a brow puckered with pain.

The prince got to his feet. January, still kneeling, put out a hand to hold him steady. The horse could be heard, whinnying furiously and, by the sound of it, trying to kick the chaise to pieces. 'Stay here,' said the young man. 'Let's see if there's enough of that chaise left to get your friend to shelter. I'm all right,' he added, gesturing to January to stay where he was.

Hannibal stirred, turned his head and whispered, *'There are few die well that die in a battle . . . Am I honorably slain?'* He coughed, and stopped at once with a noise of agony in his throat. *'O mighty Caesar! Dost thou lie so low?'* He flexed his fingers, tried to feel his ribs and stopped again. 'Please remind me never to do that again, *amicus meus*. Did our victims make their escape?'

'Mademoiselle Liesel did.' January helped his friend to sit up; last night's rain had left the mud of Perdidio Street wet and cold, and Hannibal was shivering violently. 'After giving me yeoman assistance in the fray.'

'Would that be Liesel Gautier? My sympathies lie with the attackers, then. Her escort . . .?'

'Prince Serafin is gone to fetch whatever is left of the chaise.'

'Prince Serafin?' Hannibal's eyebrows shot up. 'Well, well, well . . .'

His Highness returned, leading the limping horse and the chaise. Fifty feet away, even Nyades Street was growing quiet, as the last of the revelers went home or subsided into drunken sleep wherever they happened to be. As January got Hannibal into the chaise, he noticed that Serafin, while holding the bridle, was also carefully mopping the blood from his face with a couple of white linen handkerchiefs that flickered in the darkness like royalist banners. When he kindled the chaise-lamps again, January saw that His Highness had also taken the opportunity to comb his tousled black hair.

'Did you get a look at them?' he asked, returning from fetching cornet, violin, and music-satchels from the office doorway of Mr Marcel Ratzinger, Esq. (*Notary, wills witnessed, land sales – Ici on parle français*). 'My friend lives further along Perdidio Street, at the back of town. Can your horse make it that far?'

'I think so.' The prince held the candle down close to the animal's shins, felt cautiously along the bone. 'It's bruises only, I think – but I can't answer for that poor chaise.'

And indeed, the animal's limp grew less pronounced as they led it up the muck of Perdidio Street, toward where that aptly named thoroughfare did, indeed, lose itself in the swampy nether-regions at the 'back of town'. Lanterns and cressets still burned among the scattered shanties wrought of tent-canvas and old flat-boat planks, more or less at random among a primordial gloom of Spanish moss and cypress-knees.

Seeing the prince glance around him nervously – there were, by the sound of it, three fights in progress in saloons, and another somewhere off in the darkness – January asked again, 'Did you get a look at them, sir?' At least, he reflected, it had been dark enough that he himself could deny being there, if it turned out the attackers had been white and wanted to make an issue of being struck.

'Oh.' Prince Serafin waved with elaborate casualness. 'They were – mere ruffians. Scum.' He shrugged, not convincingly. 'One learns to expect such men, in a port, *hein?*' Two men staggered out of the Turkey Buzzard a dozen feet away and His Highness shied like a schoolgirl, and didn't emerge from behind the horse until one of the staggerers tripped and went face-down in the nearest puddle. The man's companion sat down beside his buddy, pulled his face out of the water, and proceeded to explain something to him at careful, inebriated length.

'No.' The young man pretended that he'd gone around to check a harness-buckle. 'No, I'd never seen them before in my life. Er, why do you ask?'

Kentucky Williams, proprietress of the Keelboat and nearly six feet of solid muscle, fell immediately and violently in love with Prince Serafin at first sight. After helping January carry Hannibal up to his bitter-cold attic room, and tossing down an assortment of torn towels, a bottle of whatever it was she sold out of the barrel under the bar, and a paper of pins to deal with the fiddler's broken ribs, she retreated downstairs to tenderly dab clean His Highness's bruised face and offer him a composer from the small stock of genuine cognac for which she usually charged a dollar a shot.

'I rescued your violin,' reported January, when Hannibal opened his eyes. 'Will you be all right here? You've got two broken ribs – inhale, carefully . . .' He adjusted the wrappings. 'You need to stay down – and I mean *down* – for at least two weeks. I'll be here in the morning—'

'This *is* the morning, *amicus meus*. ἦμος δ' ἠριγένεια φάνη ῥοδοδάκτυλος Ἠώς . . .'

'Later in the morning.' January groaned inwardly at the very thought. But he knew that he couldn't send Gabriel, or Zizi, or any of his relatives for that matter, into The Swamp – as the insalubrious district was called – in daylight hours. The risk of being encountered and either beaten up, if male, or raped, if otherwise, was simply too great. Particularly with everyone in a holiday mood. 'And I'm sure the prince can be counted on to reward you enough to make up for not playing—'

'I'm not so sure of that.' Hannibal leaned back on the flat pillows and shivered again – January wondered if he could drag Miss Williams away from her new passion long enough to talk her out of a couple of extra blankets.

'He's supposed to be extremely rich. He's on tour of this country, his governor . . .'

'He may be a prince,' pointed out the fiddler, 'but I doubt his reputation for wealth. Those gentlemen who organized the ambuscade – they weren't mere ruffians, as he claimed. I recognized two of them. They work for Mason Spurcid – one of the wealthiest, and least scrupulous, moneylenders in town.'

After three hours' sleep and four cups of coffee, January was just writing a note to Ti-Gall asking for his company back to the Keelboat – Ti-Gall, for all his gentleness, was a big, sturdy young man – when boots faintly vibrated the bones of the house, and from his seat at the desk in his little office, he saw a uniformed City Guard appear at the door. *Talesin*, he recognized the man. *First Municipality . . .*

Officer Talesin handed him a note, in English, in Shaw's jagged spillikin handwriting.

Mstro we hav found blod an mr grice things com hav a looke at them Shaw

SEVENTEEN

The blood was in theciprière, some two hundred feet back from the house at Les Cyprès, seventy-five from the structure farthest from the bayou, which had at one time been a woodstore. The place's original stables – built at the same time as the elegant American-style house – and an optimistic carriage-house, stood between the old woodstore and the house itself, and like the woodstore had been largely stripped of anything that could have been used as lumber. In the chilly morning sunlight, the drive and stable-yard had the look of hasty weed-cutting and new gravel, dating probably from just before Grice's arrival. Swamp-laurel and palmetto grew up thick against the walls.

A regiment of crows seemed to have taken up residence in the dilapidated buildings, their cawing like an oracles' tea party, prophesying doom.

'Miss Emmett came on this this mornin'.' Shaw glanced sidelong at Captain Barthelmy, who stood frowning grimly at the place, his inevitable uniformed officer at his side. (*It's* CARNIVAL, January protested mentally, *don't you people need every man in town?*) 'I thought, you knowin' Mr Grice an' Mrs . . . Grice . . .' again the glance at Barthelmy, '. . . as you do, Maestro, you might ought to have a look at this. See if you can see somethin' that speaks to you as it wouldn't to us.'

The Kentuckian's flat, light voice had a deliberate note of withdrawal to it. January met his eyes briefly, and saw only, *Nuthin' to do with me . . .*

He turned back to the blood.

A huge puddle of it, splashed in an area some three feet by two, in the low ground between an oak tree and a tangle of swamp-laurel. The ground on the downstream side was thick with creeper and fern, much trampled. Walking cautiously around the blood-spot, he could see no tracks of any kind on the upstream side, wetter and muddier, so presumably Miss Emmett had come upon the evidence from the downstream side . . .

'We found these scattered there, by the roots of that tree.' Barthelmy drew his attention to a fallen cypress trunk upon which had been laid a gold watch, a gold signet ring, and a 'Dutch gold' card-case that had been handsome before the thin leaf of zinc and copper had begun to fray from the underlying tin.

The signet bore the initials, L. G. 'His father's or grandfather's,' clarified Barthelmy, when January squatted to look more closely at the artefacts. 'Leonidas Grice, Miss Grice – Miss Josephine Grice – tells me.'

'They took Mrs Grice in for questionin' this mornin',' reported Shaw, his voice still unexpressive. 'Her Ladyship paid two hunnert dollars' bond for her good conduct, an' come close to havin' to pay another two hunnert for herself.'

'The Vicomtesse de St-Forgeux,' put in Barthelmy stiffly, 'might well have had reason herself to do M'sieu Grice harm. She has been a guest beneath his roof since the twenty-seventh of December, with no one but two underage girls for company; girls, moreover, who are under her protection. Who knows in what ways this man Grice may have offended against the laws of honor and hospitality?'

To say nothing of the laws of humanity, reflected January drily, *in keeping and selling and owning the bodies of men and women back in Natchez . . .*

If you prick us, do we not bleed? the Jew of Venice had cried in his anger. *And if you wrong us, do we not seek revenge?*

'The blood looks awfully fresh, sir,' he pointed out diffidently, 'to be Michie Grice's.' Even given the wet state of the weed-cloaked ground underfoot, it couldn't possibly have been shed yesterday morning before dawn – and he couldn't imagine that the searchers yesterday would have missed it.

'Not if it was shed in the small hours of this morning.' The Third Municipality captain gestured around them at the flattened foliage. 'We have no idea where M'sieu Grice was kept for the past twenty-four hours. If he was taken prisoner by the sort of ruffians that hide out in the ciprière, he might easily have escaped them and fled through the woods, only to be pursued and seized—'

Why wouldn't they have taken his signet ring and watch in those twenty-four hours? January had the wits not to ask, hearing in the man's voice how fond the officer was of this theory.

And it was true that the night would have been nearly pitch-dark beneath the trees. He supposed a man *could* have found his way that accurately back to his own house, through country he did not know, from far enough away that an all-day search hadn't uncovered his hypothetical prison.

It sounded to him, however, like the captain had attended too many blood-and-thunder melodramas at the American Theater on Camp Street.

'Have you found a body?'

Barthelmy cleared his throat. 'Not yet. If Grice managed somehow to elude his pursuers . . .'

Sufficient Damoclean blades dangled over the heads of the innocent to keep the hand of discretion in front of January's mouth. One of the first things he'd learned as a child – among parents, friends, uncles and aunties who could be beaten, tortured, or sold away forever on a white man's whim – had been, *Keep your mouth shut. You can't un-ring a bell.*

Once you say anything that puts *any* kind of idea into a white man's head, or the head of some fool idiot who's going to then turn around and blab it to a white man, you have *no idea* what's going to come of it. What that person in power is going to do with what he *thinks* he's heard.

It was the Paris Sûreté all over again.

He was aware of Shaw's pale gaze on him. Aware that Shaw – for all he respected and in some ways loved the man as a brother – was a white man and an unwavering servant of the law.

The law that said, *If a slave kills his master, all the house servants are considered accomplices in that murder.* Why would they *not* conspire to kill a man who could do to them – and to anyone they loved – utterly and absolutely whatever he pleased, without consequences?

I have to see the body – I have to know *what happened – before I speak.*

'You's awful quiet, Maestro.' Shaw's voice was barely a murmur, as January rose and Captain Barthelmy gathered up the items that had been found scattered in the blood.

'That's because I know I'd have trouble keeping my mouth shut in the face of one of the good captain's theories about where and why masked bravos would have imprisoned Grice for twenty-four hours. Or how he could have "eluded his pursuers" after losing that much blood. If it *is* his blood . . .'

'Could happen.' Shaw crammed cold-reddened hands into his pockets, followed slowly in the wake of Barthelmy's swift retreat toward the house. 'An' without drippin' a drop as he run off, neither.'

He stopped, watching the horseman who came along the bayou road at a canter – who reined in before the steps of the house as Daisy Emmett emerged from its doors (*She must have been watching for him*, thought January). She stopped short, hands flung up in horror, then fell adoringly upon the rider and touched what were clearly the bruises on his face . . .

'You think she done it?' asked the Kentuckian softly.

'I'm not sure how she could have.' January's voice was equally low. 'Both she – and Corvinus – were at the Granvilles' ball Wednesday night, and his he-nanny was watching them both like a hawk.'

'It usual' – Shaw's eyes followed the prince as Miss Emmett led him up the steps – 'for kings an' queens . . .? Is his parents King an' Queen of Hungary?'

January shook his head. 'The King of Hungary is the Emperor Ferdinand of Austria. Corvinus's father would be the hereditary prince of one of the smaller principalities of the Empire – God knows which . . .'

'Like that German feller, what was his name? That duke what came here to see the sights in '25 or '26 . . .'

January nodded. 'And yes. In Paris you'd often see German princes, doing the Grand Tour with guardians to make sure they didn't bring home some opera-dancer bride to horrify the kingdom . . . Though usually those were younger than Corvinus.'

'Hmn.' The policeman tilted his head a little, gray eyes narrowed. Persephone and Josie Grice emerged on to the porch as Captain Barthelmy climbed its shallow steps, Persephone disturbingly like her namesake in the deep sable of her recent widowhood, Josie – like Miss Emmett – frocked now also in mourning black. Miss Emmett, reflected January, hadn't worn such somber attire even for her father.

'Leavin' aside how she woulda got rid of his body,' Shaw went on. 'An' *why*. If'fn the point was for her to marry His Majesty over there, there can't be no doubt that Grice is dead. I'm for sure guessin' she's the one killed a chicken over there by the woodstore – or more like stole one already dead from the pantry – an' dumped whatever she could find in his desk into the blood. Same question goes for Miss Wishart an' Her Ladyship. I can see either of 'em doin' the deed, but not gettin' the corpse out of the house an' down to the bayou, from where they can pole a pirogue down to someplace like the Fisherman's Canal an' out into the river. Dead men are heavy. Heavier'n the livin' . . .'

And January said softly, 'I know.'

On the porch, Miss Emmett clung to the prince's arm, reached again to touch his bandaged forehead, as if she was about to summon servants to carry him into the house for her to nurse. Then she turned to Barthelmy, almost clutched at him, asked him something . . . stamped her foot ('He *is* dead! I know it! I know it!'). It was Prince Serafin's turn to soothe and comfort. To kiss her hand. Press it to his breast.

Quincy appeared in the doorway. The whole tableau passed on into the house, leaving Josie Grice for a moment alone, looking after the prince and her friend, before following them. The butler glanced in the direction of January and Shaw, then went inside himself.

Fiat justitia ruat caelum, January reflected. *Let justice be done though the heavens fall.*

But falling heavens will crush the guilty and the innocent together.

I have to know.

On his way home that afternoon, January made his circuitous way through theciprière to the Keelboat saloon, listening warily behind him. Captain Barthelmy had been far from inaccurate in describing the swamps between New Orleans and the lake as the haunt of bandits and slave stealers. It was the hour at which river-rats and sailors started to make their way to The Swamp's nefarious amenities, and Shaw – who at another time of year would have accompanied him – had to report back to the Cabildo to get ready for another night of Carnival. Flat on his back in bed, Hannibal begged him to relay his most abject apologies to Consuela Montero and to Rose. Ti-Gall, he reported, had brought him a sheaf of

Greek translations from Alice, Aglaëa, Germaine et al. and a small pail of gumbo and rice:

'So you find me well suited, *amicus meus*. Will you put off your investigation of Les Cyprès for a day or two, until I'm on my feet?'

'You will not be on your feet in a day or two,' returned January sternly. 'And, no. Miss Emmett is desperate to have the body found. Until it is, I think she'll have a much harder time finding someone to perform the marriage between her and the prince, always supposing he can get away from his pedagogue long enough to go through the ceremony. I'm certain the house servants hid the body. Whether they killed him or not, they can't let him be found. I need to know what happened, to know who the City Guards are going to go after. And I need to find that out as soon as I can.'

The fiddler stirred, and winced with pain. 'That doesn't mean you need to put yourself in danger of being kidnapped and given a nice vacation in Missouri for the rest of your life.' A spasm of coughing shook him, against which he stiffened his muscles in vain. January gripped his wrist helplessly, knowing how much of the day Hannibal must spend in agony.

'*Plura sunt quae nos terrent*,' Hannibal managed to say. 'My lungs are almost solid scar tissue at this point – I daresay you couldn't puncture them with a javelin, let alone a rib. Is there any way – any way at all – I can assist you, given my circumstances?'

'Just let Shaw know, if I don't come to see you tomorrow morning. And don't tell him – or anyone – of my theory about who took Grice's body, until I've been missing for three days. I suspect that, by that time, the house servants will have had time to make their arrangements and – as they say hereabouts – *skee-daddle*.'

'And would Friend Arithmus go with them?'

January shook his head. 'That, I don't know.'

But in his heart he did.

Over dinner that evening, he reassured Madame Montero that Hannibal would be well taken care of at the Keelboat. 'Even if Kentucky Williams has a new lover every month, she's genuinely fond of Hannibal. The girls in The Swamp look out for him, when they're not drunk or working. He writes them love poems.'

'He wrote *me* love poems,' she said reminiscently. 'And very good love poems they were. At least they were not purloined wholesale from Señor Byron or Señor Keats, like those written for me by some gentlemen I could mention. I wonder if he passes them along to these snaggle-haired harpies of his in The Swamp?'

When she left, at close to midnight (after getting the bean in Gabriel's very excellent king cake and promising to reciprocate the hospitality), January made sure there was oil in his dark-lantern, and bullets in both of the pistols that were completely illegal for him to carry. Upstairs, the girls were all asleep. His sons slept too, in their little nursery behind the bedroom. Rose said, 'Be careful.'

He kissed her, and slipped out into the dark.

It was a walk of some three miles to Les Cyprès. Up Franklin Avenue, through the straggling wooden dwellings of what had been the Marigny lands, past the street optimistically called Elysian Fields, then along the swampy stillness of the Gentilly bayou road. Now and then, through the trees towards the river, he glimpsed the pinpricks of gold that marked houses, where men had installed their mistresses less expensively than in the French town. Mostly those small cottages sheltered the free artisans of color, the wagon drivers and shopkeepers, the Germans whose parents had fled Napoleon's rampages or the threat of military service in their own principalities: Bavarians, Westphalians, Saxons, and Silesians. The Irish who managed to scrape enough money to seek land they could buy, and work that paid better than starving on an acre rented to them by an English landlord.

Then only bluish moonlight on the shell road, and night among the cypress trees, and the occasional swift stealth of owl or bobcat.

January walked with his lantern shielded, keeping to the edge of the road. The moon, nearly full, strewed pale sequins over the bayou's obsidian stillness. He listened, barely daring to breathe, for any sound that would tell him he was being stalked. Low banks had been built up by time along the edges of the bayou in places; in others, the water spread silvery mirrors over the soggy land. At least, in this cold, he wouldn't be in danger of stepping on a gator as he jumped one or another of those reedy puddles; nor did mosquitoes torment the night.

Clouds drifted across the stars.

No lights shone in the big house called Les Cyprès. Even the last whiffs of smoke from the bedroom chimneys had dispersed. Pale and square, the house was eerily reminiscent, in its stillness, of the whitewashed tombs in New Orleans' cemeteries.

He left the bayou's edge; slowly, carefully, circled the house. His feet squished in icy puddles, as he strained to match half-recognized shapes with daylight recollections.

Old stables. Carriage house. Newer stables, closer to the house. Something that had been an overseer's cottage, an anonymous vegetative heap overrun with jack vine.

The woodstore.

In the winter cold, a man dead in the early hours of Thursday morning wouldn't stink yet. But he remembered the regiment of crows, sitting on the broken frame of the fallen roof.

Palmetto had grown up thick around the long ruin, enough to shelter him from observation from the house. His small dark-lantern shed too little brightness to tell him whether the wood remaining in the store had been moved or not, and there was actually quite a lot of it left. Presumably Corena or young Geordie had been raiding it for a week now as well, not to mention previous renters and the depredations of the neighbors.

He shuttered the lantern, moved on to the old stable building. Walls torn out, doors long ago pillaged for hinges and handles. At least he didn't have to move a cord of logs to see if there was a body buried underneath. The marshy land beyond sent up its own faint miasma, almost undetectable in the cold weather. In summer, he reflected, within twenty-four hours the small vermin of the swamp would have led him to the body.

And he knew the body had to be there. Somewhere.

The remains of the overseer's cottage . . .?

'Mr J!'

The whisper nearly startled him out of his skin. He slammed the slide shut on the lantern again, dodged into the stable's darkness. He could see her just outside the stable door, moonlight on her flowered chintz frock and neat head-rag.

'Mr J!' she whispered again. 'Please. You gotta help me – you gotta help *us*.'

He half-recognized the housekeeper's sturdy shape, as much by her sweetly smoky voice as by the bulk of her, barely seen against the night. 'Corena?'

He opened the lantern again, stepped out of the old stable door, and received a crack over the back of the head with what felt like an ax-handle that dropped him to his knees.

The next instant a powerful arm wrapped around his throat and a wet rag was clamped over his nose and mouth. Metallic stink filled his nostrils, bodies pressed on both sides behind him, hands grabbed his arms. Dizziness and the weight of three men brought him down again when he tried to rise; he clawed at the hands gripping him, tried to draw breath through the damp folds of the cloth.

It felt like an eternity before he passed out.

EIGHTEEN

He came to halfway, groggy and nauseated. Darkness and the reek of swamp. He tried to move his hands and found they were tied behind his back.

Someone pressed the wet cloth to his nose and mouth again. Deeper darkness.

'Most extraordinary.' Deverel Wishart shook his head, turned on his heels where he squatted among the clutter of his bottles and jars and notebooks, his flower presses and chafing dishes, all stacked on the floor around him as he closed up his now-empty trunk. 'Ordinarily you can't get a reaction of any kind out of Arithmus – not with a painting, not with a sunset, not with ten thousand angels playing their harps. But he refused utterly to cross the threshold of this place.' His dark brows knit over the bridge of his beaky nose.

Outside in the corridor, Monsieur Mouche's valet Brachet bewailed the twilight sky, intermittently visible through the thatch of the Chateau Palongeux roof ('Now, there's the entire attic between you and those holes,' reasoned Daniel's cheerful baritone. 'And as you can see, the sky is perfectly clear . . .'). Wind had begun to sob through the ruined chambers overhead, but the air in the chamber Wishart had chosen for his own was sufficiently still that his breath, and January's, hung visible in the gold light as Belle lit the Argand lamp and set it on the chair beside the bed, there being no other furniture in the room.

'Did he say why?' she asked.

'Not a word.' The explorer began to set empty jars, pestles, twists of paper on to the shut lid of the trunk, as if on a table. 'But he backed a good ten feet away, when Grezolles and I opened the doors . . .'

Belle adjusted the lamp wick, the brighter flame winking on the brass corners of the flat-topped trunk. New, January noted; the metal sharp and shining, the leather between the brass not yet darkened with travel and time. He wondered to what state Wishart's earlier luggage had been reduced by the vicissitudes of a journey up the Nile. Nor could he help observing – almost counting – the bottles and notebooks and astrolabes and inkpots as Wishart arranged them, and nowhere among them did he see the square brownish packet of the Curse Manuscript.

In his dream he remembered thinking at the time, that he hoped Wishart had hidden it, back at the house on Rue St-André des Artes. It would be too easy for the Duc d'Aveline to pay a servant to steal it, and having seen the duc's interest in the document, he wouldn't put it past him.

But as he left the room, it was no longer twilight in the corridor outside, but pitch dark, and wind now howled through the chateau's attics. Glancing behind him, he saw, inexplicably, the room empty, changed . . .

Deverel Wishart's dead body lay on the bed, where they'd taken him – nobody had wished to leave him lying in the southeast tower chamber, with its groined ceiling lost in shadow and the bloody letters on the wall. All his chemical apparatus was stacked and jumbled around the chair, for the trunk was gone – moved, at some point, January had noted, into the cupboard under the great stair.

The trunk had been moved . . . The flickering sense of seeing something important . . .

The letter from his brother – that damning letter forbidding Belle to even think of marrying Arithmus – stood propped beside the filched kitchen candles, the fire-blackened salt-spoon.

In real life – in waking life – on that freezing-cold morning in 1825, he and Daniel had laid the blanket over Wishart's face, convulsed into that silent, gasping scream. But in his dream the blanket was gone, and the man's gaping mouth and frozen stare of horror lay naked, gazing into darkness. The bandage cut like a pale emblem across his forehead. On his left cheek, those three small oval burns seemed darker against the bluish pallor, the broken blood vessels, where ghostly fingers had touched the skin.

January turned back to the corridor, wondering how long he'd stood there, for the twilight to be now so utterly gone. The voices were gone, too: Daniel's, Ayasha's, Persephone's. The voices of his friends, lost in blackness, in silence.

And in the darkness he saw her. Topaz cat-eyes reflected the glow of the Argand lamp within the chamber. Dark braids framed the dusky velvet of muzzle, cheeks, the narrow, animal nose. The gold gaze held his, and she raised her right hand, three fingers, and reached to touch his face . . .

His shirt was wet. Not damp – soaked, as if he was lying in water.

He was, he realized, lying in water. Lying on his side, the curved bottom of what felt like a pirogue beneath his cheek, and the water also soaking the side of his face and the right leg of his trousers. The movement was the slewing rock of a boat, the lap and splosh of waves against the hull. The crying of crows.

Small boat, moving fast. No sound of oars.

Daylight brightened the lids of his eyes but he didn't dare open them, didn't dare move – *What the* hell *was that they put over my face?* His lips, and the underside of his nose, stung as if they'd been burned.

He didn't think his wrists were tied anymore, but for a time didn't dare flex his hands to see.

Listened.

No voices. (*Pity – I'd like to have that hag Corena here in the boat so I could shove her overboard and drown her . . .*)

The far-off, heavy sploshing of a steamboat paddle. Tiny as a dropped salt-spoon, the distant crack of a gun. Rifle or shotgun. *His Highness still hunting a cougar?*

More crows.

I'm on the river.

The boat turned in the current, rocked heavily. He opened his eyes.

He was alone, under open sky with clouds gathering. For a moment he closed his eyes again – please *don't have it rain . . .*

Opened his eyes. Sat up.

He was in a twenty-foot pirogue, almost mid-channel. Eight hundred feet to the eastern bank and somewhat over a thousand to the west. A paddle lay on the puddled planks beside him. On the board seat above his legs lay one of his pistols. A quick review of his pockets informed him that the little brass bottle that contained gunpowder, and the box holding a few spare balls, were gone.

He had one shot. (*I'll keep that for Miss Corena – or whoever set up that ambush . . .*)

Wind flowed over him, cold down the river toward the Gulf, adding to the strength of the monumental current. His throat and sinuses tasted of chemicals – *chlorine*? What was it Rose had told him, over a year ago now, about experiments with chlorinated chemicals producing unconsciousness? For some reason he recalled the disused bedroom at Les Cyprès, the table and the dressing table crowded with alembics and chafing dishes, jars empty and jars filled with dried leaves and sealed, a glass tube of bodkins with broken sealing wax on its rim, and twists of paper strewing the stripped mattress of the bed. One of the kitchen candles stolen from Palongeux – even the saucer and the saltspoon, plus everything that had been in Wishart's workroom on Rue St-André des Artes.

Notes of his experiments must have been there, too, for Corena to know what herbs to take. And Quincy must have read them to her . . .

The thought winked through his mind and was gone: *Later.* There was enough to think about now.

He sat up. Chill wind bit through his wet clothing.

By the sun it was mid-morning. With the current's strength, he'd be deep in the Barataria soon – the Trembling Lands, they were called. Bayous and ponds covered over with duckweed like green velvet. Islets – *flottants* – not really islands at all, but only floating mats of vegetation. Endless aisles of cypress, flooded a foot or two feet or four feet deep, knobby 'knees' sticking up like the misshapen heads of malevolent water gnomes. Turtles asleep, gators asleep. The only life was the swamp trappers, or the river pirates, who'd be quick enough to get word of a black man traveling alone.

Damn it.

Damn it, damn it.

They'd taken what money he'd had in his pockets. They'd left him his knife, his silver watch, and the blue beaded rosary with its battered steel crucifix.

This he took from his pocket, wrapped it around his fingers, and whispered, 'Thank you. Holy Mary, Mother of God, Queen of Heaven – thank you a thousand times.' He was well aware the situation could have been a thousand times worse.

And because he knew the Mother of God – not to mention his confessor, Père Eugenius – expected it of him, he added, 'Please shine your light on Quincy and Barnabas and all the others – even Corena – and lead them to safety and freedom . . .' Because he knew exactly what was going on – all except whether the servants actually *had* murdered their master – and knew that dumping him in a boat and poling it down the bayous and into the river was simply a way of buying themselves time, while they completed their preparations to flee. They did not need his ill-wishes at this point in their lives, despite his overwhelming desire to pray, *May they all catch fire and die*.

He unshipped the paddle, and began to work his way, still heading downstream on the fast current, slowly slantwise toward the river's eastern bank. It would mean a longer walk, around the outside loop of English Turn rather than cutting cross-country to take the ferry back across the river at Algiers Point. Going cross-country that way was dangerous. Though most of the professional gangs of slave stealers could be found closer to town, there was enough of a chance of running into river-pirates or pattyrollers in theciprière, away from the river, to make him deeply uneasy. And though most of the planters had gone up to their townhouses in New Orleans for Carnival, each plantation along the river road still housed its own little African village, where he might count on food, a place to hide, and people who'd lie for him in a pinch. ('No, suh, we didn't see no big tall niggah round here . . .' 'He went that-a-way, suh . . .')

It took him a day and a half to get home.

The planters might be in town with their families – those who could afford to do so left their wives and children at town residences all year – but every plantation on the river road had at least an overseer, often with two or three white riding-bosses, to make sure the field hands weren't 'idle', as they called it. Sugar harvest and *roulaison* were over, so plantation work consisted of cutting wood for next year's *roulaison* (often knee-deep or waist-deep in freezing swamp water), clearing ditches and chopping weeds in those fields that hadn't been harvested this year, shucking corn if the plantation didn't simply buy it in from up-river, butchering and preserving pork, and repairing every tool on the place. The men whose job was to keep their eye on the plantation bondsmen were warier, at this time of year, of escapes and 'disappearing' – going off to visit friends or family on nearby properties, or to hunt (illegally) in the swamps. Such men were always watching for stray men and women of color along the roads, assuming that everyone with African blood in their veins was somebody's slave – or should be.

January knew how easy it would be to simply disappear.

The river was high with winter. Paddling against the strength of the Father of Waters would be an exhausting business, and only those who had lived in these watery mazes all their lives could navigate the green labyrinth of bayous, ponds, ox-bows, and part-time semi-lakes to take even a shallow boat like the pirogue north all the way to town. He abandoned the craft and stayed off the river road; skirted, as far as he could, the higher ground that lay along the bank. Following the line of the swamp edge of the cane fields where the ground began to dip, he could stay mostly out of sight. But as he picked his way from tussock to tussock, waded with wet, cold feet in the verdant gloom among the cypresses, he heard from the cane fields away to his left the voices of the women and children hacking at the weeds in the ditches.

They had been singing, African words, learned phonetically from grandparents or aunties – words that tugged at the dark roots of the heart:

Imvula, imvula,
Chapha, chapha, chapha . . .

But the words changed, the slow, sweet chanting louder:

> *Chink, pink a-lu-la, chink, pink a-lu-la,*
> *Go wash kerchief in the bayou,*
> *Chink, pink a-lu-la, go wade out in the bayou,*
> *Kerchief spread all over the bayou . . .*

Someone had seen him. Word had gone out among the field hands that the patrols that rode the river road and the back trails knew there was a black man out walking where he had no business to be. A thief, maybe? A trader who traded for what the house servants could steal? Better pick him up and see . . .

Go wash kerchief in the bayou . . .

January turned his feet toward the swampier ground, the sheets of water ringed in with banks of reeds. Palmetto thickets would hide a man and the curving, currentless troughs of water left by some long-ago flood would fox the tracker dogs and cover his scent. As he slogged through this world of cold and wet, he cursed, not only every white man in the state (and as the night drew on, the world), but also Goddamned Quincy and Goddamned Barnabas, whether they'd actually murdered Creon Grice or not, and Goddamned Creon Grice – may he be burning in Hell this very minute.

If it hadn't been for the tale of the Nubian's Curse, Grice wouldn't have forced Belle Wishart to marry him. Wouldn't have gotten the money to become Travis Emmett's partner. He wouldn't have become the guardian of Travis Emmett's daughter. (*And who knows how many thousands of men and women wouldn't have ended up sitting under that sign in Natchez, Grice & Emmett, Prime Hands – House Niggers . . . Or would they have?* He knew there were plenty of curses out there in the world, blood-money enough to spare.)

He supposed, when it began to rain, that he should be thankful that his scent would be washed out of the earth – for he could still, now and then, hear the distant barking of dogs. He thought about that vulcanized tarpaulin raincoat the girls had gotten for him . . . *I'll never sneer at another gift, no matter how silly I think it is . . .*

Wondered if moving back toward the river would give him a better chance of shelter in the quarters (or the outbuildings) of one of the plantations. Or would this only increase his chances of being picked up by the pattyrollers or locked in a slave jail by some over-officious overseer?

When he saw the white bulk of a plantation house through the gloom on the other side of a small bayou, he thought, *Better than nothing . . .*

No sound of voices. No smell of smoke, or of animals, or of privies. He'd come through ground that had obviously been cultivated at some point – tangled thickets of scrubby cane pushing through an acre-wide granny-knot of weeds. Theciprière close to the river contained a number of bayous which had at one time been large enough to connect with the river – sufficient high ground to grow sugar on. A flood, or the silting up of the watercourse, would change things, make the land useless for crops, and the planter might move his house closer to the main river or to a larger bayou. The old place would be left to some family member (or members) who no longer wanted to live under the same roof as brothers and cousins and aunts. The land would be logged eventually to feed the fires of *roulaison*.

He circled the place carefully in the faded light of afternoon, wet to the skin and shivering. Identified what had been the quarters – a small street of broken-down huts, now crotch-deep in weeds – and the dilapidated overseer's house. Mule barn, stables, pens . . . The place didn't look big enough to have its own sugar mill, so it was probably connected with one of the larger outfits on the river road. He wondered how far it was to the main plantation, and if it was worth it, to walk there in the increasing rain.

The roof was mostly intact; most of the rooms were mostly dry. He checked each room as the light was failing, and found little that could be burned. Climbed – carefully – the ladder-like stair to the attic, and was rewarded with the desiccated remains of a few wicker hampers, such as clothes had once been stored in. Only rags remained, so damaged as to be good for nothing but burning. In one corner he found the remains of newspapers, faded and dried out as well. He took one of the candle stubs from his pocket, lighted it – with another polite Thank You to the Virgin Mary (and to Goddamned Quincy and his Goddamned conspirators, may they all rot in hell . . .) that Quincy and Company had left him with his little tin of matches – and was reaching down to see if any of the newspapers were still readable . . .

And saw a thin scattering on them of a half-dozen grains of gunpowder.

Fresh.

Ah.

The rafters sloped steeply toward the floor. He stepped carefully around them, holding up the candle, and yes, he saw now where one of the rafters had a space hollowed between it and the battens of the roof itself. He probed with his sheathed knife (*Let's not be stupid here . . .*), encountered something that gritted like a sack of pebbles, and, carefully, reached in and withdrew first a leather bag of pistol balls. Then another. Then three flat tin flasks of gunpowder.

Rifles are probably hidden up under the other rafters.
Good for you, whoever you are.

Virgin Mary, Mother of God, he prayed, *thank you from the bottom of my soul.*

His father, and several of the other men in the quarters where he'd grown up, had kept rifles or shotguns hidden for hunting, with little caches of powder and ball. Visitors to America often exclaimed at the kindness of slave masters who insisted on flooring the cabins in the quarters with planks, rather than leaving their bondsmen to simply live in the dirt. Every slave master understood that anything illicit could be buried under the floor of a house and plank floors made this more difficult. (Though not, January knew from his childhood, impossible.)

And every slave in the quarters knew that you didn't hide these things in your cabin anyway, because the Man would look for them while you were out breaking your back in the fields.

You found someplace good to cache them, someplace you could get to easily.

Like an abandoned house.

The largest flask was two-thirds empty. Using a piece of the newspaper as a funnel, he dumped as much of the powder as he could into what little space remained in the other two flasks, feeling guilty as he did so. He knew damn well how difficult it was for the enslaved to get hold of gunpowder, and how precious fresh squirrel or possum was after weeks of rationed salt pork.

The pistol balls in one of the two sacks more or less fit his own weapon. The rags he'd found would work as wadding.

He felt much, much better, scrambling down the ladder in the almost-pitch dark, knowing at least he had a re-load for his weapon.

The rain had eased. He didn't dare make a fire, but went down and gathered dry brush from beneath the house, to form a sort of bed for himself in the driest of the rooms.

Virgin Mary, Mother of God, he prayed as he pulled the scrub of weeds and scuppernong vine thick over his body, *I'm sorry what I thought about Quincy and his rat-bastard motherless stinking conspirators . . . May they have a successful escape and live happily ever after.*

He blew out the candle.

There was something in the room with him. He knew it.

He had never experienced anything like this before in his life, but he did not doubt for a moment what it was.

He lit the candle, his hands shaking a little.

There was nothing there.

He crept from beneath the brush, lit a second candle stub, and inspected the room, the room beside it, all the rooms of the house . . .

Nothing.

It took him a long time to blow out both candles and curl up for warmth beneath the brush . . .

And there was something in the room with him. And it was malevolent.

He lit the candles again. His heart was pounding.

There was nothing there.

The rain had ceased. Silence filled the bitter-cold night.

You're hungry, he told himself. *You're exhausted. There's nothing there.*

He blew out the candles.

Whatever it was, it was between where he lay, and the window. Eerie and impersonal malice.

He lit the candles again. He gathered up as much brush as he could – it took him three trips to get it all – and carried it out of the house, and waded through the choke of wet weeds to the slave cabin that he recalled as having the best roof. Breaks in the clouds filtered threads of moonlight. The owner who had built these cabins had distrusted his bondspeople enough to raise the little huts on plank floors, so the room wasn't unbearably damp.

Hungry, exhausted, and cold to the marrow, he curled up under the dry brush as the rain started again, blew out the candles, and slept until morning light woke him.

He woke knowing what had happened at Chateau Palongeux in the winter of 1825.

NINETEEN

Mid-morning, footsore and ravenous, January reached Chalmette plantation, five miles down-river from town, where almost exactly twenty-six years before, he had crouched in the freezing fog behind cotton-bale redoubts, listening for the British drums. There was a woodyard there now, and he knew some of the men who worked there ('Shit howdy, Ben, what the hell happened to you?') and he was able to get some food, and warm himself by the office fire, until the next up-river boat put in: the foreman parlayed with the deck-boss to let January aboard. In between downing coffee and bread like a starving man, January asked, what was the news along the river?

Evidently nobody had heard anything – yet – about all the servants disappearing from Les Cyprès. From the Chalmette woodyard it was only a few miles to Bayou Gentilly. He wondered if he should risk a visit to inquire, or if that would get him another trip down the Mississippi in a pirogue.

It started to rain again.

Girls, I will never say another word about that raincoat.

The *York and Lancaster* put in at the Dumaine Street wharf at two. Beneath cold silvery clouds, the bells of the cathedral chimed for Mass. January limped up the steps to his own front gallery twenty minutes later, to be enveloped before he could raise his hand to knock by Rose, his sons, Hannibal ('I told you to lie down and *stay* down!'), Dominique, and Henri Viellard (not to mention the girls). Chou-chou was sent running to Bayou P'tit-Jean with word to Belle, and as soon as January had been divested of his wet boots and presented with a kingly plate of last night's jambalaya and rice (difficult to eat with both boys clambering into his lap), Rose penned notes to Shaw and to Persephone, and sent Germaine across the street with fifty cents of Henri's money, to get the servants of their neighbors the Metoyer sisters to deliver them.

'What *happened*?' asked Rose, and January met her eyes, then glanced across at Henri.

While she didn't share January's automatic distrust of any white man's reaction when the subject was the behavior of the enslaved, Rose understood it, and only nodded when he shook his head. 'I'm still trying to figure that out,' he said, his arms wrapped tight around the boys. 'I literally don't remember anything between investigating some of the outbuildings around Les Cyprès, and waking up in a pirogue floating down the river somewhere in Plaquemines parish. I don't have a concussion,' he added, as her eyes flared in consternation. 'I have no idea what was done – I'll want to talk to you about that later.'

'As for me being on my feet,' put in Hannibal, 'I can only plead the bonds of duty. As we were hired to play at Madame Redfern's musicale last night, I couldn't very well deprive Cochon, Jacques, et al of both a fiddler *and* a piano. I covered for you on piano, Cochon did his usual excellent job with one violin instead of two, and you missed one of the most enlivening spectacles of the Carnival season thus far.'

'*How* I wish I could have been there!' Dominique clasped her hands to her bosom, and bounced a little in her chair. 'And, yes, Hannibal was very naughty to have gone to play in your place, but *you* were very naughty, P'tit, to oblige him to do so by disappearing . . .'

'His Highness Prince Corvinus,' said Henri, as January looked in bafflement from one to the other, 'was challenged to a duel by Gontran Mabillet . . . for making passionate love in an alcove to his hostess.'

'His . . . The *Widow Redfern*?'

'Well may you boggle.' Hannibal sank back into one of the several mismatched dining-room chairs, one hand pressed to his bandaged ribs. 'I certainly did. This came after the news that, in fact, Creon Grice is alive and well—'

'*What?*'

'And in Mobile, Alabama, of all places . . .'

'*What??*'

'That's what his letter said,' affirmed Henri. 'It arrived yesterday afternoon, informing Madame de St-Forgeux that he had been called away suddenly on business, and begging her to keep a close eye upon Mademoiselle Emmett. *They* arrived, I should say; the letter to Her Ladyship enclosed another for Mademoiselle Emmett, which only repeated that they should remain in New Orleans until his return, which should be, he said, on Thursday next.'

January could only regard him in thunderstruck silence, in which the rain drummed on the gallery roof like an avalanche of bird shot.

'Miss Emmett spent the early part of the evening,' continued Hannibal, 'swearing that the letters were a forgery – by whom, she declined to speculate. It was, she said, a Plot. The discovery of Mrs Redfern in the arms of His Highness, however, seemed to drive all reflection on the whereabouts of her guardian from her thoughts. La Vicomtesse and Mrs Trulove had to forcibly restrain her from assaulting the prince long enough for Mabillet to hurl the glove at his feet . . . La Redfern flung herself between the two gentlemen and begged them – not particularly convincingly – to shed no blood for her sake. I thought the only blood in danger of being shed at that moment was going to be hers, should Miss Emmett manage to wrench herself free of her chaperones.'

'But this is epic!' Rose's eyes sparkled behind her spectacles. '*Sing, Muse, of the Anger of Achilles* . . . Benjamin, I'm so sorry you had to miss it, especially to get cast adrift on the river . . .'

'Are they going to shoot each other?' demanded Cosette – the girls were clustered at the other end of the table, agog both at having missed the excitement and at not being told that this wasn't something they should be listening to. Germaine darted in through Rose's bedroom – in the proper French Creole fashion – rain dripping from the points of her tignon – and flounced down on to one of the stools at Cosette's side.

'Sabers,' Hannibal informed them. '*Arma virumque cano* . . . Dr Barnard was present in the ballroom and has contracted to be the surgeon at the duel, which, out of consideration for the Sabbath today, is scheduled to take place tomorrow at dawn near the great oak at the old Allard plantation. I'm sure if you sent His Highness a note, Benjamin, you could be hired as well. Everybody in town knows that Dr Barnard believes the best cure for a man who has been run through is to be bled . . .'

'Both of them,' said January, 'are more than welcome to bleed to death without my assistance. Tomorrow at dawn – or shortly after dawn – or *well* after dawn – I shall be paying a visit to Her Ladyship . . . and one to Mademoiselle Wishart, to make sure all is well with her. They can't possibly arrest her for her husband's murder if he's writing letters from Mobile—'

'Mademoiselle Wishart?' Henri turned in his chair, surprised.

'The former Mrs Grice,' Hannibal explained, 'has asked to be addressed by her maiden name.'

The planter blinked behind his square-lensed spectacles. 'Surely no relation to the late Deverel Wishart?'

'His niece,' said January slowly. 'I knew them in France.'

'Extraordinary!' Henri's cow-like brown eyes positively glowed with pleasure. 'I read all his articles in the *Parisian Chirurgical*, and the *Journal des Sçavans* . . . You don't happen to know what became of his work on the theory of a Nubian kingdom above the first cataract of the Nile, do you? From the little I remember reading of that ridiculous feud he had in the journals with the Duc d'Aveline – I even heard from my Uncle Veryl that the duc was supposed to have offered hundreds of thousands of francs for some documents Wishart had acquired. They certainly were never produced . . . they were supposed to prove that the Nubian kingdom had in fact conquered Egypt. Monsieur Grice *married* Mademoiselle Wishart?'

The gray drive of the Chateau Palongeux returned, like the cold of the wind that had breathed along January's bones. The way Creon Grice's gloved hand closed around Belle Wishart's elbow, almost thrusting her into the rented cabriolet. The way those cool eyes went past the little group on the lower steps, sweeping the dilapidated chateau itself.

'I've always wondered,' said Henri. 'Did Mademoiselle Wishart – Madame Grice – sell those documents to d'Aveline, after her uncle's death? Her father was dead by then, too, wasn't he? I'd heard—'

'Yes,' said January softly, and remembered to add, 'sir. Yes, he was recently dead. And yes, her husband sold the document, and the little bronze figure of the lion-goddess Menhit, to d'Aveline.'

'Who probably destroyed them.' Henri sighed. 'Such a pity. I wonder what happened to the rest of his research? He must have written half a dozen articles on poisons.'

'*Poisons?*'

The fat man nodded. 'He did a good deal of study about the poisons in use in classical times, but he also did some fascinating work with the botany of Africa. I've always wondered if that's what killed him. I remember reading – though I don't recall the details – that his body was unmarked, but that his features were hideously distorted. It's not an uncommon effect of certain vegetable alkaloids. If he were working with something like *Strychnos toxifera* or moonseed, the smallest cut, or even a bleeding hangnail, could have done it, you know. But they would have acted very quickly, and he was found in bed, wasn't he?'

January said, 'He was.'

'I would take it as a great personal favor,' Henri clasped and unclasped his chubby pink hands, 'or perhaps a great indulgence – if sometime you might introduce me to – er – Mademoiselle Wishart. When you judge the time is appropriate, of course. This whole scandal of divorce must be terribly upsetting to her, and I understand that this isn't the best time to speak of past events. But please do extend to her,' he added, 'my offer to her of help, if she needs it. I know that I speak for Madame Viellard . . .' He glanced self-consciously towards Dominique, though in fact his mistress and his wife were good friends, 'As well as myself.'

'Thank you.' January leaned back in his chair, suddenly deeply tired. 'I know she'll be most grateful.'

'And I know *you'll* be most grateful, P'tit,' Dominique stood up, and leaned down to kiss January's temple, 'if we'd all pack ourselves up and leave you to go to sleep, no? Hannibal, darling, you must let us take you to that dreadful hell-hole where you're living these days . . . *Please* don't tell me you're going to go play for the Truloves' ball this evening! Not that that cold-faced witch Anne Trulove would care if you died in her ballroom – except of course that she'd have to get her poor servants to throw your corpse into the bayou . . . or push you out of the house when you started to gasp your last, lest anyone should accuse her of letting one of her musicians die in her house . . . Do you know what she did to that poor Italian girl her husband had taken for his mistress? Not that she *was* Italian, any more than I am . . . *and* it's raining pickaninnies!' she added, glancing out the French doors into the yard. 'Rose, darling, could you lend me an umbrella, just to go out and wave to Pierrot . . .'

Pierrot was the Viellard coachman, waiting faithfully all this time in the downpour.

When they had gone, and January had obliged his sons by 'throwing' them 'out the window' a dozen times apiece, he retreated into the bedroom. Rose followed him in and closed the door behind them: 'I'll keep the boys quiet . . .'

Good luck with that, reflected January with a smile.

'They could dance around the room in a ring singing "Les Bluets sont bleu",' he sighed, sinking down on the bed, 'and I would still be asleep within moments. I trust Hannibal and Cochon between them had time to make arrangements to find another pianist – and another fiddler – for the Truloves this evening—?'

'I think they got M'sieu Hatch.'

'Ouch.'

'Anyone decent has been booked for weeks in advance,' pointed out Rose, who had heard M'sieu Hatch play. 'And Cochon will make sure Madame Trulove knows that you're only absent because you met with an accident. What did happen?'

Briefly, January outlined the events of the previous thirty-six hours.

'It sounds like you were forced to inhale what Jean-Baptiste Dumas calls chloroform,' said Rose doubtfully. 'Chlorinated lime mixed with ethanol – it can be deadly.'

'If Quincy and the Grice servants wanted me dead,' said January, 'I wouldn't have waked up on the river.'

I wouldn't have held my sons in my arms – not ever again. I wouldn't be here with Rose . . . The thought turned him sick with dread and grief.

'And maybe I waked up sooner than they'd thought I would, if they haven't made their escape by now—'

'Not that I've heard today.' She helped him off with the shirt he'd borrowed at Chalmette. He caught her hand, kissed it. Thankful that the world was real, and as it should be.

'They left me a weapon, and my watch,' he went on. 'It's clear to me they just wanted me out of the way for a couple of days, until they could get rid of Grice's body, and make arrangements for their own escape. I suppose I should feel complimented that they thought I could deal with whatever I'd meet on land.'

'Indeed you should.' She handed him his flannel nightshirt, took the grimy trousers he got up long enough to shed. 'And I shall write a thank-you note to Quincy to that effect, and even pay for a candle to burn in church in thanks for your safe return . . . I was worried.' She came back to the side of the bed, stood looking down at him. More quietly, she said, 'I was afraid.'

'I'm sorry.' He held out his hand, drew her down to his side against the pillows. *Virgin Mary, Mother of God, thank you. Thank you a thousand times.* 'But I couldn't take Hannibal with me – and I didn't want to bring Shaw in on it. And I couldn't wait. The slaves in the household might have killed Grice themselves. Or Belle might have done it, or Arithmus – maybe even Persephone, who could be lying about being sick and sound asleep at the time.'

'You're sure he's dead?'

January nodded.

'And those letters from Mobile are forgeries?'

'I'm sure of it. Quincy can write – he was doing the accounts in the kitchen at Natchez. If Persephone's at Les Cyprès tomorrow, I'll see if I can borrow the letters they got, and have Hannibal take a look at them—'

'She may not be.' Rose cocked her head, gauging the soft moan of the weather around the corners of the house. 'That wind's bringing the storm in from the south. The barometer has been falling all day. I suspect the Truloves will invite as many of their guests as they can to stay the night, rather than drive home in the storm.' Another gust stampeded more rain on to the gallery roof, and made the French windows rattle in their frames. January suspected that the moment he lay down to sleep, his wife would gather up the girls – and the ever-inquisitive Professor John – and spend the next few hours on the gallery above the kitchen, observing the storm through Rose's telescope and charting the behavior of barometers, thermometers, and the little spinning discs set up all along the gallery rail.

'I'm assuming Zizi-Marie will spend the night at Belle's as well,' Rose went on.

'How is she?' January had not missed the growing collection of chairs along the parlor wall, the half-constructed paper garlands and flowers. *The fourteenth.* A chill went through him at the thought. *Three days from now.*

And what then?

How long will it be, before Starke Hagan talks her into taking all the money she can get from young Picard – selling the jewels he gives her, the maid he'll buy to work in her house – and leaving the state with him? The young man had impressed him at once as someone who considered himself the smartest person in the room. *Is Zizi only his stepping-stone, to fund an escape? To finance some business scheme in New York or Boston or Canada?*

'Has she said anything to Ti-Gall?'

A slight crease of pain printed itself between Rose's brows. 'I don't think so. I don't think she knows herself what she wants to do. Ti-Gall knows something is wrong,' she added. 'He has faith in her.'

Faith. January closed his eyes. *Faith and love . . .*

He'd seen that kind of beaming smile, that brilliant confidence, before.

Will he even take her with him, if he runs?

And if not, what then?

He meant to say, *I'll go by Belle's tomorrow, and speak to her.* But before he got the words out, he was asleep.

TWENTY

He was back in that house in Plaquemines Parish, the house on that lost bayou (*I'll have to figure out where that is, what it was called . . .*), freezing cold and looking for something to burn. The house where whatever-it-was waited in the dark – left behind when everyone connected with its anger and its hatred were dead, including itself. Himself. Herself.

No-self.

In his dream he knew it was downstairs, waiting as it had waited for years. He knew that he'd end up creeping out in the middle of a night as rainy as this one (he could still hear the rain rattling on the gallery roof), to sleep in a half-ruined slave cabin rather than under the same roof as . . . as whatever-it-was.

*Who*ever it was.

That was why they hid the powder and ball in that house.

Because nobody would go into the place unless they had to. Maybe because everybody in the quarters bugged their eyes and hunched their shoulders when the Man was close-by: *Jeez,* nuthin' *would get me into that house, not* nuthin' . . .

(*Most extraordinary,* Deverel Wishart had said . . .)

And the overseer, having heard maybe a little about that house on the lost bayou himself, would automatically check off that place as someplace he didn't have to look into because stupid superstitious field hands wouldn't go in there . . .

(*There was supposed to be treasure hidden there,* Belle had said . . .)

In his dream, January probed at the little hollow above the rafter with the sheath of his knife, then drew out a flat packet wrapped in leather, and a tiny statue in bronze.

Under the lion-goddess Menhit's feet, the Pharaoh of Egypt lay broken, his sword in pieces in his hand.

Within the leather, brown papyrus glued to sheets of stiff parchment, the brown ink barely visible after sixteen centuries: *Diebus Tiberii Caesaris in provincia Aegypti Nubianus servus factus est . . .*

In the days of Tiberius Caesar, in the province of Egypt, a Nubian was made slave . . .

That's where Wishart put it, thought January. *That's why he got the keys from what-was-his-name . . . Grezolles? That's why he spread the rumors that the place* – of sinister reputation already – *was seriously, blood-on-the-walls, throw-you-down-the-stairs haunted, with educated witnesses to prove it.*

To have someplace safe to hide the Curse papyrus, until he could write up his theories about the conquest of Egypt and present the whole story to the Société de St-Cloud.

D'Aveline had had his house burgled. D'Aveline had bribed his servants.

He had to find another place to hide it. Grezolles was his friend, his landlord, had had him to dinner. Maybe had asked him about the 'hidden treasure' himself. *Of course he could get keys . . .*

D'Aveline had offered his business partner two hundred and fifty thousand francs to pilfer, and sell, the evidence that disproved the continuous unbroken greatness of the Egyptian pharaohs – evidence that would keep D'Aveline out of the society of men who held his patent of nobility cheap, and would not admit him to their ranks.

Dreaming, he put the Curse papyrus – and the goddess – back into their hiding place (*Let's not get* her *mad at me . . .*), and went downstairs by the light of his guttering candle stub. On the wall beside the stair, *Sauve-moi, au nom de Dieu* was written on the plaster in blood.

Not much to his surprise, he saw in one of the empty rooms a table – like the one he'd glimpsed at Les Cyprès – ranged with Deverel Wishart's chemical equipment: all of it, this time, from his workroom in Paris as well as the simple botanical presses and jars he'd had at Palongeux. Retorts and alembics, bottles and jars. A phial of steel bodkins, a bottle of green-black paste. Other jars, also sealed, as a man would seal them in the workroom of his home, to keep meddling servants from harming themselves; some of those seals were cracked.

He had to foster the place's reputation for evil, to keep the village treasure hunters away. How was he to know that the 'haunting' would scare off not only treasure seekers, but the prospective buyer?

The light clatter of Musette's toenails disappeared down the long hall into darkness.

The rattling of the window shutters made him jump almost out of his skin.

The rain had lightened. The night-light made a thumbprint of gold on the table beside the bed.

Someone shook shutters again. Rose's hand touched his shoulder, even as he reached under his pillow for his knife.

Silent as a ghost, Rose grabbed her spectacles, then her robe from off the foot of the bed. A voice outside whispered something that could have been, 'Mr J . . .'

She slipped away through the door into the boys' nursery, turned the key in the lock. Only then did January pad to the window.

'Mr J . . .'

A few strides took him to the door that led through to the parlor, and good manners be damned he opened *that* window, those shutters, and looked out.

Even with the night clouded over and pitch dark – the nearest streetlamp fifty feet away at the corner of Rue Burgundy – he knew the gawky, ill-made shape. Arithmus was alone.

'What's happened?'

It was long past curfew. By the distant clamor from the direction of Rue Royale, even the rain hadn't dampened the gambling rooms. Something desperate had to have happened, for any man of color to put himself at risk from drunken Carnival revelers and semi-drunken, resentful, grumpy City Guards.

The world smelled of wet stones, and the sea.

More rain on the way . . .

'Mr J, you got to come!' The tall African shambled over to him, caught at his arms, voice hoarse with barely controlled panic. 'It's all gettin' out of hand!'

'Is it?' January led him inside, closed the shutters and the windows. Rainwater dripped from his soaked clothing onto the waxed planks of the parlor floor. Droplets glittered in his short-cropped hair. 'Can't Quincy get rid of the body after all?'

Arithmus startled, as if January had touched him with an electrified wire, stared at him, full in the face for once, dark eyes wide.

'You know? How'd you know?' He was shaking, with cold or dread or excitement. 'We only just found her—'

'*Her?*'

Arithmus's eyes had already fleeted aside. 'Miss Emmett's friend.' With his fear, all the old gestures had returned, his big hands twisting at themselves one minute, then fluttering over his lips and throat. 'Miss Grice. Mr Barnabas pulled her out of the bayou just as it was starting to rain, forty-seven minutes after nine p.m. . . .' His glance veered to the parlor clock. 'Ninety-three minutes ago.'

'Barnabas thought it was Miss Emmett.' Arithmus's hands had calmed themselves, but he shifted from foot to foot as January pulled on trousers, boots, shirt, and waistcoat by the yellow smudge of candlelight in his bedroom. 'When it was just starting to rain, Barnabas went up to the top of the house where there's that little whatever-it's-called – a *couple-of*? I never knew a couple of what . . . Barnabas's auntie, back where he was born, taught him about how to please Kalfu and Bade, the lords of the moon and the winds. They don't really exist,' he added reasonably, 'but they're really dangerous, and Barnabas wanted to make some marks up there, to make sure they'll protect everybody and have it storm real hard tonight . . .'

'So tonight is when you're all escaping?' January slipped a copy of his freedom papers into one boot, a skinning knife into the other. In the doorway between the bedroom and the nursery shared by the boys, Rose stood, barely silhouetted against the glow of the gold-glass veilleuse burning in that chamber. January was conscious of both Professor John and Baby Xander, sitting up in bed with bright, round, fascinated eyes.

Arithmus nodded. 'Quincy says that it's going to rain really hard just after midnight – that's why I ran all the way here – that's what Barnabas was looking at, up in the *couple-of*, what the clouds looked like.'

'Cumulonimbus moving in,' agreed Rose, and Arithmus bobbed his head in earnest delight that somebody else understood the specifics. 'And the barometer's down to twenty-eight—'

'What kind of barometer do you have?'

She hid her smile at the eager inconsequence of the question, understanding it. 'I have three, actually. The one I usually use is a sympiesometer style. The storm will be heavy,' she went on, cutting in over their guest's further commentary on the taxonomy of air-pressure systems. 'There's lightning in the south. I think it's a safe bet that Miss Emmett and Madame de St-Forgeux will be staying at the Truloves' tonight.'

'A sympiesometer's more accurate than a wheel barometer,' persisted Arithmus, not to be put off his train of thought. 'Mr Wishart – Miss Belle's uncle – was working on one that didn't need liquid. Nestor was going to sneak away from Trulove's the minute it started raining,' he continued, handing January a dry and much-patched third-best jacket. 'Quincy had all his things packed and ready, with everybody else's. They had food, and fresh clothes, and even some guns, in case there was trouble with Billy Thunder – that's the man who said he'd take everybody on his fishing boat down across Lake Borgne and then through the marshes to meet Mr Wellington' – he pronounced the name carefully – 'on Cat Island, who'll take them up to Philadelphia. Is that coat tarpaulin fabric?' He reached to finger the heavy, rubberized garment Rose had turned to fetch from the nursery armoire.

'It is.'

'Jesse Wellington?' January had heard the former whaler's name from his own contacts with the Underground Railroad in New Orleans. Supposedly a coastal trader, Wellington's gray-hulled sloop, the *China Bride,* had more secret compartments in its hull than an acre of rabbit tunnels.

The African nodded. 'I was supposed to go with them,' he said. 'But I never really was going to. I promised Belle – Miss Wishart . . . I only told them I was. Quincy said, the minute we were out of there, somebody was bound to find Mr Grice's body, and then they'd hang us all, even though we didn't kill him.'

'Do you know who did?' Rose's voice was conversational, and Arithmus appeared surprised at the question.

'No. Just Barnabas went into his room on Twelfth Night – or I guess Thirteenth Morning, because it was five minutes after four – and found him dead in bed, with his eyes open and his face all twisted up, like Mr Wishart's was . . .' His hands flinched, as if trying to chase away a memory.

'There was a lot more laudanum in Mr Grice's colic medicine

than there usually is – Quincy smelled it, and said some had been added. But because he'd had colic that evening, and didn't go to the party, Quincy said, somebody would accuse us all of plotting to kill him. Quincy threw the medicine out,' he added, 'and sunk the bottle in the bayou. But he said Linney would tell the City Guards if she heard anything about it, because she thinks she's better than the rest of us. She does,' he added. 'I don't know why.'

'You'd better get going.' Rose helped January on with the cumbersome mackintosh, her voice filled with carefully concealed annoyance and regret. 'Much as I'd love to hear the rest of this, you're going to get soaked, going out to Gentilly.'

January regarded her for a moment in the murky reflection of the night-light, reading in her face what she wouldn't admit to him. Before she had borne the boys – before she had become mistress of her own school – she would have insisted on joining the expedition, and would, he knew, have been of great value for her observations and her sharper knowledge of scientific detail. Like him, as Dryden had once said, she had given hostages to the gods of fortune. This was the price she had paid, for her school, for the children she adored. For the position she held, and the day-to-day joy of passing along to those five girls sleeping upstairs the juicy meat of knowledge, the curious satisfactions of mathematics, the delight in the arts of chemistry and the otherworld wonderment of reading the sky. The price she had paid to be what she was, and to teach those curious, eager young souls to be what *they* were.

He took her hands, drew her into a kiss. 'Thank you,' he said simply, treasuring her. Treasuring her strength, the knowledge that whatever happened, she would guard the home, the sons, the true riches of their life. 'Will you do me a favor, my nightingale? When Gabriel comes in . . .' He knew his nephew wouldn't be back from Alcitoire's restaurant until after four and be damned to your curfew. 'Would you send him out to Mamzelle Wishart's?'

Rose's spectacles flashed gold ovals of firelight in the gloom.

'I don't know what things will look like when I get out to Les Cyprès,' he said. 'If there is trouble – and I have no idea what kind – I'd rather Mamzelle and Zizi were in some place less . . . isolated. Have Gabriel bring them here, at least until we know what's happened. Mamzelle Wishart is already suspected of having a hand in her former husband's disappearance—'

'She didn't do it!' Arithmus's body tensed, as if ready to physically defend his friend.

'I know that.' But in January's mind remained the knowledge that Belle Wishart very well could have murdered the man who had trapped her, used her – almost certainly raped her. She had known about her uncle's poisons. Had lived for sixteen years with them close at hand.

He shifted his shoulders uneasily within the clumsy tent of the mackintosh, listening to the ferocity of the rain increase. 'We need to go,' he said. 'There aren't more than a few hours left of the night, and I have no idea what I'm going to find at Les Cyprès.'

'She'll be here,' promised Rose. 'And I'd better hear every detail the minute you get back.'

Once clear of the new suburb of Marigny, the rainy night was bleakly still. Even at this late hour, dim lamps burned behind the shutters of some of those tiny 'shotgun' cottages, and drifts of song floated on the wet air like smoke. 'Alle Jahre Wieder' or 'Kathleen Mavourneen', to the reedy richness of concertinas or the squeak of fiddles. King cakes were undoubtedly being served, to groans or cheers when someone got the bean . . .

Islands of lamplight in the freezing night. Islands of rest, of warmth, of love, that kept the heart from drowning alone in the dark.

Further into the miprière, lantern glow illuminated makeshift canvas shelters, or made gold needles between the rough planks of huts built of dismembered flatboats. Now and then, the grimy gleam from the doorways of seedy taverns among the trees, the barely seen smolder of a lantern hung above a brothel door. January kept the slide over the glass of his own lantern, listened, as well as he could, to the night around him. Rain roaring on cypress trees, on swamp-oak, on sheets of standing water, and on the impermeable rubber sleeves of his own mackintosh, would have quenched the advancing footsteps of an army of slave stealers.

If there are slave stealers out tonight, I hope they all catch pneumonia and die and I don't think even the Virgin Mary would scold me for saying so . . .

'So what did Barnabas see,' he asked, 'when he looked down from the cupola of Les Cyprès? I take it Quincy wrote those letters and got somebody to send them from Mobile—'

'Nestor did,' said Arithmus. 'Mr Grice never knew he could write. Nobody did. Nestor's old master back in Natchez taught him, and how to copy other people's handwriting, so he could cheat them in business. He got arrested and Nestor got sold. Nestor's brother Frank is a carter, who goes back and forth to Mobile all the time. Quincy and the others hid Mr Grice's body in the old woodstore,' he went on, picking up his Twelfth Night narrative where he'd left it off, like Gabriel locating the vinegar bottle in the midst of preparing a salad, without even looking in its direction. 'I came back from being with Belle – with Miss Wishart – when they were doing that, at sixteen minutes after four Thursday morning. Nestor said Frank could get Billy Thunder and get everybody across the lake to Cat Island. But it took a couple of days to find Mr Wellington, so Nestor had to write those letters to Miss Emmett and Persephone, so everyone would think he was still alive and just out of town. Miss Emmett never believed it, though.'

'Miss Emmett needed Mr Grice's permission to marry the man she wants,' returned January thoughtfully. 'Or if he refused it, she needed him to be dead. If he were dead, and her marriage to a Hungarian prince a *fait accompli*, I don't think any of her father's second cousins could get a court to annul the marriage.' *And if Miss Emmett hadn't been at the Granvilles' ball on Twelfth Night, I'd start wondering* why *she was so certain her guardian was dead, and where* she *was . . .*

For she, he understood, would have known as well as Belle Wishart did, about the poisons among Deverel Wishart's effects even yet. She'd have seen them in Natchez, and in the house at Les Cyprès.

But we do *know where she was . . .*

And His impecunious Highness . . .

'Who brought Miss Grice back to Les Cyprès this evening?' he asked after a time. 'Was she taken ill again?' *A curious coincidence, if so . . .* 'She must have gone with Miss Emmett to the Truloves' . . .'

'She did,' agreed Arithmus. 'And Miss Emmett was swearing

she wouldn't go, she was so angry at the prince. But then the next minute she was asking Madame Persephone, would the prince be there, did she think? But why would she ask if she didn't want to see him ever again? He must have been there, though,' he added. 'Because Miss Grice was sitting on the same horse with him, behind his saddle, like little girls ride – not sideways, I mean, but with their feet on both sides of the horse, and her arms around his waist. She was in her party dress,' he added. 'The pretty green one with the wings.'

'She left the ball,' asked January, not precisely incredulous but wanting to make sure of what he was hearing, '*unchaperoned*, in the rain, sitting on the back of Prince Corvinus's horse?'

'Oh, yes.' Arithmus halted for a moment, to regard him with wide, unsurprised eyes. 'Miss Grice would go anywhere with His Highness. She's been in love with him ever since he saw her home from the Twelfth Night ball. He walked her up to the porch, and they kissed before she went on into the house, behind the pillars where Mrs Miragouin couldn't see them.'

Unseen in the pitch darkness below them, rain hammered the waters of the bayou. Veils of Spanish moss moved like rustling ghosts in the glimmer of the lantern. 'The prince brought *Miss Grice* home?' January shook his head, wondering how Arithmus's insanely retentive mind could have made that kind of mistake. 'That was Miss Emmett he brought – with Madame Miragouin. Miss Grice came home before midnight, sick, with the prince's valet—'

'No, that was Miss Emmett,' Arithmus corrected him firmly. 'She was wearing Miss Grice's dress, with those wings on it and the green mask with the flowers, but it was Miss Emmett. Her feet are smaller than Miss Grice's, so she was still wearing her red-and-gold shoes. I saw them outside the door of their room. I thought Miss Grice's dress was prettier than Miss Emmett's anyway,' he went on. 'Fairies are nice, even though there's no such thing. The goddess Menhit isn't nice. She's not real, either, but she killed all the children of Publius Antius . . .'

It took January a moment to recognize the name of the Roman master, from the Curse legend . . .

'. . . and it wasn't their fault, that their father and mother were bad people. And she killed four of their other slaves as well, just because that's what curses do.' He shook his head. 'But when Miss Emmett came home sick, she was wearing Miss Grice's fairy dress, and her own shoes. And when I came back from meeting Belle – Miss Wishart – I saw Miss Grice, in Miss Emmett's dress, get down out of the carriage. And when the prince walked her up to the porch, where Mrs Miragouin couldn't see them, he grabbed her in his arms and pushed the mask back up from her face and kissed her—'

Arithmus broke off, his face contracted with the sudden tumble of emotions, the memory of a kiss witnessed. Of passion suddenly before his eyes.

'He kissed her . . . a lot.' His voice halted, as if he were forced again to watch the kiss. Forced to witness his own feelings for Belle Wishart. What he would do, if chance ever permitted him to take her in his arms.

Or had he done that already? January wondered if it was memory that made his hands twitch again, the echo of when he was eighteen?

'He said . . .' Arithmus suddenly turned back to him, an automaton once more. His dark eyes returned to their faraway expression as he rebuilt the memories and ticked them off on his fingers. 'He said, *My God I've wanted to do that since the moment I saw you.* And she said, *Serafin, Serafin* – his name is Serafin,' he informed January unnecessarily, '*I would die for you.* And he said, *Beloved*, and kissed her again. I was just around the corner of the porch and there were candles burning in the lanterns on either side of the door. Mrs Miragouin was still in the carriage. And anyway Mrs Miragouin is so nearsighted she couldn't have told Miss Grice from Miss Emmett even without a mask.'

He frowned, concentrating on his memory of the scene.

'What time was this?' asked January softly.

'Four ten in the morning. I got back into the house at four sixteen, and Quincy grabbed me by the arm and said Mr Grice was dead and we had to get him out of his room and hide him in the woodstore. But that's how I know Miss Grice was in love with His Highness and would do anything for him, I guess, even die, though that's a lot . . .'

His frown deepened. 'I'd die for Miss Belle,' he added then. 'If she asked me to. Or if it would save her from being hurt. But

I'd rather . . .' He hesitated, and January wondered if he saw again that kiss in his mind. 'Anyway,' Arithmus went on, 'if she'd die for him, she'd sure sneak away from Mrs Trulove's party tonight with him, even though Madame Persephone would say it wasn't ladylike, and it would get Miss Emmett mad at her. But if Miss Emmett never wanted to see him again, I don't see why she'd be mad.'

He puzzled it over for a moment. 'Barnabas said she went in and got something from the house. He couldn't see what. Then they walked off into the woods. I think . . .' His face suddenly contracted with distress. 'I think His Highness must have killed her. That's what Quincy said, anyway. But I don't understand why he would have done that, if he loved her, and she loved him. She was nice,' he added sadly. 'She always spoke kindly to me. Everybody said she wasn't pretty, but I thought she was.'

'What time was this?'

'What time did Barnabas see her?' Arithmus fell into step with January once more along the shell path, the rain lightening, as if pausing for breath, before worse to come. The smell of the bayou cold and rank as the river Styx. 'Or what time did somebody kill her?'

'What time did Barnabas see them?'

The younger man frowned, mentally estimating times. January corrected himself, 'What time did Barnabas come down and tell people he'd seen them?' If the house servants were planning to decamp *en masse*, anyone who saw white folks pottering around would almost certainly come pelting down from the cupola with the warning . . .

'Eight thirty-seven. The clock in the hall is three minutes fast and it said eight forty. Quincy had Corena go back up on to the *couple-of* and watch all around the house, but nobody came, and at nine thirty-one he sent Barnabas and Joe out to have a look around, and at five minutes to ten Barnabas came back in, carrying Miss Grice's body.

'Her face was all twisted up,' he added, and again his voice cracked with distress. 'Like she'd seen something horrible, like a lion or a manticore or a dragon coming up out of the bayou, only there's no such thing. Like Mr Grice's was, and Mr Wishart's, back in France. Quincy and Corena looked for how she'd died but they said there was no marks on her, not as if she'd been strangled, or shot, or stabbed. We laid her on Barnabas's bed, because it was downstairs in the kitchen wing, and Quincy said, we'd better check Miss Emmett's room, to see if somebody was going to say we'd stolen Miss Emmett's jewelry before we ran away. And her jewelry was all gone.'

January stopped again, alarm bells ringing in his mind. A gust of wind drove rain against his back, like the ragged sleeve of a drowned ghost. *Of course. That's what Josie Grice went into the house for . . .*

Wasn't it?

Arithmus's voice went on, 'Madame Persephone's was gone, too. But that was the only thing gone from her room. But Miss Emmett's dressing table was also where she kept her letters from all her sweethearts, with different-colored ribbons around them, and the ones from His Highness were gone. They had a purple ribbon on them. Purple is a royal color,' he explained. 'The Phoenicians used to make it from the shells of the murex—'

January bit his tongue not to tell him that he knew all about the Phoenicians and the murexes. He knew from experience that this would only prolong the explanation . . .

And after several more digressions on Deverel Wishart's experiments with reproducing color-fast crimsons and purples, Arithmus abruptly returned to the original subject: 'The glass tube was gone, too. From Miss Emmett's dressing table.'

'Glass tube?'

'The one that was in the room back at Laburnum where Belle kept all her uncle's things,' explained Arithmus. 'It had five steel bodkins in it, the kind ladies used to pin up their hair with, Belle said. She'd sealed it up with sealing wax and told me never, not ever, to open it. But then after . . . after Belle left – after we came down here to New Orleans – it was in Miss Emmett's room, and Miss Emmett opened it, because the sealing wax was broken and one of the bodkins was gone.'

'When?'

'When I went to find notepaper Friday morning for Nestor to write one of those notes from Mobile,' responded Arithmus promptly. 'All the paper in the study was gone, and Miss Emmett never wrote anything. She had paper and pens in her dressing table where she kept all those letters from men. I borrowed four sheets of paper,' he went on, again ticking them off on his fingers, 'and a pen, and a bottle of blue-black Maynard and Noyes ink, and I saw then that the glass tube had been opened, and one of the bodkins taken, and that the letters with the purple ribbon around them were from His Highness. But I couldn't say anything because I wasn't supposed to be in Miss Emmett's room.'

'And did you see,' said January quietly, recalling Henri's words about *Strychnos toxifera*, 'when you brought Miss Grice's body back to the house, whether Miss Grice had a wound – it would have been a tiny pinprick, just enough to draw blood – on her neck, or her shoulder . . .'

Arithmus nodded. 'It was just like the one on the back of Mr Grice's hand when we found him,' he said.

TWENTY-ONE

'Damn it!'

January stopped again in his tracks. Arithmus stopped, too, regarding him inquiringly by that flicker of lantern-light.

'He's gone for Belle.' January turned, strode two steps back along the shell road beside Bayou Gentilly, then had to go back and seize Arithmus by the arm and pull him along. 'The prince. Prince Serafin.'

'Why would he—?'

'Because when she hears about the wounds on Miss Grice and old Creon, she'll guess what happened. Listen . . .' January cast back in his mind for anything he remembered about the paths through the ciprière, between Bayou Gentilly where they now stood, and Bayou St-John. There had to be some way to cut off the distance it would take to follow Gentilly all the way back into town.

In the dark? In the rain? With the ciprière three-quarters flooded?

How many hours' start does Serafin have?

'Do you know what day it was, that Mr Grice arrived in Paris, before Deverel Wishart died?'

'Friday,' responded Arithmus, with apparently no sense of *non sequitur*. 'Friday the eleventh of December. Mr Grice told the Sûreté he'd come on Saturday and went straight out to the chateau, but it was Friday, because later M'sieu Daucourt – the cook – and M'sieu Bloque the butler got into an argument because M'sieu went out to get fish, only it turned out Mr Grice was a Congregationalist and didn't care if he ate fish on Friday or not. But that was later, when M'sieu Bloque and M'sieu Daucourt had the argument, just before Belle – Miss Wishart – only she was Madame Grice then . . .' And his face flinched again, at the recollection of grief. 'Before we left for America,' he finished, in a beaten voice.

And then, puzzled, 'Why would the prince want to hurt Belle?'

Lantern-glow sprinkled fragments of brightness on the wet shells, the weeds beside the narrow trace along the bayou. From the dark of the woods to their right, January heard the endless soggy rushing of the trees, the clatter of the rain in growing sheets and pools between the cypresses: three miles to where Bayou St-Jean intersected Bayou Gentilly – Bayou Sauvage, it was called closer to town – where the modest wooden houses of artisans and working folk petered out towards the lake. Another two, along St-John to Bayou P'tit-Jean – which could be flooded knee-deep by this time – and thence to the muddy path that led to the house Belle Wishart sheltered in . . .

. . . with Zizi-Marie.

Damn it . . .

'Did Mr Grice have callers the next day?' asked January, knowing Arithmus would know. It is the nature of servants, he knew, to talk about their masters, and in all probability the discussion about the imposition of shopping for fish had not ended there. 'Before he went to Palongeux to tell M'sieu Wishart of his brother Stuart's death?'

'Yes,' Arithmus affirmed. 'M'sieu Daucourt said it wasn't respectable – M'sieu Daucourt didn't ever like Mr Grice. M'sieu Daucourt said, the man wore a mask but the hostlers at the Six Crows around the corner on Rue l'Éperon said that the gentleman came in a two-horse closed brougham with a matched pair of black-stockinged bays.'

'That doesn't sound cheap.' January's voice was grim.

'It wasn't,' returned Arithmus promptly. 'M'sieu Grezolles told M'sieu Wishart the last time they dined together that he'd paid two hundred francs for a carriage team that weren't well-matched, and his brougham cost a hundred and fifty francs, and it wasn't new and he said he'd have to have the upholstery redone.'

'A rich man,' said January, 'who didn't want his identity known.' And, seeing his companion still uncomprehending, 'I think it must have been the Duc d'Aveline who visited Grice the day after Grice arrived in Paris – a day earlier than he later said he had. D'Aveline would have had at least one informer in the household, to have arranged the burglary. So he'd have known that the business partner of Stuart Wishart was in town: a man who knew of the Wishart brothers' affairs and could get him information about the household. I think d'Aveline offered Grice money – a lot of money – for the Curse Manuscript, and the bronze of Menhit that went with it. And I think Grice guessed that after the burglaries, Mr Wishart wouldn't have left those things in the house. That he took them – and hid them – in the Chateau Palongeux.'

He halted again, listening. Fighting his instinct to unsheathe the lantern fully, knowing that this would only minimally increase the light it shed, but would brighten the beacon that could attract slave stealers like a lamp-flame attracts the foul, rattle-winged palmetto-bugs.

If not slave stealers, pattyrollers . . .
We can't get caught. Not now.

Arithmus was gazing at him in a kind of enlightened amazement, putting together what had, to him, for years been nothing more than discrete fragments of information, conversations remembered, details noted in the vast uncataloged library of his recollection. He said, slowly, 'You're right. You must be right. And if Mr Grice knew all that on Friday, and got the spare set of keys M'sieu Grezolles left with M'sieu Wishart that was in his desk-drawer, he could have come out to the chateau that Sunday night, when poor M'sieu Wishart was drunk . . .'

January had started off again, Arithmus keeping up easily with his long strides, his brow pulled down with anger as he recalled those terrible winter days. 'Belle's smart,' he said at length. 'Belle would remember how Mr Wishart looked, if somebody told her about how Mr Grice looked, and Miss Grice.'

'She would.' January held the lantern low as they walked – this was not the night to fall into a bayou, any more than it was a night to go striking off through the woods in the hopes of reaching Bayou P'tit-Jean before Prince Serafin did. 'And she would know what it meant. And Prince Serafin knows it.'

Serafin, he thought, who had the moneylender Mason Spurcid breathing down his neck . . . Serafin, who was in such a panic to marry money that at the prospect of delay, he would jettison his accomplices in one murder and seek the hand of the Widow Redfern, rather than do the obvious thing and write to his parents back in that vaguely defined Mitteleuropean principality . . .

Whose existence nobody, in fact, had ever seemed to be able to verify.

Not that the dazzled citizens of Louisiana had ever, to January's knowledge, tried to do anything of the sort.

Except, perhaps, Creon Grice himself.

'That's how Grice got hold of the Curse Manuscript,' he went on quietly, bending his head against a particularly vicious gust of rain. 'Once the chateau was empty, and he was married to Miss Wishart, he had the leisure to let himself in with her Uncle Deverel's keys and search the place from top to bottom. Possibly he guessed that Deverel Wishart was the man responsible for this new spate of supernatural occurrences, the blood on the walls and the wailing in the attics on windy nights. Wishart told you to pretend you were terrified of entering the place, didn't he? He had to make sure nobody from the village would go looking for that "buried treasure" and find the manuscript instead.

'I think it must have been his brass-cornered trunk that he hurled down the stairs, then dragged quickly into that cupboard under the stair before lying down himself. He probably had a little chicken or pig blood, left over from writing on the walls, to smear on the balustrade – the cut on his forehead could have been done with his own razor. Like those "ghostly fingermarks" on his cheek, which were exactly the size and shape of the bowl of a salt-spoon like the one we found in his room.'

Arithmus said, 'Ow!' sympathetically, and put a hand to his own cheek. 'It was to make everybody think a ghost went after him.'

'It was because when he saw little Musette running around the halls, he knew *we'd* guess the haunting was a hoax.'

'So that was all make-believe!' Arithmus stopped in his tracks for a moment, dazzled by the first lightning-strike of inspiration in his life. 'He only pretended he fell down the stairs . . . I liked Musette,' he added sadly. Before them, the waters of bayou and swamp had mingled to drown the track along its bank.

At least it's too cold for gators . . . Water like the leaden rivers of Hell slopped over the tops of January's boots as he waded across to the marginally higher ground on the other side of the slough. 'And she liked you,' he said, truthfully, recalling the way the little dog had always trotted to greet Arithmus in the chateau's kitchen-court. 'But Wishart didn't take his poisons with him to the chateau, did he? He brought things to study plants—'

'And his notes about alkaline cleavages of chlorine,' provided the Nubian helpfully. 'He was trying to duplicate Moldenhawer's experiments with chlorinating lime. Back at the house, he knocked himself out completely two or three times.'

'Which is where Quincy got whatever it was he used on me.'

Which had been brought down courtesy of Quincy . . . He remembered what Olympe had told him, of the casual use Grice made of the housemaids. Probably not Linney, who would chatter to her mistress, but the maid Susie. Possibly even Corena, to 'teach her a lesson' if he thought she was being 'uppity'.

Men often did that.

Arithmus nodded. 'M'sieu Wishart taught Belle – Miss Wishart – all about it,' he said. 'He must have told Miss Jondrette about it, too, back all those years ago, because the first day they were at Laburnum, Miss Jondrette told Miss Emmett not to go near any of those things, or break the seal on those that were sealed up, because they were poison. That's when Miss Emmett saw Sittina-Menhit.'

And though he knew no ghosts, no curses, no pitiless lion-faced goddess had been involved, still January shivered, remembering the agony on Deverel Wishart's face, when they'd found him on the fouled, naked mattress in the southeast turret, the empty cognac bottle on the floor nearby. *Imposuit dea manum . . .*

'Did Mr Wishart have a pinprick on him, when he was found that morning?'

'No,' said Arithmus immediately.

That doesn't mean . . .

'But the bandage on his head had been changed,' the younger man went on. 'Where he cut it on the balustrade falling down the stairs. Or maybe, like you said, he cut it himself. What you put on him was linen – that you brought in your medical kit – and fastened with pins. The one he had on that morning . . .' His slight frown deepened, calling back to himself images from among the thousands – the hundreds of thousands – that had been dumped into the fathomless well of his memory, like calling cards in a box. Unsorted and unclassified, but each as ineradicable as a first kiss or the discovery of friendship. 'It was muslin, like the sheets at the house in Paris. It was whiter than the linen, as if it had been bleached. And it was tied with knots.'

It would have been childishly easy, thought January, for Creon Grice to half-rouse a man in the drunken stupor of grief at his brother's death, to help him along the corridor in the dead of night, to the 'haunted' turret room. To push back the old bandage, roll the poisoned tip of a bodkin against the open cut that Wishart had inflicted on himself two nights before – inflicted along with the three little burns on his face before he'd tipped that brass-cornered trunk down the stairs.

'Grice must have known about the poison,' he said, 'if he worked for both brothers back in England.' That coarse-boned face returned to his mind, the dust-colored, calculating eyes. 'He'd have known that much about the contents of Deverel Wishart's workroom. And it wouldn't have taken Miss Emmett long to guess that he wasn't about to let her marry anyone but himself. You don't happen to know if he started looking into His Highness's credentials, when he saw Miss Emmett making sheep's-eyes at the prince?'

'He did,' agreed Arithmus promptly. 'He wrote to Mr Davenport – that's his lawyer – about it just before we all came down here. Madame de St-Forgeux told Miss Emmett about it, and said she'd wondered that, too.' They had reached the confluence – if such it could be called – of the Bayou Sauvage and the greater Bayou St-John, now a rain-swollen wasteland of ankle-deep swamp that stretched away between the trees. 'The day we were in the steamboat, coming down from Natchez. She said anybody could claim he was a Hungarian prince, and who could prove it if he wasn't? She said, most Americans couldn't find Hungary on a map. Miss Emmett screamed at her and said she'd have Mr Grice send her away for being impudent – I didn't know a white woman could be sent away like that, if she wasn't a governess or something—'

'She can't be.' January squatted on the edge of the sheet of water, held the lantern low, in quest of what remained of the plank bridge that he knew had been around here somewhere.

'Miss Grice locked herself in her cabin and cried. Miss Emmett said she'd die if she couldn't marry His Highness . . .'

'And His Highness' – January dug, gingerly, in the freezing

water, in quest of what seemed to be the near end of a couple of planks – 'if he *is* a Highness – was being pursued by money-lenders. Moneylenders don't often threaten to kill. A more common threat is mutilation. He *couldn't* let that happen. He had to marry the heiress *soon*. Or *somebody* wealthy. *Ibn al-harim*,' he added, as the planks turned out to be only broken ends, and Arithmus grinned suddenly, at the Arabic oath he hadn't heard in nearly twenty years.

Prince Serafin escorting Miss Grice in her green fairy-garb, and Miss Emmett in the golden robes, the lioness face of Menhit herself, to the Granvilles' Twelfth Night ball – had that been less than a week ago? The girl in the fairy-frock suddenly taken ill, driven by Gaspar – probably, like Doktor Boehler, an accomplice rather than a servant – back to Les Cyprès, to leave the goddess's red-and-gold shoes outside her door, while everyone assumed that the girl in gold, masked in the face of the lioness, was in fact Miss Emmett on the prince's arm.

He thought of that silent house, as Miss Emmett slipped in through the side door, and crept upstairs. Her chaperone sunk in laudanum-augmented dreams at one end of the upper floor, her guardian – the man who sought to keep her from her fairy-tale prince, her Own True Love – slumbering stertorously at the other end of the house. Readying the house itself to move the heiress into the room next to his, away from anyone who might hear her – as he had moved that other young girl, sixteen years before, whom he had wanted to force into marriage into a room where he could quietly enter at night.

The lion-faced goddess who avenged the wrongs done against the helpless – against those who only wanted to love and be loved – had undoubtedly smiled, watching Miss Emmett slide barefooted into her guardian's room with a poisoned bodkin in her hand. And passion in her heart.

There was silence between the two men for a time, as they picked their squishy way through the knee-deep slough along Bayou P'tit-Jean, January reflecting again on the several miles ofciprière that lay between them and that tiny cabin. *Blessed Mary ever-virgin, confuse Prince Serafin's steps. Lead him, like Puck leading those poor silly lovers in* A Midsummer Night's Dream, *now here, now there, in the rainy dark of the trees. Lead us to them in time . . .*

Olympe, he thought, would have prayed that prayer to Menhit herself.

Imposuit dea manum . . .

'The prince had to get rid of Miss Grice,' he said, after long quiet. 'She was the only one who knew that the substitution had been made. God knows what His Highness and Miss Emmett told her, either that night or when Grice turned up missing. Josie Grice knew that Miss Emmett had gone back to the house when she was seen to be at the ball. She knew that her Uncle Creon disappeared that night – and she may have wondered why her friend was so certain that her guardian was dead. If the girls quarreled over Prince Serafin, she may even have asked.'

In a sad, small voice, Arithmus repeated, 'She was nice to me. Miss Emmett is always mean. They're both kind of stupid,' he added. Accurately, January thought.

But Belle was a witness, too. Belle, who had been at the Chateau Palongeux the night her uncle died. Belle, who was almost certainly in a position to guess – as he himself had guessed – how it was her uncle had died, and why. Who could have guessed where Grice had gotten that quarter-million francs on which he'd founded his own fortune, and who might guess, eventually, what had happened to her former husband – particularly if his body were found by men searching for a dozen absconding slaves.

She was one of only four in America – two of whom wouldn't be permitted to testify in court against a white man – who had seen the expression of contorted horror on Wishart's face. Who could testify that yes, it could be caused by the action of poison and yes, it was the same as the look worn by Creon Grice, when the agent of the goddess Menhit came for him.

TWENTY-TWO

The house on Bayou P'tit-Jean was empty. Its door stood open; a single lamp burned on the table, which was no longer by the window but in a corner – the only piece of furniture in the room still standing on its legs. Every dish and pot and basket on the meager shelves had been broken, every chair overturned. Belle Wishart's sewing basket lay against a wall, its contents strewn at large. In the bedroom, the few items of clothing had been pulled from their pegs on the wall, tossed over the naked bed ropes of the bed the two women had shared. The mattress had been slit, the dried moss that had stuffed it lying in trampled lumps.

The ruffle of one of the petticoats had been torn off. Blood copiously dribbled the floorboards near where the table had been. Droplets had fallen, isolated, on the threshold, and a few in the bedroom. Kneeling, lamp in hand, to look more closely at the largest puddle, January saw grains of what looked like gunpowder among the muddied tracks on the floor.

Arithmus sobbed, 'Belle . . .'

The tracks themselves, even with the cottage's single surviving lamp held close, were barely readable in the gloom. Trying to remember everything Abishag Shaw had ever told him, January thought that one pair of feet had been shod in narrow, stylish, square-toed boots with thin soles. *Does Prince Serafin wear such boots?* The others – one set noticeably wider than the other – looked heavier, with visible stitching and broader heels. Looking again, January noted that all the tracks were much the same length.

Three men the same height . . . One heavier than the other two.

Nowhere did he see the smudges and smears, as if someone had fought and kicked against being dragged outside.

Virgin Mary, Mother of God . . .
Or Menhit the avenger of lovers . . .
Did either of you really help them get away?

Tell me what I owe you . . .

He got to his feet, strode to the windows, checked the shutters – and yes, in the front, and in the back by the rear door, and at the shutters of the bedroom window . . . all were marked with the burns of a powder-flash. Someone had opened the shutters a crack, to fire through.

'Did Mamzelle Wishart have a weapon here?'

Panic turned Arithmus's nod into a childlike jerk. 'A Brown Bess musket. She kept the powder and ball in a brass box her father had used hunting. She's hurt,' he added, staring ashen-faced at the blood. 'They came in and shot her and took her away—'

'I don't think so.' January opened the cottage's rear door, studied the dirt floor of the lean-to. A little scramble of scuffs, barely visible on the hard-packed earth. The smell of rain, the dull roaring of wind and cloudburst in the trees, audible through the lean-to's open outer door. A trail of drips that matched the muddy scuffs of the three pairs of boots. 'See? They got out the back.'

'She's hurt.' Arithmus's hands fluttered over his chin, his lips, his throat at the sight of the large blood-spot on the earth just outside the doorway, where the overhang of the roof guarded it from the rain. 'She'll die—'

'She's got a bandage over it,' January reminded him, remembering the torn petticoat flounce. 'If she was that badly hurt, she couldn't have run.' Was Zizi strong enough to carry the small and delicate woman?

Not for a long distance . . .

Raising the lamp, January saw only sheets of water, broken by the goblin heads of cypress-knees, where he had plowed five days before through creeper and fern. The trail he'd followed from Les Cyprès – the trail Arithmus had taken to meet Belle five nights ago – made a coarse trace of glittery earth, away into the darkness.

He looked back at the boot tracks, the dripped water, on the lean-to floor.

'It looks like they followed them.' As a child he had almost automatically – as a matter of survival – taken note of small landmarks, oddly shaped tree-limbs or a lone magnolia growing among palmettos. More than once he had had to find his way in near-darkness, through territory observed in the day and coming from the other direction. Following this trail with Shaw, he had mentally marked where the courses of old bayous and forgotten streams had left ridges of high ground. Had logged, as if on a mental map, old cheniers crowned with scraggy oaks; the stove-in ruin of what had looked like the shelter raised by some runaway, back when it was possible for a runaway to live this close to town, or that little cemetery on Chickasaw Chenier with its crumbling brick bench-tombs.

Can I find my way back along that trail again? In the dark and in the rain?

Zizi-Marie knows this part of the ciprière. When she was little, Olympe would take her along to collect herbs.

'See if you can find another lantern,' he said. 'They may be headed towards the lake – or they may try to find shelter downstream of here. You'll still find runaway camps up on the cheniers someplace, or trappers as you get further from town.'

Or slave stealers. He touched the pistol, wrapped in its fold of oilskin under his rubbery carapace of mackintosh.

'They're ahead of us—'

'They don't know the ground.' January recalled the prince's boasts of prowess as a hunter, his braggart quest to find a cougar (of all things!) this close to town. He, too, would be an experienced tracker. But the last thing he needed was for Arithmus to panic. 'My niece does. We may easily get to them before the prince does.'

The rain had lightened again, whispering in the marshes like the tweeting of the damned on the banks of the Styx. Arithmus located another pierced tin lantern in the back of the cabin's single cupboard, and candles lying on the floor where they'd been dumped out of a box. The tiny threads of light barely outlined the wet trunks of the closest trees, the dripping glitter of Spanish moss overhead. Something glinted in a tangle of swamp-laurel. Reaching in (after cautiously prodding the place with a stick), January drew out a pair of round-lensed spectacles. Belle's. The oak overhead had sheltered the place enough that the mud could hold a track, a long, narrow foot almost certainly Zizi-Marie's. Heavy boot-prints nearly obscured it. January wished he had Shaw's skill as a tracker, and, illogically, cursed the Kaintuck for not being on hand.

And as long as we're cursing, why don't we wish for a party of sympathetic, well-armed hunters who congenitally hate Hungarians and will shoot them on sight?

'Is that Gaspar with His Majesty?' whispered Arithmus. 'Gaspar will do anything he says—'

'If what Her Ladyship suspected is true,' returned January slowly, 'I think Gaspar may be Serafin's brother. Without that mustache he'd look very like him, you know. And Doktor Boehler as well.'

'But Doktor Boehler was always trying to chase the girls away.' The younger man sounded genuinely puzzled. 'If the prince wants to marry Miss Emmett for her money—'

'Haven't you ever had someone tell you that you can't have something?' asked January. 'And it made you want it more?'

Arithmus blinked. 'No.'

No, thought January with a sigh. Opposition had neither increased nor diminished his love for Belle: *Love is not love/Which alters when it alteration finds . . .*

Shakespeare's words returned to him. *It is an ever-fixed mark . . . It is the star to every wand'ring bark . . .*

And Arithmus always needed things explained. 'Many people,' he said, 'if you tell them they can't have something, they'll move the heavens and the earth to get hold of it – especially spoiled young ladies who want to score over every other young lady in the parish by marrying a prince.'

Arithmus thought about that. 'That's stupid,' he said finally.

'I never said human beings were smart. But that only works—'

A scream ripped the darkness, like rending cloth, terrifying and almost unreal. Arithmus seized January's arm: 'Belle . . .'

'Bobcat, I think,' January whispered. 'They can sound almost like a woman.' *Please Virgin Mother of God – St Francis the guardian of beasts – please make it be a bobcat and not a girl in terror and pain . . .*

Silence then, and the splosh of the two men's boots where the ridge they walked dipped below that rain-riddled surface of the swamp. January hated to do it, but raised his lantern, strained his eyes through the darkness for sight of another trail. Cudgeled his mind, for recollection of this route – which he'd only seen in daylight and dry weather and coming from the other direction . . .

Like the child he had been. And in those days, too, you actually *did* stand a fair chance of encountering a yellow-eyed cougar, as well as the current threats of bobcats or gators or slave stealers moving silent among the trees . . .

Far off, the crack of a gun.

January whispered, 'That way . . .'

Every instinct screamed at him to sheathe the dark-lantern he carried and blow out the candle in the one in Arithmus's hands, but he dared not. The knee-deep water ran into his boots, froze his feet; his free hand slipped a dozen times into the depths of his mackintosh to make sure he could free his pistol of its wrapping easily (*and hope to God it will fire quickly enough before the powder gets wet . . .*).

Another gunshot. The land rose a little, to another ridge. Shells crunched underfoot. *If it's only the three of them – Serafin, Gaspar, Boehler – we might stand some chance, if we can overtake them in time. As long as we're not seen. God knows what kind of story they'll come up with against us in court, if they know who we are.*

How far could Zizi-Marie carry Belle, in this cold and this rain? *It has to be Zizi. Belle couldn't carry Zizi, if it was she who was wounded . . .*

More shells underfoot. Dim with the dimness of eyes long adjusted to darkness, he saw the shapes of trees against sooty sky. Clearing . . . The little chenier where the Chickasaw had once camped, where the swamp-fishers had long ago buried their dead.

He thought there was the tiniest smitch of light there, another lantern on the ground behind the low wall. Pale squares of tombs, hazy through the darkness . . .

A gunshot exploded away to his right – within feet of him, it sounded like. The skirt of the mackintosh jerked and flapped, and January dropped his lantern and plunged off the path, into the water, tried to recall just exactly the point in the darkness where he'd seen the muzzle-flash of a pistol . . .

Another shot, from the direction of the tombs – *Good for you, Zizi (or Belle), aim at the flash . . .*

The crack of returned fire from another direction, and almost instantly the crash of another pistol from the graveyard (*They have two guns?*). Boots splashed in the water behind him and he had only half-turned when a body slammed into his; the butt of a pistol smashed the side of his head as he fell and hands grabbed his throat, held him under the water. He thrashed, bucked, the triple-god-damned-devil-festering mackintosh filled up with water like a bucket, tangling his arms, snagging his movements, holding him down. Somewhere – his lungs aching, his ears filled with water – he thought he heard another gunshot and the man above him spasmed, arched his back, fell sidelong as January twisted beneath him and broke the surface.

A dark form on the edge of the cemetery mound, another crumpled figure at its feet. Light from the lantern beyond the graveyard's low wall picked out the hard gleam of a gun-barrel as January plunged sidelong, under the water again . . . (*Goddamned mackintosh* Goddamned *mackintosh* . . .) He surfaced and saw the man closer, a blur of black mustache on a blur of white face, Gaspar . . .

In the instant that he drew breath for another dodge, he saw the gold flash of eyes in the dark behind the valet, saw the silent leap of *Jesus* Christ *is that a* cougar?

It was indeed a cougar. The valet's convulsing fingers pulled his pistol's trigger – the powder was dry enough to fire, the shot plowing wild into the water yards from where January stood – and Gaspar had time to scream once before the animal – the biggest January had seen since his childhood – seized the back of his neck and broke it with a single hard shake.

Then it stared at January, hissed like an outraged dragon, doubled on itself swift as a snake and bounded away into the darkness, leaving the man broken on the ground.

January ran forward, knowing the man at Gaspar's feet had to be Arithmus. At the same moment lantern-light jerked behind the cemetery wall. He grabbed for Gaspar's pistol – the weapon spent but it could still be used as a club – but Ti-Gall's voice gasped, 'Mr J?' Zizi-Marie came leaping over the wall like a teenaged boy, grabbed his arm, dragged him towards the shelter of the tombs. She had a musket in her other hand. January shook her free, bent again over Arithmus, who turned his head with a groan.

January dragged him up by the back of his jacket, carried him to the wall and dumped him over, then sprang after him (nearly tripping on the damned motherless Hell-begotten mackintosh),

Ti-Gall and Zizi right behind. 'Keep watch,' said January. 'Serafin's still out there.'

Zizi crouched behind the wall like a militiaman behind a cotton-bale watching for the onslaught of British troops – and it hadn't been much lighter, January reflected, in the black fog at Chalmette all those years ago. Ti-Gall hesitated and Zizi pointed with savage impatience to a spot a few yards further along the barrier. The young man dashed to it like a well-trained hunting-dog.

Arithmus sobbed in quick pain as January pulled the sodden jacket from his shoulder and saw where a bullet had grazed him. There was blood in his hair as well. He had fallen back against the wall, stunned, January guessed. He whispered, 'You're all right.'

'Belle—'

Zizi said, 'She's all right. Hurt – shot . . .'

Arithmus started to sit up and January shoved him down again.

Silence then. Green-black utter stillness, and the sea-roar of the rain in the woods. After a long time Zizi whispered, 'Mother of God, that *was* a cougar! I thought I was dreaming.'

Cautiously, January looked over the wall. The cougar – seemingly unconcerned in the rain – had returned to Gaspar's body; January could dimly make out the wet glitter of her fur but little else. Presumably, he thought, Serafin was far enough away – and probably getting farther by the moment – that his scent did not frighten her.

'Did the prince get a look at us?' He returned to crouch again beside Arithmus. A tangle of laurel near the wall gave some shelter from the rain, and January brought one of the lanterns close enough to better examine both the African's wounds. 'Did you see if he came close enough to Arithmus?'

'He was pretty close,' Zizi whispered. She'd torn off her tignon at some point in the pursuit – it must have soaked up rain like a sponge – and the ropes of hair that had been braided up underneath she'd tied in a dripping knot at the back of her neck. January noticed also that she'd cut a square of oilcloth – he dimly recognized the pattern of Belle's tablecloth – to wrap around the lock of her musket. Another packet of the stuff lay on the ground at her feet. *Powder-flask? Musket balls?* 'And there was enough lantern-light that I could see him. That was the first time we knew – knew for sure – who that was that was after us.'

'Where's Mamzelle Wishart?'

She nodded back toward the largest of the tombs, barely a foot-high bench of crumbling bricks now. When he crept near it – still keeping down, though he was increasingly certain that His Highness was halfway back to New Orleans by this time and still running – he saw that a portion of Belle's tablecloth had been anchored to the top of the bench with a couple of bricks, and to the ground two feet away with another couple, forming a minuscule shelter. Rain pattered on the oiled cloth, trickled off it in tiny rivers.

The ground under her must be soaked ...

'What happened?'

Zizi answered him quietly, but with no real effort at concealment, her eyes still on the darkness of the woods around them. 'Turns out the bravest, sweetest man in the world was sneakin' out from his mama's house every night to sit outside Mamzelle Belle's cottage,' she said, and he heard the tremor in her voice. 'Just to make sure the pair of us came to no harm.'

Embarrassed, Ti-Gall said from the other corner of the wall, 'Like I was gonna let you be out there alone, *cher*. Your mama turn me into a frog, if I didn't take care of you. Frogs is *slimy* – and then how'm I gonna explain *that* to Mama? And anyhow,' he added, 'I wasn't sittin' outside in the cold. Mostly I stayed in the kitchen where it was warm.'

January said, 'Thank you,' from the bottom of his heart. There were no other words for it. He slipped beneath the oil-cloth, lifted its clumsy folds up on to his shoulders to keep it over Belle's head as well as his own. Without her spectacles she looked younger, and very fragile. Though the tracks of the past sixteen years stitched a fine spoor around her eyes and lips, he found himself looking at the young girl he'd known in Paris. The girl who'd served coffee and macaroons to the Brotherhood of Apollo, those rainy Sundays in November of 1825. The girl who'd gone up the Nile to the yellow city of Asouan. Explored, with her uncle, the demon-haunted desert tombs.

'Anyways,' Ti-Gall went on, 'that's where I was, when I heard these three riders comin' up the shell road. Quiet, not talkin', with their lanterns all hooded down. I knew they was up to no good. I slipped round and knocked on the window, and the girls – I mean, Zizi and Mamzelle – let me in, so we had guns ready, when those men tried to break in the door.'

'They shot through the door,' said Zizi. 'Mamzelle Belle was hit in her leg, bleedin' somethin' bad. I tied it up, and tourniquet'ed it, like you and Mama taught me, while Ti-Gall shot back through the shutters—'

'I got one of 'em, too,' said the young man. 'Least I heard him cussin' – or I guess it was cussin', I couldn't make out the words.'

'Then I loaded up and shot, while Ti-Gall carried Mamzelle Belle out the back and along the trace. I ran and caught up with them, and we figured we'd try to follow the bayou out to Milneburgh. But those men were between us and the bayou, and we turned back through the siprière. There's what used to be an old woodstore, on Chitimacha Mound.'

Head bent under the rain, Arithmus crept to January's side, held the oilcloth while January turned up Belle's sodden night-rail and dressing gown, to reveal a horrible mess of soaked linen and diluted blood high on her left thigh. Higher still, a tourniquet pinched the flesh; January loosened it, pressed his hands on the squishy dressing . . .

No sense asking if anybody has so much as two square inches of dry clothing on them for another bandage . . .

'And there's that old shack Mama used to make her spells in, way back when she was a girl, out on Bayou Ouaouaron.'

'I know it,' said January grimly, having nearly been killed out there himself only a few months before.

'Is there anything you can do for her now?' Zizi sounded remarkably like her mother in her crisp competence. 'I didn't think we could do anything, except for keeping that tourniquet tight, till we got somewhere dry where we had better light. We kept hearing something behind us in the woods, that I think has to have been that cougar, coming after the smell of the blood.'

'And I think that's why it attacked Gaspar.' January felt Belle's hands – they were like ice – and brought his face down close to her lips, where he could feel on the skin of his cheek the strong, steady whisper of her breath. 'It must be him that Ti-Gall hit. He'd smell of blood as well . . . Is she still out there?'

'M'am Sauvage? I think so. I think . . .' The young woman's voice quailed, just slightly. 'I think she's eating him. Serve him right,' she added in a stronger tone. 'At least nobody can go around saying you killed him, Uncle Ben.'

'Don't you believe it.' January's fingers pressed the artery in Belle Wishart's wrist. Though rapid, the pulse there felt steady and distinct. 'I'll bet you the British Crown jewels against the hole in a doughnut that Serafin's back in town even as we're speaking, telling how Arithmus and I not only murdered Gaspar and Dr Boehler, but that it was one of us who shot Belle as well. Particularly,' he added grimly, 'if she dies.'

'She's not gonna die!' Arithmus's voice shook. 'Is she?' He looked like a man who, with very little urging, would have dropped the oil-cloth and wrapped the unconscious woman in his arms.

'We have to get her dry,' said January, with a calm he was far from feeling. 'And we have to get her warm. I think we're safe to move – I can't see Serafin letting anyone but Gaspar and Dr Boehler – who I'll swear are his brothers or his cousins, the only ones he could trust – into the secret of killing Belle. How far is it back to the cottage, or on to Les Cyprès? Serafin won't know that there's nobody at Les Cyprès now,' he added, and Zizi said,

'What?'

'Long story,' said January. 'I think it'll be safer . . . Let's go around this way.' He gestured towards the further wall of the graveyard. 'We owe it to M'am Sauvage to let her finish her dinner in peace.'

TWENTY-THREE

Ti-Gall and Arithmus took turns carrying Belle – wrapped in January's mackintosh, which he secretly vowed to donate to the poor (or feed to the nearest alligator) at the earliest possible moment – through the rainy darkness to the house called Les Cyprès. Zizi-Marie walked ahead with her musket in the crook of her arm, head tilted a little, listening to the wet blackness and studying what glimpses could be seen of trees, paths, the nearly invisible landmarks of theciprière. Listening also, January followed behind. The marshy wilderness of ponds and lakes, lost bayous and dripping cypresses, was silent. But when the wind picked up, and the rain drove hard, the noise curtained them and shut out everything else: the Three Hundred Spartans and Napoleon's Grande Armée could have been ten yards behind them and January was pretty sure he'd have been unaware of it.

Virgin Mother of God, he prayed, *hold her in your hand. Get her there safely . . .*

And between prayers, he wondered what the hell he was going to do.

By this hour – before they left the graveyard he had looked at his watch and found that it was past three in the morning – Quincy and his little band of house servants would be miles on their way across the salt lakes and marshes to meet the *China Bride* off Cat Island. Their feet would already be on the long and perilous journey north to freedom. But he knew, as if he'd seen it written in blood on a wall, that Serafin's inevitable accusation that he and Arithmus had murdered Gaspar and Dr Boehler – and murdered Belle, too, if Serafin could get a few moments alone with her – would be connected with the slaves' disappearance, particularly if and when the City Guards found Grice's body.

Bitterness and dread almost nauseated him. *The City Guards will come after Rose. The school will be closed – she'll lose the house, and where will she go? To Dominique's, with two children and Gabriel . . . ?*

And what then?

An apparent conspiracy of that size – slaves escaping, a master murdered, an adulterous ex-wife (whether alive or dead at that point) implicated, two dead white men and Benjamin January standing in the middle of it all with a gun in his hands *dammit dammit dammit dammit* . . .

Who's going to believe a story about a cougar this close to town? The rain would obliterate its tracks . . .

The City Guards would comb the landscape for him. He dared not ask the Underground Railroad for help. Helping men and women escape from bondage was one thing. Accessory after the fact to the multiple murder of white men (and possibly a white woman) was another matter. And the only witnesses in his defense were those who would be accused beside him – three of them black and one a self-proclaimed adulteress and fallen woman (and possible murderess herself).

Grimly, he returned his mind to his prayer. *Save her, dear God.* That, at least, he could pray without his mind spinning away into plans and fear. *Save her. She is innocent in this. She only wanted to love. And if you have a few minutes after that, show me the hell the way through this mess . . .*

Zizi-Marie and Ti-Gall lighted lamps and patrolled the entire house at Les Cyprès – reminding January eerily of the Chateau Palongeux in its Stygian desertion – while January sent Arithmus to the laundry for clean sheets and a pair of scissors. The Nubian also brought a bottle of spirits of wine from the bedroom where Grice had kept the chemicals from Deverel Wishart's laboratory, a packet of basilicum powder, and an assortment of small steel tools – forceps, probes, scoops, extractors – none of which January had the courage to use, remembering the sealed glass tube with its poisoned bodkins. 'Mr Quincy said he was taking the medicine-box,' said Arithmus apologetically. 'And all Mr Grice's money.'

Damn Quincy . . .

He knew the fleeing servants would need both, desperately.

January sent Arithmus to the kitchen for the thinnest filleting knife, the smallest lark-spits and the needles with which the napkins were mended. When he came back, the Nubian also carried one of Daisy Emmett's nightdresses, and looked shyly aside, as January had by that time taken off Belle's soaked and bloodstained nightgown and robe, and laid the sheets over her to keep her warm while he unwrapped and probed the wound.

The bullet had gone clean through, missing the bone and the femoral artery (*thank you, God!*) but nicking (he guessed) the *profunda femoris* vein. He washed the wound with spirits of wine, dusted everything with basilicum powder, and stitched the flesh closed. Midway through the process, Belle half-woke, struggling and crying with pain (*Where the hell is Quincy with his damned chlorinated lime when you need him?*); Arithmus, who had laid more blankets over her upper body, pressed her down gently with his arm, whispered in her ear, 'I'm here, *paka mdogo*, little kitten. I'm here. You're all right and there's nothing to be afraid of.'

Her arms wrapped tight around him and she clung to him and cried. When, half-conscious, she sobbed a name, the name she called was Arithmus.

He pinned the last of the bandages over the dressings, looked up to see wet gray light leaking through the parlor curtains, and Ti-Gall and Zizi-Marie, handfast, coming in through the door that led to the dining room. Zizi-Marie carried her musket in her free hand, Ti-Gall, a pitcher of water in his.

It was still raining.

'They'll be here soon,' said Arithmus, sitting still on the edge of the sofa, Belle's hand in his. 'Somebody'll tell them Nestor's gone, so somebody at Mr Trulove's'll have their carriage hitched up and come over here to see what's going on. And Linney'll be waking up soon.'

January looked around the parlor. He'd laid sheets down around the sofa, and beneath Belle's body, while he'd probed for the bullet and stitched the wound – would anyone think to count the sheets in the laundry and the linen room, and notice that three or four were missing?

Would Serafin accuse Belle of killing Gaspar, and being hit herself in the affray?

Damn the man. *Where's that cougar when we need her?*

What story will best fit the evidence . . . ?

'I won't leave her.' As if, following January's eyes, Arithmus followed his thought as well, the Nubian moved closer to Belle, tightened his hold on her hand. 'If they find Mr Grice's body in the woodstore, they'll say she did it.'

'I'll be there to say she was never anywhere near him.' Zizi set her musket down, began to gather up the blood-spotted sheets.

'That prince is a white man.' Ti-Gall's voice, confident as January had never heard him except when he was talking about buckles and harness-chains, cut across January's own protest. 'Miss Emmett white, too. She loves him so crazy she'll back up anything he says. And everybody knows you was out at the cottage with her, most nights, Zizi . . .'

He was going to finish that sentence with something else, then didn't, and looked aside.

Zizi finished it for him, quietly, reading the knowledge in his averted gaze. ''Cept when I was walkin' out with Starke Hagan?'

The young man said nothing. Every muscle in his bowed back and still face replied, *Yeah. 'Cept then*.

At length he continued, 'They'll say you was in on it. What you got to do, Zizi – you, an' Rithmus, an' Uncle Ben – you all three gotta hide someplace in theciprière. I'll stay here, an' tell 'em I found Miss Belle out at the old cemetery on Chickasaw Chenier, an' brought her here, an' found everybody gone. I'll find out everythin' I can about what's bein' said, an' I'll come out to where you are – maybe that old cabin on Bayou Ouaouaron, that your mama used to make up her spells in, Zizi, when she was a girl? I'll ask M'am Rose what should I do,' he added, with an apologetic glance at January. 'An' M'am Snakebones' – that was Olympe's name among the voodoos – 'an' Michie Hannibal.' Stammering a little, he added, 'I'll tell Starke Hagan you're all right—'

Zizi said softly, 'Don't.'

Her eyes met his, silent, asking nothing. After a time he reached hesitantly, took her hand where it clutched up the armload of sheets.

She added, 'You can't trust him.' Then she turned quickly, glanced at the curtained window, beyond which the rain had lessened to a whisper. 'We better go, Uncle Ben.'

To Ti-Gall, January said, 'Don't let Serafin, or Miss Emmett, be alone with Belle. Not for a minute. Tell Madame St-Forgeux that you heard me say that I think Miss Emmett might have poisoned her guardian – used Michie Wishart's poisons from his chemical kit. Find those needles in her room if you can. If

Lieutenant Shaw comes out to look at things, tell him the same thing: that you heard me say . . .' He cast his mind hastily back, 'You heard me say last night that I thought Miss Emmett had traded places with Miss Grice on Twelfth Night, and had come back here and used poison on a bodkin to kill her guardian.'

If Abishag Shaw was a member of the First Municipality Guards, not those of the Third, in which Les Cyprès lay . . . Bayou P'tit-Jean was in the First. *Damn the idiots who thought it was a good idea to split New Orleans into three separate towns with three separate police forces; damn them damn them . . .* Would they send out men from the municipality where the crime had been committed . . . ? Or would they spend the next twenty-four hours arguing about whose jurisdiction it was in?

Somewhere, distantly, in another corner of the house, he heard a woman's voice call out sleepily, 'Corena? M'am Hauser?'

Damn it . . .

'What was you doin' out in the cemetery where you found Miss Belle?' asked Zizi sharply, and Ti-Gall stared at her, flummoxed.

'Uh—'

'You was diggin' up goofer-dust,' provided January. 'To lay a curse on . . . on someone who did you wrong.'

'I wouldn't,' protested the young man. For a moment, Starke Hagan's name hung in the air between them.

No, thought January. *No, you wouldn't . . .*

'You were going to sell it to Queen Régine.' He named one of the best-known voodoos in the French town. He almost added, *To buy flowers for the wedding . . .* and changed it to, 'To buy your sister Tienette a birthday present. You got to been out there for something, in the middle of the night,' he added, when Ti-Gall looked about to object that under no circumstances would he dig up graveyard earth for anybody . . .

'Now let's go.'

He winced at the thought of the other blunders he was almost positive the young man would commit, but somewhere in the dark, Linney's voice called again, 'Where you gone, Corena?' She would, he knew, see the glimmer of the lamplight, follow it to the parlor . . .

He caught Zizi by the arm, shook free the jumble of sheets from her grip, put his hand on Arithmus's back and pushed him toward the window. 'Don't leave Miss Belle alone,' he added in a whisper, and – praying that nobody in the Third Municipality Guards would look at the muddied wet tracks all over the parlor rug – pulled his accomplices through the French window to the portico. Leaving them in the shadows of the pillars, he doubled back inside and grabbed the mackintosh, which he guessed could have been identified as his.

The rain was easing as they disappeared into the sodden night.

Bayou des Ouaouaron lay several miles downstream on Bayou Gentilly. It was full daylight when they reached it, working their way through the morass of cypress and cheniers, shell mounds and laurel-hells, wading through mud and water and tangled jack vine underfoot, to stay off the shell path along Bayou Gentilly itself. Olympe's old hiding place had been barely more than a shed even in its youthful glory days, and now, half-buried in laurel saplings and scuppernong vines, it was barely to be distinguished from the surrounding foliage.

The rain had ceased, but everything in the landscape – including the interior of the roofless dwelling – dripped as if God had thought better of his storied wrath and had resurrected Lyonesse or Atlantis from the bottom of the sea. January tried to calculate when last he'd gotten a full night's sleep, and failed – *last Tuesday?* And he knew that between Prince Serafin's skill as a liar, and Ti-Gall's hopeless inexperience at the same art, he dared not doze off.

A posse would be scouring the countryside for them within hours. He spread out his loathed mackintosh – the only more or less dry item among the three of them – in the least-sodden corner of the hut, where the remaining square yard of roof had offered a little protection, and tried to think of a line of retreat, in case he heard someone coming. There was a sugar mill at the old St-Gemme plantation, deserted at this time of the year, and far enough from the Big House that, with care, he and his companions could reach it from the edge of the woods . . .

He woke suddenly, to see mid-morning sunlight glinting on the drops that still jeweled the curtains of moss hanging through the broken roof.

By the light, he'd been asleep for at least three hours.

Against the frieze of dangling vines, Zizi-Marie's back was a dark silhouette in what had been the door of the hut, musket cradled in her arms. January turned his head, saw Arithmus scrunched on to the remains of what looked like a broken table, which had also been in the hut's single dry(ish) corner, his back wedged in the corner itself. He was looking out through another gap in the wall, shivering with anxiety and rubbing and twisting something between his hands.

January knew, even before he saw it, that it was the little bronze of Menhit, the Nubian goddess who brought misfortune to all who harmed those in her care.

'Did you find her among M'sieu Wishart's things?' he asked.

Arithmus startled, then nodded, and held the little image up. 'I got her back last night. She was in Miss Emmett's dressing table. M'sieu d'Aveline sent her back to Mr Grice in March of 1828, after his son hanged himself. He said he didn't want her under his roof anymore. Mr Grice laughed about it, and said M'sieu d'Aveline never did get into the Société de St-Cloud, and nobody ever asked him to teach at the Faculté des Sciences. He said, "A fool and his money are soon parted." But she really is mine. The only thing I have left from Uncle Tafiq, and Asouan, and the desert. He kept her because he wanted to sell her to Mr Adams in Washington, that used to be president, who's trying to make a collection of ancient things for a national museum.'

January had to smile, thinking of what that pale-eyed old scholar back in Washington would make of the tale of ancient curses and ancient loves. 'Did M'sieu Wishart borrow her back from you, to hide at the chateau?'

'He said one of the servants was working for M'sieu le Duc, and would try to steal it from me. He said he could use her to prove that M'sieu le Duc was wrong, that the manuscript was true – that the Curse was real and that it all really happened. He promised to give her back when it was all done. I told him it was silly, because there's no such things as curses and ghosts.'

January thought about whatever it was that had stood in the room with him at the old house on the lost bayou, and said, 'No.'

Thought about a young girl dead, bearing a baby in the convent to which she had been sent to hide the shame of bastardy. And only months later, a young man dangling at the end of a rope.

A girl slipping into her guardian's room in the green garb of her friend's fairy costume, a poisoned bodkin in her hand and crazy passion for a fairy-tale prince in her heart.

... *magnum malum omnibus habitantibus in domo illa*, the manuscript had said.

Bringing great misfortune to all who dwelled in that house.

'No,' he said again.

And to me, he thought, his sick dread returning. *Who merely dabbled the ends of my fingers around the edges of Menhit's business: trying to figure out where I'm to flee if accused of Dr Boehler's murder; Rose losing the school that is her life for a second time; our sons left with nothing.* The money he'd earned so far through the Christmas season – thirty-five dollars, hidden in one of the oil-jars in the cellar, along with the first quarter's school fees for the girls ... Rose would need that.

Olympe will know someone who can get me out of town. Or Ti-Gall, down at the wharves, will ...

It was hard not to panic.

He crossed the weed-grown floor, leaned a shoulder against the wall beside Arithmus. Looked down into the pitiless face of the goddess, the dead pharaoh lying with a broken sword beneath her feet.

Maybe I can get Olympe to talk to her for me, he thought wearily. *Or Hannibal.* He'd never yet met a woman Hannibal couldn't sweet-talk – though, come to think of it, God help the fiddler if he came in contact with that ancient lioness ...

Wasn't His Highness supposed to be fighting a duel this morning with another one of Mrs Redfern's suitors? Maybe I'll be really lucky and he'll be run through ...

He closed his eyes again, and this time he saw her, standing beside the broken cemetery wall on the old chenier, watching Prince Serafin and the thick-shouldered, glowering Gontran Mabillet dueling in their white shirtsleeves in the rain. She wore Mrs Redfern's mourning gown and diamonds. A cougar, licking bloodied whiskers, lay at her feet.

TWENTY-FOUR

'Dead?' exclaimed Zizi-Marie.

January opened his eyes. It was evening.

'*Vile and ingrate! Too late thou shalt repent,*' quoted Hannibal, from some blood-and-thunder Baroque poem,

'the base injustice thou hast done my love . . .
Heav'n has no rage, like to love to hatred turn'd,
Nor Hell a fury, like a woman scorn'd.

'The prince's body was found dead on the floor of the guest-room occupied by Miss Emmett at the Trulove home this morning,' he went on, leaning on the remains of the vine-grown wall and looking very white around the lips. 'Although she insists that she woke to find his corpse there – and in fact had hideous nightmares of his being struck down before her eyes by spectral shapes – both Henri and Chloë Viellard advanced the theory that the shocking distortion of his facial muscles argued for some kind of toxin. Lieutenant Shaw – according to the lovely vicomtesse – was in the process of searching the grounds when Madame de St-Forgeux left the place to come to your house.'

He held out his hand to help Rose over the wall but it was she who had to help him: 'You should be in the gig,' she said.

'He should be home in bed,' added January firmly, rolling to his feet and crossing to his friends. 'Has anyone been to Les Cyprès?'

'You mean, in the uproar over the discovery of His Highness's body – his real name was Fabio Haspel, by the way, and he was no more a Hungarian prince than you are,' Rose lifted her brows, 'did anyone send a carriage to investigate the disappearance of Grice's coachman, carriage, and team?'

'Yes,' returned January. 'That uproar.'

'Miss Emmett's maid Linney turned up at the Truloves' just as Madame was getting into her carriage to come to me – actually to come to you. She said she wanted to ask you what you might know of the affair, before the Guards came in with all sorts of questions . . . and thank heavens the good lieutenant was preoccupied at the time, poking around the flower-beds below Miss Emmett's window. Linney was nearly in hysterics, as well she might be. She woke in the small hours of the morning, she said, to find the house deserted and Mrs Grice – Mamzelle Wishart – unconscious and wounded in the parlor . . .'

'Is she all right?' Arithmus crowded forward, hands closed upon one another to keep them still. 'Belle – Mamzelle Wishart . . . She isn't—'

'She's well.' Rose took his hands, smiled up into his eyes before his glance ducked shyly away. 'She will be well. Ti-Gall had the good sense to send Linney to the Truloves' – you should have heard her on the subject of what the walk had done to her shoes! – and Madame de St-Forgeux stopped at our house only long enough to collect me, Hannibal, Gabriel, Germaine, and Marie-Evaline, before going on to Les Cyprès. And yes, I told Hannibal he should be in bed—'

'*Labor omnia vincet*,' retorted the fiddler. 'And I thought you might need a witness who'd be listened to in the courts.'

'We picked up Olympe on the way – it was rather a crowded drive. Starke Hagan was there at the house,' she added more quietly, with a glance at Zizi-Marie. 'He said you and he were to have met for coffee . . .'

'We were.' The girl shook her head, like one half-waking from a dream. 'I'd forgot about that. But I-I'll have to . . . to speak to him. I don't suppose he'll be there when we get back.'

Rose studied for a moment the stillness of her face, the downcast look in her eyes under the long, wet straggles of her hair, then only nodded. 'We can send him a note tomorrow.'

Zizi started to say, 'I . . .' and stopped herself, as if unable to frame what was in her heart. 'I have to speak to him tonight. Soon.'

'Of course. You can send a message from the house.' Rose stepped forward, and took January's niece in her arms. 'You look tired to death, sweetheart.'

Zizi nodded, her lips set hard. Through the soaked awfulness of the night, through the long day of waiting, she had been like Olympe, feral as the cougar that had sprung from the darkness by the cemetery, and tough as stone. Now January saw her tremble, and tears shimmer again in her eyes.

Rose added practically, 'And you're probably starving.'

'I am,' agreed Arithmus at once. 'Is Madame with her? At Les Cyprès? Is it all right for me to go there?'

'It is.' Rose hid her smile at this display of literal-mindedness – or perhaps at the joy in his usually wooden features. 'They'll probably welcome your help. When we got there, there was no one but Ti-Gall present, keeping watch over Mamzelle Belle. Madame St-Forgeux sent Gabriel back to the Truloves', asking for the loan of a couple of servants. I expect when we get there,' she added, 'we'll find the City Guards as well. Once that was done, Madame took Germaine and Marie-Evaline and retreated to the kitchen, so presumably we can all get dinner when we arrive. Are you all right?' She turned to January, took his hand in hers. More quietly: 'You look terrible.'

It was not the reaction of any heroine of those novels so beloved by Miss Emmett and Dominique – but it filled January with delight like the warmth of the sun. And in her gray-turquoise eyes was deep relief, to see him unhurt and on his feet.

'I feel terrible.' He rested his hands on her shoulders, thought about the words. 'No,' he corrected himself, 'I actually feel wonderful, to see you here. To know that I'm not going to have to flee the state.'

He helped Rose back over the broken wall, then supported Hannibal down through the dripping tangle of weeds to the trace – barely a trail across puddled ground at the bayou's edge – where a gig waited, drawn by one of the showy chestnut coach-horses that he recognized from Grice's stables. Evidently Nestor had brushed, fed, and stalled the carriage team before he and the others had fled. 'Rithmus and I will walk,' he said, helping first Rose, then Hannibal and Zizi-Marie up on to the small vehicle's seats.

Rose gathered the reins, glanced sidelong down at him. 'Did you think you were going to have to flee?'

'I'm pretty sure His Highness saw me, yes,' he said in a low voice. 'Do you know if anyone has been out to the old cemetery on Chickasaw Chenier?'

'Probably by this time, if the Guards have gotten to Les Cyprès and Ti-Gall told them about the bodies there. As it is, there's nothing to show who shot Gaspar – if that was really his name. You'd probably better get rid of that musket, Zizi,' she added. 'All the firearms, in fact . . .'

'I'll take them.' January took the two pistols and the musket while Rose drew rein, and sloshed through the weeds to the largest oak tree he could see from the trail. He scrambled into its branches and wedged them in a clump of foliage where they wouldn't be seen from below. And if they were, he reflected, springing down with a splash, losing them was still better than being found with them on or near his person.

'Remember,' said January to Arithmus, as the first scents of woodsmoke and cooking drifted through the gathering dusk, 'you don't know a single thing of what happened at Les Cyprès. You woke in your room with a horrible headache, it was still dark, and the whole house was empty. To your horror, you found poor Mamzelle Grice's body . . . In Barnabas's room, you said?'

'It's downstairs so it was easy to carry her into. They laid sheets over the bed but her dress was soaking wet, so it'll all have soaked through by this time. They left the chain around her,' he added. 'It was one of the trace-chains from the stables, Quincy said. It was just to weight her down so she wouldn't float. Her face was awful.' His voice broke again from its customary monotone. 'Like she was screaming, or wanted to scream and couldn't. Her eyes were open.' He flinched, and shook his head. 'She was good to me,' he repeated. 'And now she's dead, and I don't think any of it was her fault. Did Miss Emmett give the prince the bodkin to do that to her?'

'Not necessarily.' The gig stopped, as the lights of Les Cyprès appeared before them through the trees. Shadows crossed and recrossed the glowing windows, and January heard a man's voice call out something in French. *City Guards*, he thought. 'He knew about the poisoned bodkins. He certainly had access to wherever Miss Emmett had them. Whether Daisy Emmett put him up to killing the girl who doubled for her on Twelfth Night, or whether he was just taking precautions—'

'That would make sense,' put in Rose, 'if he'd decided he – or his creditors – couldn't wait for however long it would take to prove Grice's death. That could be months, or years, if those letters kept coming from Mobile or Nashville or wherever else in the country . . .'

'And obviously' – Hannibal, who had been leaning back in exhaustion, reached gingerly around to touch his bandaged side – 'Mason Spurcid and Associates weren't going to wait. And without permission of her guardian, it would be . . . What *is* the age of consent in Mississippi?'

'I should think,' said Rose, 'that would depend on the terms of Travis Emmett's will. If it was something like twenty-one, the prince would *have* to find another target . . .'

'Hence that melodrama behind the curtains at Mrs Redfern's musicale,' agreed the fiddler. 'And the duel with Gontran Mabillet, which obviously didn't take place this morning—'

'And hence,' concluded January softly, 'Serafin's decision – what did you say his name really was? – to get rid of the only witnesses who could have proven Grice's murder on to Miss Emmett. It may be,' he went on, 'that in fact Miss Emmett was saving her own life, when he came to her room last night. Because if he seduced and entranced Mrs Redfern, he wouldn't have been able to let Miss Emmett survive, either.'

He took the bridle of the carriage horse, led her forward; she followed with the air of a duchess performing an act of noblesse oblige at pulling a mere gig.

'Don't you think it,' said Hannibal. '*Amor et melle et felle est fecundissimus: Love abounds in honey and poison*. Miss Emmett was within two yards of the musicians' dais when Mabillet pulled that curtain aside and revealed the Widow Redfern in Prince Charming's sinewy arms. *Rabidem livoris acerbi / nulla potest placare quies* . . . Miss Emmett let out a scream they doubtless heard in Boston. Her wrath would have put Medea to shame . . . and we all know how *that* turned out.'

'Uncle Ben!' Gabriel reached them, grabbed the rein. 'You all right?'

'They found M'sieu Grice!' Germaine seized January's sleeve, looked from him up to Rose in the gig. 'It was awful! He'd been hid in the woodstore, and M'am St-Forgeux wouldn't let us see him, but Timmy – M'sieu Trulove's coachman – says his face was all twisted up, like as if he'd seen a ha'nt—'

January wondered if, after seven days, the puncture-wound

would still be visible on the man's neck. As cold as it had been, it should be . . .

He turned to remind Arithmus that if he mentioned Grice's body at all, it should only be to say that in addition to finding poor Josie Grice's corpse in one of the servant bedrooms above the kitchen, he had only accidentally come across Grice's body that morning . . .

But the Nubian had glimpsed, through the lighted parlor window, the small, rather fragile, dark-haired figure sitting up a little on the sofa, pillows behind her back and her spectacles gleaming in the candle-glow. And he'd left the gig, strode across the weedy lawn . . . Through the French door, January saw Belle turn on the sofa, saw the look in her face and how she held out her arms to him.

Saw them come together, crushing in an embrace as if neither would ever let the other go again.

'Maestro?' Lieutenant Abishag Shaw ambled from the direction of the distant woodstore, to join the little group beside the gig. January had the feeling that the cold gray eyes took in the state of his clothing, torn and rumpled and smirched all over with bayou mud. 'Miz Wishart tells me you was acquainted with her uncle back in France – the one as she says fooled around with poisons.'

'It wasn't only poisons,' said January. 'He was a scholar of many things – M'sieu Viellard can show you all the articles he wrote for scientific journals, about herbs and languages and mathematics and mummies in ancient Egypt. But yes, he did work with poisons also. I have reason to believe that Mr Grice killed him – back in 1825 in France – with one of his own poisons, administered by stabbing him with a poisoned bodkin . . . It's a long story.'

And one I hope I can keep straight while concealing how I know half the things I know . . .

'I would purely like to hear it. But first . . .' The Kentuckian turned toward the gig, and executed his usual inexpert bow. 'Mamzelle Corbier, ain't it? Zylemia Corbier?'

From the corner of his eye, January saw a thin shadow that had to be Olympe, silhouetted against the gold of the open hall door. Only standing, arms folded, watching . . .

'I'm Mademoiselle Corbier.'

January almost felt her glance go towards her mother, then back to him. Reassured at their presence.

'My understandin' is that you know a man name of Starke Hagan? Valet to Marc-Antoine Picard?'

'Yes. He's a . . . a friend of mine. As is his master, M'sieu Picard.'

'He run off this mornin',' said Shaw. 'Took seventy-three dollars of his master's money an' household silver – silver-back hair-brushes, a gold card-case, stick-pins an' cuff-links an' sech truck. I was wonderin' if he ever spoke to you, regardin' men in town as might buy plunder like that. If ever it seemed to you as he had . . . money he maybe shouldn't'a had, 'fore this.'

Zizi-Marie sat very still, very silent on the seat of the gig, and in the twilight January guessed, rather than saw, Rose take her hand. In a voice stiff as a steel rod she finally said, 'No, he never spoke of such things.'

Shaw spit into the weeds that tangled the lawn. 'Ain't my business if a man runs off,' he said quietly. 'Well, it is . . .' He glanced back at the house, the dark silhouettes of the trees, where the woodstores were hidden, and the little bayou where Josie Grice's chain-wrapped body had been thrown. 'An' there's things here that surely need clearin' up an' sortin' out. Theft is serious business – an' murder is serious business. You look like you had a strenuous day today yourself, Maestro, an' I won't keep you here long. But if'fn you could see your way clear to takin' a look at the bodies we found – Grice, an' that poor niece of his – an' the chemical truck that's up in one of the bedrooms upstairs, I would surely appreciate hearin' whatever you have to tell me about it all.'

'I can take Aunt Rose and Zizi home,' offered Gabriel. 'If it's all right with M'am la Vicomtesse, I can put the horse up at Valentine's Livery and bring the gig back tomorrow. Michie Trulove's servants are here—'

January sighed. 'All right.' All he wanted was a night's sleep in his own bed with Rose, but he realized that this would be the easiest way to make sure the policeman saw the puncture-wounds and understood the whole tangled sequence of events. 'On the condition that somebody gives me dinner—'

'Maestro . . .' Shaw grinned a slow gargoyle grin. 'It'll be small payment for hearin' the tale. Miz Janvier . . .' He touched his hat-brim to Rose. 'Mamzelle . . .' His glance went to Zizi. 'It might go easier with your friend, if'fn at least Mr Picard ain't spittin' mad over losin' his hairbrushes. An if'fn you should remember anythin', about where Hagan might have sold or left or hid his plunder . . .'

'I will tell you, yes.' She even managed to put warmth into her voice. 'But truly, it was not something we spoke of. I . . . did not know him very well.'

TWENTY-FIVE

January reached the old Spanish house on Rue Esplanade at slightly after ten that night, to find it still lit up like the Fourth of July in Boston. In this it was no different from pretty much every other house in the French town, and the streets between them alive with noisy gangs of ersatz Turks and Mohawks, Cavaliers and paladins of Camelot. Shaw's men having returned to town earlier in the evening, in the end it fell to Herr Sigerist – who rode with Shaw, January, and Ti-Gall back to town – to take their borrowed horses and retrieve the gig from Valentine's Livery. His only comment, as they wove their way through the gaudy throng on Rue Esplanade, was that none of this compared to what went on in Venice during the carnival season. 'This is all' – his gesture seemed to take in two murders, switched identities, *crimes passionnels*, and non-consensual voyages down the river in pirogues, to say nothing of counterfeit Hungarian princes and ravening cougars – 'very ordinary indeed.'

In addition to the medicine-box and the money-chest, Quincy and his companions had carried off all the foodstuffs they could from their master's larder. But enough had remained for Persephone and Gabriel – ably assisted by Herr Sigerist and Fräulein Hauser – to put together a serviceable feast of roast chickens, 'dirty' rice, stewed apples, and gingerbread, and January felt considerably better. Nevertheless, he longed for nothing so much as his own bed and no further adventures that week. (*And I'm playing at the Almonasters' party tomorrow night, damn it damn it damn it . . .*)

He and Ti-Gall waved farewell to Shaw, Sigerist, and the horses – Shaw lived over the livery stable – and mounted the steps: 'I should go.' Ti-Gall stopped behind him.

January turned back, regarded him in the reflected glow of the windows.

'He was here this morning,' explained the young man quietly. 'Starke Hagan. Germaine told me. Maybe left her a note, an' she'll

'... She may have gone off already to meet him. To leave with him.' He looked up at the house above them. 'Listen. There's lights on, but I don't hear voices talking.'

Then long silence, the young man gathering his words. 'She loves him, Uncle Ben. I see the way her eyes light up, when somebody only says his name. I'll take oath she knew nothing of him bein' a thief, but I know she'd have gone to be plaçée to that Michie Picard, only to be near Starke. She did say she was meeting him this morning, only but for that prince fellow trying to kill Mamzelle Belle. She'd have gone anywhere with him – for him – if he'd asked, and I think he meant to ask this morning. With the house all decorated for the wedding Thursday, and the punch-bowl and the cake-plates all washed ... I don't think I could stand to hear them all talking about it.'

Softly, January said, 'I think you're wrong.'

'Maybe.' He shook his head, a big, clumsy, rough-handed young artisan. Dark like her mother, awkward in his heavy boots. 'But he hurt her, running off. Hurt her bad. If I went up there I couldn't keep from saying what a bastard I think that man is, what a coward, what a ...' He stopped himself. 'I don't want to hurt her worse.'

January descended the step or two that separated them, put his hand on Ti-Gall's shoulder. 'People make mistakes,' he said. 'If they're lucky, they get saved from what could have happened. It'll be all right.'

A gang of Greek gods reeled past them on the banquette, Zeus and Hermes, Aphrodite and Athene, an over-age Cupid dancing in front of them, flapping cardboard wings. Their voices blended, with surprising melodic beauty:

> *L'aimable Harlequin*
> *Frappe chez la brune*
> *Elle répond soudain.*
>
> *Qui frappe de la sorte?*
> *Il dit à son tour*
> *Ouvrez votre porte*
> *Pour le Dieu d'Amour ...*

> *Harlequin knocked at the dark lady's door:*
> *'Who's there?' she cried, he called in his turn,*
> *'Open your door, it's the God of Love'* . . .

They left a trail of white feathers behind.

Ti-Gall sighed, and followed January up the steps.

Even as he approached the French door of his study, January perceived that Ti-Gall was right. Candles were lit in the parlor, but there was no sound of merriment, or chatter, or excitement. Only someone's footsteps crossing the floor told him the place wasn't empty. Then Gabriel's voice said, 'Well, shit.'

January opened the French door to his study, crossed through it – Ti-Gall on his heels – and into the parlor.

All the girls were there, Zizi-Marie, Rose. Gabriel had just brought in the coffee-pot. As Ti-Gall had said, the paper garlands, the flowers of twisted wire and beads, adorned the walls and decorated the piano and the harp. The faces that all turned toward him were relieved to see him, but unsmiling.

Gabriel said, 'That f—' He groped for an adjective that could be said around his Aunt Rose's pupils.

And Aglaëa put in quickly, 'We didn't know, M'sieu J! We didn't even think!'

Zizi-Marie said, 'I'll get the milk' and, getting to her feet, walked swiftly to the pantry and disappeared.

January asked, 'What happened?' From the corner of his eye he saw the faces of his two little sons, peeking around the nursery door. Solemn with the shadow that seemed to cover the room.

'He just said he wanted to leave her a note!' Cosette's voice was pleading.

Rose said, 'It seems that after I left him here this morning, Starke Hagan went through the house – while the girls were quite properly at their lessons in the workshop above the kitchen – and took all the jewelry the girls had in their rooms – mine as well – and all the money from the cellar, the pantry, and the attic. He took your pistols, too, and that silver coffee-pot the girls got for Zizi and you hid in the cellar. I think the only reason he didn't take your rifle was because he couldn't carry it down the street.'

Shocked, sick, exhausted, and cold . . . it still wasn't as bad as the desperate dread he'd felt that morning at the thought of having to flee the state.

January concentrated for a moment on the faces of the girls: round, pugnacious Cosette, fairy-like Germaine, Aglaëa with her blue eyes and honey-dark hair, little Alice . . . and reminded himself that one did not say words like *Fucking son of a whore-bitch pig* in front of one's pupils. *And that's probably not a very nice thing to say about whore-bitch pigs, either, who can't help what they are* . . .

He took a deep breath, let it out.

'I'm playing at the Almonasters' ball tomorrow evening,' he said, in his most reasonable voice, though his heart was screaming, *All the first quarter fees for the girls* . . . 'And at the Villères' on Friday. That's food for the rest of the week. Lent doesn't start for another five weeks.' He saw their faces change, their stiff bodies relax. As if, swept adrift in a hurricane flood, they'd felt their feet touch bottom.

In their eyes he saw it: Trust. He was strong, and they were safe. He could almost feel them draw breath.

'We'll manage.'

'Mr Sefton said he'd give the school all his money if he could sleep in the laboratory,' provided Germaine. 'If we all promised not to tell anyone he was there, because he isn't respectable.'

All the girls – even the pious Marie-Evaline – crossed their hearts.

'And we're supposed to be fasting after that anyway,' added Marie-Evaline.

Cosette put in, 'I can help with the laundry.'

'Your grandmother would pull you out of the school before you could rinse the soap off your hands,' retorted January, with a manufactured grin. 'And nobody wants that. We'll manage. You all stay here.'

He walked into the pantry, and, finding the little room empty, out on to the rear gallery.

Zizi-Marie stood, a shadow by the rail in the dark, looking out across the yard and listening to the tumult of singing and laughter from the Metoyer Sisters' house on the other side of the street.

> *Plaisir d'amour ne dure qu'un moment,*
> *Chagrin d'amour dure toute la vie . . .*
>
> *The joy of love lasts only for a moment,*
> *Its pain endures all through life . . .*

Quietly, he said, 'Père Eugenius at the cathedral always says, when you can't think of anything else to say, say, "Thank you."'

Her voice was barely a whisper. 'I'm so sorry. I was such a stupid fool and I'll pay you back, Uncle Ben, I'll pay you and the girls and Aunt Rose and everyone back, every penny, if it takes me ten years. I'm so sorry . . .'

'I'm not.' January stepped across, to stand beside her. 'That money was well spent, to get rid of a man who would have made you unhappy for the rest of your life. He can have every penny of it, for breaking the . . . the spell he had over you. The spell that people can place on each other, with kisses and words, promises and dreams.'

'I should have known better! I should have seen what he was!'

'At your age I hope to hell you wouldn't have. That you wouldn't have had the experience that would let you know what he was. Did you know he was planning to run?'

She moved her head a little: *no*. 'Not really. He talked about leaving New Orleans sometimes, talked about getting Michie Picard to manumit him. Talked about going to New York or Boston and making his fortune. He asked me, Sunday, if he were to go, would I come with him? I said I would. I said I'd follow him anywhere, go with him anywhere . . . And I would have. Just . . . I couldn't imagine not . . .'

She shivered, and turned her face away. 'He wasn't like anyone I'd ever met.'

'That's because you've always been around respectable people,' said January, and it surprised her into laughing a little.

'It's not that . . .'

January could take a good guess what it had been. His voice very quiet, he asked, 'Did you make love?'

'Not all the way.'

Silence between them then for a time, with the jangle of Carnival on all sides. The shutters on the back of the house were all closed, only a thread or two of gold leaking through in the dark. The yard was a bottomless well of ink, the reflected glow of lamps and lanterns and flambeaux in the streets like the glimmer of dawn beyond the wall. The midnight of the year was over. It was time for light to return.

'You don't have to tell anyone anything,' said January. 'Not until you're ready. Not until you've thought about it a little. You may want to go to confession, and talk to Père Eugenius. God has seen a lot of bad behavior, Zizi; he's seen a lot of mistakes, with a lot of consequences more terrible than you or I would ever be able to imagine. Do you think this will make God surprised? Or angry?'

And again she chuckled softly, in spite of herself. 'I guess not.'

'Ti-Gall loves you,' said January. 'He loves you with the whole of his heart. I don't think anything you say will change that.'

They were crossing back through the pantry to the parlor again when Aglaëa's voice said firmly, 'Well, your Mama's a voodoo, Gabriel. I'll bet she could put a really good curse on Starke Hagan, and that'll show him!'

'Oh, good,' sighed Zizi, her shoulder resting against January's arm in the dark of the tiny room. 'Something else to tell Père Eugenius.' Already she sounded more like herself.

Through the half-open door in the candlelit room beyond, Ti-Gall turned his head at the movement in the pantry, got to his feet. His heart – as they say in novels, thought January – shining in his eyes.

He remembered the little bronze of the goddess who avenged lovers, buried – like Olympe's balls of black wax and fishhooks – under the floor of a Roman house . . .

Imposuit dea manum . . .

'Will you?' he asked.

Zizi sighed. 'No. You're right, Uncle Ben. I did get out cheap. And I won't start my life with Ti-Gall – if he'll still have me – with poison on my fingers or in my heart.'

She stepped through the door into the candlelit parlor, and two steps brought her into Ti-Gall's arms.

Zizi-Marie Corbier and Ti-Gall L'Esperance were married on the fourteenth of January and lived happily ever after. After the wedding, Belit-Ilani Wishart took passage on the brig *Aphrodite* for France, en route to Egypt, with Arithmus Sudirja. In April, Daisy Emmett was convicted of the murders of Fabio Hansel, of Vienna, and Creon Grice, and sentenced to life imprisonment in the State Penitentiary at Baton Rouge. Litigation among her father's surviving relatives for control of the Emmett family assets continued until well after the Civil War.

Prince Serafin Corvinus was buried by Orleans Parish under his true name – Fabio Hansel – along with the men who were identified the following year – through extensive correspondence with the Vienna police – as his brothers, previously known to the Viennese and Paris police as confidence tricksters playing the roles of his valet and his 'guardian'. No trace of the cougar which had killed 'Dr Boehler' was ever found, and it was presumed to have wandered from the state. Quincy Taylor, Barnabas Morraine, Joe Burley, and the other Grice bondsmen were never recaptured, nor was Starke Hagan.

Olympe Corbier – the voodoo Olympia Snakebones – took charge of the bronze Curse statue of the goddess Sittina-Menhit, and put it on the altar in her parlor, among the shells and the salt, the graveyard earth and the beaded gourds. Though a good Catholic, Benjamin January periodically brought it offerings of whiskey and tobacco. And there it slept, having finished its job.